She perused him in a leisurely manner. It was the first time she had ever been close to a man of his size and physique. Odd how she wasn't in the least bit intimidated, by his proportions or his masculinity. She immediately understood why. He was a ghost, a person just a bit more tangible than her imagination but not substantial enough to be a threat. Yes, this was the kind of man she could deal with. He was arrogant and impossible, but he had a kind of teasing manner about him that was utterly charming. And he looked at her as if he actually found her appealing. Desirable was pushing things, but appealing she could believe.

She saw Kendrick's hand lying on the armrest, just an inch or two from her chair and found herself suddenly overcome by an utterly ridiculous idea. Would he feel it if she touched him? Would she feel him?

Hesitantly, she put her hand over his. A tingle, like a hint of static electricity touched her. Her hand went through his to rest on the chair. She looked down, speechless. Kendrick's hand surrounded hers, like an aura. Real, but not real. What if it had been? She leaned her head against the back of the chair and closed her eyes, giving her imagination free rein. The century didn't matter, she had Kendrick and that was the only thing important to her.

Turn to the back of this book for a special sneak preview of

The Very Thought of You

Available in paperback from Berkley Books!

Titles by Lynn Kurland

STARDUST OF YESTERDAY
A DANCE THROUGH TIME
THIS IS ALL I ASK
THE VERY THOUGHT OF YOU
ANOTHER CHANCE TO DREAM
THE MORE I SEE YOU
IF I HAD YOU
MY HEART STOOD STILL
FROM THIS MOMENT ON
A GARDEN IN THE RAIN
DREAMS OF STARDUST

❦

Anthologies

A KNIGHT'S VOW
(with Patricia Potter, Deborah Simmons, and Glynnis Campbell)

LOVE CAME JUST IN TIME

THE CHRISTMAS CAT
(with Julie Beard, Barbara Bretton, and Jo Beverley)

CHRISTMAS SPIRITS
(with Casey Claybourne, Elizabeth Bevarly, and Jenny Lykins)

VEILS OF TIME
(with Maggie Shayne, Angie Ray, and Ingrid Weaver)

OPPOSITES ATTRACT
(with Elizabeth Bevarly, Emily Carmichael, and Elda Minger)

TAPESTRY
(with Madeline Hunter, Sherrilyn Kenyon, and Karen Marie Moning)

STARDUST OF YESTERDAY

LYNN KURLAND

BERKLEY BOOKS, NEW YORK

If you purchased this book without a cover, you should be aware that this book is stolen property. It was reported as "unsold or destroyed" to the publisher, and neither the author nor the publisher has received any payment for this "stripped book."

This is a work of fiction. Names, characters, places, and incidents are either the product of the author's imagination or are used fictitiously, and any resemblance to actual persons, living or dead, business establishments, events, or locales is entirely coincidental.

STARDUST OF YESTERDAY

A Berkley Book / published by arrangement with
the author

PRINTING HISTORY
Jove edition / April 1996
Berkley edition / April 2001

All rights reserved.
Copyright © 1996 by Lynn Curland.
Excerpt from *The Very Thought of You* copyright © 1997
by Lynn Curland.
This book, or parts thereof, may not be reproduced
in any form without permission.
For information address:
The Berkley Publishing Group, a division of Penguin Putnam Inc.,
375 Hudson Street, New York, New York 10014.

ISBN: 0-425-18238-X

BERKLEY®
Berkley Books are published by
The Berkley Publishing Group, a division of Penguin Putnam Inc.,
375 Hudson Street, New York, New York 10014.
BERKLEY and the "B" design are trademarks
belonging to Penguin Putnam Inc.

PRINTED IN THE UNITED STATES OF AMERICA

10 9 8 7 6

To Lynn R., my should-have-been-sister,
for ten years of unfailing friendship

To Elane, my dear friend,
for unflagging support

To Gail, my editor,
for never giving up on this book, or on me!

And to Matthew, my sweet husband and beloved friend,
who is living proof that reality is indeed better than fiction.

Prologue

"Damn you, man!" Kendrick of Artane exclaimed. "Have you no idea who I am?"

Matilda's lover looked at him blandly. "I know perfectly well who you are. It hardly matters, as your illustrious father is not here to save you."

"He will have your head for this," Kendrick spat, his pale green eyes blazing. "You won't live out the year once he discovers what you've done." He jerked against the chains that bound his wrists and ankles to the cold, damp wall.

Richard shrugged. "Perhaps he'll think wolves found you, or ruffians. The possibilities are numerous."

"You'll rue this day, Richard. I'll see to it myself."

Richard smiled and raised his crossbow. "I appreciate the gold you brought so discreetly to give Matilda a dowry. You've made me quite a wealthy man."

"Wait," Kendrick said. "I want Matilda to witness this. I want to be looking at her when your arrow finds my heart."

1

Richard laughed. "Of course. She is eager to be here." A motion of his hand sent his squire scurrying up the cellar stairs. Kendrick continued to look at Richard, unable to believe the events of the past few hours.

Was it only yestereve that he had ridden through Seakirk's gates with such a light heart, pleased the king had awarded him Seakirk and Seakirk's lady as a bride? Was it merely yestereve that he had gazed upon Matilda, bewitched by her beauty, only to watch her expression turn to one of hatred and satisfaction once Richard of York had entered the great hall with his guards? Even though Kendrick had killed many of his attackers, he and his few companions had been hopelessly outnumbered. Now he stood, chained to the wall, awaiting certain death.

Kendrick met Matilda's eyes as she came down the steps, and cursed himself for his foolishness. Why had he been so blind? Surely her treacherous manner should have been plain to him: the coy way she batted her lashes, the sly way she had of twisting words and avoiding plain speech. And that smile. A shudder went through him. Her smile chilled him more fully than the stone at his back.

He shook his head, cursing himself again. Aye, he had been a fool indeed and perhaps deserved what was coming.

He swung his gaze back to Richard. He looked his murderer full in the face and waited, daring him to release the arrow.

Richard did.

Chapter
One

It was good to be home. Genevieve set her suitcase on the curb, propped her portfolio against her leg and sighed in pleasure at the sight of her office. The sign had been painted to perfection, the flowers behind the windows were blooming obediently and the door was ajar, beckoning clients to enter. Yes, it looked like the kind of place a homeowner would come to with pictures of his dilapidated house, hopeful some kind of magic could be done to restore it to its former glory. And without exception, every such homeowner left satisfied. Genevieve knew her business and she had hired others who knew it just as well. Her clients were never disappointed.

Genevieve lugged her baggage inside the front door, then laughed at the sight that greeted her. "Welcome home, Gen" was painted on a huge banner taped across her office door. She set her things down and went into her office. Flowers covered her desk, balloons hung in great bunches against the ceiling.

"Surprise!"

Her small staff crowded around her. A plate of cake was put into one hand and a cup of punch in the other as she was herded to her chair. Questions came at her from all sides.

"So, did you see any stars?"

"What did they think of the proposal?"

"Did you bring us anything back?"

Genevieve laughed as she looked around her. How good it was to be back among friends. On her right was Kate, who had been with her the longest and was mainly concerned about what kinds of celebrities hung out in old houses. Then there was Peter, carpenter extraordinaire, who was interested strictly in the details of each job. Angela, who held down the fort, was twenty going on ten when it came to presents. She stood on Genevieve's left, practically salivating with anticipation. Genevieve smiled.

"Well, as for stars, I saw only the big dipper. They loved the plans, and, Angela, your present is in my suitcase." She took a bite of cake and looked at the three of them crowded around her desk. "Does that satisfy you?"

"I want a better report," Peter said, "but I can see I'll have to wait. Angela, go get that phone. Gen, I'm going to the Murphys' this afternoon. Don't eat too much cake. Chocolate makes you sick."

"Yes, Dad," Genevieve said, with a mock salute.

"I'm out too," Kate said, moving to the door. "I have things to put together for your trip to Carmel this afternoon. You remembered that, didn't you?"

"Right," Genevieve said, with another salute. "Thanks for the reminder."

"That's what I'm here for," Kate said, smiling. "It's nice to have you home. We'll have to do a long lunch tomorrow and you can give me the scoop."

Genevieve nodded and then leaned back in her chair with a sigh. Life was too good to be true. After eight years of hard work, her business was booming. What more could she want?

She looked around her office and sighed. Actually, a knight

in shining armor might have been handy. Maybe he could have saved her from the mess surrounding her.

She closed her eyes in self-defense. Despite its charm, *Dreams Restored* was a tiny place scrunched between other tiny shops in one of the quainter areas of San Francisco. Tiny was fine when it came to how much square footage she paid rent on, but it was a problem when it came to storing all her supplies. Her desk was piled with fabric swatches, paint sample cards and photocopies of her tax forms from 1991. The floor around her desk boasted everything from half-stripped moldings to books on medieval architecture. At the moment, it was also piled high with flowers and balloons. Everyone else's desks were tidy. Maybe that knight should come along with a Day-Timer and some file boxes while he was at it.

"Gen, you have a call on line two. Some attorney with a great British accent." Angela was breathless. "Think he's a royal?"

So, the cavalry had arrived. Genevieve laughed at the absurdity of her previous thoughts. "I'll let you know."

"Well, take the job anyway. I bet Buckingham Palace has great souvenirs."

Genevieve picked up the phone. "This is Genevieve Buchanan."

A man cleared his throat. "Ah, Miss Buchanan, my name is Bryan McShane. I represent the firm of Maledica, Smythe and deLipkau, based in London. I am in San Francisco this week and I wondered when it would be convenient for me to drop by. I have a legal matter to discuss with you."

"A legal matter?" she echoed. Who in the world would want to sue her? And for what? For leaving them with uneven floorboards in the kitchen or stenciling that wasn't quite up to snuff? She was certainly as human as the next person but she considered herself a far sight more meticulous. She took her restoration work very seriously.

"About an inheritance," the man replied. He lowered his voice, as if he were afraid others were listening in on the conversation. "This is a matter that needs to be discussed in person, Miss Buchanan. Are you free this afternoon?"

"Mr. McShane," she said, slowly, "I think you have the wrong person. I'm an only child and my parents were only children. They have both passed on and I have no other relatives."

"Miss Buchanan, I assure you that you do have an inheritance and it is quite substantial. You are the last living direct descendant of Matilda of Seakirk. Rodney, the last earl of Seakirk, passed away recently and I have been sent to inform you of what awaits you."

"Who? Are you certain?"

"The earl of Seakirk. And yes, I'm quite certain. My research in that area has been meticulous. When would it be convenient for you to meet and discuss this?"

Genevieve shook her head. "But there must be thousands of Matilda's descendants—"

"Regrettably, all others have either passed on or are otherwise unable to claim the inheritance."

"Otherwise unable?"

Mr. McShane was silent for a long moment. "Insanity seems to run rampant in the family, Miss Buchanan."

Genevieve was sorely tempted, despite that last little morsel to make her think twice about having anything to do with her ancestors. Unfortunately, reality had other plans for her that afternoon. She'd promised the Campbells she would take a look at their property in Carmel. She cradled the phone between her shoulder and ear as she set to work on a jumbled pile of paperwork.

"I'm sorry, Mr. McShane," she sighed, "but this afternoon is impossible. Is there something you could mail me and let me look over?"

"I fear I was specifically instructed to speak to you about this in person. Perhaps later in the week?"

The man was persistent, she would give him that. And despite her doubts, she was intrigued. The thought of inheriting some bauble from an ancestor of noble blood set her mind working furiously. What could it be? And the history behind it? What if it were an ancient treasure?

"Perhaps over dinner?" Mr. McShane prompted.

"Dinner would be fine," she heard herself saying. Well, she *could* make it back for a late supper. She gave Mr. McShane the name of a restaurant downtown and hung up the phone.

Maybe it was some gaudy dinner ring. The meager contents of her safety deposit box could use some company. She would sign the papers, claim her prize, and that would be that.

The restaurant noises around her seemed magnified far beyond what they should have been. She heard silverware clanking against china, the sound of liquid being poured into glasses, people chewing, swallowing, burping discreetly. She noticed the redness of Bryan McShane's watery blue eyes, the pinched lines of strain around his mouth, the unfortunate lack of hair on top of his head. And, most notably, the way his hands fluttered over his silverware and around the crystal stem of his wineglass like little butterflies, too timid to land on something that might suddenly come to life and have them for a snack. And this new awareness was all due to the shock she felt over his announcement.

"A castle?" she repeated in a strangled voice.

"A castle," he nodded, his hand fluttering up to pull at the knot of his tie. "Seakirk once boasted a nunnery and one of the finest halls on the coast of what is now Northumberland. The abbey is in ruins, but the keep is in almost perfect condition. It merely awaits your loving touch."

Genevieve moistened her lips, realized it was a futile gesture, then downed the contents of her water glass in two gulps. A castle? No, she was dreaming. Things like this didn't happen in real life.

"You're kidding, right?" she managed.

Mr. McShane shook his head. "The castle is yours, Miss Buchanan. All you need to do to claim it is live there."

Genevieve ruthlessly squelched the exuberance that flooded her. She put her hands on the table and pushed her chair back a bit, shaking her head.

"I couldn't," she said, shaking her head again just in case her words hadn't sounded convincing enough.

"Please don't be hasty," Mr. McShane said quickly. "By all

means, take a few days and consider it. Did I mention that
along with the castle, you have inherited a blank cheque?"

"I beg your pardon?"

Mr. McShane pulled a handkerchief out of his pocket and
wiped off the fog that had suddenly accumulated on his
glasses. "Miss Buchanan, the bank account that awaits you is
so large, I doubt you could spend a tenth of it in your lifetime.
In essence, you have free rein with more funds than you can
imagine, to use any way you want. Perhaps in the refurbish-
ment of your castle." He deposited his glasses back onto his
nose and peered at her intently, waiting.

"Oh, no," she moaned, clutching the edge of the table. "This
can't be happening to me."

"A stroke of marvelous fortune, if I might venture an opinion. Certainly an opportunity not to be missed."

Genevieve grasped frantically at her fast-disappearing
shreds of reason. "I can't just up and leave my business," she
said, mentally making a list of all the travails she had gone
through to build it up. "Do you have any idea how many years
it's taken me to convince people I was a restoration artist, not
just a glorified interior decorator? I have clients all over the
country."

There, that was beginning to sound reasonable.

"I love my work," she said, warming to the topic. "Discovering the personality of the original structure, scraping away
all the layers of living and old paint is what fires my imagination. How could you possibly ask me to give that up in return
for spending the rest of my life in a castle I might hate at first
sight?"

"But, Miss Buchanan, what could be more stimulating than
doing restoration work on a marvelously preserved thirteenth-
century castle?" He looked at her pleadingly. "Just think of all
that money and the fine antiques you could buy with it. Why,
you could even restart your business in England."

Oh, a lawyer's logic. Genevieve felt her fine resolutions
begin to slip away from her like water down a drain. Heaven
help her, she was actually considering it!

She had to escape—quickly, before she did something she'd

regret. Her business was her life. She'd worked hard to build it from nothing. It was the one thing she had done on her own, without any help from anyone. Money and property weren't more important than that.

"Mr. McShane, I'm going to have to say no."

"But—" The butterfly fingers set to rapid, helpless flight. "If you do not take the castle, it will go to a distant relative of the late earl's. Surely you don't want that to happen."

Genevieve stood. "I have to go," she said miserably, then turned and ran from the restaurant.

A half hour later, Genevieve walked into her apartment and shut the door behind her. She bolted it by feel, then leaned back against it, letting the darkness envelop her. She let her bag slide to the floor. Her jacket followed.

She pushed away from the door and started down the hallway, counting the doorways by touch. Second on the right. She put her hand on the knob, then turned slowly. She stepped inside the room, then closed the door behind her. It was only then that she reached for the switch. Pale, golden light immediately filled the room, throwing the shadows back into corners and crevices.

She sat down on the floor right where she was and simply stared at what surrounded her. Castles. Castles of all sizes, shapes and colors. Paper castles she had taped, puzzle castles she had laminated, primitive wooden castles she had hammered. Then there were the castles she had purchased, replicas of ones that had existed in times past, castles that were only shells now on that distant isle.

She smiled faintly. It was her shrine, the place where she came when life wasn't going so well. No matter what had really happened in the Middle Ages, to her a castle represented security. It was a place of refuge from the storms of life, a place full of family and laughter and love.

And now she had been offered one.

Was Bryan McShane a fairy godmother in disguise? Good grief, the structure alone was enough to send her mind reeling. What would it be like to own something so deeply coated with

layers of history that she could never have scraped away all
the signs of living? Not that she would have wanted to. No,
she would have restored the structures and their interiors to
their original glory, searching for months for the perfect piece
to go in that corner, or the perfect tapestry to line that wall. It
would have been a restoration expert's dream. And if that had
been as deep as her feelings ran, it might have been easier to
walk away from the opportunity. Unfortunately, her fascination didn't stop with just the stones and mortar.

In grade school when the other girls had been playing with
dolls, she had been daydreaming of dragons and knights. In
high school when the other girls had been worrying about
makeup and boyfriends, she had been daydreaming about
dragons, knights and their medieval abodes. During college
when the other girls had been either trying to catch a man or
hopping on the fast track, she had been busily designing,
sketching and furnishing medieval dwellings for her knight to
come home to after a hard day of dragon slaying. Castles had
always figured prominently in her imagination, and certainly
no castle had been complete without a charming, chivalrous
and handsome knight who loved only her.

Freud would have had a field day with her daydreams. She
didn't want to speculate on why she continually felt the need
to be rescued, but she suspected it had a great deal to do with
the fact that most people tended to walk all over her and she
tended to lie down and let them do it.

Well, that wouldn't happen this time. Who knew what kind
of domineering kin waited for her on yon isle, ready to leave
footprints on the back of her shirt? No, it was best she stay
right where she was. Her business was her life. She had
sweated and slaved to get where she was. Her work had eased
the pain of having lost her parents, distracted her from
thoughts of a lover, kept her from agonizing because she had
no children.

Her staff had become her family. They loved her, fussed
over her, gave her a sense of belonging she'd never had, even
in her own family. Her work demanded all her energies. What
love she would have given to little ones, she lavished on the

houses she restored. No detail was too small or insignificant. Old wood became beautiful under her hand, weathered stone threw off Sheetrock coverings, brick emerged from under layers of paint. Houses blossomed and took on a homey feeling. No matter that she created such a feeling for others. It was her joy.

And no amount of money was worth giving that up. Her father had been obsessed with money, her mother obsessed that he didn't make enough. He'd had a heart attack at fifty and her mother had soon followed him to the grave. After the estate had paid the bills, the attorney had handed Genevieve her inheritance. The irony hadn't escaped her. Two lives spent chasing after things that hadn't lasted just to leave her a five-hundred-dollar legacy. She still had the check. It helped her keep her perspective.

No, she wouldn't give in to temptation. She rose and walked back to her front door. After flipping on the lights, she picked up her purse and retrieved Bryan McShane's card from her wallet and carried it into the kitchen. She turned on the faucet and started the garbage disposal.

And she froze. Well, perhaps that was a bit drastic, even for her. Maybe she could bargain for visitation rights. She shut the disposal off and turned off the water. Perhaps a month during the winter, when things were slow.

She hesitated.

Then she put her shoulders back. She did not need this distraction. It was best to just walk away while she still had the determination. Foolish or not, she had her reasons and she was very clear about what they were. She threw Mr. McShane's card on top of a pile of papers she intended to recycle.

And it was with only a slight twinge of regret that she turned off the kitchen lights and went to bed.

Chapter
Two

"But—"

"We have nothing further to discuss, Miss Buchanan. Good day."

There was a click and then a dial tone. Genevieve looked at the phone in her hand and felt the urge to take it apart and see just what kind of bug had been put inside to torment her. That was the third client in a week who had dropped her like a scalding potato.

Her office door opened and Kate walked in. Genevieve pushed aside her concern. "Well, how did it go?" she asked.

Kate shrugged helplessly. "It was going fine until the phone call, then they threw me out of the house. No explanation, just good-bye and good riddance."

Genevieve sighed and replaced the receiver she still held. "Maybe it's something in the air. I just lost the Montgomery account."

Kate sank down into the chair facing Genevieve's desk. "You're kidding."

"I wish I were."

"Gen, that was a half-million-dollar account! What in the world did you do?"

Genevieve pursed her lips. "I didn't *do* anything."

"But you must have! Why in the world would they have dumped us unless you offended them or something? You know how touchy they are."

Genevieve knew exactly how touchy her clients were because she'd been hung up on by several of them over the past two weeks. "If you're trying to help, Kate, you're doing a terrible job."

"I think you should take some kind of class, Gen. Maybe you need to work on your delivery. I can't afford to work for someone who offends everyone she meets. In fact, I don't think I can afford to work for you at all." She stood up. "I quit."

Genevieve watched in complete astonishment as Kate left her office and slammed out the front door.

The phone rang. When it continued to ring, Genevieve frowned. Where was Angela? She finally reached for the receiver and picked it up.

"Dreams Restored, this is Genevieve."

"Gen, it's Peter. I'm at the airport. In Denver."

"What's up?"

"They fired me, that's what's up! What did you do to these people?"

Genevieve could hardly believe what she was hearing. "I didn't *do* anything." Hadn't she just said the same thing to Kate? This was starting to become a bad habit. "Listen, Peter, let me call the Johnsons and see what's—"

"Don't. Don't do anything else. They want nothing to do with you and told me they would sue for harassment if they heard from any of us again. I quit, Gen. You're ruining my reputation."

"But—"

"I'll clean out my stuff when I get back. Sometime when you're not there."

The phone went dead. Genevieve could hardly believe her ears. She replaced the receiver slowly. The phone began to ring almost immediately. Where was Angela, anyway? She got up and walked out to the tiny reception area.

Angela's souvenir collection was gone, but there was a note secured to the computer screen with well-chewed gum.

I quit, too, Gen. Sorry. Angela.

Genevieve put her head in her hands and tried to groan. It came out as more of a whimper. Business reversals were one thing. Having the entire crew abandon ship was another thing entirely. She sat down heavily at Angela's desk, staring at the phone lines that were blinking furiously. Maybe she could get a temp in for the day until she could find someone permanent.

But until she took a few calls, she wouldn't have a phone line free to get out on. She picked up line one, steeling herself for the worst.

Eight hours later, she wondered how she could have under-estimated how bad things could get. Kate had reappeared about ten A.M. with moving boxes and cleaned out her desk. At noon, a messenger from Kate's attorney had delivered a demand for two-months' severance pay, with the threat of a lawsuit if Genevieve didn't comply. Genevieve had been so numb, she'd cleaned out her savings account to do it.

It had been the afternoon for attorneys. Genevieve had heard from at least a dozen of them, representing various clients who never wanted to hear from her again. If it hadn't hurt so badly each time she pinched herself, she would have been certain she was in a very prolonged, very vivid nightmare.

And so, eight hours into the dream from hell, she still sat at Angela's desk. The phone lines weren't blinking anymore. Angela's office keys were in a tidy pile. Kate's were in another tidy pile right next to them. Genevieve tried to smile at her organizational skills. Somehow, she just couldn't manage it.

So she put her head down on the desk and cried.

She couldn't find it.

Genevieve paced back and forth in front of her fireplace,

frantically gulping down spoonfuls of double fudge ice cream. Her spoon came up empty and she cursed the container for being so small. She set her spoon on the bare mantel, then tossed the carton into the fire and watched the flames consume it. It was going up in smoke just like her life.

She rubbed her hands over her face, trying to concentrate. She had had a nap that afternoon, so weariness wasn't an excuse. It was just hard to think with the rain beating so incessantly on the windows. It was unseasonably cold for September, as if a sinister force had taken control of the elements and was now taking delight in torturing the poor mortals doomed to walking the streets. *She* would be out walking the streets if she didn't do something very soon. If she could just find that damned business card, and if it weren't too late to say yes, she might be able to pull herself out of her current mess.

She looked around her living room. How hard could it be to find one simple piece of paper? Her furniture was gone, sold to provide refunds for incensed clients. Her office junk was piled in one corner of the room. Her *Dreams Restored* storefront sign leaned drunkenly against one wall. She turned away. Even though it had been over two months since she had closed up her shop, it still hurt to think about it.

She had to find Bryan McShane's business card. It was her only hope. She was broke, furnitureless, and losing weight by the day. With any luck, Mr. McShane had been vacationing all summer and hadn't been able to find anyone else to give that pile of stones to. She was more than ready to take it now. She had no more family, no more business and definitely no more money. Moving to England was sounding better by the minute. She could learn to like tea.

She'd thrown the card into the recycle pile, she knew that much. But there were no less than two dozen piles of papers occupying various bits of floor. Her mother would have been appalled, but at least the piles were neatly stacked. Genevieve had had a lot of time on her hands, and it showed.

She started on a pile near the doorway, ignoring the panic

that threatened to overwhelm her. The card could be found. It would just take patience.

An hour and two piles later, she began to wonder if it would take more patience than she would ever have in a lifetime.

Three hours and four piles later, she knew it wasn't going to take patience, it was going to take a miracle.

By dawn, she began to wonder if even a miracle would cut it. She had looked through every stack of paperwork in her house. She had checked the recycle pile near her phone and come up with nothing. She had checked the pile of cards by the sink, almost certain she would find Mr. McShane's card there. Surely she wouldn't have thrown it out. When would she have had time, with all the disasters going on around her?

By noon, her place was a wreck. She was a wreck. For the life of her, she couldn't remember the name of Mr. McShane's firm. She had called a London operator looking for his home number, but with no success.

She had blown it.

What she needed was brain food. She unearthed her change jar and started counting out pennies. If she could just come up with enough for a pint of chocolate-chip cookie dough ice cream, she was sure things would look better. At least she would have enough energy for another round of searching.

She had one dollar and six cents. Hardly enough for a good-size candy bar, much less gourmet ice cream.

She started to cry.

The phone started to ring.

Genevieve ignored it. It was probably another attorney calling on the off chance there was any meat left on the bones. She was sorry to disappoint him. If someone was keeping score, they would probably have shown it as: Dragons, a bunch; Buchanan, nothing. Oh, where was her handsome knight on his black destrier?

And still the phone rang. Maybe selling her answering machine hadn't been such a good idea. Call screening came in handy now and then.

She finally gave in. She could always hang up.

"Hello?" she croaked.

"Miss Buchanan?"

Genevieve jumped to her feet.

"Mr. McShane?" she squeaked.

"Yes. I was in town and I was wondering if we could perhaps meet again?"

She laughed out loud. "When?"

"Um, yes, well, are you free for dinner?"

Now, that was a question for the annals. With only a soggy head of lettuce and some ketchup in her refrigerator, she was certainly free for dinner. All right, so Bryan McShane wasn't exactly her ideal knight; he would certainly do in a pinch.

"How about a late lunch?" She didn't care if she sounded desperate. Whatever he had to offer had to be better than what she had right then, which was nothing. "Say, in ten minutes?"

"If you're certain you'll have time—"

"Oh, I'm sure. Do you know where the China Bowl is?"

He did. Genevieve was still laughing when she hung up the phone.

Miracles never ceased.

Twenty minutes later she faced the attorney again, this time over an abundance of Chinese food.

"Well?" she asked with her mouth half-full. It would have been completely full had she been shoveling in the food as fast as she wanted to. What a nice change from generic macaroni and cheese.

"Seakirk. I've come to see if by chance you might have changed your mind."

That was what she wanted to hear.

"I have," Genevieve said. "I'll go."

Mr. McShane's eyes went wide with surprise. "You will?"

"Yes. It's a godsend."

He looked around the room furtively before he leaned forward and spoke. "You know, Miss Buchanan, you needn't accept if you don't wish to."

"How bad can it be?" she said with a smile, surprised at his change of heart. "You said the castle was in good shape. Don't you want me to accept?"

"To be honest," he said, lowering his voice to a whisper, "the castle does possess an odd quirk or two."

Genevieve felt a grin tug at her mouth. "Are you telling me it's haunted?"

"I'm not at liberty to say."

She laughed. "Don't worry, Mr. McShane. I won't sue you if I hear anything go *bump* in the night."

Mr. McShane looked like he wanted to have the entire affair over with as soon as possible. She took pity on him and called for boxes for the enormous amount of food they hadn't consumed. Genevieve almost felt guilty about having ordered half the menu, then stopped herself. Her dinner companion was probably charging his entire trip to her inheritance anyway.

Mr. McShane looked shocked once they reached her apartment and he saw the lack of furniture in her living room. His gasp was particularly audible when she put away the food and he saw the bareness of her refrigerator. Genevieve smiled.

"You see, Mr. McShane, it *is* a godsend. Now, how soon should I come over?"

"How soon can you be ready?" he asked nervously.

"A week." She had renewed her passport two weeks before. It had seemed nothing but wishful thinking at the time.

He crooked his finger between his collar and his neck and tugged. "If you're sure . . ."

"I am," she nodded firmly.

"Very well, then. A ticket will be waiting for you at the airport. I will return to England and assure that all is in readiness."

Genevieve saw him out, then locked the door behind him. She waited until she heard his footsteps recede before she broke into an impromptu celebration dance. She danced her way back into the kitchen to check out what was left of the fortune cookies. Emptying the bag onto the counter produced one cookie and ten one-hundred-dollar-bills. Now, *that* was chivalry for you.

She cracked open the cookie and popped half of it into her mouth before she unrolled the small slip of paper.

Beware of ghosts sending gifts.

She laughed out loud. Obviously they had meant, "Beware of *Greeks bearing* gifts." An oddly coincidental mistake, but a mistake nonetheless. Bryan McShane was certainly no ghost. She pointedly ignored the tingle that went down her spine. Castles possessed quirks. She didn't care if hers possessed a basement full of vampire-filled coffins.

She had just inherited a castle of her very own.

It was a dream come true.

Bryan McShane made his way down the hallway to the study, cursing weakly under his breath. Of course, *he* had to be the one to come to Seakirk. It wasn't enough that he had taken his life in his hands to travel to the States. Of course not. Now he was taking his life in his hands a second time to give the current tidings to Maledica's newest client. There wasn't enough sterling lying about to compensate for this kind of distress. He fished his rumpled handkerchief out of his pocket and mopped his brow, trying to get hold of himself. Ten minutes and he would be back in his car and on his way. He could last ten more minutes.

His timid knock was answered only by a gruff command to enter. He entered hesitantly and looked at the television that dominated most of one wall. American football players were grunting and snarling as they fought for territory, their glories and failures portrayed vividly, thanks to the satellite dish on the battlements.

"They fight like nuns, don't you think?" a deep voice demanded.

"Aye, my lord," Bryan squeaked, finding, as usual, that his voice did not work properly in the presence of the admitted lord of Seakirk.

"Well, don't just stand there and shake, man. What are the tidings?"

"She's on her way, my lord. She should be here the first of next week."

The television flicked off and Bryan's client stood and faced him. Bryan never could get over how tall the man was, nor how intimidating. It wasn't just the coldness of the pale green eyes, nor the intimidating frown that usually sat on the brow. It wasn't even the rippling muscles that cloth couldn't conceal, or the hands that could have easily broken a man in two. No, it was the mocking smile. It was a dangerous smile, lacking any semblance of warmth whatsoever. When the man smiled, Bryan wanted to run for cover.

"I trust you will see to the necessary details for Worthington?"

Worthington was an elderly gentleman who possessed the dubious title of steward. Bryan wouldn't have traded places with him for any money.

"Aye, my lord. I'll see to it first thing."

"And you've paid yourself?"

"Aye, my lord," he said, looking anywhere but at his client. "And not a pence over what is due me."

"I never thought you would. Your fee is exorbitant, but I can't argue with the results you've produced. I feel certain I will have further need of your firm's assistance. I trust I may reach you at the office in London?"

"Of course, my lord. I am always at your service."

Only a grunt answered him, and the television flicked back on. The man lowered himself with feline grace into the chair and propped his feet up on the stool in front of him. Bryan knew he had been dismissed.

Perhaps the entire episode wouldn't have seemed out of the ordinary, but Kendrick of Artane was not an ordinary man. No, he wasn't ordinary at all.

He was a ghost.

Chapter
Three

Genevieve was, quite frankly, overwhelmed. They had been on the grounds a good fifteen minutes before she even saw the castle. When she finally caught sight of it rising up in the distance, she squeezed her hands tightly together to control the urge to hop up and down in Mr. McShane's front seat. It was even better than she had expected!

If she hadn't known better, she would have sworn she was on her way to Camelot. An outer wall complete with towers, battlements and a drawbridge enclosed a taller inner wall. The castle itself rose up austere and forbidding. In contrast, a black-and-silver flag flew merrily in the breeze from atop the tallest tower of the keep. She half expected to see mounted knights come thundering across the grass toward them, demanding to know who dared trespass on Seakirk's soil. Seakirk. Even the name made her smile.

The drawbridge was lowered as they approached the first wall. Not a soul was in sight. Genevieve certainly didn't believe in ghosts, but she found the lack of personnel a bit unnerving just the same.

"There is some sort of staff here, isn't there?" she asked casually.

Bryan swallowed. "Of course, Miss Buchanan. Excuse me, *Lady* Buchanan."

"Oh, I don't think I have the right to lay claim to that title."

"I assure you, my research was meticulous. You are the last surviving direct descendant of Richard of Seakirk, a thirteenth-century earl. You have every right to claim the title and all that goes with it."

All that goes with it? Why did that sound so ominous?

Genevieve pushed aside her ridiculous thoughts and concentrated on what was going on around her. Once the drawbridge was lowered, a metal grate was raised and they drove across the bridge and through what had originally been the gatehouse. Barbican, Genevieve reminded herself. Might as well keep the jargon straight. The passageway soon opened onto an extensive piece of land surrounding the inner walls.

They approached another gatehouse and another metal grate was raised.

"Portcullis," Bryan identified.

"I know," she said, her eyes already glued to the courtyard now visible through the thickly walled tunnel. "I know a bit about medieval architecture," she said, modestly. It was an understatement, of course, but there was no use in bragging. Mr. McShane looked like he was ready to break down and bawl as it was; a blow to his ego might just push him over the edge.

The castle was a mixture of the best designs of medieval engineering. The main building was no less than four stories high with rounded towers on each corner. There were only a few windows on the lower two floors but the upper floors more than made up for that lack. Genevieve could hardly wait to see what sort of window seats were set behind those beautifully beveled panes of glass.

There was a large garden to her right, full of the very last flowers of summer and numerous large trees. It did seem a bit overgrown though, and Genevieve could hardly wait to get her hands into it.

The courtyard leading to the castle was inlaid with pale

ivory-colored stone. It was obviously very old but also very well cared for. She crawled out of the car in a daze, shivering at what she had almost passed up. The entire estate was in excellent condition, and it was hers. Unbelievable. She had a hard time suppressing the urge to leap from the car and do a little gratitude dance right there on the front steps.

Bryan was out and fishing for her baggage in the trunk almost before the car had stopped moving. He deposited her pair of suitcases on the wide steps leading up to the hall.

"Best of luck to you," he said, then hopped in his car.

"But—"

He waved, then beat a hasty retreat.

Genevieve stood on the steps and watched him go, feeling decidedly uncomfortable. It was something akin to what she'd felt when her mother dropped her off for kindergarten for the first time, but this was much worse. What if no one were home? Worse yet, what if there were bodies inside, but they were dead?

She took a deep breath and turned to face the door. She had to get control of her imagination before it ran away with her and didn't come back. This was her home. She had every right to knock on the door and expect a normal, everyday person to open it and welcome her in.

Before her knuckles made contact with the wood, the door was opened, leaving her standing face-to-face with a dour-looking butler. He could have been none other than the butler. He wore a dark suit with a crisp white shirt and a prim black bow tie. His white hair was trimmed neatly above his ears, and not a hair was out of place. She was certain he would accept nothing less. She laughed before she could stop herself.

"Oh, you're *perfect*."

He didn't blink. "Lady Buchanan, I presume," he said drolly.

Genevieve felt her smile fade. So the help wasn't exactly gushing over her at present. It was probably considered impolite to gush on the first meeting. She nodded and held out her hand.

"You have the last name right at least. And you are?"

"Worthington, my lady," he said, ignoring her hand. "The steward."

"Ah, the steward," she said wisely. "I'm pleased to make your acquaintance."

"No doubt, my lady," he said dryly as he moved past her to gather up her baggage.

"No, I can—"

The words died on her lips at the look he gave her. She felt like a child who had just screamed an obscenity in Sunday school. Obviously Worthington took his job very seriously.

"This way, my lady," he said, moving past her and heading into the hall.

She followed him inside and then stopped short at the sight that greeted her. A shiver of delight went through her. The great hall. None of her castles in the boxes that would eventually catch up with her could do justice to the kind of room she was seeing. It was at least two stories high with enormous fireplaces on either side. Enormous perhaps wasn't the word for them. She could have thrown half a tree on each and still have had room to roast a boar or two.

Stone floors lay under her feet, floors that would have been strewn with hay in the Middle Ages but presently had been swept and polished until they positively gleamed. Tapestries bearing medieval designs and stretching almost from floor to ceiling hung on the walls. They were either authentic or very impressive replicas. She was walking toward one wall, her hand outstretched to touch the fabric, when Worthington cleared his throat imperiously. She looked longingly at the wall, then at her steward. He looked a bit impatient. Well, the tapestries would keep. It was probably close to time for tea, and she had the feeling Worthington·was a stickler about serving on time. She obediently followed him up the steps.

The staircase was a winding one, just as she always imagined Camelot would have had. She trailed her fingers over the cold stone as she followed Worthington's lead. The stairs opened up onto a long hallway. Lights in the shape of torches gave relief from the darkness. She found she couldn't keep the disbelieving smile off her face. With a little imagination, she could believe she really was the lady of the keep, spending her afternoons sewing with her ladies in her solar, waiting for her warrior husband to return from his adventures and shower her with hard-earned spoils.

"Your room, my lady," Worthington announced, setting the bags down in front of a door and turning the knob.

Genevieve stepped in front of him and peeked inside. Then she gasped. It was the most horrific thing she had ever seen in her life. The room was wall-to-wall Louis the Fourteenth, complete with a gilded birdcage in the far corner. The carpeting was pink, matching the pink chairs, pink bedclothes and pink wallpaper. She felt as though she had just eaten far too much cotton candy.

She took a step back into the hallway and shook her head.

"I can't do it."

"I beg your pardon?"

"The room," she said. "It's awful. I'll stay anywhere else: the guest room, the servants' quarters, the cellar. Anywhere but in this bedroom."

One silver eyebrow went up in surprise. "It doesn't suit you?"

"It nauseates me."

The other eyebrow went up to join the first. "Indeed. Then perhaps you would care to have a look at the other bedchambers? We have several you could choose from."

She nodded. He showed her the room next to the first one. It was done in the same period furniture, only this time in blue. Visions of Smurfs dressed in French finery chasing her in her dreams made her shake her head quickly.

The next room was a dreadful combination of yellows and oranges. The knickknacks and baubles covering every available surface made her flinch. She suppressed a powerful urge to hurry into the room and dust, then begged Worthington to show her the barn. He ushered her down the hall to the last two guest rooms. They were no less disgusting than any of the others. Genevieve threw up her hands in despair.

"But they are all so *gaudy*," she exclaimed.

What might have been a glint of approval appeared in his eye.

"My lady, each of the past five mistresses of Seakirk decorated a different chamber. You don't find anything redeeming about any of them?"

"I'm sure the ladies were quite nice but their taste in furnishings was atrocious," she said firmly. "The only thing redeeming about any of those rooms is the fact that I have the money to do them over again, which I fully intend to do. Now, show me the stables. It won't kill me to sleep out there for a few nights."

"The stables would be too cold for you, my lady," Worthington said with a thoughtful frown. "Perhaps I could prepare one of the servants' rooms for a night or—"

Genevieve walked away before he could finish his sentence. Worthington had been studiously avoiding a door further down the hallway and she wanted to know why. Though it was probably nothing but a storage room, it couldn't possibly be as tacky as what she had seen so far. Being rolled up in a blanket for a night or two wouldn't be so bad.

"Lady Buchanan," Worthington said quickly, "you cannot . . ."

She turned and lifted one eyebrow superciliously, determined to start things off on the right foot in her new home. Worthington was her butler, not her boss. Though he'd spent the last half hour ordering her around, he wasn't going to get away with it any longer. It was best he learn right off that she wasn't the kind of girl to be walked all over.

It didn't matter that she'd just made that decision. She was head of her home and by golly her butler was going to realize that.

"I cannot what?" she asked in her most imperious tone, trying to imagine how Queen Elizabeth I would have said those words.

"My lady," he pleaded, "you will detest that room. I'm sure of it."

"That is for me to decide."

"I beseech you—"

She was already turning the handle as the words left his lips.

Worthington, her fine resolves and the fact that she needed air to survive were all completely forgotten in the magic of what she saw.

It was the most amazing bedroom she had ever seen, and she had not only seen but decorated some doozies. A massive hearth dominated one entire wall to her right; it was easily as large as the fireplaces downstairs. Huge windows with heavy drapes flanked one side of the room. An enormous wooden desk sat under one of the windows; with any luck that window would overlook the garden. Draperies had been pulled back from another window to reveal the most comfortable-looking window seat she had ever laid eyes on. She could hardly stop herself from running over and curling up on the spot.

The bed was a huge four-poster affair, complete with bed-curtains. Maybe the tapestries downstairs were replicas; the curtains surrounding this bed were not. Without even stepping any closer, she could see that the cloth was exceedingly old, yet in astonishingly good condition. All in all, Genevieve felt as though she had stepped back in time hundreds of years.

"I love it," she breathed.

"But my lady, 'tis very drafty here," Worthington said. "You'll catch a chill."

"The fire will be more than adequate," she said. "Worthington, the room is perfect." She turned a brilliant smile on the steward, all her former irritation with him forgotten. "You did this on purpose, didn't you? You know, I doubt I would have appreciated this as much if I hadn't been treated to the other monstrosities first. Thank you so much." She reached out and gave his hand a grateful squeeze, picked up her bags and closed the door in his face.

She turned and leaned back against the door. It was perfect. And it was hers.

If she'd had any more tears to shed, she would have, but they would have been ones of happiness. This bedroom and this marvelous, magical keep were worth every single moment of anguish she had gone through over the past three months.

It was worth it all.

She was home.

All Worthington wanted to do was hasten downstairs, sequester himself in the wine cellar and drink himself into oblivion. Unfortunately that simply would not do. His Lordship would have to be told and soon, before he discovered the truth himself.

He sighed deeply and turned back down the hall. The steps to the third floor had never seemed so steep or so many before. He dragged his feet all the way down the hall to Lord Seakirk's study, then stopped and knocked smartly.

"Come in and be quick about it," Kendrick bellowed.

Worthington sighed and cast a pleading look heavenward before he entered the room. Kendrick was pacing back and forth, his hands clasped behind his back.

"Well?" he demanded impatiently. "Which chamber did she choose, old man? Hopefully the blue one. I've always wanted to scare a woman witless in a blue chamber."

"Nay, my lord, she did not choose the blue room."

Kendrick folded his arms over his chest and smiled grimly. "Tell me then that she chose the yellow bauble room. Lady Emily worked so hard on that room before her untimely demise."

Worthington couldn't help his sigh. "My lord Kendrick, I think perhaps you should reconsider."

Kendrick frowned in displeasure. "Ridding myself of this final Buchanan is my only hope, as well you know."

"She's not like the others."

"She's a Buchanan. Nothing more needs to be said."

"She has spirit."

"And she no doubt looks just like Matilda."

Worthington shook his head. "She doesn't. She has dark hair and the most beautiful pair of hazel eyes I have ever seen. She's certainly not a woman you'd want to kill, not that you've ever been able to do it in the past."

Kendrick's scowl darkened considerably. "I see she's already begun to work her magic on you." He strode to the window and looked out. "All the Buchanan women were bitches, beginning with that first bitch I almost wed. It may well be that murder won't be necessary, but I will have what I want from her." He turned around and pinned Worthington with a chilly glance. "Now, tell me which out of the five chambers she selected. I've no more head for riddles today."

Worthington realized the futility of arguing. Kendrick was incapable of listening to reason when it came to Matilda or any of her hapless descendants. Worthington had long since given up trying to change his lord. His father hadn't been able to do it, nor had any of his father's fathers.

Worthington turned away with a sigh. "She took none of them, my lord," he threw over his shoulder as he pulled the study door open.

Time passed in silence for several moments, long enough for Worthington to descend to the second floor.

Kendrick's shout of fury could be heard all over the keep.

Worthington smiled to himself as he sauntered down the passageway. Perhaps the young lord of Seakirk would think twice about killing the girl if she were to bleed all over his own bed.

It was midnight when Kendrick appeared in her chamber. *His* chamber, he thought grimly. Genevieve was reading by the light of a candle. Bloody romantic. There was a lamp right by her bed if she had just taken the time to look.

He stood in the shadows and gave a last thought to what he was about to do. Aye, it was the only way. He planned to see the last of the Buchanan bloodline either gone, insane or dead by the end of the week. In truth it mattered not to him how the deed was accomplished, though the thought of having a bit of revenge for his trouble was tempting. If he tried hard enough, he could likely pretend that Genevieve's screams were actually Matilda's.

He took another look at his ensemble. Perhaps he could have been more clever, but the arrow was a nice touch. It was a nasty-looking bolt that jutted straight out from his chest. The blood he was drenched in was always good for a throaty scream or two. Aye, it was creative enough for the first fright. He smiled darkly at the thought, imagining young Mistress Buchanan's bloodcurdling shriek and what was sure to be an abrupt flight from his bed.

Perhaps she would scream all the way down the passageway, through the great hall and out the front door. He'd parked the car right there with the keys in it, for just such an occasion. Once she had fled the keep, he would call Bryan McShane and have him seek her out with the proper documents to sign. She would be more than willing to sign a statement saying she had seen the castle and did not want it. It would be perfectly legal and perfectly final.

And then, thanks to a meticulously forged birth certificate, the keep would be his, as it should have been seven hundred years ago.

And then he would be free.

Genevieve snuggled deeper into the pillows and held the book closer to the flame of the candle. Reading by candlelight might have been romantic but it was certainly hard on the eyes. She smiled anyway. So what if she got a headache? It was the principle of the thing that counted. This was how she'd imagined it; sitting in her medieval castle in her medieval bedroom, reading by candlelight. All she needed was a medieval manuscript to make things feel completely authentic.

Her first day at Seakirk had gone off without a hitch. Of course, there had been that hair-raising bellow during the afternoon, but Worthington had assured her it was only the pipes creaking. After being grateful that some efficient soul had actually installed pipes, she'd made Worthington promise to call the plumber first thing in the morning. Too many hints by Bryan McShane had made her a bit jumpy. The fewer things that went bump in her home, the better she'd like it.

Out of the corner of her eye, she saw a shadow shift by the hearth. Instantly her head jerked up of its own accord. She let out a shaky breath. Nothing. She pushed her bangs back off her face. Tricky little beasts. It was amazing how they danced around and made the skittish think they were seeing things they really weren't.

The candle flame began to flicker wildly, as if someone were blowing softly on it. A thrill of fear went through her, then she expelled her breath with a great whoosh.

"Don't be stupid," she said aloud. "It's just a draft."

Just saying the words made her feel a hundred percent better. The flame stopped flickering and she relaxed, willing her heart to stop thumping so loudly against her chest. Worthington had been right about the draftiness. She'd have a closer look at the room by the light of day and see just where the breeze was coming from. No sense in catching her death.

Thump.

Worthington was puttering around in the kitchen again. She'd have to talk to him first thing about the hours he kept. A chill crept down her spine like a spider, making her jerk nervously.

Thump.

Was he cleaning the other rooms? At midnight? Oh, yes, she'd chat with him *very* first thing.

Thump. Grumble.

Grumble?

She wasn't going to look up. It could have been a very large rat or a very large creature from a B movie. Either way, she had no desire to make its acquaintance. She stuck her nose back in her book doggedly.

Thump. Grumble.

Oh God, she prayed, her palms suddenly slick with sweat, *let me be dreaming.* A quirk? Had Bryan McShane actually said the castle possessed an odd *quirk* or two? What an unfortunate understatement!

The creature cleared its throat pointedly.

Genevieve looked up. Had she been capable of it, she would have screamed her head off. Instead, she could only squeak.

It was huge. It was drenched in blood. It was glaring evilly at her. It reached its arms out and continued its relentless approach, just as Frankenstein had done in every one of his feature films. Genevieve would have gasped with horror at the arrow protruding from the monster's chest but she just didn't have any spare breath. She shrank back against the headboard and pulled the sheet up to her chin. No, this wasn't a movie. This wasn't the vampire show she had watched in grade school, sitting close enough to the television to change the channel when things got too hot to handle. This was real and she was going to die.

The creature stopped just short of the bed and waved its arms menacingly. Genevieve didn't think twice. She flung away the covers and bolted from the bed to the door. The lock slipped under her trembling fingers as if it had been greased.

"Begone, wench, if your life means aught!" a deep, wraith-like voice bellowed from directly behind her.

Genevieve shrieked and jerked open the door. Her bare feet slapped against the stone as she fled down the hallway, but she didn't notice either the pain or the coldness. She had just seen a ghoul and there was no way in hell she was going to spend another night under the same roof with it. First she'd find a nice comfortable inn, then she'd track down Bryan McShane and kill him for lying. *Quirk?* Sweet Mary, it was a ghost!

She pounded ungracefully down the winding staircase as fast as she dared, tripped on the last step and stubbed her toe. The pain made her gasp but she kept on limping, right to the front door.

"Lady Genevieve, good heavens!" Worthington's voice echoed in the great hall. His voice startled her so badly that she shrieked again. "What are you thinking to be up without your slippers on?"

Genevieve struggled with the lock on the hall door.

"Got to get out," she panted. "Ghost . . . upstairs . . . ."

"Now, my lady, you're overwrought," Worthington said soothingly. "Come let me prepare a bit of tea. A dash of brandy added to it will be just the thing to calm you."

Genevieve shook her head vigorously. "Not . . . on your life. I'm not staying . . . another minute . . . in this place."

Worthington put his hand over hers and stilled her frantic movements. "My lady, you cannot go out without your shoes. And you cannot go out tonight."

She slowly realized she was not going to get the door unlocked without help or reason, neither of which she possessed at the moment. She stared up at the ceiling and let out her breath slowly.

"I can't go back upstairs," she whispered.

"Of course not. We're going to the kitchen. Come out of the hall, my lady. 'Tis a drafty place."

Genevieve couldn't make herself release the door. Letting go of the cold metal of the bolt felt too much like letting go of her only hope of escape.

"He tried to kill me, Worthington."

"Come have some tea, my lady. It will help you sleep."

"I don't want to sleep."

"You're overwrought from your travels and the excitement. Tea will soothe you." He looked at her expectantly, then gestured with his head toward the doorway near the back of the hall, as if the very motion would induce her movement.

"My lady?" he prompted, when she didn't budge.

She sighed and nodded. With an effort she pried her fingers from the lock. She followed her butler across the great hall and into the kitchen, then sat and waited. She watched Worthington heat the water, steep the brew, then add a jigger or two of brandy, all without really paying much attention. All she could see was the huge blood-covered monster upstairs, the one who had come at her with death in his eyes. Without thinking, she drained the cup Worthington had set down before her, then she gasped and coughed at the burning of her throat.

"More," she rasped. Anything to help her forget.

Two cups later, she felt much better. And she was starting to feel very foolish. Ghosts weren't real. It had been her imagination. After all, she did have a graphic one. And what had she been reading? *Night of the Bloody Ghouls*. It was no wonder she'd been spooked.

"I'll see you to your room," Worthington offered, standing.

"Thanks," Genevieve smiled, but her smile was weak. Talking brave and being brave were two entirely different things.

"I think we'll need to hire a carpenter," she continued as she forced herself to walk from the kitchen. "The room is drafty."

"Of course," Worthington nodded.

Genevieve walked with him up the stairs and down the hall

to her room. No, she didn't want to go back in there, but what was she supposed to do? Tell her butler she'd just seen a ghost and would he mind sitting in a chair next to her bed and playing bodyguard? Genevieve felt foolish enough after her ridiculous flight downstairs. There was no use in making a bigger spectacle of herself.

After only a moment's hesitation, she pushed open the door and peeked inside. Empty. She couldn't suppress her sigh of relief.

"A good night to you, my lady."

"You too," Genevieve responded, lingering by the doorway. Suddenly the thought of giving up company wasn't appealing in the least. "Worthington . . ."

"You are safe here," Worthington reassured her. "Perfectly safe. Sleep is what you need, my lady. Jet lag is hard on a body."

That was what she wanted to hear. He was probably right. Jet lag was causing her hallucinations. She smiled, shut the door and walked back over to the bed. The room looked perfectly normal. The candle on the nightstand burned just as brightly as it had before and cast just as soft a light over the room. A look around—a casual look, of course—revealed that everything was still in its rightful place.

Genevieve crawled beneath the blankets and snuggled down, pulling the comforter up to her ears. Perfectly safe. Nothing in the room but furniture and her imagination.

"I'm perfectly safe," she said aloud. "Nothing will harm me."

The candle flame on the nightstand extinguished itself abruptly.

"Don't be so certain, wench."

Genevieve shrieked and pulled the covers over her head. She curled up in a little ball and prayed for a sudden loss of consciousness.

The deep voice echoed in her mind again and again, reminding her that there was more than furniture on the other side of the down comforter she held over her head like a shield. Whatever was out there was big, bloody and bothered.

And it wanted her dead.

Chapter Four

Genevieve woke with a gasp. She lay perfectly still. When she heard nothing but her own pounding heart, she gingerly wiggled the fingers of her right hand. They worked. She didn't feel any pain from gaping wounds, so it was a safe bet that she wasn't bleeding to death.

So he hadn't killed her. Why? Had the ghoul taken pity on her, or did he intend to frighten her into a heart attack? It would have been a clean homicide. Or was it ghoulicide? She managed a weak smile at her own cleverness. Too bad the world would never know just how scintillating she had been because the ghost was probably waiting for her to show her face so he could decapitate her.

Or was he merely nocturnal? Well, that would certainly be true to beastly form, wouldn't it? There was no telling what time it was unless she poked her head out from under the covers, and she wasn't quite ready to do that yet.

She needed a plan. To-do lists always made her feel better, even if she ignored them the split second after she'd made them. First on the list: pray it was morning, then run and open

the windows to shed some light on the situation. Second, face
whatever still awaited her in her room (either the creature or
the gory mess he had left behind). Third, run like hell downstairs and beg Worthington to let her sleep on his floor for the
rest of her life. Four, forget all three, run out the front door,
down the road and never set foot inside Seakirk's gates again.

No, Number Four was not an option. This was her home.
She wasn't about to walk away from it.

Without giving herself time to think any longer, she threw
back the covers and bolted from the bed to the window. Her
hands trembled as she jerked open the drapes. She'd never
been so glad for the sight of sunlight in her life.

She put her hands on the warm panes of glass and took several deep breaths. How bad could her floor look? She'd get
Worthington to help her scrub the blood off. At least the floor
was made of wood. Getting that kind of stain out of carpet
would have been murder.

Murder? What a poor choice of words.

She turned slowly, dreading coming face-to-face with death.
Instead, she came face-to-face with her bedroom. She
frowned. It certainly didn't look any different than it had yesterday. She crossed the room to the side of her bed where the
creature had been. Perfectly clean. She dropped to her knees
and smoothed her hand over the floor. Nothing. No blood, no
guts, no gore. Absolutely nothing.

She sat down with a thump. This was nuts. She *had* seen a
zombie/ghoul last night and he had frightened her silly. She
jumped to her feet, prepared to do battle. There had to be some
evidence left behind: a scuff mark, a bit of torn clothing, a
drop of blood.

Thirty fruitless minutes later, she conceded the match.
There was nothing. Had she dreamed it all? She walked back
over to the window and sank down on the window seat, letting
the sight of the garden below soothe her. Too much television?
Maybe it was dinner. Worthington had prepared a mousse of
sinful richness for dessert and she had eaten two helpings of it.
Maybe it was a sugar hallucination.

And maybe, she thought with a rueful smile, it was just her

imagination playing tricks on her. Hadn't she always been prone to nightmares as a child? Every monster she had ever seen in the movies or on television had always come back to haunt her at night. Last night was just a heck of a dream. It had to be a dream. Her castle was *not* haunted. She didn't believe in ghosts.

Get a grip on yourself, Buchanan, she chided sternly. Good grief, what a fool she'd made of herself. Worthington was probably making her an appointment at the local sanitarium right now. She couldn't blame him. Hopefully in time he'd forget about it and chalk it up to jet lag and too many novels. That was certainly what she intended to do.

During a decadently long shower, she concentrated on her plans for the day. The sooner she catalogued the items in the other bedrooms, the sooner she could get rid of the furniture and do something different. Ideally, she wanted to find medieval replicas to use. Or perhaps she'd search out authentic pieces. Her bedroom was perfect and she wanted to redo the others in the same manner.

After all, when you've got a blank cheque, why not use it?

That evening Genevieve sat in the high-backed chair Worthington had pulled close to the hearth for her, and watched as her butler carefully laid several more pieces of wood on the fire. There was probably a cozier room than the immense great hall but she hadn't had the time to find it during the day and, despite her earlier rationalizations about ghosts, she wasn't about to look around at night. The huge hearth would keep her warm enough for now.

Worthington straightened and made her a small bow. "If there won't be anything else . . . ?"

She sat up quickly. "Oh, don't leave yet. Stay and enjoy the fire with me."

"My lady, I wouldn't presume—"

"Presume or you're fired," she answered, only half-teasing. She wasn't ready to relinquish the comfort of human contact and she was willing to go to great lengths to make sure she kept it. Worthington only blinked a time or two before he obediently pulled up another chair and sat down to keep her company.

Actually, company hadn't been her problem that day. An entire army of cleaning people had come in and scoured the castle from top to bottom. Worthington had overseen the activities with the skill of a garrison captain. The personnel from the village were quick and very thorough, working as if they couldn't wait to get out. Genevieve hadn't missed the pitying looks they had thrown her way. What did those looks mean? Did the villagers pity her for her newfound wealth? She had seen the bank records. All the zeros after that pound sign had made her positively dizzy. Whichever Buchanan had amassed that kind of staggering wealth had been one smart cookie.

Or did they pity her having such an immense home to look after? She'd only had time to go through the five monstrous bedchambers that afternoon but had the feeling the castle contained ten times that many rooms.

Or did they pity her for the fact that once the door to the great hall was locked, she probably didn't stand a snowball's chance in hell of getting out?

The hair on the back of her neck stood up and she squelched the urge to look over her shoulder or above her head. There was nothing in the house. Worthington didn't look spooked. In fact, he looked positively serene sitting there with firelight glinting on his silver hair and a peaceful expression resting comfortably on his face.

"Worthington?"

"Yes, my lady."

"Have you noticed anything odd about the castle?"

"Odd?" he echoed, looking puzzled.

"Odd," she repeated. "You know, as in strange. Unusual. Paranormal," she threw in casually.

Worthington smiled blandly. "The castle does possess an odd quirk or two."

"Quirk?" Why did everyone insist on using that word?

"My lady," Worthington said gently, "this keep has been standing more or less in perfect condition since the Middle

Ages. How could it not have acquired a bit of character along the way?"

Character. Of course. She should have seen that for herself. And so what if that character just happened to be in the form of a ghost? She could learn to live with it. And once it had accepted the fact that she wasn't going anywhere, it could probably learn to live with her too. All things considered, it could turn into a rather amicable relationship. *You don't scare me and I won't call in the paranormal squad to exorcise you.* Sort of an unfriendly truce, but it might work.

Genevieve felt decidedly better. In fact, she felt so much better that she didn't protest when Worthington stifled a yawn and begged to be excused. She waved him away good-naturedly and settled back to enjoy the fire. She pulled her legs up into the chair with her and wrapped her arms around her knees. Yes, this was the life.

Things would get even better when she finally discovered where her library was hiding. A full day of reading was sounding better all the time. It would be just the thing to cure her of the last traces of jet lag. She closed her eyes and smiled in anticipation. A full day of daydreaming of her wonderful castle and imagining that it contained a handsome, brave knight—

Thunk!

Her eyes flew open. She scrambled over her chair, looking with alarm at what was quivering in front of her, only an inch away from where her toes had dangled off the edge of the seat.

It was a sword. A fat emerald gleamed in the hilt. And across the crossbar was engraved in medieval-looking letters:

ARTANE

"I'll not miss my mark a second time," a deep voice grated from behind her.

She whirled around, bumping her arm against the back of the chair in the process. The excruciating pain of smacking her funny bone was forgotten in her astonishment at what she saw.

He stood well over six feet, easily, weighing in at probably two hundred twenty-five, and those two hundred and twenty-five pounds were covered in impenetrable armor. A long, heavy broadsword was held in one hand, resting point down on the floor, while the blade of an axe winked in the light from the fire as it occupied his other hand.

It was her knight.

It was also her ghost.

She backed up sharply against the chair, a feeling of terror starting at her scalp and sweeping down to settle in her knees. No, it wasn't his size that terrified her, or his armor, or even his weapons.

It was the murderous look in his eye.

"Begone, wench!" he bellowed suddenly, raising the sword and holding it over his head.

Genevieve fled. She didn't know what her direction was until she smacked her toe against the bottom step of the stone staircase. Not even the rush of pain stopped her. She blinked back tears and crawled frantically up the stairs, using her hands and feet both to help her in her flight.

An eternity passed before she reached the second floor. She whimpered in relief as she saw the light of the torches revealing nothing but the floor and the walls. He hadn't followed her—

"Are you deaf, woman?" a disembodied voice demanded angrily from behind her. "I command you to leave!"

Genevieve shrieked, jumped to her feet and stumbled down the passageway. Suddenly, the lights went out. She lost her sense of direction and went down heavily to the floor. A brush of air went over her. She pulled her knees up under her, ducked her head and covered her neck with her hands. She could already feel the agony of cold steel against her flesh, severing bone and sinew, separating her head from her body.

It didn't happen. She knelt there for several minutes, her heart pounding wildly against her ribs, her breath coming in gasps, waiting for death. It didn't come. In fact, nothing was coming. No touch, no wound, no pain. Nothing.

Good lord, was she losing her mind? She *had* just seen him again, hadn't she? And he was a ghost, wasn't he? She lifted her head slowly and tried to make out the shadows in the gloom. It was impossible. She carefully inched to her right, holding out her hand until she made contact with the wall. Then she slowly rose to her feet. For several moments, she merely leaned back against the wall and drew breath. Who knew how long she would be around to enjoy the pleasure?

When she heard nothing else breathing in the hallway, she began to move to her right, in the direction she knew her room had to be.

"Damnation, wench, that is not the path to the door!"

Genevieve froze, waiting for the telltale whistling of the blade coming her way. Blades always whistled in the movies; they probably did the same thing in real life.

"To your left, demoiselle! Go to your left!"

He was really exasperated now.

"I can't see anything," she whispered.

The lights in the hallway came on and she gasped as she caught sight of the ghost leaning against the opposite wall, his arms crossed over his massive chest, a fierce frown of displeasure on his face. Good grief, how he must have intimidated others when he was alive! He lifted his right arm and pointed back down the hallway toward the stairs.

"*That* is the direction to take."

Genevieve's lips refused to form coherent sounds. Her mouth worked silently for several moments, eliciting a darker frown from her ghost.

"What?" he barked.

She gulped. Going down the stairs again was entirely out of the question. She'd fall and break her neck.

"Can you get through a locked door?" she blurted out in a sudden flash of inspiration.

His brows drew together so fiercely, they became a dark slash over his eyes. "I fail to see what that has to do with it."

That was answer enough. Genevieve turned and sped down the hall in the direction opposite from where he wanted her to go. If he couldn't get through a locked door, then that's just what she'd put between them. In the morning she'd call the paranormal exterminators and have them come out right away.

A ghost was just too much character for her keep. At this point, she much preferred dullness.

She'd almost reached her bedroom door when the ghost appeared before her, standing with his hands clenched in fists by his sides.

"Damnation, woman, I want you gone!" he thundered.

Genevieve skidded to a halt a hand's breadth in front of him and then backed up a pace or two. At least he'd lost his sword and his axe somewhere downstairs. Now, if she could just distract him long enough to slip past him into the room . . .

"It's k-kind of late to be g-going out," she said, her teeth beginning to chatter.

The ghost scowled. He looked the faintest bit indecisive, then scowled some more.

"You'll leave tomorrow?"

She nodded quickly.

He grunted. "Tomorrow then. At first light."

"I'm not really a morning person—"

"At first light!" he bellowed.

"At first light," she agreed quickly. "I'll be there with bells on." *Now, just get out of my way and let me into my sanctuary.*

The ghost vanished. Genevieve gaped for several minutes at the place where he'd been. Then she whirled around and looked behind her. The hallway was empty. She put her hand on the door, then stopped.

"You're sure you'll stay out of my room tonight?" she asked the empty air.

"The chamber is *mine*, wench!"

"Yours," she corrected herself hastily. "Of course it's yours. But you'll leave me in peace tonight anyway, won't you?"

A pause.

"Aye." The grumble hung in the stillness of the hall.

"Thanks," Genevieve whispered.

Only a dissatisfied grunt answered her.

She fled inside the room and locked the door. Then she leaned back against it and heaved a huge sigh of relief. Safe. Her door was locked and her ghost had promised to leave her alone. He would be as good as his word, she was sure of it. After all, a knight never lied.

She felt her knees give way and she sank to the floor, grateful it was solid underneath her. It was the only thing that had reacted appropriately that evening.

Before she knew it, she was crying. She looked up at the ceiling and let the tears slide down her face. Four months ago, she'd had a beautiful home, a wonderful view and a fabulous business. Now she had nothing. Less than nothing. She had acquired a perfect castle only to have it taken away from her. Her dream had been given to her, then ripped away mercilessly.

She drew her knees up and rested her forehead on them, her arms hanging limply by her side. What was it with life lately? Circumstances were completely out of her control. She had been controlled by outside events for weeks. And if outside forces weren't browbeating her, everyone else certainly was. First her staff had left her high and dry with demands for severance. Then she'd been backed into a corner by her clients until she had no alternative but to allow Bryan McShane to dump her off in a drafty old castle with a bossy butler and a despotic ghost!

Her head came up sharply. Damn it, it was going to stop. She was sick to death of people telling her what to do, taking advantage of her good nature, leaving tread marks on the backs of her clothes. Genevieve jumped to her feet and began to pace, her affronted feelings boiling over into a fine, indignant rage. Worthington was not going to tell her what to eat anymore, or where to sleep, or when she would and would not have tea, and that damned ghost—well, he could take his autocratic self and go straight to hell!

Her pacing became more furious. How dare he try to throw her out of her own house! Whoever he was, he sure as hell wasn't the direct descendant of Richard of Seakirk. The jerk was probably some ill-begotten stableboy with delusions of grandeur. Well, she'd show him a thing or two about who was boss! She almost wished he would appear again so she could give him a dressing-down he wouldn't forget for the rest of his days. She'd had as much of his terrorizing as she was going to take. If he didn't behave, she would take away all his weapons.

His other sword. She pulled up short at the thought. The sword still imbedded in the chair downstairs. It was probably too heavy to swing but having it in her possession instead of his might be a step in the right direction.

She returned to the door and put her ear to the wood. There was no sound in the hall. She unlocked the bedroom door and carefully opened it. It made no sound of protest. She peeked out into the corridor. The torches were out. Just as well. If she couldn't see him, he couldn't see her. With any luck at all, he was downstairs in the servants' quarters giving Worthington a fright.

Genevieve scowled as she stepped out into the hall and shut the door behind her. Worthington and his *character*. The old busybody knew all about the damned ghost. Well, he'd have an earful first thing. Right after she told him she wasn't going to have oatmeal for breakfast again. It was about time he became acquainted with the virtues of Pop Tarts.

The great hall was empty, except for the two chairs near the hearth. The fire had died down, almost far enough to not be any help at all in Genevieve's search. She crossed the room mainly by feel and paused behind what had been Worthington's chair earlier that evening and her mouth fell open.

The sword was gone.

She stepped forward and dropped to her knees, looking at the front of the wooden chair she'd occupied. She ran her hand over the place where her toes had been and her eyes widened in disbelief.

There was no mark. No indentation. No evidence that a heavy sword had been thrust into the timber.

She sat back on her heels, stunned. Though it was tempting to think her imagination was again playing tricks on her, she knew that wasn't the answer. There had been a sword. She'd heard it being driven home and she'd seen the firelight flicker off the steel. She'd read the word ARTANE on the crossbar.

But it was no longer there, nor was there any record of it having been there.

Suddenly, a most astonishing revelation occurred to her. The sword left no trace because the sword really *hadn't* been there. It was something the ghost had conjured up to frighten her, just as he'd conjured himself up out of thin air.

He couldn't hurt her.

Because he had nothing to hurt her with.

Genevieve wanted to laugh. And she would, just as soon as that damned ghost had received a healthy piece of her mind. She rose quickly and walked purposefully back up the stairs and down the hall to her bedroom. She saw nothing and heard nothing.

By the time she had locked the door behind her, she was seething. The hell he'd put her through! And with what? Imaginary toys.

Leave the castle? Ha. Not in this lifetime. It was *her* home and she wasn't going to give it up to humor some foul-tempered jerk with no chivalry in his soul.

No, her ghost would just have to ingest a helping or two of humble pie, then learn to accept her. Because she wasn't going *anywhere*.

Chapter Five

Kendrick de Piaget, formerly the second son of the earl of Artane, lately the default lord of Seakirk, sat in his study with his feet up on the stool in front of him, stared at the television that dominated the facing wall and scowled. By the saints, he was going soft in the head! That was the only reason he had allowed Genevieve to stay the night. If he'd possessed even a smidgen of intelligence, he would have forced her to leave on the spot.

He mentally manipulated the electrical currents to change the channels, flipping through them with a speed that would have made a mortal dizzy. Damn, no American football. Not even any hockey. A bit of savagery would have soothed him immensely, but it was obviously not to be so. With a deep sigh, he flicked off the television and rose.

He made his way up the stairs and through the door to the battlements. In life, walking along the roof had always soothed him. In death, things were not so different. Despite the obvious differences, of course. In life, the sea breezes would have ruffled his hair, tugged at his cloak, slipped through the weave of his garments to caress his skin. He would have smelled the tang of salt in the air and felt the chill of the night wind. He would have tasted the wine from dinner on his tongue and savored the fullness in his belly. And his body might have craved a different kind of pleasure, something that any number of his father's serving wenches would have been happy to help him with. Aye, in life, this kind of evening could have finished most pleasantly.

In death, there was nothing. No use of the senses his strong body had provided him with for over thirty years; no sense of taste, of smell, of touch. Death was a void, an empty place, a cage that had tormented him for seven centuries. Not even the full use of his mind and its strange powers made up for the simpler, more prosaic blessings his body had once furnished.

Soon. Soon Genevieve would leave, the deed to the castle would be in his name and he would be free to stop his interminable haunting and pass on to the other side, no longer bound by the chains of earth, no longer bound by the curse Matilda had muttered over him as he lay dying in Seakirk's dungeon. The castle would finally be his and he would leave it willingly. He was so very tired of living yet not living.

And he was weary of the bitterness. In life he had been a fairly agreeable sort, as agreeable as a warrior could be while spending so many years killing others to save his own sweet neck. He'd never lacked companionship at night when he wished for it; surely that said something about his character. A pity all that charm and gallantry had disappeared with a single bolt from a crossbow.

How he despised Richard and Matilda! And of the pair, he loathed Matilda the more. The witch. Scheming, conniving little harlot with her greedy outstretched hands. Kendrick swore harshly. Aye, it was because of her that he had become so acrid in his ways. In life he never would have raised a hand against a woman, nor used one ill. It made him slightly sick inside to think of the terror he had caused poor Mistress Buchanan. What he had been reduced to!

He forced a frown to his face. He'd had no choice. It had been instantly obvious to him that she couldn't be driven daft.

She certainly possessed a constitution much stronger than any of her ancestors. Frightening her had been his only recourse. Regrettable, but necessary.

Odd how he had never suffered such pangs of remorse with any other Buchanan.

He started to walk before that thought had any chance to bloom into further speculation. In a few hours, she would be gone. He would have Worthington call Master McShane and have him bring up the proper documents. Then Kendrick could lie down and sleep forever. The very thought brought tranquillity to his heart. Oh, how very tired he was of haunting!

He walked until darkness began to yield the skies to the faint light of dawn. Suddenly he was overcome by a feeling of weariness, not of the mind but of the body. But he didn't have a physical body; how in the world could he be tired? The only time weariness ever tormented him was when he made the effort of trying to move something from the physical world. Once he'd tried to use the telephone. Simply lifting the receiver had taken him an hour, then he'd been in bed for a week trying to recover from the exertion. He hadn't been desperate enough to try the like again.

Perhaps a small rest wasn't such a poor idea. Of course his bedchamber was forbidden him at the moment, but there was that comfortable table downstairs in the wine cellar. Aye, that was the place for him. It would also give him ample opportunity to see if Worthington was imbibing more of that Gascony vintage than was good for him.

"Kendrick, merciful heavens, what are you doing?"

Kendrick was sure he'd only closed his eyes for a moment or two. He glared at his steward. "Trying to rest, old man. A task in which, I might add, you are not aiding me in the slightest." He rubbed his forehead in an unconscious gesture, then realized what he was doing. As if he could actually have a headache! He scowled anyway, on principle. "What is all that bloody racket?"

"The lady Genevieve found a buyer for the blue room, my

lord. Said buyer is now departing with Lady Agatha's collection."

Kendrick sat bolt upright. "She did *what?* She was to be gone by first light!"

Worthington brushed a bit of lint from his jacket. "I think she changed her mind, my dear boy."

Kendrick leaped to his feet. "Bloody hell, Worthington, why didn't you tell me?"

"I never cared for Lady Agatha's taste. An opinion you share, I believe."

"I wanted Genevieve out, damn it, and you knew it."

"Indeed," Worthington observed, unperturbed.

Kendrick shot his steward a displeased glare and stomped up the stairs, wishing he had a body, for he would have made a fine, satisfying sound of irritation if he'd had feet to do it with. He stopped at the entrance to the kitchen and watched his prey charming an old crusty couple whose blue blood was so thick it made their skin match the horrendous blue furniture that was just disappearing out the front door.

"I'm so pleased the furniture is going to a good home," Genevieve gushed. "I did so want to find the right buyer for it."

"Rest assured, Lady Seakirk, that we will take painstakingly good care of the items," the older woman replied, her words dripping with self-importance. "Of course, we have only a few pieces of our own we would consider parting with in trade, some of the lesser items, you understand."

"Of course, I understand," Genevieve assured her. "Perhaps later in the month I might drop by."

"Not without an appointment, my dear. So many important people to see and so little time in which to do it. I couldn't possibly see you on less than two weeks' notice."

Kendrick's anger was transferred momentarily from Genevieve to the blue blood who was currently belittling her so thoroughly. He was half tempted to jump out of hiding and scare the woman and her retiring husband witless. On second thought, that wasn't such a bad idea.

"What is the meaning of this?" he thundered, striding out into the hall.

The woman promptly got the vapors. Perhaps she'd heard about Seakirk's illustrious reputation, one Kendrick never hesitated to augment every chance he had. The more people who believed the keep to be haunted, the more peace and quiet he'd have.

Genevieve flashed Kendrick a glare before she turned a solicitous glance on her customer.

"It's just the wind, Lady Hampton. Lord Hampton, I believe your car has arrived. I will phone you later. Good-bye."

With that, she hustled them both out the door and shut it firmly. Kendrick marched over and gave her his most ferocious frown.

"I demand to know what you're doing!"

She leaned back against the door and yawned. It wasn't a ladylike yawn, it was a yawn of pure weariness. Or boredom. Kendrick wasn't sure which it was, but he knew she was trying to insult him with it and he didn't like it.

"Damn you, wench, answer me!"

Genevieve pushed away from the door. "Boy, moving is hungry work. Worthington," she hollered, "I'm ready for lunch now."

"It isn't time yet, my lady," Worthington called from the kitchen.

"I don't care," Genevieve said crossly. "I guess I'll have to fix it myself."

Kendrick's mouth fell open when she walked past him as if he weren't there. She had completely missed his glare, which he was sure had been formidable. He could only watch stupidly as she sauntered across the floor, her well-formed shape clad in jeans and a long sweater. Her hair was caught up at the back of her head in something that greatly resembled a horse's tail. He watched it bob with irrepressible pertness as she continued on her way into the kitchen.

Her disappearance galvanized him to action. Damn the wench if she thought to walk away from him! He strode angrily across the floor and into the kitchen, placing himself next to her as she reached for the handle of the icebox. He couldn't remember the last time he'd been so irritated.

"I grow weary of your disrespect!"

She opened the door so quickly, he flinched. Had he possessed a body, the door would have smacked him in the face. As it was, it left welts on his pride.

"I will not be ignored!"

"Worthington, we're out of ice cream and I really wanted a milk shake. Can you go to the store for me?"

"My lady, ice cream is bad for you."

The door slammed shut. "I don't care," Genevieve said very distinctly. "You're not my mother and I will not be told what I can and cannot eat. If I want ice cream, that's what I want and it's your job to get it for me. Got it?"

Kendrick folded his arms over his chest and waited to see what Worthington would do. Now Genevieve would see who was at the head of the culinary garrison. Worthington's word in the kitchen was law and it was past time Genevieve realized that.

"Of course, my lady," Worthington said humbly. "Your wish is my command. Chocolate milk shakes morning, noon and night if it pleases you."

Kendrick snorted in disgust. So much for spine.

Genevieve gave a very satisfied *hrumph* and marched out of the kitchen, nose high, horse's tail bobbing arrogantly. Kendrick grunted.

"Pitiful, Worthington."

Worthington only smiled contentedly. "She has spirit, that one. You have to admit that."

"I don't have to admit anything," Kendrick muttered as he left the kitchen. His heart grew heavier with every step he took toward his third-floor study. She hadn't been driven conveniently insane. Frightening her had obviously been a dismal failure. After the insulting lack of respect and disturbing lack of fear she had shown that afternoon, Kendrick knew there was only one choice left him.

He'd have to kill her.

*   *   *

Genevieve wiped her hands on her jeans as she sat in front of the fireplace in her room much later that evening, waiting for her ghost. She had no doubts he would appear that night and be furious over her treatment of him that afternoon. If there was one thing he obviously couldn't bear, it was to be ignored. Well, she wouldn't ignore him any more. Once he appeared, she'd invite him to sit. They would talk calmly and rationally. There was certainly nothing a bit of communication couldn't solve.

Was he testing her, just to see what she was made of? Or was he trying to frighten her into leaving? Well, that just wasn't going to happen. She could learn to put up with him. It could work out tolerably well for the both of them.

She felt the hair on the back of her neck stand up and knew he was in her room. Then she looked in the long mirror hanging on the wall and caught the reflection of a blade hovering in the air behind her. She gulped.

Then the dagger positioned itself over her back. She closed her eyes in self-defense.

"That's sort of the cowardly way of doing it, isn't it?" she squeaked, clinging to the arms of the chair. At any moment, she was sure she would hear the sound of wood splintering from the force of her grip.

The knife jerked up suddenly. "I beg your pardon?"

"Stabbing me in the back," she choked, praying she could distract him with a bit of mindless chatter. "Sort of a spineless way to go about it, don't you think?" She winced. *Oh, yes, Genevieve, insult him.*

"As my only thought was to kill you as quickly as possible, I truly did not care how the deed was accomplished."

"Wouldn't you rather look me in the eye while you're at it?" she offered, trying to buy more time.

"Damnation, but you are a saucy wench!"

Genevieve felt, rather than heard, him move. She soon found herself staring at thick, heavy thighs on a pair of long legs that put his groin about level with her nose. He had obviously opted for comfort that night, because he was out of armor and into faded denim. She hastily forced her eyes up past his slim hips, past the waistband of his jeans, then took in the view of his sweatshirt. Her blood pressure rose several notches. The sweatshirt was black, a bit on the ratty side, and emblazoned with the words *Death to the Buchanans*.

"How clever," she said weakly.

He grunted. Well, at least his arms were still down by his sides. She followed them up, noting the width of his chest and shoulders, then the thickness of his neck. Then she saw his face.

How in the world had she ever had the presence of mind to even think around him, much less ignore him? He was so ruggedly handsome, he stole her breath away. Now, *this* was the way to die if she were going to go. She looked past the dark hair that hung below his shoulders, then looked up to his square jaw, firm lips and sculpted cheekbones. Such a strong face, with rugged, masculine features. Yes, indeed, this was her knight. Oh, how devastating he must have been in real life! She lifted her eyes to his again and their color caught her off guard.

"Your eyes are the most amazing shade of green," she blurted out.

"My mother's," he said shortly.

"Your mother's?" she echoed, suppressing the urge to fan her cheeks and cool down her blush.

"My eyes," he growled impatiently. "I have my mother's eyes." He growled again, muttering a curse under his breath. "My father used to say they were the color of sage after it had been in the sun too long."

"How romantic," Genevieve said, smiling in delight. "But he was joking, of course." With parents like that, surely this ghost couldn't be all bad.

He was speechless for a moment or two. Then he managed an unconvincing grunt.

"Aye, he was."

"You have a lovely accent, you know."

He clapped his hand to his forehead, exasperated. "This is possibly the most ridiculous situation I have ever found myself in," he exclaimed. "I come to kill a woman and now I stand chatting with her as calmly as if we strolled in the king's garden. By the saints, demoiselle, you are making me daft!"

"Oh, but I'm sure you really don't want to kill me," Genevieve said quickly. "I'd really like to chat. In fact, why don't you have a seat and let's talk—"

"You foolish twit," he sputtered in frustration. "I *do* want to kill you! Why do you think I brought this bloody knife?"

Genevieve was hard-pressed to stifle her indulgent smile. Why, the man was a pushover. He'd tried to intimidate her for three days with pretend swords and things and now he was trying to make her think his weapon was real? Not likely. Her courage returned in a rush. She held out her hand.

"I'm Genevieve."

"I know who you are!"

She smiled, unperturbed. "How nice. And you are . . ." she trailed off encouragingly.

He dropped the knife onto the chair facing her, then threw up his hands in despair.

"You, my lady," he said with a pained look, "would drive a lunatic to madness. By the saints, will you look what I've been reduced to?" He turned and walked toward the door, muttering as he went. "A gelding, that's what I've been reduced to. At least my father cannot see my sorry state. Saints, how he would roar!"

He vanished, the echo of his deep voice hanging in the air.

For several moments Genevieve stared at the place where he had been. Amazement was the only word she could come up with to describe her feelings. Not only had he not truly brandished his pretend knife, he had hardly shouted at her at all and their conversation had been almost polite. There was hope for him after all.

And how that knowledge pleased her. Cleaned up from all the blood and gore, he was certainly an extraordinarily handsome man. An extraordinarily handsome *ghost*, she corrected herself with a smile. Yes, encountering him now and then would be a pleasure. A gorgeous man who would never bother her with physical demands she wasn't sure she knew how to satisfy. Nice, safe conversation and nothing else. Life just got better all the time.

She smiled indulgently at her memories of the evening. Her ghost had brandished that knife initially as if he actually meant to do her harm. And yet, despite his gruff demeanor, he didn't look as though he had the heart to truly hurt a woman. A man perhaps, but not a woman.

She looked at the knife in the chair opposite her. Strange how he had managed to leave it behind when all his other weapons had disappeared. If she touched it, would her hands slide right through it as if it weren't there? She rose slowly, not wanting to disturb any kind of illusion he might have set up for her benefit. The firelight gleamed dully on the blade, which was indeed lying on the cushion. Taking a deep breath, Genevieve reached down and touched the slim hilt.

It was cold under her fingers.

She picked up the knife and began to tremble. Her trembles turned instantly into violent shudders. The dagger slipped from her fingers and she felt the room begin to spin out of control. Good grief, it was real! He could have killed her!

She felt comforting blackness descending and she didn't fight it. Maybe he'd take pity on her and kill her while she was passed out. She'd wake on a fluffy cloud with a harp in her hands.

Go ahead, handsome ghoul. I'll never feel it.

Kendrick stood over the crumpled heap of his latest victim. A trace of a smile flitted over his features. How his grandmother would have liked the young woman who had stood up to him so bravely. Grandmother Gwen never could abide a girl without spunk.

He sighed. He'd rouse Worthington and have him put Genevieve back to bed. There was no sense in her catching her death from the cold. He left the knife on the floor next to her. Worthington would have to get that too. Holding it for so long had exhausted Kendrick. It was one thing to wield a weapon conjured up out of thin air and a great amount of imagination;

it was quite another to pick up something from the physical world.

He sighed and dragged his hand through his hair. Ah, when had it happened? When had he become such a spineless woman that he couldn't take a blade and plunge it through his enemy's heart?

Since his enemy had turned out to be a fetching maid with a sharp tongue and a vast amount of courage, that's when. By St. George's knees, he couldn't bring himself to kill a woman, no matter what her parentage.

"Pitiful, Seakirk," he chided himself. "Truly pitiful."

He made Genevieve's inert form a small bow, conceding the battle. The outcome of the war, however, was yet to be determined.

He had the sinking feeling he wasn't going to win this one.

Chapter
Six

Bryan McShane unfolded his handkerchief and refolded it, looking in vain for a bit of fabric that wasn't already damp with sweat. How he hated being called in to Maledica's office, especially when the news he had to deliver was not what his superior was expecting!

"Go on in, Bryan," a sympathetic voice encouraged.

Bryan stole a look at Cecelia, Mr. Maledica's secretary, and managed a faint smile in the face of her understanding expression. How in the world did she manage to work for the man? Bryan would have permanent hives if he were in her place.

His timid knock was answered by an impatient bark to enter. He did, mopping his hands a final time on his handkerchief and slipping it into his pocket. He stared at the coat of arms hanging behind his employer and tried not to let the sight of the dragon rampant unnerve him. At least watching the red dragon was less unnerving than watching Maledica.

"G-good m-morning, sir," he squeaked.

"News," Maledica demanded. "Don't quiver, McShane. Stand still and report."

Bryan didn't dare come any closer to the massive wooden desk than he already was, not even to use one of the heavy leather chairs as a shield. Maledica probably could have reached across the desk and throttled him before Bryan would have been the wiser.

It was only by chance that he had uncovered just how dangerous his employer was, though it was something that should have been apparent by the man's appearance. Maledica was tall and very broad, something his suitcoats did nothing to hide. Along with his physique was a face that gave nothing away, features built for concealing facts, for encouraging the curious to keep their questions to themselves. The only thing that might have alerted anyone to the true nature of the man was his eyes, eyes that glinted with a continually smoldering anger and bitter amusement, as if to say *I could reduce you to nothing without an effort.* Bryan might have been able to ignore the warning in Maledica's eyes had he not come out of the office late one night, following his employer by a few purely coincidental steps. A thug had jumped out from the alley. Maledica had leveled the chap with one powerful blow to the face. Bryan hadn't loitered about to see what was left of the poor bloke, for fear his end would be along the same lines.

And now Maledica wanted news.

"A-as far as, er, news is concerned—"

"Has she signed the papers or not?" Maledica asked curtly.

"Not yet, sir, but I expect to hear from her any day now—"

"You fool!" Maledica bellowed, then shut his mouth abruptly, as if he regretted the display of emotion. He leaned forward with his wide hands splayed on the desk. "Hear me well, young McShane. Those papers must be signed and they must be signed quickly, before she escapes back to the States. You will go immediately to your car and drive to Seakirk today. You will call on Miss Buchanan and, if she is still sane, invite her to settle for the stipulated amount."

Bryan nodded with a gulp and suppressed the urge to loosen his tie. If the choice were between saying no to Maledica and possibly facing Kendrick de Piaget again, Bryan just wasn't sure what would be worse.

"And if she is no longer there, you will track her down and offer her compensation. I think she will be more than willing to accept it, don't you?"

"Yes," Bryan nodded vigorously. She'd be a fool not to take the money and run.

"Should she have departed for points unknown, you will search for her. Do not return without her signature. Is that understood?"

The unspoken threat hung in the air like a disembodied soul, sending tingle after tingle down Bryan's spine. He had no illusions about what his fate would be should he return unsuccessful. It was enough to make a grown man weep with fear.

"That will be all, McShane."

Bryan turned and scuttled over to the door.

"Do not betray me, McShane."

Good lord, a mind reader too! Bryan fled.

Maledica sat back in his comfortable leather chair and smiled at the breeze that crossed his face, a breeze created by the abrupt flight of his flunky. How little intelligence McShane possessed if he thought to doublecross in this deed! No, the events were set in motion, and victory was almost within his grasp. No sniveling simpleton would cost him this prize, the one he had waited so very long to have. He swiveled his chair around and stared up at his crest, the one his family had borne in the Middle Ages. The dragon winked back at him from the surface of the burnished shield, and Maledica laughed. He could taste triumph on his tongue and nothing would stop him from savoring it fully this time.

By now the last of the Buchanans was undoubtedly frightened witless and would be more than willing to give up any right to Seakirk. And then once Seakirk was his, William Sedgwick Maledica (and oh, how he loved his invented surname!) would finally have what he had sold his soul for.

Revenge.

Chapter Seven

Genevieve bounded enthusiastically down the stairs. What an incredible adventure she was living! She rubbed her hands together as she walked quickly across the stone floor of the great hall. Now was the time to have answers to all the questions she hadn't had the presence of mind to ask before. Who was her ghost? What would he do now? What had made him so irritable, besides the obvious reason that he was no longer alive?

Worthington was puttering about near the stove, muttering under his breath.

"Smells wonderful," Genevieve said brightly, sitting down at the long worktable.

Worthington turned and looked at her closely. "How do you feel this morning?"

"I've never felt better."

"Did you sleep well?"

"Who is he?"

The corner of Worthington's mouth tipped up in a smile. "Who is who?"

"Don't play games with me, Worthington," she warned.

"You know who I'm talking about. You've been withholding information and I'm sick of it. I want answers and I want them now." Wow, she really *was* starting to sound like Queen Elizabeth. Genevieve put on her most formidable frown. "Tell me who he is."

Worthington turned back to the stove. "I'm not at liberty to say, my lady."

So, her butler wasn't going to give. It sounded like he had taken the same courses in *lawyerese* Bryan McShane had. Well, it was only a minor setback. Surely there were others who knew something about the castle. All the cleaning people from the village at least knew the rumors. If Worthington wasn't going to spill the beans, she'd just look around until she found someone who would.

"Well, then I won't nag you," she said, feigning an air of indifference. "Could I use your car today? I need to run into town."

"Mine's in the shop," he said, pretending great interest in what was in the pan. "Take His Lordship's Jaguar. It's out front with the keys inside."

"You mean Rodney's car?" Genevieve prodded. "The *late* earl of Seakirk?"

She could tell by his profile that he was fighting his smile. "Nay, my lady. Not Rodney's."

"Rodney was the only earl I know of," Genevieve snorted.

"I know of another," he said serenely.

"Come on, Worthington," she cajoled. "Give it up. Don't make me fire you."

Worthington smiled indulgently. "All in good time, my lady."

Genevieve wasn't about to acknowledge her ghost as anything as lofty as an earl, but it was entirely possible that the man had a penchant for expensive automobiles. "What does a ghost need with a car?"

"His Lordship loves his toys."

"Well, I'll try not to drive it into a ditch."

"I don't think he'd appreciate that."

"I don't think so either. And," she added, "just so you

know, I'm off to the antique shop. Research for my business."
She'd seen an ad in the paper and had the feeling if anyone
would know about what sort of antiques, living or not, were in
her home, it would be an antique dealer.

Worthington gave her a skeptical look as he set down a
plate of eggs and ham in front of her. "Miss Adelaide is a
tremendous gossip. You shouldn't believe all her prattle."

"And how am I to tell truth from fiction if there is no one
here to help straighten me out? Unless you'd care to clear
things up for me. Would you, Worthington?"

"His Lordship has a point," Worthington grumbled. "You
are a saucy wench."

With that, he glided from the kitchen, his very proper, mid-
night-black coattails trailing behind him like an entourage.

The trip into town was one Genevieve would have preferred
to forget. Quickly. Having the steering wheel on the wrong
side of the car was uncomfortable. Driving on the wrong side
of the road was damned dangerous. Knowing that she was sitting behind the wheel of a hundred-thousand-dollar car made
her feel light-headed. Perhaps her undead host didn't want to
kill her now, but he certainly would if she totaled his favorite
toy.

After only a few brushes with death and the oncoming traf-
fic, she reached Adelaide's Ancient Acquisitions. The acquirer
herself was waiting on the step, as if she'd known Genevieve
was set to arrive. Genevieve began to wonder if the entire village were haunted.

"Come in, dear child, and sit," Adelaide said encouragingly,
drawing Genevieve inside and shooing her over to a chair instantly. Adelaide had to make tea before she would even begin
to talk about anything at all, and Genevieve was almost beside
herself with anticipation. Perhaps now she would know who
the man was who continued to haunt her even when he was
away. Adelaide took her time preparing refreshments and then
settled her substantial self into the chair opposite Genevieve.

Genevieve hardly had time to open her mouth to ask her
most pressing question before she was inundated with gossip.

There were the usual items of interest: the grocer's affair with the constable's wife; the dressmaker who had lengthy private sessions with the mayor; the school superintendent's children who had just set fire to the library. Genevieve found herself warming to the woman instantly and laughing at her tales of small-town English life.

"Now, tell me," Adelaide said, her eyes twinkling. "Have you met him?"

Well, now this was what she'd been waiting for. Why then had she all of the sudden become reluctant to speak of him? By golly, he was *her* ghost. The last thing she wanted was a pack of tourists and paranormal investigators camping out on her front stoop.

But it looked as if Adelaide wasn't to be deterred. She was waiting expectantly for Genevieve's answer.

"Who?" Genevieve asked casually.

Adelaide smiled. "My dear, I do tend to chatter on, but I chatter selectively, believe me. I will not betray your confidence."

Genevieve found herself smiling. "Do you know who he is?"

Adelaide's eyes took on a dreamy look. "Is he truly as handsome as they say he is?"

"When he isn't covered in blood and brandishing a battle axe."

Adelaide's eyes widened and then she giggled a most undignified giggle. "He's up to his old tricks then."

"Can you tell me more? My butler is hopelessly close-mouthed and I'm not about to ask my ghost."

Adelaide pushed her teacup aside and leaned forward conspiratorially. This was serious gossip. Genevieve leaned forward too, not wanting to miss a single syllable of what would no doubt be gripping revelations.

"His name is Kendrick de Piaget of Artane," Adelaide said in reverent tone. "Sir Kendrick was a son of the most powerful earl in England in the thirteenth century, Robin of Artane."

Genevieve was grateful she hadn't been sipping her tea or

she would have choked on it. "The thirteenth century?" she gasped.

Adelaide nodded, her eyes full of barely suppressed enthusiasm. "Aye, and there wasn't a family more powerful on the island at the time, or more feared and respected for their prowess in battle."

"Wow," Genevieve breathed. She could certainly believe that, if Kendrick's sword were any indication.

"Now, 'tis said that Kendrick was set to wed the lady of Seakirk, Matilda. How it happened exactly has never been revealed but somehow she betrayed him and he was murdered because of it. He swore vengeance on her descendants and he's been tormenting them a generation at a time for centuries."

"I see," Genevieve said, finding it difficult to swallow suddenly. And she was Matilda's descendant. Pieces were starting to fall into place.

"I've never seen the man, of course, but I've heard the tales of his hauntings. When His Lordship is on one of his rampages, Worthington is wont to hie himself off to the pub and have a bit of peace and quiet. After a mug or two of ale, he tends to ramble." Adelaide smiled in spite of herself. "Not that his rambling yields much. He's too tight-lipped for that."

"Yes, I'm well acquainted with his unwillingness to divulge details," Genevieve nodded. She realized then that she was clutching Adelaide's lace tablecloth as if it were a life preserver. She forced her fingers to unclench. "Can you tell me any more?"

Adelaide sighed. "I wish I could, child. Whatever else you learn about the man will be through your own doing, I'm afraid. All I know is that it's rumored that Sir Kendrick is the rightful earl of Seakirk."

"But how can he be the earl of Seakirk—" Genevieve started to ask, then answered her own question. "I see," she said thoughtfully. "Then a Buchanan stole the title from him."

"I'm sure it's more complicated than that, my dear, but I haven't the details to prove it."

Genevieve nodded thoughtfully. She had the feeling those details were precisely what she needed to know if she hoped to understand the man who had haunted those solid walls near the sea for the past seven hundred years.

She drove home and then left the castle to walk along the beach. She walked until the sun set, trying to understand the man she was now sharing a home with. Had he loved Matilda? How old was he when he died? How had the murder been committed? Was there more to it than that?

She walked for hours, or what seemed to her hours by the time she was good and lost. Damn, when had it become so late? She watched as the sky turned a dark blue and the stars came out. Not even a moon to help her. Why hadn't she thought to bring a heavier coat? She turned to go back the way she had come only to find that the tide had come in and the beach had disappeared. It was oh so tempting to sit down and cry.

Suddenly the flame from a candle appeared before her, hovering in midair.

"Lost?" a deep voice asked gruffly.

If he'd been made of flesh and bone, she would have thrown her arms around him and hugged him. "Very," she replied hoarsely.

Kendrick de Piaget materialized, revealing the hand that held the candle aloft.

"You're still on my land. Fortunately. A few more paces north and I wouldn't have been able to come for you."

"Thank you," she murmured, looking up into his pale green eyes. She found herself smiling. They really were the color of sage.

"I don't want you dead before I can kill you myself," he said shortly. "Follow me. By now I should hope I know the way home."

She nodded and scrambled after him up the slope. "Are you really Kendrick de Piaget?"

He hesitated only slightly before continuing to walk. "Aye."

There was no more conversation for a good hour, as Genevieve didn't have the breath for it. Kendrick obviously had forgotten that she possessed a pair of very mortal legs and couldn't keep up with him without running. His pace was drill-sergeant swift.

She followed him through the gates and into the courtyard. The lamp hanging outside the hall door bathed the surroundings in a pale, golden light. Genevieve stopped to catch her breath.

"Did you love her?" she wheezed, hunching over with her hands on her thighs. There, the question she had been burning to ask him was finally out.

Kendrick turned a chilling glance on her. "If you had any idea how I felt about the woman, you would not dare ask."

"Oh," Genevieve gulped. "I see."

"So you do," he said curtly and promptly vanished.

Genevieve did nothing but breathe until her side ceased to ache and she was no longer gasping for air. She straightened and frowned. Getting answers out of this man would be more difficult than she had anticipated.

"Well," she said, after stewing for several moments, "if you loved her so much, why do you hate me? I mean, I'm her descendant and all, but—"

He appeared instantly, towering over her. "I despised Matilda," he said, his eyes flashing. "Not even when I thought I loved her did I truly love her. She was a sniveling, whining bitch who thought of no one but herself. Thanks to her, my life is hell."

"Why?"

"Because I cannot leave Seakirk!"

"But what has that got to do with me?"

"You live and breathe."

"Do I remind you of her so much?"

Kendrick's frown was fierce. "You look nothing like her. And that isn't the point."

"Then what is? Whoever said trying to kill me would solve your problems?"

"I deduced it myself."

"You deduced wrong, buddy," she said, glaring at him. Rude *and* unreasonable. Maybe it would be best to leave him alone until he was in a better mood. She walked right through him, then gasped when she realized what she had done. She turned slowly to face him.

He looked as astonished as she felt. "No one has ever dared such a thing before," he said.

"You were in my way," she said, regaining her composure. "Maybe you'll move the next time."

She made it back to her bedroom without seeing him again. Her preparations for bed were made by memory; she was far too preoccupied. Now she knew who was haunting her and she knew why. At least part of the why. Worthington would have to provide her with the rest of the answers.

No, she thought decidedly, she wouldn't ask Worthington. It was Kendrick's story to tell and she'd just wait to hear it until he was ready to tell it. Knowing him even as little as she did, she had the feeling she shouldn't hold her breath. Well, it didn't matter. She wasn't going anywhere and he certainly didn't look to be going anywhere. They'd have plenty of time to talk in the future.

She lit the candle next to the bed and slipped under the covers. Reading didn't appeal to her so she simply lay there and stared off into space.

"We are quite civilized here at Seakirk," a deep voice growled. "You needn't use just a candle."

He was leaning against the footpost of her bed.

"Don't you ever knock?"

"This is *my* chamber."

"I wasn't about to take any of the others," she said with a shudder. "And, as I seriously doubt you sleep any, you surely don't need this bed."

"It hardly matters whether or not I use it. Seakirk belongs to me and I decide the activities that go on within these walls. And," he said, looking at her pointedly, "I don't like you in my bed."

"Kill me then," she said, with a shrug.

"You'll bleed on my sheets."

"Then drag me downstairs and kill me outside."

A dark frown appeared on his face. "I cannot."

"You held the knife."

"It took an enormous amount of energy. Carrying you is quite beyond my capabilities."

"Learn to live with me then," she said, "because I'm not going anywhere." She leaned over and blew out the candle. "Good night, Kendrick."

Genevieve lay as still as a corpse, praying she wouldn't soon feel the sting of a blade across her throat. Had she been a complete idiot by standing up to him? She knew he wouldn't kill her. Didn't she?

There was no sound in the room, and finally she began to relax. She carefully pulled the covers up over her ears. Got to protect that jugular from vampires. Or would her ghost protect her? He might if he thought the alternative would leave him with blood on his sheets. Not exactly a paragon of chivalry, but with a little patience, perhaps he could be taught manners.

Was he still out there? Genevieve didn't dare lift her head to look. So instead, she contented herself with a determined set to her jaw.

"I'm not leaving, you know," she said, to no one in particular.

A dissatisfied snort answered her. "I gathered as much."

A hint of humor. So Kendrick de Piaget wasn't a completely lost cause.

"Good night, Kendrick."

She waited for several minutes, then felt weariness steal over her like a soft mist. She was almost asleep when she heard his deep whisper echo in the room.

"Good night, Genevieve."

Chapter Eight

Bryan McShane clutched the sweat-slippery steering wheel as he passed under the inner curtain wall and saw the keep proper of Seakirk jut up before him like a headstone suddenly erupting from the earth. He squeaked in fright and reached for another handkerchief. How he hated this place with its ghosts! If it wasn't Lord Seakirk coming up behind him, it was one of his other undead cohorts. Bryan vividly remembered the first time he had come to Seakirk and been chased away by a Saracen warrior waving a pair of bloody swords. The rental car company hadn't been at all pleased with the condition of the driver's seat.

The embarrassment of having soiled himself was only one of the reasons Bryan hated Seakirk with all his heart. Seakirk's lord was the other. Bryan didn't like to be intimidated. There was a lion inside him, begging to have a chance to display its courage. Even his lion skittered off in terror when faced with the formidable frown of de Piaget. One day de Piaget would pay for what he'd put Bryan through. Yes, he'd pay dearly.

But not today. Today Bryan would get Miss Buchanan's

signature on Maledica's papers. Tomorrow he would figure out a way to transfer that signature to papers with his own name under the RECEIVED BY line, then he would sell the castle right from under de Piaget and Maledica both. Then he would take a very long, very secluded vacation. For the rest of his life.

That was tomorrow. Today was another trip inside Seakirk's great hall, something he had put off for over a week. At least he wouldn't have to make the trek to de Paiget's study down the Hallway to Hell.

Bryan hadn't even put his knuckles timidly to the wood before Worthington was there, opening the door. How did the old man stand his living conditions? Maybe he had nerves of steel. Bryan suspected there wasn't anything in this world or the next that would force even a single strand of Worthington's hair out of place.

"Mr. McShane. A pleasure."

Bryan nodded weakly. "I'm here to see Miss Buchanan."

Worthington stood back and gestured for Bryan to enter. Bryan did, then jumped when the door closed behind him. His inner lion was bolting with its tail between its legs. Bryan wanted to do the same thing.

"Lady Genevieve is not here at present, Mr. McShane—"

"Worthington," a deep voice said from across the hall, "I'll handle him."

Bryan forced his fingers to uncurl, then quickly wiped his clammy hands on his trousers.

"M-my lord," he stammered. "I didn't expect to see you."

"Obviously," Kendrick said as he walked across the floor, not making a sound. "I remember telling you quite specifically that I would call you when your services were required again."

"Ah, you d-did." Bryan nodded quickly. "I merely came to call as a courtesy. All is going as you had expected? I brought the papers for Miss Buchanan to sign."

Kendrick's frown only deepened. "As I said before, when your services are required, I will alert you. Until then, you are not to return to Seakirk."

Bryan blinked. "Then she's still here? You haven't fright-ened her off—"

"Enough!" Kendrick bellowed suddenly. "Have you gone daft, man? When I need your aid, I will demand it."

"But, my lord—"

Kendrick took a step forward and Bryan fell back. Death at Maledica's hands seemed a pleasant thing compared to the fu-rious ghost he was facing.

"Begone, dolt!"

Bryan turned and fled, blessing a serene Worthington for holding the door open for him. He jumped into his car and screeched out of the inner bailey, down the road through the outer bailey, through the gatehouse tunnel and over the draw-bridge. He didn't breathe until he was safely off Seakirk land and had turned onto the road leading to the village.

Genevieve Buchanan was either dead or an unwilling pris-oner within those twelve-foot-thick stone walls and, either way, Bryan wasn't going to rescue her.

France was nice this time of year, wasn't it?

Kendrick watched the dust created by McShane's hasty flight. Pitiful rabbit. The man should have rather chosen a bak-ery as his life's work. He was surely not equal to handling any but the most pedestrian of tasks.

"My lord, what was young master McShane babbling about?" Worthington asked, straightening his immaculate suit coat.

"Idle chatter, old man. Alert the outer gate guards not to let him pass again unannounced. I don't care for his brand of ser-vicing."

Worthington shot him a skeptical look, then pursed his lips. "Just what is it you're planning?"

"You know exactly what I planned, Worthington. I wanted Genevieve to sign the papers and free me. By the saints, hadn't we discussed this at length?"

Worthington lifted one silver eyebrow. "You seem to be speaking in the past tense, dear boy. Can I take that to mean you've changed your mind about your sweet houseguest?"

Kendrick scowled. "You can take it to mean I think you are an interfering old busybody with nothing better to do than to poke your nose into my affairs, a place your nose certainly doesn't belong."

"If your affairs do not concern me, my lord, I don't know what does."

Kendrick ignored the attempt at drawing out further information. He knew that if there was one thing Worthington couldn't bear, it was to be left in the dark. Kendrick wasn't about to oblige him on this. All his steward needed to know was that Bryan McShane was better left outside Seakirk's gates. Kendrick wasn't about to let Genevieve fall into his attorney's hands. The less she knew about what Bryan McShane's activities had been over the past few weeks, the better off she'd be. Even though Kendrick wasn't sure he wanted her in his house, he wasn't above admitting that she wasn't a bad temporary guest.

How could anyone not admire her spunk? Or that stubborn set to the jaw she acquired when she was digging in and preparing to hold her position? Ah, and then there was that delightfully insolent way she flipped her mane of hair caught up in the ribbon like a horse's tail, as if he were nothing but an annoying fly she had put up with for much too long.

He wandered across the great hall and up the steps, curious to see what chamber contained his houseguest at present. As he walked, he pulled his sword out of thin air and belted it around his hips. Perhaps it was only vanity that made him wear it when he could have conjured it up and brandished it at any time. Or perhaps it was to see what kind of reaction he would get out of Genevieve. He had the feeling he wouldn't be disappointed.

It had been over a week since he had followed her down to the shore, and, despite himself, his fascination with her had grown more each day. She was like no other Buchanan woman he had ever met. At least she wasn't afraid of hard work. She had spent three days going through the other bedchambers, labeling all the items and spending hours on the phone looking for buyers for the remaining furniture. By the end of the week, the monstrosities were just bare rooms, waiting for a loving touch. Kendrick knew very well what she was capable of doing and actually found himself looking forward to seeing her work her magic on his home.

He walked through the upstairs solar door and hung back in the shadows. Genevieve was curled up in one of the window seats, staring out over the ocean. The sunlight fell softly on her long, dark hair. It was hair made for a man's hands, to be brushed, caressed, tangled between fingers and smoothed across whiskered cheeks. Aye, the thought of her hair was only one of the things that had left him pacing on the battlements far into the wee hours that morning. It was preposterous, but he could not rid her image from his mind. And he had seen her as she was now with her long legs tucked up on the bench with her, her slender fingers clasped around her ankles, her stubborn chin resting on her knees.

Why had no man claimed her for his own? Perhaps she wasn't beautiful in the classical sense of the word but there was something earthy and secure about her. It was a pity he hadn't met her when he was alive. She was the kind of woman who would have inspired him to give up his roaming ways and enjoy innumerable evenings together with her in front of a cozy fire. Ah, what a painful thought.

She looked as pensive as he felt. He felt a twinge of regret over what he had done to get her to the island. No doubt she missed her home very much. At least she wasn't pining after a lost love. Kendrick's research had been thorough enough to discover that there was no man in her life who would come chasing after her. For some insane reason, that thought pleased him.

Only because it showed that she had made her way in the world on her own, he justified quickly. Nay, there was no relief at knowing she belonged to no other, none indeed. Kendrick knew he hadn't gone as daft as that. He folded his arms over his chest and scowled. Damnation, but he hardly cared if she was another man's. She was a Buchanan and he needed her only for her signature on a piece of paper that would relinquish her claim to his home. He had no other interest in her besides that. He had to remind himself of that several times before he came close to believing it.

She caught sight of him and jumped, putting her hand to her throat.

"You startled me."

"I keep forgetting to knock," he said gruffly.

Her smile began in her eyes. Worthington was right; it was nothing short of enchanting. Her eyes were a beautiful hazel; deep green with flecks of gold in them. Her grin appeared briefly and then abruptly left her face as she caught sight of his sword.

"Good grief," she breathed.

He walked over to her with a swagger, pleased at her reaction. So he intimidated her. It was soothing to his ego to know he could still make a woman back up a pace or two and take notice.

"I thought you weren't going to kill me," she said.

"I'm still pondering the matter."

"Oh," she said, lifting her eyes to meet his. "Well, let me know when you come to a final decision."

He pursed his lips, trying to fight his smile. By the saints, the wench was cheeky. "You'll be the first to know, believe me," he assured her. He sat down on the opposite end of the bench and leaned back against the wall, letting his hand rest casually on his sword hilt. She continued to steal looks at his blade from under her eyelashes. He found that extremely satisfying.

Time stretched into an uncomfortable silence. Finally Genevieve spoke.

"I wish you'd make up your mind."

"I'd prefer to keep you guessing."

"I really don't think killing me is going to make you feel any better," she said.

What genuine concern there was in her eyes. It made him feel doubly low for having used her so ill.

"What you ought to do is talk about it," she continued earnestly. "I'm a great listener, you know."

Irritation replaced his guilt. As if talking would solve his problem! He stood swiftly.

"How dare you give me advice," he snapped. "You who know nothing of what I've endured."

"Killing me is not the answer," she repeated, looking at him unflinchingly.

Damnation, but this wench was much too frank for his taste. Never mind that all the women in his family had been just as frank. What he wanted was a woman who knew her place and, more to the point, when to keep silent!

Then he realized what his last thought had been and he swore. As if he actually wanted a woman, and a Buchanan at that!

He vanished from the room, cursing furiously.

Two days later he was still in a foul mood. He'd locked himself in his study and not come out, not even to answer Worthington's queries. Let them both think he was dead. He would certainly be better off that way. He tried to ignore the way his pride was stung knowing Genevieve hadn't bothered to come looking for him. She was no doubt pleased not to have him around her. Just as well. The very last thing he needed was a mortal woman fouling up the smooth running of his undeath.

A dark shadow shifted by the window. Kendrick looked up at the captain of his guard.

"What news, my friend?"

Royce of Canfield crossed the room and sat down in the chair opposite him. "I only have a few hours—"

"Royce, you've been saying that for the past seven hundred years," Kendrick said crossly. "Don't you think that by now I know just how many hours you can remain?"

Royce leaned back against the chair and smiled. "Touchy, aren't we? Is your new Buchanan giving you grief? I caught a glimpse of her as I was haunting the airport. She's a comely thing."

"She's no concern of yours," Kendrick said, glaring. He frowned even more fiercely at Royce's grin. There were times he missed his dearest friend and then there were times he didn't. Like now.

That wasn't entirely true, though Royce tended to remind him of things better left forgotten. Kendrick sighed and leaned back against his chair. He and Royce had been inseparable as children. Royce had fostered with the same lord he had. They'd both gone home to Artane when allowed and Royce had been treated as another of Robin of Artane's sons.

After they had won their spurs, Royce had announced he would become Kendrick's captain. Kendrick could not have been more pleased. They had gone crusading together, wenching together, warring together. Just how many times had Royce saved his life while they had hired out as mercenaries? Too many to count.

And now this. Together in life, together in undeath. Kendrick's only regret was that Royce had been cursed to roam while he had been cursed to remain at Seakirk. Matilda hadn't seen fit to leave them even the comfort of each other's company.

Royce stretched out his long legs. "Popped over to the ancestral digs."

Kendrick smiled. How he loved tales about Artane and its illustrious inhabitants. "And?"

He laughed. "Kendrick, you should see Lord Artane's youngest son. If he'd looked any more like you, I would have thought I was seeing a ghost."

"Your humor is, as always, sadly misplaced. How is the dear earl of Artane? My father would be shocked to see what a pantywaist his descendant is."

"The lad seems to be managing rather well. Of course, he looked a bit spooked when I asked him for refuge for the night."

"You didn't."

Royce grinned. "I did. And Nazir almost gave him apoplexy when he started waving those bloody swords of his about."

"Where is he?"

"I lost track of him—"

"Royce!" Kendrick exclaimed. "Your duty is to control him. *You* can leave Seakirk to keep him in hand. I cannot."

"Kendrick, he'll come 'round sooner or later. He always does."

Kendrick was hardly pacified. Nazir was one of the more uncontrollable members of the undead, and Kendrick shuddered to think of the mischief the Saracen warrior could stir up. If only Kendrick weren't bound to Seakirk—

"It isn't all it's cracked up to be, you know," Royce said.

"What isn't?" Kendrick asked, unnecessarily. Royce could read his thoughts as easily as he could read Royce's. It was amazing the things a mind could accomplish when not fettered by a mortal body.

"Roaming. At least you have a home. I'm unable to stay in one place more than a night."

"At least you can travel about as you wish," Kendrick grumbled.

"Roam and roam and roam. It grows tiresome after a few hundred years, my friend. Be grateful for the beauty of your hall and the woman you share it with. You could be much more unfortunate."

Kendrick didn't have an answer for that. He hardly knew which fate was worse, but he suspected it wasn't his. He smiled sadly at his friend.

"I'm sorry. 'Tis my fault you cannot—"

"*Merde*," Royce said with a smile. "I chose to remain and you know it. It was nice of Matilda to give me a choice, wasn't it?"

"You think she was a witch?"

Royce laughed as he rose. "I'll give you my answer the next time I see you. Farewell, Kendrick. Kiss that sweet wench of yours a time or two for me."

"Hell would have to freeze over first," Kendrick muttered, knowing it would be just that long before he would ever have a body again to kiss with.

After Royce had gone, Kendrick wandered up onto the battlements, hoping the sight of the sea crashing against the shore would soothe him. He wasn't surprised that it didn't.

Perhaps it was the visit from Royce that had so undone him. A wistful smile touched his lips. How sweet had been those days when Artane had been filled to the brim with his family, grandparents, aunts and uncles, cousins and siblings. There had always been some child about a bit of mischief or amusement. Nay, he had never been lonely in those days. He and Royce had been as close as two friends ever could have hoped to be, closer even than Kendrick had been with his brothers. Their only disagreement had been over Matilda. Royce had detested her. Kendrick had called him a fool.

Nay, he had been the fool. Matilda had been a witch. Kendrick didn't believe in witches, but he couldn't deny the strange feeling that had come over him as Matilda had cursed them both. She'd bid Royce to roam forever, never finding peace. She had only suggested to Kendrick that it was past time he found hearth and home to stick close to. Prophetic bitch.

Only Nazir had escaped such restraints. Perhaps his infidel beliefs had kept him safe. Kendrick knew only that his Saracen servant had a penchant for stirring up trouble and took that much more delight in knowing that Kendrick could not come after him. He scowled fiercely. The bloody wretch would regret it one of these days.

But nay, he could have called to Nazir at any moment and his loyal slave would have been forced to heed him. Somehow he just didn't have the heart or the energy to restrain him. Nazir's troublemaking was the only amusement left for him. Hearing the Saracen's tales of glory was worth his own chagrin at having loosed such a naughty member of the undead on the world.

"Kendrick?"

Genevieve's voice startled him so badly that he almost fell off the walkway. He looked over his shoulder to see her standing not ten paces from him.

"What?" he asked gruffly. So he was lonely. And so she had come to seek him out. He squelched the sudden twinge of pleasure that knowledge brought. He'd be damned before he'd settle for Buchanan company.

Genevieve approached hesitantly and tilted her head back to look up at him.

"I'm sorry," she said. "I never meant to offend you, or hurt your feelings."

"I've no feelings to be hurt."

"Perhaps you don't but I was still out of line. I have no idea what you've been through and it was presumptuous of me to pretend I did. I would like you to forgive me."

How sweetly she trembled as she stood near him, and how strenuously she fought to hide those trembles. He'd frightened her badly over the past two weeks, yet she had braved another fright to talk to him. Astonishing.

Even more astonishing was that she had apologized. He felt the ice around his heart begin to thaw just the tiniest bit. Not a great amount, mind you, but a tiny bit. It wasn't actually Genevieve's fault that Matilda had been such a bitch. She certainly couldn't be blamed for his current situation.

He sighed. He hadn't been able to carry through any of his plans. He couldn't kill her, nor could he make her daft. At the moment, he had too much pride to ask her bluntly to sign the castle over to him. Ah, what a sorry state he was in!

Perhaps in a few days he would try again, after he had overcome this foolish desire to see her smile, after he had regained in his breast the ache that her coming into his home had somehow filled, or perhaps after he had lost the yearning to lose himself in her deep hazel eyes. Aye, then he would demand that she give up what was rightfully hers in order for him to finally be free of Seakirk's hold on him. If she found him in a particularly fine mood, he might even allow her to live in the keep after he had gone.

But not now. He looked down into her sweet face and winced at the rapidness of his surrender.

"I'll forgive you if I must," he said, trying to sound ungracious. There was no sense in letting her think she had the upper hand. Perhaps she had a body of flesh and bones, but that hardly meant he would let her take over the running of the keep for as long as they were both there. Despite what might be in the Crown's records, Seakirk was *his*. He had paid for it in blood and he fully intended to keep it. Genevieve had best realize from the start that he was lord.

Genevieve gave him a hesitant smile. "Should you find yourself bored, or just in need of company, I would . . . well, I'll be here."

"In my bed," he said darkly.

She actually grinned. "Yes, in your bed. You shouldn't have a hard time finding me." She took a step back. "Good night, Kendrick."

How sweetly his name rolled from her tongue. Had he never before listened to the way a mortal voice whispered against his ears? Nay, it was Genevieve's voice that gave such music to the word, that husky voice of hers that made his traitorous knees want to buckle.

She turned to walk away. Suddenly, he very much dreaded being alone.

"Genevieve?"

She turned to look at him. "Yes?"

Nay, he could not admit wanting to have her stay. He'd lost everything else, but he still had his pride. No sense in bidding that *adieu* quite yet.

"Good night," he said, hoping he sounded confident and a bit aloof.

She looked puzzled. "Good night, Kendrick. And thank you for not killing me."

"Tomorrow is another day."

Damn her if she didn't laugh right in his face. Then she had the gall to wink at him! Before he could recover his wits, she had walked away.

Damnation. He turned back to his dark contemplation of the water below him, and did his best to muster up a frown.

Instead, a grin crept over his mouth. By the saints, she was a cheeky wench! First she flattered him with an apology, then teased him with a mocking wink, as if he were now completely under her spell and she were free to act with him how she pleased.

"Hell," he muttered under his breath, then his sigh turned into a chuckle and his chuckle turned into a laugh. Aye, the last of the Buchanans certainly had come away with all the fire. He laughed again at the memory of her grin and felt his heart begin to shake off some of the shackles that had fettered it for centuries. Perhaps it was time he took advantage of the situation and availed himself of some company.

Of course it would only be for as long as she continued to intrigue him, which surely wouldn't be long. Then he'd demand her surrender and be on his way. But, as that time would certainly come quickly, there was no reason not to tarry a few more days and enjoy Genevieve's companionship.

After all, Buchanan company was better than no company at all.

Especially when that Buchanan was Genevieve.

Chapter Nine

Genevieve sat on a stone bench in the garden, enjoying the shade provided by an ancient tree. Sketching designs for the bedrooms had seemed like such a good idea that morning but somehow she just couldn't take much interest in it. She twirled the pencil around her fingers idly, wondering what she was waiting for. And she was waiting for something.

Or, more to the point, some*one*. It had been two days since her conversation with Kendrick on the roof. She was beginning to wonder if he would ever appear to her again. Had she offended him again? Did she care? She tapped the end of the pencil against her thigh thoughtfully. Why shouldn't she care? He was *her* ghost, after all. A girl couldn't be expected to ignore such a handsome quirk.

She lifted her eyes from her sketchbook and caught her breath. As if he had materialized from her very thoughts, Kendrick himself walked down the path toward her. She wondered how in the world Matilda had resisted him. He was nothing short of breathtaking.

His black leggings did nothing but show off his long, muscular legs. A white tunic hugged his broad chest and thick arms. His long hair was pulled back and she could see the tail of a black ribbon falling over his collarbone. His sword belt was slung low over his hips, making him look like a sexy pirate. He walked with an arrogant swagger, as if he were master of all he surveyed. Perhaps there was truth in that. If Seakirk belonged to anyone, it was to Kendrick.

And how real he looked. If she hadn't known better, she would have thought him a flesh and blood man. What a pity he wasn't. Matilda had been a fool. Even if she could have ignored his handsome face, she shouldn't have been able to resist his magnetism. Genevieve had stood next to him on the roof for only a few moments and she had felt suspiciously like swooning. How could anyone stare up into those sage-colored eyes and not feel a bit faint? No matter if the man did nothing but frown. He was a stunner. In fact, Genevieve sincerely hoped she never saw him smile. The sheer kilowattage would probably kill her.

The lord of Seakirk stopped just short of her and made her a low bow. Was this the same man who had come at her two weeks ago with an arrow jutting from his chest, then threatened her with both a broadsword and a very tangible knife? And now he was *bowing* to her? She was half tempted to pinch herself just to make sure she wasn't dreaming.

"Good morrow to you, my lady," he said gravely.

It was preposterous, but Genevieve found herself blushing furiously. She felt like a fourteen-year-old girl being noticed for the first time by the captain of the football team. She ducked her head, pretending to be mightily interested in the grass at his feet.

"Same to you," she said.

Out of the corner of her eye, she saw him sit down next to her on the bench. She wiped her clammy hands on her jeans, realizing that it was hardly from fear that her palms were damp. Oh, she just wasn't good around men who weren't tucked safely away in her daydreams!

" 'Tis a fine day out, isn't it?" he asked.

"Yes, it is."

"How does the garden smell at present? The last blooms of the summer are almost faded, it seems."

That surprised her enough to force her to look at him. "You can't smell?"

"What would I smell with, Genevieve? When I lost my body of flesh and blood, I also lost use of those senses you take so much for granted."

Genevieve saw her opening. Now was the time for questions, before Kendrick ran out of patience and drew his sword.

"But I hear your voice," she countered. "How do you speak without vocal cords?"

"Ah, well, it's fairly complicated. I don't know that I understand it all myself."

She waited. She was a college graduate, for heaven's sake. Surely it wasn't that hard to understand.

Kendrick smiled at her, as if he understood exactly what she was thinking. That made her squirm. Surely he couldn't read her thoughts. . . .

"You see," he began, "the essence of man is a powerful thing. When housed in a mortal frame, the spirit finds itself fettered and bound. Not that it objects, mind you. There is much to be said for the pleasures a body can provide."

Genevieve smiled to herself. She had the distinct feeling Kendrick had fully enjoyed those pleasures when he was alive.

"There is a price for being housed in flesh," Kendrick continued. " 'Tis much like a man's ability to move less freely while wearing armor that he can unbound."

"Go on." Why hadn't he ever written a book? The money he could have made with these revelations!

"I did," he said. "Not a best-seller, I fear."

Genevieve gasped, her worst fears coming true. "You can read my mind?"

"The mind is powerful, my lady. You only use a small portion of yours. I have full use of my faculties. And what I wouldn't give to trade those powers for the feel of a rose petal against my cheek or the smell of salt air in my nostrils. The ability to read your thoughts is a poor substitute for your faculties."

"I had better watch what I think around you."

"I already know you think I'm foul tempered, arrogant beyond belief and, let's see . . . what else did you call me?" He gave her a lazy smile. "Breathtakingly handsome?"

"I was having a bad dream at the time."

He laughed, a full-throated laugh, sounding not in the least bit offended at her slur. When his mirth subsided, he leaned back against the wall and smiled at her. Oh, that smile was nothing short of lethal. Genevieve felt light-headed.

"You've had quite a few nightmares since you came and I'm almost to the point of apologizing for them. And to answer your first question, what you hear is the image of my voice that I project into your mind. 'Tis a simple enough thing to do."

If you're a ghost, she thought dryly.

"Exactly. Now tell me, my lady, how does the garden smell? It looks fragrant enough."

Genevieve swallowed with difficulty over the lump in her throat. She did take so much for granted: the feel of the early autumn sun warming her hair and back; the delicate perfume of the roses before her; the rough feel of the stone bench under her hands. How could Kendrick not be vengeful, having been denied all that for so long?

"Don't pity me," he said, beginning to frown.

"Stay out of my mind," she retorted, then grimaced. "I'm sorry. I didn't mean to be rude."

He waved away her apology. "I have no feelings to bruise, remember? I never should have told you. I'll try not to eavesdrop so often. Please tell me of the day."

"It smells like roses and dirt," she began slowly. "And I can smell the smoke from the fireplace a bit too. It's almost chilly here in the shade and the bench is actually quite cold." She looked at him and shrugged. "That's it, I suppose."

"Ah," he said, nodding. "Very pleasant indeed."

The sun glanced off the hilt of his sword and Genevieve stiffened. "Why do you wear that thing?"

"Habit, I suppose. When I was alive, it was never out of

reach, even while I slept. A weapon close at hand saved my life more times than I care to remember."

It was strange to think that the man facing her had lived in another time, another world really.

"What was it really like?" she asked. "In your time?"

He smiled. It was a boyish smile, full of mischief and exuberance. She was completely charmed by it. Then there was his dimple. How his mother must have loved that sweet mark in his cheek.

"Would you like to see my time?"

"How do you mean?"

"Look."

She blinked and then gasped. Where the garden had been, there was now nothing but dirt. Men and animals roamed about the courtyard freely. She could hear the clank of a blacksmith's hammer against his anvil. There was a tremendous crash to her right and she jerked her head around in time to see an armored man go flying twenty feet off the back of his horse, still holding onto a lance. She pulled her knees up to her chest, then gasped again. She was not in jeans, but a dress.

"How . . . ?"

"I call it illusion. Or delusion, if you prefer."

"But your clothes seem real enough."

"There seem to be various levels of these illusions I am able to conjure up. This, for example"—he drew his sword, and the sunlight winked off the blade—"is what I call a permanent illusion. Like my clothing, once it is created, it remains from day to day without changing. The yard before you is more of a momentary illusion. It will remain only for a few hours, longer if I pour more energy into the fashioning of it. Your gown is fashioned of that type of illusion."

Genevieve shut her mouth and looked down at the dress she was wearing. It was a historian's dream. The dress was green and looked to be made of coarse wool. The fabric was heavy and rough under her fingers. The bodice was worked with pearls and precious stones that would have been worth a small fortune. She trailed her fingers over the gems, marveling at the cold hardness of them.

The sound of hoofbeats startled her and she looked up to see two horsemen approaching. They dismounted and stood before Kendrick.

"Allow me to present one or two of my more permanent illusions." He gestured to the man on the far left. "This is a sturdy version of my cousin, Jamie. He isn't really here—'tis but my imagination and memories which have found home in the mock body I created for him."

Jamie was taller than Kendrick and built like a house. His long blond hair hung well past his shoulders and he carried a battle-ax in one hand and a deadly-looking sword in the other.

"Jamie was a fine fighter," Kendrick mused. "We went waring together for many years. And the other," he gestured to the smiling young man standing with his hand on his horse's neck, "is my younger brother, Jason. He doesn't do much but remind me of how I felt when I was younger and could best him in a sword fight without my sword."

Genevieve smiled. Kendrick's ego was healthy. He winked at her.

"I know."

She frowned. "Mind your own thoughts, Kendrick, and stay out of mine."

She was preparing to give him a more thorough lecture when another man thundered up on a white horse and leaped to the ground before the beast had stopped. He was dressed all in white robes and looked exactly as she had always imagined a Saracen would look.

"This is Nazir, troublemaker extraordinaire," Kendrick said with a grumble. "He tried to kill me many times when I still possessed a body of flesh and blood. It was only after I almost killed him that he became my devoted slave. Isn't that right, Nazir?"

"I am no slave," the man said stiffly and his voice was an eerie whisper.

Genevieve gasped. "Good grief, he speaks?"

Nazir looked at her, and she had the distinct impression he was just as real as Kendrick.

"Who is the woman, my lord?" Nazir asked in a husky voice. "Her beauty stirs my desire." He took a step closer to her, his dark eyes hot with something that made her definitely uncomfortable.

Kendrick stood up, his hand on his sword hilt. "The woman is mine. You will not touch her, nor will you approach her when I am not by her side. Your only duty to her is to protect her if I cannot. You will kill anyone who tries to harm her but you will not take her for yourself. Is that understood?"

"Aye, my lord," Nazir said curtly. He made Kendrick a low bow and then straightened. "If that is all?"

Kendrick's scowl was formidable. "What havoc have you wreaked as of late?"

Nazir's eyes immediately took on an unholy twinkle. "Deeds worthy of song, my lord."

"The saints preserve me," Kendrick groaned, lowering himself to the bench wearily.

"Aye, that was what most of my victims cried also."

"Nazir!"

One corner of the Saracen's mouth tipped up in the slightest of smiles. "Just a bit of mischief in London, my lord. I'll tell you of it, when you wish to be amused."

Genevieve leaned closer to Kendrick. "He can leave Seakirk?"

"Aye, beautiful one," Nazir said in his unearthly voice. "I bring His Lordship tales from near and far to amuse him. If you would care to hear—"

"Later," Kendrick grumbled. "Beat it, Nazir."

"Beat it?" he echoed.

"Depart hence. Disappear. Make haste to another part of the castle where I am not."

Nazir disappeared. With a flick of his wrist, Kendrick sent his cousin Jamie and his brother Jason wandering off too. He looked at Genevieve.

"Nazir takes some getting used to."

"So I see. Why is he with you?"

"He pledged fealty to me in life and still seems to be bound by that vow. He will not harm you, if that concerns you. He is as good as his word."

"He looks merciless."

"He is. Or was." He sat back and stared out thoughtfully over the dirt field in front of them. "I made the mistake of stealing a kiss or two from his sister while I was in the Holy Land, and Nazir swore vengeance. He hunted me tirelessly, always just a step or two behind me, never coming out in the open where I might have fought him like a man."

"Lies!" an invisible being shouted angrily.

Kendrick chuckled. "We fought many times but neither could gain the advantage. And that says much about his skill, for my father was the finest swordsman in England and I had learned well his craft. The final battle between Nazir and me came one moonlit night in the desert. We fought until I thought my arms would fall off. Then behind him I spotted a poisonous serpent. I pulled the knife from my belt and flung it at the beast before it could strike Nazir. When he realized what I'd done, saving his life in spite of his poor treatment of me, he dropped to his knees and pledged me his fealty." He shrugged with a smile. "My father almost had apoplexy when I came riding through the gates with a Saracen in my guard."

Genevieve looked at his sword and sighed. "It must have been a harsh world to live in. I can't imagine always having to look over my shoulder to make sure no one was coming after me."

He held up his blade and turned it this way and that, watching the sun glance off it. "It never seemed that bad, most likely because we had nothing else to compare it to."

Genevieve gasped softly. There was an emerald the size of a silver dollar in the hilt. "Good grief. Was that there originally?"

He lifted one eyebrow arrogantly. "I was a wealthy man. Would you care for proof?"

"What do you mean?"

"Come with me and I'll show you."

She gathered up her things and then jumped as she noticed the garden was once again a garden and her dress was once again her jeans and sweatshirt. She frowned at him. "I wish you'd tell me before you do that kind of thing. It's unnerving."

"You're a bit skittish, Genevieve."

"You would be too if you were in my shoes," she replied, trying to remain unaffected by his deadly dimple and his mischievous grin.

"Knowing your fondness for fainting at the slightest provocation, I'll try to keep my illusions down to a minimum."

"I never faint. Except for that once and you would have fainted too," she added as she followed him back to the house. "I thought you were going to kill me!"

He turned around so fast, she almost walked through him.

"And you think I've given up on the idea?"

"You wouldn't have rescued me on the beach if you'd still wanted me dead," she said, tilting her chin up to give herself courage. Oh, how grateful she was that he was a ghost. She would have been quaking in her Keds if he'd been made of flesh and blood. He was much taller than she was and built like a football player. Not the ones who threw the ball, but one of the burly ones who tried to mow down all the other ones. Her knowledge of football was scant but she knew how big they looked on television. Kendrick was that kind of big.

"I could have rescued you just to have the pleasure of killing you," he said.

"You know it won't solve your problem."

"And letting you live will?"

"I never said that. But at least you have some company. That has to be worth something."

His expression softened. "Aye, it is. And you are very beautiful company." He smiled and motioned to the house with his head. "Let's go inside and I'll show you my den of iniquity."

Genevieve hesitated, feeling as if she'd never before encountered the ghost before her. Was he being nice to her just so he could kill her later? Had he suddenly been possessed by a knight in shining armor or was this what he was really like underneath all those grumbles?

"Genevieve?"

She looked up at him and smiled reflexively at the smile he

wore. Whatever else he might be, he was certainly being pleasant this afternoon. It was probably a good idea to take advantage of it while she could. She followed him obediently, as if she'd spent the whole of her life dealing with the undead.

"Lord Kendrick, Lady Genevieve," Worthington bowed as they passed, speaking as if there were nothing at all odd about the fact that she was walking with a ghost.

To her surprise, she found she was beginning to think of it as normal too. She might have begun to forget Kendrick's undeadly status if it hadn't been for his disconcerting habit of walking through whatever was in his way. It was lucky he'd never come back to life; he'd be nothing but bruises until he reaccustomed himself to a body.

She followed him up the stairs to the third floor and down the hallway. The lights came on magically as they passed.

"How do you do that?"

He winked at her over his shoulder. "Centuries of practice." He stopped before a door and bowed. "My lair. After you, my lady."

Genevieve looked at the door and frowned. It was one she'd been trying to open for a solid week. So this was Kendrick's hiding place. She could hardly wait to see all the cobwebs and dust gathered in the corners. Did he have a coffin too?

She opened the door and stopped so suddenly that Kendrick walked right through her. His passing left the oddest sensation in the pit of her stomach.

Well, so much for cobwebs and inches of dust. Kendrick was obviously a man who liked his creature comforts. There was a fireplace, several bookcases lined with dust-free books, a large chair with a footstool and a pair of chairs flanking a side table supporting many crystal decanters.

"Shall I give you the tour?"

She nodded, curious about what it was he wanted to show her. She followed him across the room, then stopped behind him as he paused in front of another door.

"The shrine," he said with a deprecating smile. "Enter at your own risk."

Genevieve opened the door hesitantly and peeked inside.

She sucked in her breath suddenly as the torches on the walls lit themselves, revealing a narrow room that ran probably the length of the castle. It was filled to overflowing with antiques—weapons mostly, but here and there a few pieces of furniture, and numerous suits of armor.

"Good grief," she breathed. "Where did you get all this stuff?"

"Off the dead bodies of all the Buchanans I killed."

She whirled on him and he quickly put up his hands in a gesture of surrender.

"That was a jest, Genevieve. I've managed to acquire most of it in various *legal* ways, though I'm not above admitting that a few of the acquisitions were a bit on the unsavory side." He motioned to a doorway on her right. "In here are my personal things. Open the door and go in." He sighed as he followed her. "A Buchanan in my private study. I think I've gone daft."

A retort was on the tip of her tongue but it fell off at the sight of the small, intimate room. The walls were paneled in a dark wood, making the room seem just that much more private. One wall sported bookshelves, but she didn't take the time to look at the volumes. The painting above Kendrick's desk was what drew her attention.

"My family," he said, following her eyes.

She easily identified his father, whom Kendrick strongly resembled. Gray eyes twinkled and the man looked to be on the verge of grinning. A beautiful woman stood next to him, her long blonde hair flowing over one shoulder like threads of fine silk. Genevieve stood on her tiptoes to get a good look at Kendrick's mother's eyes.

"I'll be darned," she breathed. "They were green."

Kendrick chuckled. " 'Tis only now you believe me?"

She smiled and then continued to study the painting. "I recognize you and Jason but who are the rest?"

"My mother and father, Anne and Robin, and my older brother, Phillip." He moved to stand next to her. "That deceptively angelic-looking girl is my sister, Mary."

"She's very beautiful," Genevieve murmured.

"Aye, she was," he said wistfully. "She died of consumption the year before I was murdered. It was very hard on my sire. He ever pretended gruffness in public but underneath he was very tenderhearted." He sighed and put his shoulders back. "They're all together now, a fact about which I am very envious."

"How do you know?" she asked, turning to look up at him.

"They each came in turn to say farewell to me as they passed over to the other side."

"That's good to know," she said quietly.

"For some, I'm sure it is. Now," he said, "you can have a look at my mail and then I will show you my sword."

"Who painted that portrait?" she asked, following him.

"Jonathan, Matilda's grandson. He's one of the few of her children I could tolerate. He came along about the time I finally resigned myself to the fact that I was indeed very unalive. He captured my family from my descriptions better than I could have with a photograph."

She followed him over to a glass case. It contained a well-preserved suit of medieval chain mail and clothing obviously from the same time period. It was hard to fathom that what she saw before her had actually belonged to Kendrick while he was alive. She looked at his surcoat, which was embroidered with a black lion rampant. The turquoise color of his eye startled her.

"My grandmother's eyes were that color," Kendrick said. "That is how my grandfather honored her."

"He loved her very much."

"Aye, very much. And she him. She died only a few hours after he did in their advanced years. My father begged her to tarry, for he loved her deeply, but she would not. She said the light of her life had been extinguished; what need had she to remain? And so, after they had laid my grandfather Rhys out in the great hall and the villagers had come to pay their respects, my grandmother stretched herself out beside him and put her hand over his. She closed her eyes and slept, never to wake again. My mother swore she saw my grandfather's spirit take his lady's hand and lift her spirit up, but I never believed it. Until later, of course. It's amazing how blind we are when our spirits are housed in mortal flesh."

Kendrick seemed to find the sentiment a bit uncomfortable. He cleared his throat and managed a gruff sort of grunt. "Now, I will show you proof that I was once a wealthy knight capable of putting a precious gem or two in my sword." He led her over to a long wooden case resting on a tall side table. He made a motion for her to open it.

Lifting the lid revealed a very long, very old, very well-kept broadsword. It was polished into almost painful brightness. And there, in the hilt, was an egg-sized emerald. She reached out and ran her finger over it in awe.

"Wow," she said, at a loss for words. "This was yours?"

"Aye," he said proudly. "And a fine weapon it was. The balance was perfect. The edge could cleave a stone in twain, or a pesky infidel, whichever happened to be in my way at the time."

She nodded and ran her fingers over the edge of the blade. She jerked her hand back in shock, watching the blood squirt from two out of three fingers.

"Woman, have you gone daft?" Kendrick exclaimed. "Tear off your sleeve and bind your hand!"

It was amazing how much blood could come out of such tiny appendages. Damn, she had bled all over the beautifully lined case. Well, perhaps soap and water would take that out. Or maybe some vinegar. Wasn't that what her mother had used to clean off stains? Or was it lemon juice? No, lemon juice was to drink. And vinegar was for salad dressing. Oh dear, now she was bleeding onto the floor.

"Genevieve, tear off your sleeve!" Kendrick bellowed.

Maybe some prewash detergent. She felt like giggling. Hell, maybe she'd just throw the whole thing into the wash. She looked at her hand again. Wow, was that bone?

"Genevieve!"

She winced at the force of his yell and then felt her sweatshirt sleeve being pulled down around her wrist. Kendrick gave it one final tug and then collapsed to the floor.

"Bind your hand," he said faintly. "Have Worthington take you to the infirmary."

"Kendrick—"

"Now!" he coughed. "Make haste!"

She wrapped the cloth around her fingers, then sank to her knees beside him. "Are you hurt?" she asked anxiously.

"Bloody hell, woman, will you just go?" he thundered, his voice echoing off the walls.

She stumbled to her feet and then hesitated. "You're sure . . ."

"Aye," he said, pointing toward the door. "Begone!"

She staggered from the room, praying she'd find Worthington before she went into shock. Somehow she managed to work her way down to the main floor before she began to tremble violently. Worthington was standing by the long table in the great hall, polishing a silver tea service. He turned as he heard her and then went white as a sheet.

"My lady . . ."

"My fault," she whispered. "You drive, Worthington. I think I'm going to faint."

He caught her as she pitched forward.

Chapter
Ten

The excursion into the village was quick and relatively painless; painless only because Worthington produced a flask of brandy and poured half of it down Genevieve before they reached the hospital.

The stitching was something she would have preferred to forget. The worst thing about it was listening to the nurses marvel at the severity of the gashes. Fortunately the doctor was deft and quick. Worthington gave him a solemn promise that Lady Genevieve would not be allowed into the kitchen again nor anywhere else where she might be tempted to reach for the wrong end of a knife.

"It was his bloody sword, Worthington," she muttered crossly as he helped her into the car.

"I know, my lady," Worthington said in his droll voice. "And it's not nice to say *bloody*."

"Bloody hell," she grumbled as he shut the door. He was her butler, not her mother. She was thirty years old, old enough to decide for herself how she'd swear.

By the time they were home, she was feeling the full effects of the pain shot mixed with old brandy. She giggled all the way up the stairs and then did a shaky swan dive onto Kendrick's bed.

"The judges give it a perfect ten," she slurred just before she began to snore.

Worthington took off her shoes and covered her up with a blanket, clucking his tongue and shaking his head. But how could he be anything less than pleased with the spirited Colonist who snored so charmingly? She was just the thing to bring Kendrick out of the foul humor he'd been in for the last seven hundred years.

Worthington knew all about it. He was the direct descendant of the man who had been Kendrick's squire in the thirteenth century. He'd grown up at Seakirk listening to his father grumble about Kendrick's moods for years. When his father had passed on, Worthington had taken over the job of steward without hesitation. He was actually very fond of the young lord and did what he could to ease Kendrick's pain.

And now there was Genevieve. Worthington had fallen under her spell the moment she claimed Kendrick's chamber as her own. Her spunk since then had only raised Worthington's opinion of her. It was a pity there was no hope for the pair. Out of all the Buchanan women, Genevieve was certainly the only one who could have made a fitting wife for Kendrick. And Kendrick needed a wife. In all the years Worthington had known him, he'd never known Kendrick to smile other than grimly or bitterly. Laugh? Never. Grumble? Continuously. And all those poor Buchanans he had driven insane. Worthington shook his head as he closed the bed curtains and made his way to the door. No, it was high time Kendrick allowed his heart to thaw, and Worthington was convinced Genevieve was the woman who could help His Lordship in that task.

Worthington mounted the steps to the third floor and entered his lord's study. Kendrick was barely discernible as he sat sprawled in his massive chair.

"How is she?" he whispered.

"Rather inebriated at the moment, my lord. She came very

close to severing the fingers completely. The physician assured me, however, that she would mend. I left her snoring in a very ladylike manner in your chamber."

Kendrick closed his eyes. "Thank God," he said, sounding extraordinarily relieved. "Do take care of her, Worthington. It will be several days before I regain my strength and can see to her." He opened his eyes and pinned Worthington to the spot. "You will watch over her carefully, won't you?"

Worthington could have sworn he heard a distinct sound of urgency in his lord's voice.

"Of course, my lord. She won't make a move that I don't know it."

Kendrick nodded and allowed his eyes to close again. "Don't let anything happen to her, Worthington. I couldn't bear it."

Worthington watched as his master surrendered to slumber. Had he been a duller man, he might have suspected he was beginning to bore people. Having his two charges fall asleep on him within the space of a quarter hour was almost insulting.

He smiled as he left the study. It was the first time he had ever heard Kendrick inquire about the well-being of anyone, himself included. And with such fervor! It was a most auspicious sign.

Genevieve's only memories of the next two days were ones of intense pain in her hand and Worthington forcing pills down her. He seemed to materialize out of thin air each time she woke in agony. She managed to stay awake long enough to inquire about Kendrick and learn that he was upstairs recovering before healing sleep again claimed her.

Three days after her accident, she dragged herself out of bed. After an eternally long shower, she dug in her drawer for her favorite pair of fire-engine red feety pajamas. Now, *these* were clothes made for pampering. All she needed was a container of Häagen-Dazs and a toasty warm fire, and life would be good.

The stitches in her fingers pulled when she flexed her hand, and that gave her the chills. She carefully uncurled her digits and looked at the ugly red slashes across two of her fingers and at the black thread that held the flesh together. Oh, how close she had come to cutting them completely off. It would be a very long time before she came close to Kendrick's sword again.

She dropped her hand to her side and crossed to the door. The sooner she had some ice cream, the better she'd feel. Maybe Worthington had a spare oven mitt she could wear on her hand so she wouldn't have to look at the evidence of her stupidity.

Worthington was just coming up the steps as she was going down them. He bore a silver serving tray on which sat a pint of chocolate chocolate-chip ice cream and a silver dish full of steaming hot fudge sauce. Her laugh was more a half-sob of relief.

"Don't tell me you're reading minds these days too," she groaned.

Worthington came as close to grinning as he surely ever would. "My lady, your likes and dislikes are so simple as to border on dull. You really should try a different flavor. Have you never been tempted by Raspberry Truffle?"

"Not on your life. Wouldn't want to waste the calories on something not dark and sinful. Are we going to eat that downstairs?"

"Actually, His Lordship has been pestering me so about your condition, I thought perhaps you might want to join him in his study and ease his mind."

"He has?" she asked, feeling a blush creep up her cheeks.

"Constantly. He's about to make me daft with his nagging."

Genevieve had a hard time fighting her grin. "Well, we wouldn't want you daft, Worthington. I'll go put him out of your misery."

Worthington nodded approvingly, then led her up the stairs to Kendrick's study. He didn't bother to knock. Instead, he opened the door and ushered her inside.

Kendrick was there, but he was almost transparent.

"What happened to you?" she asked, hurrying over to kneel next to his chair.

"I'm just a bit pale," he said, smiling faintly. "I'll mend."

"Pale?" she echoed incredulously. "Kendrick, you're hardly there!"

"I'm simply weary," he whispered, the effort of talking obviously tiring him further. "You might compare my tearing off your sleeve to your lifting a car off the ground. It was an effort of enormous proportions."

"I'm so sorry," she said miserably. "Kendrick, this is all my fault. I never meant to hurt you—"

He put his finger to his lips and then dropped his hand back to his chest. "Rather you should be rejoicing. I've never in all my days of haunting done a nice thing for a Buchanan. You, my lady, have the dubious honor of being the first."

"That doesn't make me feel any better. You look terrible."

"It looks much worse than it really is," he assured her. "Worthington," he said, lifting his eyes to look at his steward, "just what is it you have there for my lady to eat?"

"Nothing healthy, my lord."

Kendrick frowned. "Then by all means take it away and prepare her something else. She needs her nutrients."

"I want my ice cream," Genevieve put in.

"Make haste, Worthington," Kendrick said, ignoring her. "And bring it here when you have it ready. I can see I will have to watch her closely if she is to mend properly."

"I want my ice cream," Genevieve insisted, throwing Worthington a warning look.

Kendrick threw Worthington a warning look of his own. "Begone, old man. Return only when you've something in your hands fit for Genevieve's consumption."

"Damn it, I can decide for myself," she said, rising and folding her arms stubbornly across her chest. She was instantly aware of what a ridiculous picture she made in nightclothes intended for a toddler, her hair in a ponytail and her chin thrust out indignantly. Both Kendrick and Worthington looked like they were trying to hide very amused smiles. Genevieve knew it was too late to retreat graciously, so she stood her ground.

Kendrick lifted his eyebrows and looked at his steward. "Her ladyship has spoken."

"So she has," Worthington agreed.

"I have the feeling we shouldn't tangle with her. She looks powerfully fierce."

Worthington set the tray aside, pulled up a heavy wooden chair next to Kendrick's, then gestured for Genevieve to sit. She had no dignity left, so she sat. The tray was deposited on her lap with all due haste.

"Fetch her something healthy for dessert, Worthington," Kendrick said wryly. "I'll see she saves room for it."

Genevieve ignored Kendrick as she poured hot fudge sauce over her ice cream and savored a decadently rich spoonful.

"Good?"

She was ready and willing to be miffed, but after one look into his pale green eyes and an eyeful of his faintly amused smile and adorable dimple, she gave in and smiled.

"It's heavenly."

"What does it taste like?"

She looked away and tried to put it into words. "Smooth, creamy and sinful."

"It sounds dangerous."

She started to agree, then sobered slowly. Tragic really, all the things he would never experience. And now to see him weak and pale and know it was her doing . . .

"I'm really sorry," she said softly.

He shook his head. "Nothing to apologize for. But there is something you can do to assuage your guilt, if you wish it."

"Anything."

He grinned. It was a faint grin, but a grin nonetheless. "Make your promises carefully, my lady. My mother always warned my mates that I was a merciless bargainer."

"I'll keep that in mind. Now, what can I do for you that isn't illegal, disgusting or immoral?"

He laughed. "You narrow my choices drastically. Actually, I was hoping you would turn on the telly and find a football game for me to watch. Unless there's something else you'd be more interested in?"

"I don't know much about football but I'll stay and keep you company if you want." She rose and put the rest of her ice cream on the side table near the door, then walked back over to her chair.

"How could I say no to a woman in such fetching night-clothes?" he murmured, letting his gaze roam over her baggy pajamas.

Genevieve dropped into the chair and began flipping through the channels frantically, looking for something that would distract him. She hadn't thought twice about coming up in her pajamas and now she wondered why she'd been so dumb. Kendrick might have been a ghost, but he was a one-hundred percent *male* ghost. His blatant perusal and slow, wicked smile were enough to send heat to her cheeks immediately.

"There," she said triumphantly. "Is that good enough?"

"University ball," he sighed regretfully. "And not for another half hour. Well, it's the best we can hope for."

She set the remote control near his hand, then blushed when she caught sight of him watching her.

"Will you stop that?" she hissed, embarrassed.

"I'm only looking, Genevieve. You can't blame me for that. It's a bit like a young lad looking in a toy shop window—desiring mightily but unable to have."

She snatched a blanket off the arm of the chair he was occupying and draped it over herself. "Voyeur," she said primly.

He burst into hearty laughter and laughed until his voice began to weaken again. "You, my lady, are a woman of the finest breeding. I will endeavor to lust after you with a bit more discretion."

He then launched into an animated discussion of the rules of football, completely ignoring the new blush that came to her cheeks. She was desperately grateful he was not a man of flesh and blood. The thought of him holding her with those strong hands, touching her with those long fingers, kissing her throat with his firm lips—

"Genevieve, you're not paying attention," he said. "You'll never enjoy the game if you don't learn something about it."

Genevieve forced her eyes back to his with an effort. "I was paying attention," she lied.

"Then tell me what a running back does."

Well, that was a stupid one. "He runs, of course," she said, feeling very pleased with her quick thinking.

"Wide receiver?"

"He receives."

"What?"

Damn, he was getting technical. "The ball?" she ventured.

"Right answer, but it was a guess. I don't think your heart's in this, my sweet."

"Oh, but it is," she assured him. Who was he kidding? She would have listened to him expound quantum physics if it had allowed her to just sit and listen to his deep voice, watch his pale features light up animatedly, know that she had his full and undivided attention. Oh, yes, she would certainly learn a little football in return for that pleasure.

"All right, then," he said, sitting up. "Let's go over the offense again. First you have your down-linemen. Remember who they are?"

"The burly ones who bend over," she nodded.

He smiled, as if he found her answer somewhat amusing. "That's close enough. And the running backs?"

"The ones who take the ball and get clobbered by all the big guys in the other colored jerseys who want to have it."

Kendrick began to grin. "Well-done. Now, what of the wide receivers?"

"They catch the ball, hopefully in the end zone, then they do those ridiculous little dances and let themselves be jumped on by their own teammates. I never have understood that, Kendrick. And why do they pat each other's butts all the time? You didn't do that when you were a knight, did you?"

He laughed. "No, Genevieve, but it's a different world at present. And I apologize for doubting you. You've paid a good deal of attention. Now tell me what you know about the quarterback."

That was insulting. She'd lusted after Steve Young often enough in the past.

"Kendrick," she began patiently, "I know who the quarter-back is and what he does. I'm not completely football illiterate."

"So I see," he chuckled. "Then why don't you tell me about the defense."

She squirmed. "I'd rather listen to you tell me."

"I already know all about it."

"Which makes you the perfect one to discuss it."

He pursed his lips, but it seemed to be in an effort not to laugh. "You're stalling."

"And doing a fine job, if I do say so myself," she agreed.

Kendrick did laugh then. "All right, I'll explain it. But pay attention. The game is almost ready to begin and I'll expect you to be able to point out the different positions. We'll work on plays during halftime."

"Whatever you say, my lord."

He dove into another detailed explanation of who did what, where they did it and to whom. Genevieve knew she'd have to see it to believe it, but that was obviously his intention. He wound up his little speech just before the kickoff.

Genevieve was torn between watching the game and watching Kendrick watch the game. He was by far the more entertaining of the two choices.

Before she was aware of it, the game was finished and Kendrick's eyelids were drooping. He gave her a sleepy smile.

"Would you be offended if I nodded off for a few moments?"

She shook her head. "I'll go."

"Nay," he said quickly, "stay. Please?"

How could she say no to that? She resumed her seat slowly. "I probably should keep an eye on you for a while. You're very pale."

He nodded solemnly. "I need to be watched closely, 'round the clock if possible."

Genevieve couldn't stop the blush that stained her cheeks. Fortunately Kendrick seemed not to notice. He closed his eyes and relaxed back in his chair. She couldn't hear him breathe but she saw that the rise and fall of his chest soon became shallow and regular. He certainly knew how to sleep at the drop of a hat.

Once she was sure he was sleeping deeply, she turned sideways in her chair to face him and allowed herself the luxury of gaping. He was like no one she'd ever known before. Most of the men she had known over the course of her lifetime had either been wimps, like her father, or tyrants. Though it wasn't as if she'd had a great selection to choose from. When she'd finally gotten around to dating in college, she'd given it up almost instantly. She'd spent so much of her life being bookish, dreamy Gen Buchanan that she found she didn't have the skills or the inclination to deal with real men. It was much safer to stick to the ones in her imagination. Not to say that she hadn't had male friends, but they had been few and far between. And none of them had ever considered her anything but a sister.

Unlike Kendrick. If he considered her anything besides a pest, that anything was definitely not a sibling. The look he had given her while taking in the full view of her pajamas still brought heat to her cheeks. She knew the look. She'd seen men wear it in the movies and seen her few male friends give it to women they were in hot pursuit of. But never had she seen a look of that kind come her way. Until today.

She didn't think she was beautiful; that was something she refused to let bother her. She was good at her job and she was good at her dreams. Over the years, she'd convinced herself that was all she needed to survive.

And then her dreams had become reality. She'd been swept from her everyday existence into a world where nothing was the same. She had a castle, more beautiful than anything she had ever conjured up in her imagination. And she had her knight. His gruffness had unnerved her at first, but she was beginning to see that some of it was due to his understandable bitterness over his situation and some of it was just a means of playing tough. Kendrick wasn't as hard-hearted as he would have had her believe.

She perused him in a leisurely manner. It was the first time she had ever been close to a man of his size and physique.

Odd how she wasn't in the least bit intimidated by his proportions or his masculinity. She immediately understood why. He was a ghost, a person just a bit more tangible than her imagination but not substantial enough to be a threat. Yes, this was the kind of man she could deal with. He was arrogant and impossible but he had a kind of teasing manner about him that was utterly charming. And he looked at her as if he actually found her appealing. Desirable was pushing things, but appealing she could believe.

She saw Kendrick's hand lying on the armrest, just an inch or two from her chair, and found herself suddenly overcome by an utterly ridiculous idea. Would he feel it if she touched him? Would she feel him?

Hesitantly, she put her hand over his. A tingle, like a hint of static electricity, touched her. Her hand went through his to rest on the chair. She looked down, speechless. Kendrick's hand surrounded hers, like an aura. Real, but not real. What if it had been? She leaned her head against the back of the chair and closed her eyes, giving her imagination free rein. The century didn't matter, she had Kendrick and that was the only thing important to her.

Perhaps the thirteenth century. She would have been the lady of Seakirk, orphaned, besieged from all sides by vile suitors who wanted nothing but her land, not caring a fig for her personally. At the moment of greatest jeopardy, Kendrick would have ridden up on his black warhorse and scattered the scoundrels with a few well-dealt blows of his great broadsword. Genevieve saw herself standing on the front steps in the gown Kendrick had shown her in the garden a few days earlier, waiting patiently for him to come to her. He would have ridden up and remained mounted, looking down at her with that heartbreaker grin of his and said something like, "Now that the pond scum has been swept away, my lady, perhaps you'd care for a swim?"

No, Kendrick wouldn't say something like that. He probably would have ridden up, held down his hand toward her and frowned. Then he would have said gruffly, "Come up here, wench. That light exercise before supper has left me too weak to walk to the chapel to wed you. We'll have to ride." Then he would have hauled her up into his arms, grumbled a time or two about all the minor exertion she'd put him to, then kissed her until she couldn't see straight. Genevieve smiled to herself. Yes, that was easy enough to imagine.

Or would she have met him in her day? She might have found herself dragged to one of those schmoozing parties she found so dreadfully uncomfortable and taken up her usual post in the far corner of the room where no one could bother her. She would have seen him across the crowded room; he would have been surrounded by a bevy of beautiful women, charming them with only half an effort. He would have lifted his eyes and met hers, then sparks would have flown. Without apologizing, he would have left his entourage and come to her. They might have circled the globe in his private jet or sailed the seven seas in his yacht. The place wouldn't have mattered; he would have had eyes for only her.

Or would he have been a recluse, a novelist perhaps who had need of restoration of his medieval castle? She smiled; that was starting to sound a bit familiar. It would have been love at first sight. He would have courted her with silly little gifts, sweet notes, handpicked flowers from his garden.

Genevieve sighed. Somehow she just couldn't picture Kendrick grubbing in the garden. It was best to leave him up on his horse, his hair plastered to his neck with sweat, his mail groaning as he moved. He belonged in his world with the dangers he had obviously mastered so well. It was no wonder he liked football. It was probably the only thing left that reminded him of battle.

She opened her eyes to look at him. Then she froze. He was awake. And looking at her. Oh, the gentle, loving look on his face! Genevieve felt herself falling into the warmth from his eyes as if she'd tripped and plunged into a huge marshmallow. Soft and warm and so very inviting.

Suddenly she felt heat flood to her cheeks.

"Have you been l-looking"—her voice broke with embarrassment—"into my thoughts?"

He shook his head slowly, his eyes never leaving hers.

She closed her eyes briefly in thanks, then pulled her hand back.

"Don't—"

Her eyes flew to his.

"—move," he finished. He turned his hand palm up. "Put your hand in mine again, love."

The warmth suddenly became stifling heat. What if he had seen all her foolish imaginings? She wanted to bury her face in her hands and weep from humiliation. All the courage she'd summoned up to face Kendrick while he was waving swords at her vanished, and she did the most rational thing she'd done all afternoon.

She fled.

She ran all the way to her room, praying he was too weak to follow her. She locked the door, dove for the bed. She pulled the covers up over her head, as if that would somehow shield her from Kendrick and from her own stupid imagination.

Heaven help her.

She was falling in love with a ghost.

Chapter
Eleven

Kendrick sat on his newly acquired love seat and tapped his foot impatiently. Well, perhaps it was more nervous tapping than impatient tapping. He knew Genevieve would be coming up soon and he honestly wasn't sure he wanted to see her reaction to what he'd replaced his great chair with. Would the love seat seem too personal?

"Dolt," he muttered, "what's it supposed to imply? Isn't that the reason for the bloody thing?"

Which was, of course, why he was tapping his foot, a gesture of nervousness that had never before been in his repertoire. What need had there ever been for nervousness? The women of his time had hunted him down like defensive linemen rushing a poorly defended quarterback. He had spent more time fighting them off than he had worrying about how to attract them. His reputation for prowess in battle and in bed—as well as the rumors of his wealth—had drawn them from as far south as Italy. Rich widows, bored noblewomen, wide-eyed virgins: aye, they had all planned and schemed to woo him to their beds. And now he was nervous? Because he was afraid of frightening off a woman he couldn't even *touch*? It was the most preposterous situation he had ever encountered. How his father would have roared with laughter at the tale.

A week had passed since Genevieve had fled his study, and during that week several things had happened. He'd regained his strength. It had actually come back quickly but he'd dragged the entire affair out much longer than necessary, finding it a convenient excuse to have Genevieve hovering over him at all hours.

Once he'd managed to lure her back to his lair, that is. He'd been sorely tempted to have a peek inside her head and find out just what had sent her scampering from his study, but somehow he'd found the self-control to refrain. Whatever she'd been thinking, she certainly didn't want him knowing it. Perhaps it was just as well. For all he knew, she'd been thinking what a toad he was. He shifted uncomfortably on the couch. That thought hardly sat well with him.

The other monumental happening had been the realization of what he was feeling. For a solid se'nnight he'd told himself that his fascination with her was only temporary. It would pass quickly enough and then he would demand she sign over the castle to him. He'd anticipated that the entire process would be completed in less than a fortnight.

Until he'd realized he was falling in love with her.

It hadn't taken much effort to determine exactly when he'd first known. It hadn't been when she'd tried to bolt for his chamber when she thought he couldn't get past a locked door. It hadn't been when she'd almost clobbered him with the door of the icebox. It hadn't even been when he'd allowed her into his private study and she'd been so fascinated with his personal things and his family, though he was pleased she found them to be a friendly-looking group.

Nay, it had been when he'd woken from his dozing to find his hand covered by the slight fingers of a woman in ridiculous-looking nightclothes, a woman who was smiling contentedly, as if she'd just found what her heart sought. Then she'd opened her eyes and he'd seen the remains of her dreams still shining brightly there, and somehow he had known he'd been a part of those dreams. Saints above, he'd wanted to haul her into his arms and kiss her until she couldn't breathe!

He sighed and dragged his hand through his hair. Leaving now was unthinkable. Having Genevieve leave was inconceivable. For better or worse, they'd have to endure whatever fate had in store for them. In the end, perhaps she would sign over the castle to him and he would proceed on ahead to the next world and wait for her to join him.

Assuming, of course, that she was like-minded.

A soft tap on the door sounded barely a moment before Genevieve entered. Kendrick hastily slung one leg over the other, hoping to achieve a casual pose. He stole a look at her and prayed he wouldn't see disgust. She was the only woman in seven hundred years he had wanted to win. He wasn't sure how he would react if she shunned him.

She was smiling. Shyly. Oh, she was still a bit on the uncomfortable side with him, and had been since the afternoon she'd touched him. But that would pass. He was a very patient man. She would come to him in time. At least she was smiling and not bolting at the sight of the intimate bit of furniture. A grin crept over his mouth. His ego was still intact and that relieved him more than he really wanted to admit.

"Comfy," she nodded approvingly, coming to stand at the back of the sofa and then running her hand over the fabric. "But how in the world did you get it up here? Or maybe the better question is when?"

"Last night. The merchants in the village are used to what they think are Worthington's odd hours. I was beginning to feel sorry for you sitting in that hard chair so I bought this."

She smiled. "You are far too kind, my lord."

"Come try it out," he said, trying to sound as if he actually couldn't care less if she sat next to him or not. *Steady, Seakirk. For heaven's sake, don't look so desperate.*

Genevieve came around slowly, then sat. If she'd sat any further away, she would have been sitting on the other side of the armrest.

"You had the stitches removed today?" he asked politely. "Might I see?"

She held out her hand, then jumped nervously when he bent over it to look.

Distraction. He had to distract her and quickly or she would run again.

"Football?" he offered. "Raiders and 49ers on videotape. I haven't watched it yet. It could be exciting."

"It sounds great," she nodded. "Might be some playoff hope for my 49ers if they win today."

Her 49ers, indeed. Kendrick felt himself begin to frown. "Steve Young is a weak-kneed woman," he said distinctly.

"No, he's not."

"Aye, he is. I could throw twice as far as he does and twice as hard. And I wouldn't need a front line to protect me," he added arrogantly.

She gave him an amused smile. "Of course, my lord."

Kendrick scowled at her for her patronizing tone and received a laugh in return. Fortunately he wasn't so annoyed that he didn't notice that she had relaxed and was no longer hugging the far armrest. He did his best not to let his scowl turn into a grin. It looked as if distraction was going to be the way to woo and win Mistress Genevieve Buchanan.

The game began, and it took only minutes for Genevieve to become fully engrossed in the play. He laughed at her outrage over poor calls for she was easily as opinionated as he was. Then he fumed over her appreciation of hulking male bodies in tight uniforms. Their forms weren't *that* fine. By the saints, he would have cut a rakish figure in such garments. He was tempted to conjure up a suit just to show her. If he hadn't thought it would have seemed a bit obvious, he would have done it.

During halftime, her interest evaporated and he sent her off into the shrine, taking secret pride in her boundless fascination with all his acquisitions. The day before, he'd followed her after a few minutes to find her running her fingers lightly over a tunic he'd worn in life. The sight had left a suspicious lump in his throat and he'd quickly retreated, not wanting to disturb or embarrass her. He'd fled to the battlements where he'd indulged in a tear or two of regret, then tormented himself with visions of Genevieve running her fingers over a tunic he happened to be wearing.

He sighed as he propped his feet up on the stool in front of him and put his hands behind his head, relaxing back against the couch. Despite the frustration of not being able to touch her, he couldn't remember the last time he'd been so content. For the first time in centuries, he felt like his old self. Gone were the all-consuming thoughts of revenge that had plagued him from morn 'til eve. Gone was the bitterness toward Matilda and Richard for their scheme. Gone was the resentment he had harbored toward the Powers Above who had left him in such a sorry state.

Instead, he was grateful. How could he have known that seven hundred years of waiting would bring him a treasure like the woman who hummed as she puttered around in his past? He wasn't sure he was up to admitting it, but, aye, there was even gratitude for the darkness of his ghostly past. If there had been no darkness, how would he have appreciated the light Genevieve had brought with her?

She had hurtled into his existence with the force of a hurricane and swept him up along in her joy before he knew what was happening. How could he not love the way she laughed at his poor jests? How could he do anything but admire her drive, her enthusiasm, her pleasure in the simple things he had long since ceased to mark? Through her, he smelled the tang of salt air, felt the dirt in the garden under his fingers, tasted the simple fare Worthington prepared with such restrained gusto.

And then there was the woman herself. Her shy smile delighted him, her laugh enchanted him, her bewitching hazel eyes held him captive. He adored watching her pad around in those ridiculous red nightclothes, looking like an overgrown child.

Aye, the only pain came from knowing he would never be all the things to her he wanted to be. He would never hold her, touch her hair, lift her face up for his kiss. He would never lie beside her at night and hold her slender body next to his. He would never pick her up in his arms and carry her to the beach to love her in the warmth of the summer sun.

Perhaps it had taken seven centuries to pare away at his soul and leave him capable of feeling such regret for joys lost. In life perhaps he would never have looked at her twice. He'd had his spurs to win and a quest to fulfill. When the Crusade had left a poor taste in his mouth, he'd roamed the continent hiring out as a mercenary. It had been a harsh life, full of danger, blood and death.

He had become cynical. He'd never seen it before, but that's what had happened. Women had been nothing but conveniences for him. He thumbed through the catalog of memories in his head, skimming over the dozens of women who had sought him out for one reason or another. For many, luring him to their beds had been nothing but a coup. That hadn't hurt his feelings. Beautiful women bragging of his prowess only augmented his reputation.

Then there had been the women of vengeance, the ones who had used him to spite another. He'd faced more than one livid husband in the morning and lived to tell the tale. Those were the women he preferred to forget.

Only a handful of others stood out in his mind. Two or three had been dreamy-eyed virgins whom he had bluntly told there was no hope of marriage. Eventually he'd taken them, realizing that they would probably be trapped in a loveless marriage anyway. It had been his gift to them, albeit a fairly selfish one. The others had been either wed or older, women who had appreciated his wry jests, women who had considered themselves his equal and not stooped to playing foolish games. It had been mutual seduction, no commitment, pleasure while it lasted and friendship once it was finished.

He realized, with a start, that Matilda was not among any of the women who paraded before his mind's eye. He smiled faintly. Nay, he'd never loved her truly. She had been nothing but a means to an end.

A means to Genevieve.

He dropped his hands to his lap and closed his eyes. And

what would Genevieve say when he told her he was falling in love with her?

Genevieve wandered around Kendrick's private den, touching everything she saw and wondering if it had been something he'd touched during his life. She wandered over to the cabinet containing his clothes. As she had done almost every day for the past week, she opened it and gently touched a worn tunic.

She shut the glass and tried to distract herself. She was losing her mind. There was simply no other reason for the feelings she was having lately. Kendrick was a ghost. Even if he hadn't been, he was way out of her league. Friendship was something he seemed willing to give her, but anything else? She shook her head. It probably wouldn't occur to him.

She strolled over to his desk and looked up at the portrait. What a wonderful family it must have been. She could just imagine Phillip reaching over to give Kendrick a wet willy, or Kendrick snapping Jason's jock strap. Even in the painting, the boys looked to be full of mischief. As full of it as was their father. Robin of Artane grinned down at her and she grinned right back. He had probably been the worst of the bunch.

And Lady Anne. There was something ethereally beautiful about the woman. It had nothing to do with the pale gold of her hair or her eyes the color of dried sage. There was a beauty of spirit, a gentleness that reached out to whomever gazed at her likeness. Genevieve wished she could have met her. Time in her company would have been time well spent.

She looked over Kendrick's desk and found nothing of great interest. There was an accounts book lying open but she hardly cared what it contained. She was turning to walk away when a piece of paper caught her eye. She bent and picked up what looked to be a receipt.

Lord Kendrick de Piaget, receipt for services rendered, £25,000.

It was signed by Bryan McShane.

She stared at the slip of paper in shock. *Don't jump to conclusions*, she warned herself as a number of ugly scenarios leaped immediately to mind. Maybe it was a coincidence. Surely Bryan McShane had offered her the castle in good faith. Surely Kendrick hadn't sent him to make her an offer she would have been stupid to refuse just because he wanted to kill her. Before she let her imagination really run wild, she took the receipt and marched out into the television room. Kendrick looked to be sleeping but that didn't deter her. She cleared her throat imperiously.

He opened one eye. "You rang, madame?" he drawled.

She shoved the receipt at him. "Explain this."

A flicker of something might have crossed his face but it disappeared so quickly she was fairly sure she had imagined it. Kendrick sat up slowly and peered at the paper she held.

"It greatly resembles a receipt from my solicitor."

"You know him?" she screeched. "He works for you?"

Kendrick gave her an amused smile. "Love, why else would he have approached you about this keep? Of course I sent him to track you down. I will admit that my motives were not the purest in the beginning but you don't fault me for it now, do you?"

She groaned and sank down on the couch next to him. "Don't give me that deadly smile of yours. I'm immune to it." Had he called her *love*? Genevieve ignored the flood of pleasure that brought to her and concentrated on remaining irritated with the frighteningly handsome man sitting next to her, who was currently attempting to look innocent. She waved her finger at him. "Don't you dare try to weasel out of this. You sent a man to find me, knowing full well that he was going to bring me here to meet my end. Isn't that true?"

He gave her a solemn, little-boy pout, obviously something he thought would induce sympathy on the part of the receiver. She frowned darkly at him and he sighed.

"Come on, Gen," he said coaxingly, leaning closer to her, "you know I'm sorry for frightening you all those times. I had no idea what a wonderful person you were or I would have never done what I did."

"What *else* did you do?"

He smiled gently. She wanted to close her eyes in self-defense. The man had no scruples whatsoever.

"I misjudged a person I'd never even met, then regretted my actions sorely. Won't you forgive me for that?"

She threw in the towel. "All right," she sighed, defeated. "You're forgiven. And you're missing the game. Your Raiders are losing without your support. And," she added, "I still don't think what you did was very nice. You put that poor man under a great amount of stress." She sighed, realizing he was only half listening to her. "But I guess it worked out for the best. Your offer certainly got me out of a jam."

Kendrick pretended not to have heard her and heaved a silent sigh of relief over the disaster successfully avoided, praying she wouldn't feel the need to thank him for appearing in her life at the moment she was left with nowhere else to go. *Merde*, that had been close!

He hadn't really lied about what had happened; he'd just left out a big chunk of truth. But it was truth that would put Genevieve forever beyond his reach if she learned of it. He made a mental note to ring Bryan McShane first thing in the morning and warn the man to keep his mouth shut.

About the time Genevieve discovered Kendrick had been the one to turn all her clients against her, he'd be in a hell he could only imagine in his worst nightmares.

Chapter
Twelve

Bryan McShane lifted one side of the shade away from the window and peeked outside. Almost dawn. Maledica would soon be at work and the streets would be safe. Bryan had wanted to flee his flat last night but being out in the dark with his employer possibly lurking about hadn't been appealing in the least. No, it was best he wait for daylight.

He hadn't wanted to come back to his apartment after his latest failure at Seakirk, but he hadn't had a choice. In the first place, all his money was stuffed in his mattress. He could hardly get across the Channel without funds. Also stuffed in his mattress were his forgery tools. Who knew what the future held? Should he by some quirk of fate stumble someday across a document with Genevieve Buchanan's signature on it, he didn't want to be unprepared.

The phone rang. That had to be Bobby. He'd called his former school chum and begged a ride to the docks. He prayed nothing had gone wrong with the plans.

"Hello?"

"McShane? Glad to find you at home. I've a matter to discuss with you."

Lord Seakirk. Bryan immediately began to sweat. Surely the ghoul hadn't found a way to get off his land, had he?

"My lord," he squeaked, "where are you?"

"Where do you think I am, dolt?" Kendrick said curtly. "By St. George's throat, man, have you gone daft?"

"Forgive me, my lord," Bryan said quickly. Tempting as it was to hang up on the man and be done with it, that wouldn't do. Who knew what sort of undeadly minions de Piaget was capable of commanding. "How may I serve you?" The very words were dragged from his mouth by force.

"I want you to keep your mouth shut about what transpired to get Miss Buchanan to England."

"Ah, you mean calling her clients?" Bryan said, puzzled. "But, my lord, what could that possibly matter—"

"It matters because I wish it to remain strictly between you and me," Kendrick cut in. "I've transferred a substantial bonus to your account, McShane. Should you prove to be trustworthy, I might see fit to do it again in the future. But," he said, and his voice dropped to a menacing rumble, "should you prove false, rest assured that there isn't a stone large enough for you to hide under. You would regret mightily having abused my good will."

Substantial? Bryan's mind was reeling. De Piaget might have had his faults, but understatement and stinginess weren't among them.

"Of course, my lord!" he exclaimed. "I won't say a word, I promise you!"

"Good," Kendrick grunted. "See that you don't. Worthington, hang up the bloody phone for me."

The line went dead. Bryan replaced the receiver in the cradle and slumped back against the wall, sweat pouring down his face. He didn't bother with a handkerchief. He dragged his sleeve across his forehead and started toward the bedroom to fetch his luggage. Bobby wouldn't mind a side trip to the bank.

Just as he set his suitcases down, a knock sounded on the

door. Thank heavens his old chum had arrived on time! Bryan flung open the door in relief.

Maledica stood there, his dark blond hair combed neatly, his expensive Italian suit immaculate. Good lord, the man was huge. A pity Maledica would never stir himself to travel to Seakirk. He and de Piaget would have been fitting matches for each other. Now, that was the kind of standoff Bryan would have liked to see. Unfortunately, he probably wouldn't live that long.

Maledica came into the flat and closed the door. It sealed with an ominous click.

"I've missed you at the office, McShane."

"Ah, er, sir, I was, ah—*arrgh*!"

Bryan couldn't breathe. Probably because Maledica had him by the shirtfront, hoisted half a foot off the ground.

"Sir, I can explain—"

"Silence. I see you're prepared for travel. Back to Seakirk, I assume?"

Bryan nodded as vigorously as he could.

"I daresay you've packed garments for a long stay. I don't wish it to be a long stay, McShane. Surely you don't want to disappoint me again, do you?"

"No, sir," Bryan gasped.

Maledica didn't release him. "You've failed again, haven't you?"

"I tried, sir, but de Piaget—"

"I don't want excuses!" Maledica thundered. He took a deep breath and let it out slowly. "Hear me, little woman, and hear me well. 'Tis past time the keep was mine. I grow weary of waiting. You will attempt the feat again and this time you will not falter. Understood?"

"Aye," Bryan squeaked.

"Do whatever you must. I find the idea of a kidnapping rather appealing, but that is simply my opinion. I suggest, however, that my opinion become your opinion. Surely you see the wisdom of it."

"I think he's holding her prisoner," Bryan managed, struggling to suck in air.

"*Merde*," Maledica said, with a snort. "He's a ghost, for pity's sake." He gave Bryan a shake. "Have you lost your wits, man? She will leave the keep soon enough, for one reason or another. Lie in wait for her. Saints, must I do the deed for you?"

"No, sir!"

Maledica set Bryan on his feet. Bryan tried not to flinch as his employer straightened the jacket, shirt and tie his fists had rumpled. Bryan could only stare up into Maledica's eyes and shudder at the cold, icy anger there. The man's gaze was made all the more frightening by the different color of his eyes, one brown, one blue. Bryan preferred to stare into the brown one. The blue made him think of something unearthly, evil, demonic. God help him should he ever truly cross this man!

"Not even God can help you if you do," Maledica growled. He turned and strode from the room. The door shut with a bang.

Bryan dashed for the bathroom. After losing his breakfast, he rinsed his mouth out and stared at himself in the mirror. His hair was disheveled, his eyes red, his mouth tight with strain.

Too much stress.

It was going to kill him one of these days.

Chapter Thirteen

Genevieve trailed her fingers idly over the wood of her chair, remembering the last time she had sat there. It had been the night she had decided she and Kendrick would talk, the night he had shown up with a real knife instead of a pretend one. How he had frightened her.

But now Kendrick was sprawled in the chair facing hers, his head turned toward the fire in the hearth. He looked as harmless as a sleepy cat. His long, jean-clad legs were stretched out in front of him, far enough for him to tuck his feet under the front of her chair. He wore a white oxford shirt, unbuttoned a bit—for her benefit no doubt. His hair was tied in a queue, and both hair and black ribbon fell over one shoulder. He would have looked like a preppie pirate if he'd had a gold hoop in his ear.

The firelight flickered softly over his features, highlighting the beautiful sculpting of his cheeks and jaw and the relaxed line of his full lips. She was staring at his mouth when she felt his eyes on her. A blush stained her cheeks before she even met his glance. He winked and she blushed some more.

"Stop it," she said.

His smile deepened into a grin. "Why?"

"Because it's not nice to tease."

"I like to watch you blush."

She didn't have a good comeback for that one. Kendrick had been teasing her like that for days, as often as he could—and that was plenty often. Since the night she had found the receipt they had been inseparable during the daytime. Genevieve was still waiting for him to get bored, but it didn't seem to be happening. If she wasn't up early enough to suit him, he woke her. If she wanted to go to bed early, he made enough noise for sleep to be an impossibility. Heaven forbid she should want to read during the day. Kendrick was at his most obnoxious when being ignored. She made sure to chew him out often for being such a pest but secretly she treasured every grumble, every medieval drinking song bellowed in her ear at dawn, every moment he spent vying for her attentions.

"What are you thinking about?"

She leaned her head back and smiled. "Absolutely nothing."

"It isn't nice to lie."

"You wouldn't want to know."

"Shall we wager?"

She shook her head. "Just idle thoughts."

"Then you won't mind if I read them—"

"Don't you dare!"

He grinned. "You make it very tempting, Genevieve."

Distraction. She was fast discovering the best way to get Kendrick off an uncomfortable subject was to distract him.

"Do I look like Matilda?" she blurted out without thinking. Then she gasped. Good grief, what a poor choice of topics!

Kendrick was only momentarily taken aback, then he shook his head and gave a short bark of a laugh. "Merciful saints, nay. She was tall and slender, like you, but she possessed an abundance of mousy-blonde hair and blue eyes that could freeze a man at twenty paces. She was, on the whole, an impossible woman to endure. How Richard managed it all those years is beyond me."

"Richard?"

"Her lover."

"Oh," Genevieve said. "Did you know him previously?"

He smiled. "You want the entire tale, do you?"

She squirmed. Want the tale? She was dying for it! "If it wouldn't bother you."

"A month ago I couldn't bring myself to speak of it. Now I find it holds little bitterness for me. And to answer your question, nay, I did not know Richard before I saw him in Matilda's great hall that fateful day."

"What happened?"

Kendrick looked into the fire, his expression sober, as if he were witnessing the events again. "I had come to tell Matilda that the king had awarded me Seakirk for my valor in the Crusade and that, in return for her hand in marriage, I had paid off her creditors. I had assumed, arrogantly I suppose, that she would be overcome with gratitude."

Genevieve waited while he paused. There was nothing she could say to comfort him and she didn't want to push him to go on. She'd opened the can of worms but it was entirely his decision to pull them out.

"I'd come with only a few men. It never occurred to me to bring more. After all, I was coming to see my betrothed. What need had I for men to guard me?"

"Kendrick," she interrupted, "maybe talking about this wasn't such a great idea."

"You've a right to know, Genevieve. For curiosity's sake, if nothing else." He turned back to his contemplation of the flames. "Royce, Nazir and I were standing in the great hall with a handful of my personal guardsmen."

"Royce?"

"My captain." He smiled at her apologetically. "I'm sorry I haven't introduced you to him yet. He can't stay anywhere longer than a few hours so he tends to appear infrequently. I'll present him to you the next time he comes."

She nodded and waited for him to go on.

"I stood in the great hall and waited for Matilda to come down to greet me. Instead, her men-at-arms swarmed into the hall. They cut down all but Nazir, Royce and me. I hardly had the wits to react, I was so astonished. We were hopelessly out-numbered, but the three of us had been in like situations before. Nazir killed a score of men before he was overcome. Royce's tally was at least a dozen before he was disarmed. I have no idea how many I killed but the bodies were in piles six-deep around me."

"Downstairs?" she whispered.

He nodded.

"And it doesn't bother you?" She quickly shook her head. "Sorry, that was a stupid question." What could he do about it? It wasn't as if he could leave Seakirk to find somewhere else to live. But surely seeing the site of such a terrible tragedy had to bother him.

"For better or worse, Seakirk is my home," he said simply. "I daresay I wouldn't go anywhere else even if I had the choice. After we were subdued," he continued, "we were taken downstairs and chained to the walls in the cellar. Richard came down and thanked me kindly for all I'd done for him, which included bringing a few bags of gold along with me. He then let loose arrows into Royce and Nazir, then me. Once he was finished with his part in it, Matilda came down." He grimaced. "She smiled as she whispered her black words over the three of us. I stood there in the spirit and listened to her weave her black spell."

The hair on the back of Genevieve's neck stood up. "She was a witch?"

"If I believed in witches, I would have to say aye."

Genevieve shivered. She didn't believe in witches either, but she had a vivid mental picture of a medievally garbed woman standing over three dying men and muttering her black incantations. Whether she had used witchcraft or not was debatable. Whatever the case, she had certainly caused a far-reaching tragedy.

"But why did they do it?"

"For the money, I suppose. My family was enormously wealthy." He trailed his finger over the small scar on his cheek. "I had my share of enemies."

"Who gave you that scar?" she asked quietly.

Kendrick smiled grimly. "An honorless whoreson from Sedgwick named William. He surely hated me enough to want revenge, but I daresay he wasn't clever or brave enough to have thought of murder. Nay, it was for the gold, and Matilda was the one to see it done."

A life ruined, simply for money. Genevieve wished she could get her hands around Matilda's neck. The greedy witch.

"And how old were you when you," she took a deep breath, "when Richard . . ."

"When he killed me? A score and twelve."

"Thirty-two? And you were just getting married? Wasn't that pretty old to still be single in those days?"

"I had my reasons, I suppose." He met her eyes and smiled innocently, all grimness gone from his expression. "Having my pick of hundreds of women who were all begging to spend a night in my bed made marriage seem a bit too confining for my taste."

Genevieve wanted to slug him. "You were quite the Don Juan then," she said shortly.

"Aye," he grinned. "I am very skilled between the sheets."

"You son of a bitch."

He laughed. "You've nothing to be jealous of. They're all dead now."

"I'm not jealous. I'm just appalled at your promiscuousness."

"And how many lovers have you had?" he teased. "Come, Genevieve, you're thirty years old. You can't tell me you're still a virgin."

Genevieve was on her feet and out the door before the thought of moving had even taken shape in her mind. She ran down the hall and up the stairs to the roof. Not even the shock of the cold November air cooled the fiery heat of her cheeks. She leaned against the wall and blinked back embarrassed tears. There was nothing wrong with being a virgin, damn it! And damn Kendrick for making fun of her because of it!

"Is it true?"

His deep voice washed over her like a warm wave.

"Go to hell," she said, brushing the tears away from her cheeks.

Kendrick's hands came to rest on the wall, flanking her body. "Sweet Gen, I didn't mean to grieve you."

Genevieve folded her arms over her chest and blinked furiously.

"I never dated, damn it."

"Gen—"

"How was I supposed to sleep with anyone when I never dated?"

"Genevieve—"

"I wasn't just going to go out and do it just to do it! I don't care what you think of me, either."

"But, I think—"

"I'm not a prude. I'm just choosy. Good grief, I'm picky about chocolate chips. Why wouldn't I be picky about this too?"

She stood there and fumed. *Go ahead and say something insulting. I'm ready for you.*

Kendrick was silent for several minutes.

"Have you finished, my love?"

My love? Genevieve frowned. Just what did he intend by that? She set her jaw and nodded. Let him take his best shot. She could handle it.

" 'Tis a wondrous thing. I would never make sport of it."

Genevieve felt some of the tension inside her ease. "Well, you shouldn't. There's nothing wrong with it."

"Nay, there is not." He paused. When he spoke again, his voice was hushed. "It pleases me that I would have been the first."

Genevieve couldn't help but smile a little. He was certainly sure of himself.

He was silent for a few moments. "You waited because you never found someone to your liking, aye?"

She nodded.

"Never? Not even recently?"

She shook her head, then froze. What was that supposed to

mean? No, Kendrick wouldn't have looked at her twice if she hadn't been the only woman for miles around. She sighed.

"I suppose I was waiting for a dream." She watched the moon spill its light onto the surface of the ocean, watched the way the light shimmered and shifted with the swells and eddies of the water. The motion soothed her, stole her inhibitions so fully that she found herself putting into words the beautiful, haunting fantasies she'd entertained over the course of her life.

"From the time I was small, I dreamed of castles and knights," she whispered. "I pretended I had a castle of my own, a place where I was safe, where I was loved. It was a beautiful place, like I had always pictured Camelot to be, only this was real and it was mine." She smiled to herself. "The older I got, the more specific I became in my dreaming. My castle was medieval in design and filled with all the trappings. I spent my imaginary days roaming in my garden or walking along the battlements, enjoying the feel of the sea breeze on my face and the sun on my back. And when the winter chill set in, I retreated to my solar with its enormous fireplace and walls lined with bookcases and there I passed my time with my favorite characters from other worlds and other realms."

She fell silent, caught up in the memories and in the sound of the sea against the shore.

"And were you alone there?"

"What is a castle without a handsome knight to defend it against dragons?"

"Of course," he murmured.

Genevieve closed her eyes. "He was someone who thought I was beautiful," she whispered. "Someone who understood what I'd saved for him. He didn't care that I couldn't flirt, that I wasn't very good at relationships, or that I would probably embarrass him at parties. And it didn't matter to him how many dragons he had to go through to win me. They would seem like nothing."

"Tell me what he looks like."

His voice was so soft, Genevieve hardly heard him. "Tall," she said, just as softly. "And strong, strong enough to frighten his enemies, yet he would never hurt me with that strength.

His hair would be long and dark. I'm sure it would be some-thing he would like brushed, but he would never admit as much to me."

"What color are his eyes?"

"Green," she answered without thinking, then she bit her lip and woke completely from whatever had induced her to bab-ble like a brook. Good grief, what had she said?

"Dark green?"

She hesitated. Then she bit her lip some more. Well, what had she got to lose? Her pride? No, that was already gone. She looked down at her hands, hands that were resting on the wall between other hands; Kendrick's wide, strong hands.

"No," she said quietly.

"Perhaps . . . the color of sage?"

She nodded, mute. *Lord, please don't let him be teasing me now!*

"Tell me more of this lad," he demanded. His voice next to her ear sent chills down her spine. "Is he handsome?"

"Oh, Kendrick," she pleaded.

"I want to know," he rumbled. "I will know if there is an-other man I must needs kill this night for taking you from me. Now, tell me of your knight. Is he handsome?"

Kill a man for taking you from me? Genevieve felt a warmth spread through her chest, a delicious feeling of be-longing she had never before experienced. A smile started deep within her and worked its way out, bringing tears with it.

"Genevieve, speak," he repeated gruffly. "Is he handsome?"

"Tolerably." As if Kendrick didn't know that already.

A catch of breath, then a soft grunt. "Arrogant?"

She smiled again. "Very."

"Foul-tempered?"

"Not always," she said, feeling her smile turn wistful. "No, he can be sweet when he wants to be."

"Genevieve." Kendrick's voice had suddenly become very hoarse. "My love, you have your castle of dreams. Here, be-neath your feet. And you have your knight. If he pleases you."

Genevieve turned slowly. Never had she wished for flesh-and-blood arms to hold her more than she did at that moment.

She leaned back against the wall and looked up at Kendrick. The light from the moon fell down softly on them, casting Kendrick's face in shadows. But there was enough light for her to see the gentle expression he wore and the honesty in his eyes.

"Shall I slay your dragons for you, my lady?"

"Oh, Kendrick . . ."

"Yea or nay." He held up his hand and his sword was immediately there, winking at her in the moonlight. "My sword is drawn and ready. Shall I wield it? Shall you be my lady and give me reason to fight?"

Genevieve stared up at him, mute. Her dreams were coming true right before her eyes and she hardly knew what to think. She'd wished on enough stars in the past, politely suggesting the delivery of someone who would love only her. Stardust was rumored to have powerful wish properties, but she'd never really believed it.

Until now.

"Oh," she said, wiping at her eyes, "yes. I would like that very much."

The sword disappeared. He lifted his hand and put it against her cheek. A shadow of longing crossed his features and he quickly dropped his arm. But he did not move away.

"If I had the power," he murmured, "I would kiss you senseless."

She shivered at the thought.

"You're cold," he said, stepping closer to her, as if he could warm her himself.

"No, not exactly," she breathed. Those shivers definitely weren't from the cold.

He stared at her for several moments in silence, his expression grave. Finally he smiled, a wistful little smile that made her want to cry all over again.

"Come," he said softly, "let us descend. I have no cloak to put around you. If you make ready for bed, I'll tuck you in."

She nodded and followed him along the parapet.

"Will you sing to me tonight?" she asked.

"Name your pleasure."

"That song you sang yesterday morning."

"Which one?" he stalled.

"You know which one. About the bawdy wench who drinks all the knights under the table, then takes their armor off them and sells it. I really liked that one."

Kendrick groaned as they walked through the door and started down the stairs. "Only if you promise never to mention it to Royce when you meet him."

"Why not?"

Kendrick flashed her a grin. "Because it happened to him."

Genevieve smiled back, then allowed her thoughts to wander as Kendrick began to sing.

The irony of her situation made her smile again. She'd finally found a man who respected her and what did he have to be? A ghost. Just as intangible as the knights in shining armor she'd spent her life dreaming about.

Somehow it just figured.

But she certainly wasn't going to complain.

Chapter
Fourteen

Genevieve woke and stretched, smiling at how rested she felt. No nightmares. No ghosts brandishing battle-axes and threatening her with death. The only thing her gallant ghost had been brandishing over the past week was a wry wit and a knee-buckling smile.

No, calling him her ghost just wasn't true anymore. He was her champion. She had the insane desire to get up and sew a ribbon for him to wear on his arm. Would he and Nazir stage a mock tournament for her benefit?

She'd woken during the night to find she had fallen asleep on top of the covers after spending half the night talking to Kendrick, something that had happened regularly for the past few days. The blanket that covered her was certainly nothing she'd put there herself. Kendrick had been watching her with a gentle smile. He'd dismissed her worry over possible aftereffects from the exertion, saying, with a wink, that he'd been working out. How could you argue with a man who pumped iron so he could cover you up when it was required?

"Kendrick?" she said aloud.

Aye, love. His voice whispered across her mind like a caress.

Where are you?

On the roof. Do you miss me?

She smiled. And this from the man who'd had her death on his mind not a month earlier. Things change.

"So they do."

She jumped as she heard his voice next to her ear. He had materialized next to her on the bed. That any man should look so lazy and satisfied so early in the morning had to be a sin. His grin deepened as he looked at her.

"Did you dream of me?"

"You would know."

"You told me to stay out of your mind. I've been behaving."

"Why do I have the feeling it's a stretch for you? I shudder to think of the gray hairs you gave sweet Lady Anne."

Kendrick grinned again. "My mother thought me to be a most perfect child. It was my father who did most of the yelling over my antics."

Genevieve turned on her side to face him. Oh, how she loved mornings in bed with him. It made her never want to get up.

"Tell me more," she prodded.

"The list of my escapades is long."

"Bore me for a minute or two."

He propped his head up on his palm. "Well," he said, posturing as if he expounded some deep concept, "I suppose you might have labeled me an inquisitive child—"

"Troublemaker," she translated.

"Highly intelligent—"

"Bratty—"

"Enterprising—"

"Your poor mother," she laughed.

"She found me charming," he said, pretending offense. "It didn't bother her in the slightest when I took apart the drawbridge to see how it worked."

Genevieve gasped. "You didn't. How in the world did you manage it?"

"Did it at night," Kendrick said proudly. "I was only fortunate none of our enemies knew of it or you wouldn't have such a handsome knight at your disposal."

She ignored his vanity. "What did your father do?"

"Praised me for my questioning mind, then shouted at me until I thought I would go deaf. I was let off lightly that time. He actually looked like he wanted to beat me when I dismantled the smith's forge."

Genevieve groaned at his unholy grin.

"Phillip, my brother, was with me." Kendrick laughed at the memory. "I can still hear him pleading: 'Kendrick, Father will take a switch to you! I beg you to reconsider. Oh Kendrick, please, please, *please* do not do this.' Phillip never was one for straying too far out of the bounds of propriety."

"Did your father spank you for that?"

"He got drunk instead and threatened to disown me."

"Did he ever hit you?"

"Nay, but he certainly shook me vigorously when I took apart his favorite suit of chain mail on a dare from my sister Mary." He winked at her. "I told you she was deceptively angelic-looking."

"You were very fortunate that your father had such control."

He sobered instantly. "Yours didn't?"

"My father hardly stirred himself to speak, much less anything else. He and I both were too busy being ordered around by my mother. She wore the pants in my family."

"A bit on the headstrong side, aye?"

"You could say that."

"She just needed to be taken in hand. Like you. A strong woman needs a stronger man."

"Like me?" she echoed. "What are you talking about? And who are you to think you need to *take me in hand*, as you so charmingly put it?"

He smiled as he leaned forward until their noses would have been touching had things been a bit different.

"I am your lord. My duty, and pleasure, is to protect you, care for you and see that you lack for nothing."

"In return for what?"

"Complete obedience," he said with a straight face.

"Kendrick, that is the most medieval attitude I have ever heard!"

"What else could you expect from me?" he asked with a smile tugging at his mouth. "Get dressed, my lady, and let me show you just how sweet having me lord over you can be."

She pulled the covers up to her chin. "Leave."

"I'd rather stay."

"Go," she said, pointing to the door. "And don't you dare peek." She stopped suddenly. "Do you watch me shower?"

"Though I've been sorely tempted, I haven't," he said solemnly. "Should I start?"

She pointed again at the door. "Walk through it so I know you're not just hanging around where I can't see you."

He obliged her with a regretful sigh. Genevieve bolted from the bed and hurried through her morning routine. She pulled on her favorite pair of jeans and groaned at the snugness. Looking in the full-length mirror near the armoire only showed her the thoroughness of the damage. Too many healthy meals at Worthington's table had contributed to this problem.

"Nonsense. You look ravishing."

She whirled around in surprise. Kendrick was leaning lazily against the footpost of her bed.

"You promised you wouldn't peek!"

"Genevieve, you're completely dressed."

"How would you have known?" she demanded.

He grinned sheepishly. "I peeked."

She opened her mouth to retort, then shut it. Why bother? After all, it was his bedroom.

"*Our* bedchamber," he said softly.

Genevieve felt herself begin to blush. "Don't you get any ideas about taking up residence in here, buster. You don't sleep anyway."

"I do on occasion. Just out of habit, of course."

"Well, do it somewhere else. Yours is the only bed in the house at the moment."

Kendrick walked toward her slowly and stopped when he was only a hair's breadth from her. "You are a saucy wench, aren't you?"

Genevieve suppressed the urge to gulp. He was just so *big*. She looked up into his eyes and felt herself sway. It was an effort not to just give in and let him have what he wanted. It was especially hard in light of the fact that she really wouldn't have minded having him around twenty-four out of twenty-four hours each day.

But ghost or not, she just wasn't ready to give up that much privacy.

"You can't sleep here," she managed.

He folded his arms over his chest and frowned down at her. "Already you forget who is lord here."

"Possession is nine-tenths of the law," she reminded him breathlessly.

"I at least want napping rights," he rumbled. "I can become very out of sorts if I don't have a rest just before tea."

She had to fight her smile at his stubbornness. "Nothing else?"

"Nothing else," he muttered, "though I hardly believe I'm saying the like."

Whew. A nap in the daytime was one thing; sleeping through the night was another. She could handle the first.

"Very well, then, my lord," she said. "Napping rights are yours."

"That was easy enough. See you how sweet being obedient is?"

"Oh, yes," she said dryly.

"And now I will show you how indulgent I can be. What is your pleasure for the day?" He backed up a pace or two and made her a low bow. "I am your willing servant."

"Actually, I was thinking of starting on the other rooms. Do you want to help?"

"I don't know how much help I'd be, but I'll come along."

"I'll be glad to have you," she said.

*   *   *

Genevieve hadn't had the courage to tackle the walls and floors of the other guest chambers. Carpet would have to be torn up and wallpaper torn down. It was a job she knew she couldn't do herself. She looked up at Kendrick as they stood in what had been the French Smurf room.

"If I bring in men to do the dirty work, will you behave?"

"Your doubt wounds me. Why would I frighten unwitting souls?"

"I seem to remember screaming a few times when I first arrived."

"You were different. I planned to scare you s—"

"Kendrick!"

"Witless," he finished with a grin. "I was fairly clever about it, even if I do say so myself."

"Clever doesn't quite cover it." She looked around the room, trying to imagine it with wooden floors and stone walls. "Where did you get the furniture in your room?"

"Jonathan had it made for me. You remember, Matilda's grandson who painted my family's portrait?"

"Impossible. Furniture can't last that long."

"It can, when it's taken care of. Besides, no one used the chamber, it being the master's and all. Whoever tried found out swiftly that they'd made a serious mistake."

She couldn't help but laugh. "Kendrick, you are a horrible man, haunting hapless souls like that. Was it fun?"

"Excruciatingly amusing. I wish I'd taken more time to enjoy it, though I doubt I could have." He looked at her and his smile was full of love. " 'Tis only recently that I've found joy."

She smiled weakly, feeling a familiar blush stain her cheeks. Would his comments never fail to make her redden? She took a deep breath and put on a bright smile. She didn't have the stamina for this conversation now. Maybe when her blush had faded, say, in a few weeks.

"Do you know of any good antique stores nearby? Or perhaps an old castle we could ransack?"

"You are changing the subject, but I will humor you. I can send Royce and Nazir furniture hunting. Once the enemy is identified, it would be a simple thing to storm the keep with a staggering amount of money in hand. Though I would worry about Nazir's taste in furnishings."

I HAVE EXCELLENT TASTE!

Genevieve shivered as the echo of the shout died away. "I thought he was a roamer."

"He's become a homebody since he saw the new attraction at Seakirk," Kendrick said, with a grumble. "Be warned that the only place I managed to forbid him to watch you was in my bedchamber. He won't appear to you unless you call to him, and he certainly won't harm you, but I can't guarantee anything else. He can be a pest."

I AM NOT A PEST.

Genevieve laughed at the petulant tone that echoed in her mind. "He seems very sweet."

"And how do I seem, Lady Genevieve?" Kendrick asked softly, catching her gaze and holding it effortlessly. "I vow it's been an eternity since you last mentioned it."

"You seem a bit on the lazy side," she breathed, seizing on the first thing that came to mind. "Help me plan, would you? The day's a wastin'."

He laughed. "Saints, Genevieve, you've no romance in your soul. Very well, what will you have me do? And pray make it something that requires your undivided attention."

"Give me some ideas," Genevieve suggested. "Should I do all the bedrooms in a medieval style or would you prefer they each have their own time period?"

"Anything but Louis Fourteenth," he said, with a shudder.

She couldn't help her laugh. "No arguments there."

Kendrick turned to stand shoulder-to-shoulder with her and stroked his chin thoughtfully. "Perhaps you should do something like that farmhouse you did in upstate New York. You know, I actually am very fond of the Shaker style. The lines are simple, almost peasantlike in their lack of ornamentation. Aye," he said, warming to his topic, "and then maybe a room done all in that country look that's so popular in the Colonies these days. Like the Montgomery place in Ohio." He began to pace, talking animatedly and gesturing now and then to emphasize his point.

Genevieve was speechless.

"Can you quilt? If not, we'll hire someone to do it. And then perhaps a room done in a sort of a nineteenth-century, old rich look. Mahogany tables. Tapestry-covered chairs. Beveled mirrors. Aye, I've always had a fondness for beveled mirrors, even if I can't see myself in them."

"You know the Montgomerys?"

"Of course. Pay attention, Gen. Where was I? Ah, beveled mirrors."

"Do you know the Allans, too?"

"Of course," he said, waving aside her question. "Talked to them on the phone while I was trying to get . . . you . . . over," he said, his little speech winding down as though he were a marionette in sad need of a cranking. He looked at her helplessly. "Genevieve, I . . . I never meant . . ."

It couldn't be. Genevieve shook her head in disbelief. Kendrick strode over to her and she backed up until the wall stopped her movement. He looked down at her with an expression of anguish.

"I never meant—"

"Never meant to what?" she demanded, recovering her powers of speech. "Ruin my business? It was you, wasn't it?"

"You wouldn't accept my offer—"

"So you took my dream, the only thing I had ever loved and ruthlessly smashed it to pieces."

"Genevieve, I never meant to hurt—"

"You called them all, didn't you?" she asked, her voice cracking.

He paused, then nodded, mute.

The emotions bubbled up inside her, churning like a mess of noxious waste in a mad scientist's beaker. Kendrick had ruined the only thing she had built with her own hands, simply to bring her to her death.

"You bastard," she said, choking on a sob. "*Damn* you!" She brushed past him and fled from the room. He was right behind her, pleading for her to listen, but she wouldn't. She

put her hands over her ears in an effort to drown out the voice
that went straight into her mind.

"Stop it!" she cried shrilly, bursting into his room and slamming the door behind her. She dug her suitcase out from the
wardrobe and threw it on the bed. Then she reached into the
trunk under the window and grabbed armfuls of clothes. She
flung them haphazardly into the suitcase. Kendrick appeared
next to her.

"Genevieve, I beg you—"

"To what? Start another life so you can ruin that too?"

"I didn't know you—"

"As if that excuses you," she cried.

"Genevieve, damnation, will you just let me explain?"

"Just leave me alone! And after everything I told you. How
could you have been so cruel?"

Clothes started flinging themselves out of the suitcase as
fast as she could shove them in.

"Nazir, I need no aid!" Kendrick thundered.

Nazir was obviously not listening. If she hadn't been so
devastated, Genevieve might have laughed at the struggle she
was having with Kendrick's servant. She continued to ignore
Kendrick as she fought to retrieve her clothes. Finally she just
shut the lid and dragged the suitcase off the bed.

"Genevieve, you can start over again here," he said firmly,
as if his was the only opinion that mattered. "I'll help."

"I don't *want* to start here," she said through gritted teeth,
giving her suitcase a mighty tug. It wouldn't come off the bed.
Nazir became visible, holding onto the handle and fighting to
pull the suitcase his way.

"Don't be ridiculous," Kendrick said, brushing aside her
words as if they'd been an annoying bit of dust. "Your business will be twice as fine here. Why, we'll use the garrison
hall as a shoppe of sorts where people can come and see all
types of furniture—"

Genevieve let go of her luggage and turned to face
Kendrick, hoping that her anguish was plain to see. "I don't
want to start over again here," she said. "My life was there."

"But—"

"You're a cold, calculating bastard, Kendrick of Seakirk. I don't know how you can look me in the face after what you've done. Don't you have any shame?"

"I did what I had to do at the time. You know I wouldn't have done it had I known you."

"And that excuses you?" she retorted.

"Can you blame me?"

"Yes," she cried. "It was *my* life you ruined."

"And what of my life? I had to have you here, one way or another."

"To kill me!"

"Nay," he said, shaking his head sharply. "To sign away your right to the castle."

"Sign away my right to the castle?" she echoed. "But why?"

His expression tightened into a grim mask. "Because it's the only way I can be free. Once your signature is on the deed, Matilda's curse will be broken and I can join my family in the next life."

Genevieve put her hand to her mouth. "That's the only reason you did it? The only reason you ruined my business?"

He nodded.

A half-sob escaped her. "Why didn't you just ask? Why did you have to ruin my life while you were at it?"

"I didn't think you'd help me willingly."

"So, now it's either your dream or mine, isn't it? I give up living here in this castle and you have your freedom, or you give up your freedom and I keep my dream."

He wore the grimmest, most world-weary expression she'd ever seen. His answer was terse.

"Aye."

"Then forget it," she spat. "Keep it all. My dream and your chains. I'm not signing a damn thing."

"Genevieve, that's not what I want—"

"I don't care what you want!"

"If you would listen to reason," he said hotly, "you would see that we can work this—"

Genevieve turned and ran to the door. Only instinct made her grab her purse. She'd buy other clothes once she was

away. As long as she had her passport and a hefty amount of
Kendrick's money, life wouldn't be so bad.

"Master, stop her!"

"Let her go," Kendrick snapped. "She won't listen to reason
anyway."

It was only sheer luck that kept Genevieve on her feet and
not tumbling down the circular staircase. She was still weeping as she fled through the great hall. She collided with Worthington at the front door.

"My lady!" he exclaimed.

She pulled back and glared at him. "Did you know too? All
in on this together, huh? You, Bryan and His Bastardship?"

"In on what?" Worthington asked, genuinely confused. "My
lady, what by the blessed name of St. George has happened?"

"Let Kendrick tell you about it since he's the one who
ruined my life."

"Oh, my lady, you're overwrought. Let's have a nice cup of
tea and you'll tell me the story," he said soothingly.

"I don't want any tea. I want the keys to the Jag."

Worthington hesitated, then nodded. Genevieve watched
him go, her eyes burning with unshed tears. How could
Kendrick have been so cruel? Dreams Restored was the only
thing in her life that had ever worked out right for her. Her
business had taken the place of her parents, her friends and a
lover. It had been her life. And Kendrick had destroyed it.

He'd been about as compassionate as Matilda.

Worthington stood with his hands clasped behind his back
and watched as Genevieve descended the steps. She looked as
if everything she'd ever loved had been ripped away from her.
Perhaps that wasn't so far from the truth. And after how happy
she and Kendrick had become together. Worthington shook
his head again. What a disastrous turn of events.

"You'll call?" he asked quietly.

She nodded.

"And you'll be home soon." He tried to make it sound like
an inescapable eventuality.

How bloodshot were those sweet hazel eyes. Worthington's heartstrings were pulled uncomfortably taut.

"I don't know, Worthington," she said in a whispery voice, rough with grief. "I'll let you know when I find out."

Worthington nodded, knowing there was nothing else he could say. "Drive carefully."

She smiled grimly. "I won't wreck His Lordship's toy."

"The car be damned."

Genevieve walked to the low-slung Jaguar. She stopped and looked up suddenly. What she saw evidently grieved her, for she hastily turned away and slid in under the wheel of the car. She started it up and it purred sweetly, just for her. Worthington watched with moist eyes as she drove down the road and through the inner curtain gate. He walked down the steps, then looked up, wondering what she had seen.

Kendrick stood at the window, with his hands pressed against the glass.

"What a mess you've made of things, my lord," Worthington said, shaking his head sadly as he reentered the house.

Chapter
Fifteen

Kendrick stood on the battlements in his usual place, hoping against hope that the waves would soothe him. He'd been standing on the roof for a solid week, hoping for the same thing. But how could the waves comfort him when he had never more in life or death deserved misery? He wiped his hands over his face, sucked in a deep breath and looked up into the heavens. God help him, he should have told her about the deed to the castle. He should have shouted out the words as he was trying to frighten her into leaving. That would have sent her packing in record time.

But nay, he had given in to the selfish desire to keep her near him. Instead of letting her go as he should have, he had plotted and schemed to keep her close. And what had it earned him? A week of bliss immediately followed by the most hellish week he had passed in over seven hundred years.

Keeping her close wasn't what he'd done that was so terribly wrong. His offense lay in not being honest with her. He should have curled up in bed with her one night and gently told her of the curse and how he could be freed from it. She might have shared in his relief that after seven hundred years of haunting, he had finally come up with a legal means to break the malediction that had bound him to the stone of the castle only for so long as it did not belong to him in truth. She would have understood his motives for having treated her so poorly, and then she would have listened to him give her the most sincere apology of his life. Assuming she accepted it, he would have then looked deep into her eyes and told her the words that had gotten stuck in his throat that disastrous afternoon in the blue room when he had revealed his role in the scheme of things.

He didn't want her to sign the deed.

He groaned, a sound that came from deep within his soul. Not even those words would have ever compensated for what he'd done to bring her to England. He had ruthlessly and methodically destroyed her reputation. Aye, he was a fine warrior indeed. He'd identified his prey, scrutinized her perimeter, then systematically destroyed the walls that surrounded her, all with the precision and detachment of a seasoned mercenary. She might have forgiven him for other things, but she would never forgive him for that.

How he wanted her to! He looked down at the stone under his fingers, remembering how Genevieve had leaned against that very stone and poured out the deepest dreams of her soul. And somehow, beyond reason and beyond hope, he had become a part of those dreams. How he had adored her then! And how earnestly he had made his vows, vows to make her happy, to see that she lacked for nothing, to do everything in his power to keep her safe. Useless vows now. She would never accept anything from him, which meant he had nothing to give her.

Except restitution.

"My lord?"

Kendrick turned a weary look on his steward. "Any word?"

"Nay, my lord. I was hoping Nazir would have followed her and returned with a report."

"Nazir said, and I quote, 'I don't like you very much at

present, Master. I think I will shadow the Mistress for a time.'
He won't come back unless she does."

"Do you want her back?"

"Merciful saints above, Worthington, have you gone daft?"
Kendrick bellowed, feeling his anguish coat every word as if
with blood. "Of course I want her back!"

"Perhaps it would not be inappropriate for you to search."

Kendrick turned a stone-faced expression toward the sea.
"Don't be cruel, Worthington. It doesn't become you."

"I wasn't suggesting you try to leave the keep, my lord.
What is that commercial they have in the Colonies? *Let your
fingers do the walking?*"

With that, Worthington turned and walked away.

Kendrick clapped his hand to his forehead and cursed himself for his stupidity. Why hadn't he thought of that? He
turned and sprinted toward the battlement door.

"Damn you, Worthington, wait! I can't dial the bloody
phone myself!"

Genevieve lugged her shopping bags over to a taxi and
gratefully allowed the man to help her. Once her purchases
were settled, she collapsed into the back seat and groaned at
her protesting muscles. Shopping was backbreaking work.

After giving the man a tip that made him grin from ear to
ear, she had her purchases sent up, then made her way to the
small tea shop. She'd never been particularly fond of tea back
in the States, but she'd definitely acquired a taste for it in England. The only thing she didn't like was that it relaxed her
enough to allow her to think. Thinking was hardly her favorite
activity as it invariably led to remembering and that led to
pain. At least it had initially.

When she'd arrived in London a week ago, she'd been bitter
and hurt. Not even spending thousands of pounds on clothes
and jewelry had made her feel any better. As the hours had
trudged by, she'd become first numb, then thoughtful. For the
first time, she thought she understood a bit of the pain
Kendrick felt. Hadn't Matilda ruined his life just as he'd
ruined hers?

But was her life truly ruined? At least she still had a body—and what a precious blessing that was! She could still travel, see new places, taste foreign foods, smell strange and marvelous fragrances. Kendrick could do none of those things. Perhaps Kendrick had destroyed her dreams, but hadn't he, in his own way, restored them? He'd shared his home with her. He had taught her about football. He'd even offered to fund her business ventures.

But he'd given her more than that. He had made her feel beautiful. He had looked at her with love in his eyes and offered to be her champion. He had teased her, sung to her, ordered her around arrogantly. Wasn't that worth a bit of forgiveness?

And after all, he hadn't known her, had he? If he had, he would have known a mere smile would have brought her to him. It was only out of ignorance that he'd ruined her life. If she were to be completely honest with herself, she had to admit that he hadn't really done even that. He'd ruined her business, yes, but not her life. Her life was far fuller now than it ever had been before.

She set her teacup down and pushed it away from her. In a few more days, she would go home and if he wanted her to sign the papers, she would. If not, she would hug him as best she could and tell him just how much she loved him.

She made her way up to her suite. It was a beautiful room. She'd have to take the brochure with her so Kendrick could see. He'd be surprised at what a change it was from the inn where the bawdy wench had swiped Royce's mail.

The phone rang.

Genevieve looked at it, knowing without even picking it up who was on the other end of the line. She wiped her hands on her jeans and took a deep breath. There was no reason to be nervous. It was just Kendrick. She'd talked to him before. She could handle this. Except that she felt as if she were on the verge of something very momentous. She walked over to the bedside table and looked down at the phone.

It continued to ring.

She reached out and snatched up the receiver.

"Hello?" she said breathlessly.

"Do you have any idea how many bloody hotels, inns, youth hostels, boardinghouses and rooms for let there are between Seakirk and London?"

She sank down on her bed, her knees not up to the job of keeping her standing.

"I don't, but I have the feeling you do."

"Genevieve, I hardly know—"

"Kendrick, there's no need—"

"Please," he said, hoarsely, "let me finish. What I did to you was unforgivable. I wouldn't blame you if you never wanted to see me again. If I could leave Seakirk, I'd give it to you and never darken your door again."

"Kendrick, really—"

"I'll buy you whatever you need to start over again. Pick a city, find a house and all the trappings and I'll see that it's yours. I'll spread your reputation far and wide as the most marvelous of restoration experts. You'll have so much business, you'll need a garrison of assistants to help you. I think New York might be best, but if you want to go back to San Francisco, I'll see that you have your old home back. Or I'll find you a new one if you like. Whatever pleases you."

Genevieve felt numbness start at her hairline and work its way down. This wasn't what she had been expecting to hear. He was supposed to want her back, not want to send her further away.

"I see," she said, tonelessly.

"It will never replace what I took from you, but unfortunately there are limits to the restitution I can make."

"I see," she repeated, wondering why she couldn't say anything else. "Then you want me to move back to the States."

"I know you don't want to come back here."

She was silent. Her hurt was like bitter bile in the back of her throat. He didn't want her back. She blinked furiously to keep her tears from falling.

"I'll send your things along if you wish it. I know you don't want to come back to get them—"

"Well, you don't know everything now, do you?" she

snapped and slammed the receiver down. Damn him to hell! He was supposed to apologize, then promise her undying love, tell her he couldn't bear life without her, that the thought of facing another day without her by his side was just more than he could take. He wasn't supposed to call to tell her she didn't have to bother coming back to get her things. Why didn't he leave them out by the moat while he was at it?

The phone began to ring again. She let it ring a good twenty times before she yanked the receiver up.

"What?"

First there was silence, then the sound of a deep voice echoing in her ear.

"Come home."

No request, no please, just a demand.

It was the sweetest demand she had ever heard. Genevieve let out her breath slowly.

"Of course, my lord."

More silence.

"I love you."

"Oh, Kendrick," she said, fumbling for a Kleenex, "I do too."

He cleared his throat gruffly. "I don't hear you packing yet."

Genevieve hugged herself. What did she need with flowery phrases when she had a demanding, arrogant, impossible knight waiting for her at home? She laughed, feeling wonderfully cherished.

"I have a bit more shopping to do yet."

"More?" he choked. "Genevieve, I'll have to start robbing unwary travelers if you don't take pity on my funds."

"Liar," she said as she lay back on the bed, smiling up at the ceiling. "Where are you?"

"Face down on the table in the kitchen. Worthington was good enough to dial and then lay the receiver down where I could lean my ear on it."

"Why didn't you just put your voice in my mind, like you do at home?"

"You're past Seakirk's boundaries. And I don't like that, by the way. I've given the term *restless spirit* an entirely new meaning the past fortnight."

"Is Worthington ready to quit?"

"I wouldn't know. He's been spending most of his time down at the pub. What have you been doing? Besides spending my money," he added darkly.

"Looking in antique shops," she said. "I wish you could see some of the stuff. I got a few catalogues to bring home."

He was silent for a moment. "Then you had actually considered coming home? To me?"

"Kendrick, I forgave you a week ago," she said softly. "Everything you said was true. You did what you had to do. You were out to destroy that last faceless Buchanan. I shouldn't have taken it personally."

"I'm sorry, Genevieve. I wish to heaven you knew how very sorry."

"It's forgotten, Kendrick."

"If I had known you, I never would have done it."

"If you had known me, you wouldn't have had to."

His soft chuckle rumbled over the line. "Are you telling me a mere crooking of my finger would have brought you running?"

At least his arrogance was still intact. "You're pretty sure of yourself, aren't you?"

" 'Tis merely a bluff to hide my insecurities."

"Kendrick, I don't think you have any."

"Until you're back home where you belong, I daresay you're wrong. Leave the car in London and take the train home. I'll send someone down after it later."

"I still have some things to buy."

"Christmas presents?"

"Would you let me stay another day or two if I said yes?"

"That all depends on what sorts of gifts you plan to purchase for me. Only twenty-eight more shopping days, you know."

"Like you really need anything," she teased.

"What I need is you," he said, his voice suddenly husky. "Hurry home, Gen."

"Missing a Buchanan?" she whispered. "Kendrick, you're going soft in your old age."

"If it were possible, you'd be a de Piaget before you knew it." He sighed. "Perhaps 'tis fitting that I love the last Buchanan the most. My mother would have thought it romantic."

Genevieve closed her eyes as she listened to the low, soothing sound of his voice. How easy it was to imagine he was her flesh-and-blood lover, whispering promises to her in the dark.

"Gen?"

"Yes?"

"You know, I can be a very chivalrous knight when the circumstances call for it."

"Does this mean you're going to woo me, Kendrick?"

"Come home and see."

"I can hardly wait."

There was silence on the other end of the phone for so long that she wondered if he had regretted his words.

"Kendrick?"

"I'm still here," he said quietly. "Genevieve, you know what you're getting in for, don't you?"

"I'll survive."

He was silent for some time. "Gen, perhaps it would be well if you rethought this. It isn't as though I have much to offer."

"Stop it—"

"I could never give you comfort at night, a family—"

"Kendrick, I said stop!"

He paused only for a moment. "I don't even think we could find a priest daft enough to wed us."

"Kendrick, if you don't shut up right now, I'll hang up and take the phone off the hook."

He was conspicuously silent.

"Those things don't matter to me."

"You cannot mean that."

"Kendrick, somehow it will all work out. Don't give up before we've even given it a try."

"Is that a proposal, my lady?"

"Jerk. You're the one who's supposed to do that."

"Make haste on your return and see what St. Nicholas slips in your stocking."

Genevieve felt a laugh bubble up inside her. "You really are a romantic soul, aren't you?"

"I come from romantic stock. Now, do you want to continue this expensive conversation or do you have other things to see to, such as packing?"

"I'll leave day after tomorrow. And this is on your bill. Let's talk some more."

He grunted. "I'll tell you of how I passed my time and perhaps that will inspire you to finish your shopping with all due haste."

Genevieve rolled on her side with the phone under her ear and grinned as her brave knight outlined in the most glorious of detail all the hellish hours he had passed since her abrupt departure.

She pointedly ignored the reality of her situation. For now, Kendrick was as real as any other man and the caress of his voice was the most wonderful thing she had ever felt. It was as if he were kissing her mouth with gentle lips, touching her with strong, callused fingers, holding her close to a body as real and tangible as her own.

She'd face the truth later.

And hope to survive.

Chapter Sixteen

Genevieve peered into the glass case and frowned at the choices there. "Don't you have anything less conservative?" she asked the saleswoman. "I'd even settle for plaid at this point."

The saleswoman smiled. "Trying to get your father into the swing of things?"

"My butler."

"Ah, then perhaps something truly daring." She reached in and pulled out a black watch plaid bow tie. "Very adventurous."

Genevieve suppressed the urge to roll her eyes. "I'll take that one too, but haven't you got anything livelier? Like tiger stripes or polka dots? He needs a walk on the wild side."

A half hour later, Genevieve left the department store. In her shopping bag were half a dozen bow ties of various levels of wildness, from black watch plaid to a cute little paisley she was sure Worthington would hate on first sight. She could hardly wait to give it to him.

"Lady Seakirk?"

She almost didn't look up, then she realized that, for better or worse, Lady Seakirk was who she'd become. Bryan Mc-Shane was standing in front of her, looking as if he'd seen a ghost. What she wanted to do was give him a good old-fashioned tongue-lashing, but she stopped herself. What good would it do? Maybe it would be more fun to play dumb and let him hang himself. She had the feeling he'd do it soon enough.

"Why, Mr. McShane," she said, smiling brightly. "What a *pleasure* to see you again. How are you doing?"

"Very well, thank you," he said faintly. "Ah, perhaps you would allow me to buy you lunch? I'm interested in hearing how you're adjusting to English country life."

I'll bet you are, Genevieve thought with a smirk. Shame on him for sending a poor, innocent girl into a lion's den. Genevieve smiled as she listened with only half an ear to Mr. McShane's ramblings. Fortunately the lion in her den just happened to be the most wonderful man ever created. Genevieve was tempted to give Bryan a kiss right there in the street.

"Here we are," he said, indicating an exclusive-looking restaurant. "My treat."

I should hope so. He'd made enough money off Kendrick to eat breakfast, lunch and dinner in this place for the rest of his life. Maybe it was time Kendrick looked for a cheaper attorney, now that he wasn't head-hunting any more Buchanans.

Genevieve settled into her chair and smiled at the lawyer.

"How is business?" she asked.

Bryan looked as though he'd just gone bankrupt. "Ah, I need to slip away and make a phone call. If you'll excuse me?"

He rose, beating another of his hasty retreats. *Typical,* Genevieve noted, remembering how quickly he'd bolted after dropping her off at Seakirk.

Bryan returned with just as much haste, but looked decidedly better. He took his seat and gave her a smile.

"Seakirk seems to agree with you," he said, sipping at his water and watching her closely.

"I can hardly believe I almost passed it up. I'll be eternally grateful to you for tracking me down."

Bryan squirmed a bit. "It was nothing, really. I'm simply re-lieved to know that the situation has worked out so well. I had heard rumors that the keep had a quirk or two." He looked at her from under his eyelashes. "Have you noticed anything odd?"

"What castle doesn't have a few quirks?" she asked, trying not to laugh. "There's nothing at Seakirk that I can't handle. And I'm already planning a bit of restoration work on the in-side. The next time you're in the area, feel free to drop by. I'll give you the grand tour."

"That would be very kind."

And that was that. They ate their lunch making polite small talk. Genevieve knew no more about Bryan when she left the restaurant than she had when she entered. It was just as well. She'd actually thought him to be not too bad-looking when she first met him. Wimpy, but not too bad. Now he struck her as being a very nervous, very edgy little man with small dreams and an even smaller imagination.

Then again, compared to Kendrick, who wouldn't be?

Two hours (and a few stores) later, she made her way to her hotel. What she wanted was a hot shower, a hot cup of tea and a phone call from Kendrick, not necessarily in that order. Then she'd go to bed early so she could start back first thing in the morning. Kendrick's Christmas present was set to arrive by the end of the week and she wanted to be home before he saw it. She knew if she weren't there when it arrived, she would find Kendrick trying to open the thing himself. He would be transparent for a month as penalty. The computer had been horribly expensive, but she hadn't blinked when she'd plunked down the money for it. It was state-of-the-art technology, al-lowing the user to speak his commands instead of typing them in. Money had spoken loudly and she'd even been introduced to the programmer and been offered a few test games for her trouble.

She had sent all of her other purchases home too, finding that taking advantage of the services offered the idle rich was a sweet thing indeed. All she had to do was pack the few clothes she had kept out and go.

She walked into her room and closed the door behind her. Immediately the hair on the back of her neck stood up. There was someone in her room and she had the feeling it wasn't the maid. Forcing herself to keep moving, she laid her purchases on the bed and then flicked on the light.

The room was a shambles. The bedclothes were shredded, pillow feathers scattered everywhere, furniture overturned. The mirror looked as if someone had put a sledgehammer through it.

Then she saw him. He stepped from the shadows and walked across the room, crunching the rubble underfoot. He held a rope in his hands. She had the feeling she'd be dangling from the end of it very soon.

Her "Stop or I'll scream" came out as nothing but a squeak. An obviously very ineffectual squeak, as it didn't deter her attacker.

Before she could do anything besides force herself not to faint, another form appeared in the room. He was dressed all in white and wielded two deadly-looking blades.

Nazir.

Just the sight of him brought the man up short. Then the Saracen came at him, shouting and waving his swords.

The man pulled out a knife and waved it menacingly. Nazir didn't pay any attention to it, he merely continued his assault. The man stumbled backwards, tripped and hit his head on the corner of the dresser. He groaned as he fell to the floor, then slipped into unconsciousness.

"Bind him quickly, Mistress!"

Genevieve couldn't do anything but stand there and tremble.

"Mistress, now!"

"I d—don't know h—how," she stammered.

"Fetch his rope. Mistress, you must do this while he is senseless!" Nazir resheathed his swords in the scabbards on his back. "Come. I will show you what to do."

Genevieve approached. When she saw that the man was truly out, she gathered her courage in hand.

"Turn him over, Mistress. Now hold his hands together and wrap the rope around them. Yes, well-done. Now the other end around his ankles."

Genevieve finished, then looked at her handiwork. Not a bad job for a woman on the verge of hysterics.

"Call the Master," Nazir hissed in his ghostly voice.

Genevieve nodded and picked up the phone numbly, thanked every saint she could remember for having made the man so stupid that he didn't cut the cord, then called Kendrick.

Worthington answered.

"Worthington, get Kendrick," she said, her voice quavering. "Please hurry."

Kendrick was on the line immediately. "What's befallen you? Genevieve, what has happened?"

"Someone was in my room," she said, her teeth beginning to chatter. "Nazir scared him and he hit his head."

"Genevieve, I want you to hang up and ring the concierge," Kendrick said tightly. "Tell him to send the authorities. Once you've done that, ring me again and I'll wait with you."

She made her call to the front desk and had hardly connected again with Seakirk when there was a pounding on her door.

"Go answer the door, love," Kendrick said soothingly. "And tell Nazir to make himself scarce. He's liable to frighten the poor bobbies to death."

"I think he'd like that."

"I *know* he would. Go on, Gen. I'll hold for you."

Genevieve put the phone down, then paused as she saw that Nazir looked to have every intention of remaining visible. "Nazir, you can't let them see you. It's just the police."

Nazir looked at her skeptically. "I will hide behind the draperies."

"They'll still see you. Be a good ghost and do like Kendrick would want you to."

I AM A GHOST, NOT A CHILD. He vanished but his grumbles hung in her mind as she hurriedly went to the door.

The police were in her room and handcuffing the unconscious man before she had a chance to explain. A pudgy, red-nosed man took her in hand.

"There, there, miss," he said sympathetically. "I'm Inspector O'Mally, New Scotland Yard. Tell me the story from the beginning."

"I'm on the phone," she said, feeling a bit embarrassed. "It won't take a moment to finish." She retrieved the phone and put the receiver to her ear. "Kendrick?"

"Put the inspector on," Kendrick said firmly. "I'll settle this."

Genevieve handed the inspector the phone, not knowing how to introduce her housemate.

"Inspector O'Mally here." He listened for a moment, then one eyebrow went up. "She's your fiancée?" He nodded, then sat up a bit straighter. "Of course, Your Lordship. Though I will have to ask her a few questions." He listened some more. "It's a bit out of the way—no, of course not. Right away, my lord. I'll have her home in no time. Yes, I'll put her back on." He handed the phone back to Genevieve. "His Lordship wishes to speak again with you, my lady."

Genevieve took the phone. "What?"

"Inspector O'Mally will bring you home."

"All right," she whispered.

"I'm sorry I wasn't there."

"No one could have prevented it."

"Gen?"

"Yes?"

"I love you."

"I love you, too," she whispered.

"Say it again."

She smiled. "I love you."

"I'll never hear that enough. Make haste, before I wear a trench in our great hall from pacing."

"I'll do my best. I'll see you soon."

"I'll be the one standing on the front steps, wearing the besotted look."

She smiled. "Thanks for the tip."

*   *   *

Four hours later, they were on the road. Inspector O'Mally had brought two other men to help with the driving. Genevieve couldn't have been happier about it. She spent most of her time gazing out the window and thinking. How odd were the quirks of fate. Just when she finally found the perfect man, providence had to throw a monkey wrench into things and make him a ghost. Though she knew she should have been weeping, she just couldn't bring herself to do it yet. She'd shed her tears soon enough. Now was the time to imagine just how sweet it would be to see Kendrick again, to know that his smile was for her alone, to imagine all the lovely afternoons they would spend up in his den, talking and laughing softly with heads close together as lovers do.

Yes, there would be time for tears later.

Chapter
Seventeen

Genevieve sighed in relief as the drawbridge lowered itself when the car approached. Even though it was barely dawn, they were expected. She leaned back against the seat and stared out the window as the car wound its way up to the inner bailey. Just a few more minutes and she would be home.

Home. How strange it was to think of a thirteenth-century castle as home. And to think of a medieval ghost as her love. She smiled to herself. Somehow it seemed perfectly normal. Would the rest of her life be just as normal? She sincerely hoped so.

The young driver looked around frantically for the sight of human beings.

"Don't worry," Genevieve reassured him. "Flesh-and-blood staff."

"I heard the place was haunted," he said in a hushed voice, as if he expected all the ghouls from hell to appear and give chase.

"You shouldn't believe everything you hear," she said, then she lost her train of thought as the keep rose majestically in the distance. They drove through the inner gate and into the courtyard. Genevieve let out a long, weary breath, which did nothing to settle those pesky butterflies in her stomach.

Kendrick was standing outside the hall on the steps, wearing jeans and a black leather jacket. He looked like he was shivering. More than anything, Genevieve wanted to throw her arms around him and make him warm.

She crawled from the car and tried to walk sedately across the flat stones of the courtyard. That lasted about two steps. She ran the rest of the way and came to a teetering halt on the stair below Kendrick. He waited until she'd regained her balance before he bent his head and kissed her.

She didn't feel anything but the slightest bit of static go through her, but it was enough. She looked up at him and gave him her most brilliant smile. By golly, he looked good. His dark hair was just as long and just as unruly as ever, with a few stray bangs hanging in his eyes. His eyes were still that dusty, pale green. His face was just as handsome and his body just as drool-inducing. The difference was, he loved her.

"I'm glad you're home," he whispered roughly, trying to frown. "Worthington's thoughts aren't nearly so pleasing to me. Did you miss me?"

You haven't seen for yourself? Did you miss me?

Let me get you alone and I'll show you how much.

"Welcome home, my lady," Worthington said, making her a low bow.

Busybody, Kendrick grumbled.

Genevieve smiled at him before she leaned over and kissed Worthington on the cheek. "Thanks, Worthington. Is there anything to eat? I haven't had a decent meal in two weeks."

Worthington was still trying to pretend he wasn't blushing from her display of affection.

"I'll put tea on right away, my lady. With your favorite little pastries. I took the liberty of preparing some early this morning."

Kendrick laughed as Worthington fled inside the house, leaving the door wide open. "Gen, I don't think he realizes it's

too early in the morning for tea. I've never seen him so flustered."

"You must have driven him completely crazy these past
couple of weeks." She looked over her shoulder to find her
three escorts standing uncomfortably at the bottom of the
steps. She looked back instantly at Kendrick with wide eyes.
Well, at least he looked solid enough. As long as the Inspector
didn't try to shake his hand—

I'll take care of it.

Talking like this is hardly fair to them, she chided.

*It will be vastly amusing. They'll leave thinking we've gone
daft when we sit and giggle at each other all morning while
saying nothing.*

She smiled. *You're enjoying this, aren't you?*

*I'm glad to see you. The sweetness of your voice in my mind
is merely an added pleasure.*

Kendrick clasped his hands behind his back. "Inspector
O'Mally, gentlemen, please come in." *Gen, will you close the
door? It's an ungentlemanly thing to ask—*

Don't be silly. She passed into the house first, then waited
until all the men had filed by her before she closed the door.
Fortunately Worthington was at the table and he pulled out
Kendrick's chair for him. He waited until Genevieve had approached, then did the same for her. Once she was seated, he
leaned down and whispered in her ear.

"My lady, 'tis a bit early for tea. Shall I prepare breakfast
instead?"

"Please," she nodded. "I'm starved."

Inspector O'Mally cleared his throat and launched into his
questions. Genevieve gave up trying to concentrate on what he
was saying and simply stared at Kendrick. He leaned back to
one side of the chair with his hands folded casually in his lap,
looking for all the world like a man who had everything.
Every now and again, he would bring his hand up and brush
his hair back from his face. She wanted to do it for him. Goodness, how could Matilda not have loved him instantly and
never wavered?

She was a fool, Kendrick said with a wink thrown her way.

The little wench was just lucky she let you go. You would have had one heck of a catfight on your hands had she stuck around long enough for me to fight her for you.

Kendrick choked and then recovered himself in time to answer the Inspector.

"I have no enemies that I know of," Kendrick said. *At least none that are still alive.*

Enemies? Since when had this become so serious? Genevieve looked at the Inspector. "I'm sure it was just a random thing. Doesn't this happen often?"

"No crime should go uninvestigated. Now, our first step will be to look for clues," the Inspector stated. "Sometimes it's what's most obvious that we overlook."

After fielding a few more questions about his travel habits, Kendrick put his hands on the table, signaling that the interview was over. Worthington was instantly behind him to pull out the chair.

"I appreciate your assistance, Inspector," Kendrick said in his most lordly tone. "I would offer you lodgings, but we're presently restoring the other chambers. Worthington will take you down to the inn and see you settled. I'll have train tickets waiting for you tomorrow morning."

"Very gracious of you, my lord," the Inspector said, rising also.

Later Genevieve would swear that a member of the undead had tripped her, but at the time she had no one to blame but herself for her clumsiness. She moved to stand next to Kendrick, then suddenly found herself falling through his arms. She jumped up in horror to the accompaniment of a shriek coming from the younger of the investigator's assistants. The poor boy fled from the great hall as if an entire host of werewolves had sprung up and picked him out as an entrée.

The Inspector remained admirably calm. "Jones, go after him and tell him he was seeing things."

"Yes, sir!"

Once the second young man had fled, Inspector O'Mally sat back down. His face was ashen and he was shaking.

Genevieve had to admire his merely remaining in his seat and not bolting like his men.

Kendrick looked down at Genevieve. "Take your seat, love."

Genevieve sat back down in her chair and looked at him miserably. *I'm so sorry! This is all my fault.*

The man seems to be fairly discreet. It will be for the best. You can never have too many mortal allies.

Kendrick sat back down and looked the investigator straight in the eye. "As you have seen, our situation is rather unique."

"Are you the earl of Seakirk?" Inspector O'Mally asked bluntly. "I've never been one to keep up with the antics of the nobility, but Seakirk has acquired a rather peculiar reputation. I was under the impression that it belonged to the Buchanans."

"I purchased Matilda of Seakirk's debts in the year 1260," Kendrick said, just as bluntly. "If Henry III's records were correct, they would show as much. But what they will not show is that I was murdered by Matilda's lover in this very keep that same year. Seakirk is mine."

Inspector O'Mally swallowed convulsively. "What does your betrothed think of that?"

"Kendrick is the rightful earl," Genevieve said quietly.

"And you are truly betrothed to him?"

"That, my good man," Kendrick said firmly, "is none of your affair. I have a birth certificate placing me on the earth sometime before 1962. Now unless you can find me a man of the cloth who won't try to exorcise me the moment he claps eyes on me and have him wed me with my lady, you need only concern yourself with this investigation and not my private affairs."

Inspector O'Mally sat back and folded his hands over his belly. His trembles began to subside. He looked down at the table thoughtfully for several moments, then met Kendrick's eyes.

"This changes the situation greatly. How many people know of your existence?"

"Definitively? Very few. As I am unable to leave the keep, I have scant contact with the outside world. Rumor is a bit more widespread, I fear, though I doubt many believe the tales."

"And your fiancée?"

"Genevieve knows very few people in England. Though she was a well-known restoration expert in the States, I hardly think anyone would come here to harm her."

"Well, that gives me more to work with at least," Inspector O'Mally said with a nod. "I'll need complete lists of all your acquaintances. I'll run checks on all of them and see if anything looks odd. I trust I can reach you here?"

"Day or night," Kendrick sighed. "We'll work on our lists and have them sent 'round first thing." He rose and walked through the chair without giving it another thought.

Genevieve suppressed her smile at the Inspector's renewed loss of color, then took pity on him and tried to draw him out into small talk as they made their way to the door. Worthington was there with keys in hand. Kendrick waited until the car had pulled away before he shut the door.

"I could have done that," Genevieve said quickly.

"It gives me an excuse for being tired enough to go take a nap. Shall we go up?"

Genevieve nodded and walked with him to the stairs. By the time they reached his bedroom, Genevieve could barely put one foot in front of the other. It was all good and fine to pretend she was coming home to her lover. The reality of their situation was like a sharp slap in the face. He was dead. There was no getting around that.

The door opened as they approached.

"Kendrick, stop," she said softly. "I can do it."

He ignored her and merely waited for her to pass into the room. She shut the door before he could get to it. He smiled ruefully.

"Is this how the rest of our lives will be?" he teased. "You fighting me for control?"

She felt tears burning at the back of her eyes. "Kendrick," she began helplessly.

"Genevieve, things will be fine," he said soothingly.

"But it's so hopeless."

"Gen, perhaps some day some angel will take pity on us. Until then, we'll just have to make do. Now," he said, with forced brightness, "let's lie down and you will describe in great detail all the things you brought home for me from London. I've always been terribly fond of presents."

She couldn't even manage a decent smile. Kendrick ducked his head to catch her gaze.

"Come on, then, love."

Genevieve nodded as she kicked off her shoes. She turned back to find Kendrick lying on the bed with his ankles crossed, his hands behind his head. His shoes were gone and his bare feet looked hauntingly real. He turned toward her as she approached and she saw the muscles flex beneath his jeans as he moved.

"You're lusting after me again, love," he said with a half-smile. "Come pull up the blanket before you chill."

She lay down, then pulled the blanket up over both of them. She stared in surprise at the sight of Kendrick's form, which was actually discernible beneath the covering.

"I'm a ghost, not a pure spirit," he explained. "My body is the same as yours, 'tis simply made of more refined matter."

"Then how is it you are always walking through things?" she asked.

"It used to be sort of an effort. Now it just tickles." He grinned at her. "I rather like the feeling."

She couldn't help but return his smile. "You gave poor Inspector O'Mally a start when you walked through the chair."

"I know."

She closed her eyes, wishing with all her heart that just once, if for only a split second, she could feel the touch of his hand on her face. She opened her eyes and looked at him miserably. She knew he was reading her thoughts.

"Stop," he begged.

"I can't help it."

"We can't spend the rest of our lives wishing for what cannot be," he said hoarsely. "I can't touch you, Genevieve, and I'll never be able to. I'll never be able to hold you, kiss you, or make love to you. If we both don't accept that right now, we'll never survive. All we have is love. Is that going to be enough for you?"

"I don't think we have another choice."

"You're absolutely right."

"Is it possible to love someone so quickly?"

He smiled and his eyes were moist. "It is when you've been waiting seven hundred years to find her."

She couldn't help the miserable half-laugh that escaped her. "You are the most wonderful man."

"And?" he prompted, his eyes beginning to twinkle.

"I love you," she whispered. "Foolish or not, I love you."

" 'Tis fate, Genevieve, not foolishness. If I had known what all those centuries of agony were going to bring me, I would have passed through them cheerfully, not killing off Buchanans by the scores."

"You're very sweet."

"And you're very beautiful."

"And?" she smiled.

"I love you," he said. He frowned, pretending to look gruff. "Now, go to sleep. I'm not one for sentimentalities, and you've had more than your share from me today."

She closed her eyes, a smile still firmly fixed on her face. There was more to life than touching. She'd just learn to get used to it.

She woke to the sound of snoring. She was coherent instantly, too surprised to even have to give herself a list of reasons to wake. Kendrick was lying on his back, snoring!

"Kendrick," she hissed. "Wake up."

He mumbled something intelligible, smacked his lips a time or two and continued to sleep. Genevieve no longer wondered where the phrase *sawing logs* came from. Kendrick was about to bring down the entire forest.

That isn't nice, you know.

She laughed as he opened his eyes and winked at her. "I take it His Lordship grew weary of watching me sleep?"

He turned on his side and smiled at her. "I could watch you sleep for hours, my love. I just had the feeling that somewhere in the world there had been some football on and that my VCR had caught it. I thought you might wish to watch with me. As shaking you awake was a bit beyond me, I tried the next best thing."

"Well, at least you aren't bellowing songs in my ear any longer."

"That is a joy I reserve for your mornings only. A nap merits nothing more than a snore."

"I get the hint already. And I suppose we should start working on those lists while we're at it."

"Mine will be enormously short," Kendrick said as he rolled from the bed. "I'll go on up while you take care of your needs."

Genevieve rolled from the bed, cheeks flaming. "Will you give me some privacy, for heaven's sake?"

"I was just making polite conversation."

She threw her pillow at him. It went through him and bounced harmlessly off the wall. Kendrick smiled in amusement.

"A bit grumpy, aren't we, love?"

She pointed to the door and waited. He made her a low bow and walked through the wood. Genevieve put her hands to her cheeks and took a couple of deep breaths, trying to cool her embarrassment. Well, there were some things she'd have to get used to, and one of those was Kendrick's ability to read her mind. If he weren't so painfully blunt it might not be so bad. Perhaps in the future he would refrain from pointing out to her when she needed to use the bathroom. Heaven help her when her period caught up with her again.

I couldn't agree more.

"You stop that!" she snapped, trying to muster up anger and only coming up with mortification. She laughed miserably. "Kendrick, I'm serious. At least leave me a bit of privacy. This is worse than being married!"

Ouch.

"This mind-reading business is like you looking through my underwear drawer," she muttered under her breath as she walked toward the bathroom.

Much more exciting, surely.

Kendrick!

She could have sworn she heard him chuckling. She went into the bathroom, then paused. Damn, this was unnerving! She turned the water on and used the toilet as quietly as possible. This was going to take some getting used to.

A few minutes later, she ran down the corridor and up the steps to the third floor. She lifted her hand to knock on Kendrick's study door.

Just come in, Gen. No need to knock.

She opened the door and slipped inside the room. A fire was roaring in the fireplace and a blanket was already draped over one arm of the couch. Kendrick was sprawled there with his feet up on a stool in front of him. He tilted his head back to smile at her.

"Cowboys and Dolphins. Mildly entertaining."

"Sounds boring to me. Give me my 49ers or give me death," she said. "Have you got something to write with in your lair, or dare I look?"

"I've nothing to hide, Genevieve."

She walked over and leaned on the back of the couch next to him. "No more nefarious plots I should know about? Nothing more to confess?"

"Other than an insane desire to wed you and bed you?" he asked with a smile. "Nay. All my secrets have been revealed."

"Wed me and bed me?" she asked, blushing. "Whatever happened to romance?"

"You've only been home a single day. Allow me time to conjure up a few ideas. There's a notebook and a pen on my desk. Fetch it and we'll work on the list during commercial breaks and halftime."

"Demoted to serving wench already," she grumbled as she made her way across the room and through the doorway that led to Kendrick's museum. She opened the door to his private study and jumped as the lights went on by themselves. *Thanks.*

My pleasure.

She looked down at his desk and blinked. Then she did a double take. There was a notebook all right, and a pen sitting on top of it. Along with a pair of diamond earrings. No box, no fancy wrapping paper. Just sitting there as if she had merely taken them off and forgotten to put them away.

"Kendrick!"

"It's first and goal, love. Can't this wait?"

She laughed. "No, this cannot wait. Get in here."

He took his sweet time about ambling into the room, then he leaned back against the doorframe and gave her a lazy smile.

"Her ladyship rang?"

"What," she said, pointing pointedly at the earrings, "are these?"

"I was afraid what you brought with you would soon turn your ears green. Just trying to save you from yourself."

She reached down and picked one up, smiling involuntarily at the sweetness of the gift. Her jewelry was a bit on the ratty side, but she'd never had the money or the inclination to change that. Earrings were an intimate gift. That Kendrick had been the one to give them to her pleased her very much.

"Put them on," he suggested, "and let me see if I like the size." She did and he came close to peer at her ears. "Why, I can hardly see them! I suppose I'll have to buy you a larger pair tomorrow."

"Any bigger and I'm sure they would blind you."

"As well as dragging your earlobes down to your shoulders," he agreed with a grin. "Perhaps we'll save gaudy for the tiara and matching necklaces."

"Don't you dare," she warned. "I'll never have anywhere to wear them and it's a waste of money."

"I have more money than either of us could ever spend."

"You haven't seen what I bought you for Christmas."

"If the Jag didn't put me under, I doubt your Christmas presents will."

Genevieve touched the diamond studs in her ears. "These are beautiful. Thank you."

He reached out to touch her, then stopped himself. He forced a smile to his lips as he dropped his hand to his side. "You are the beautiful one, and I'm happy the earrings please you. Now can we go back and watch the game? All this woo-ing is exhausting me."

"Oh, go on," she said, shooing him away with a good-natured smile. "Wouldn't want to wear you out your first day." She snatched up the pen and paper and followed him back into the den.

Kendrick was already engrossed in the game by the time she had the lid off the pen, so she started with her list first. The number of people she knew was staggering. Where to start? Fortunately she was an expert list maker and it took her little time to write down all her previous clients. Four pages later, she turned to personal acquaintances. That didn't take up much space.

The people she had come in contact with in England were few. She started from the moment she had set foot on English soil and finished with Inspector O'Mally.

The sound of the television went off and Genevieve looked up at Kendrick with a smile.

"Halftime?"

"Aye. How goes your list?"

"Finished. I'll start yours. Who's first?"

"Alive or dead?"

She tried to smile. "Dead?"

"There are more ghosts rattling around on the island than you'd care to know about. We'll dismiss them, however. The good Inspector's constitution would not take kindly to para-normal investigation. Let's start here. There's Worthington—"

"Kendrick!"

"The man wants names—I'll give him names. We'll skip the villagers. They only believe the rumors anyhow. Now, let's see about London."

"London?" she echoed.

"There's Bryan McShane, who you find so charming."

"I do not. He's a wimp."

"But he's manageable."

"And expensive."

"He's intimidated. That's the way I like him. Then there's

my banker, young master Beagley. A very honest, forthright lad. Completely trustworthy."

"And intimidated?"

"He thinks I'm a rich recluse pretending to be nobility," Kendrick said with a wink. "I daresay my circumstances wouldn't matter to him if he knew of them."

Genevieve tapped the pen against the pad. "I still think it was a fluke."

"Perhaps."

"You don't agree?"

He looked at her seriously. "Out of all the rooms the man could have chosen, he chose yours? I don't like those odds."

"But who would want to hurt me?" she asked, aghast. "I don't know anyone here!"

"I'm wrong," he said quickly, soothingly, "It was probably a mistake. Let's put the list away and we won't think about it any more. Look, halftime's over," he said, flicking the sound back on. "The Dolphins are being soundly trounced."

"You're changing the subject."

"I know."

She chewed on the end of the pen for a few moments, then turned sideways on the loveseat to face him. What if there were more to it than simple coincidence? What could anyone possibly want with her? It wasn't as though she had any money or any possessions to speak of. Had some nefarious villain sunk so low that he was willing to strip the Cole Haans off her feet? Her shoes were probably the most expensive of her belongings at the moment, other than the purchases she'd made in London.

The castle.

And the estate that went with it.

It was all in her name, wasn't it? Though the Buchanan fortune could never come close to rivaling Kendrick's, there was still a substantial amount of money in her name at the bank. What if someone knew that and planned to kidnap her, then hold her for ransom?

"Kendrick, where are the papers for me to sign?" The best

way to assure her safety was to make sure she was worth nothing. That would give the thugs no reason to come after her.

"What?" he asked, his attention riveted to the screen.

"The papers for me to turn the castle over to you."

He froze. Then the television went blank. He turned his head and looked at her.

"I don't want you to sign them."

"I think I should."

"I forbid it," he said, an edge to his voice.

"Why? What does it matter? You aren't going to kick me out, are you?"

"You don't understand," he said, turning to face her. "I would be free. Owning the castle in truth would allow me to finally pass on, Genevieve."

"Oh," she said soundlessly.

"I don't want you to leave you."

"I don't want you to go," she whispered.

"No more talk of that. I never should have said anything about the papers in the first place. I want you to forget I did."

"All right," she nodded.

"And give no more thought to the other problem. Inspector O'Mally will sort out the mystery for us."

"You don't think that possibly these guys are after the castle and they think they can get to it through me?"

Kendrick's expression softened. "Nay, love. I don't think so. I've had McShane working for months on those documents that we aren't going to discuss again. I hardly think a simple criminal could conceive of such a plan, much less act on it. Now, let's allow the good Inspector to puzzle over the problem. He seems very capable."

She nodded and leaned her head against the back of the couch. Kendrick was right. There just wasn't much more they could do.

The phone rang. Bryan fumbled for it as he turned and tried to make sense out of the numbers on his alarm clock. Three A.M.? Who in the world would be calling at three A.M.?

"Hello?"

"McShane," a rough voice growled, "I'm in the cooler. Get your ass over here and get me out!"

Bryan groaned mentally and dropped his head back onto the pillow. "How in the world—"

"Some monster with a pair of bloody swords came at me from out of nowhere! You never said I'd be dealing with swords! Just the girl. I just had to get her and get out. Now look what you got me into! Get me out o' here!"

"Calm down, Mr. Starkey. I will come immediately with bail. But your job is not finished, nor will it be until you have Miss Buchanan in hand."

"Bloody hell, you say!" the man bellowed. "I ain't going close to the bitch again!"

"Then, regrettably, I won't be able to post bond. Good night, Mr. Starkey."

Bryan hung up the phone. The lion had come out and been victorious. He hadn't liked Starkey's airs from the first. No, he'd have to hire another man, perhaps two, with a bit more spine.

He sighed as he rolled from the bed and headed toward the loo. *Just don't think about Maledica, lion. He doesn't have to know about this blunder.*

Though Bryan had the feeling he'd know anyway.

Chapter Eighteen

Genevieve put the finishing touches on the last of her Christmas packages. Though it was only the second week of December, she wanted to be ready. It was the first time in her life she'd had the time and the peace of mind to get ready for Christmas early. Next on her list was to introduce Kendrick and Worthington to chocolate chip cookie dough. Not cookies, but the dough. Once dough reached cookie stage, she always lost interest. Kendrick might not be able to taste the food of the gods, but she could describe it well enough for him. And then she'd have to make sugar cookies and fudge and whatever else Betty Crocker could help her come up with. Worthington was already shuddering in anticipation, though no doubt it was anticipation of the mess she would make.

She placed the last package in her trunk, then shut and locked it. After putting the key in her pocket where Kendrick couldn't get it, she left the bedchamber and descended to the great hall. Worthington was reading the paper in front of the fire.

"Where's Kendrick?"

"Outside, my lady. Run upstairs and fetch your cloak if you intend to join him."

"Yes, Mother," she sighed as she ran back up the stairs, pulled her worn pea coat from the closet and ran back down to the hall. Worthington didn't spare her a glance as she walked by.

"I'd suggest gloves, my lady."

She ignored him and continued on her way. She walked to the front door, opened it and gasped. The courtyard was back to thirteenth-century style. She walked down the steps in a daze, then realized she'd walked through someone only because the ghost laughed. She whirled around, her hand to her throat.

The man took off his helmet and pushed the mail coif back from his fair hair. His blue eyes twinkled as he smiled and made her a low bow.

"Royce of Canfield, lately of Artane, at your service, my lady."

"Oh, hello," she said, flustered. "I'm Genevieve."

"I know, my lady. A pleasure it is to gaze upon your loveliness at close range. I espied you at the airport but hesitated to make myself known to you. Indeed, my lord Kendrick's tales of your beauty do you a disservice. Your loveliness exceeds anything words could describe."

Genevieve stared at him, openmouthed. "Wow," she breathed. This guy sure knew how to pay a compliment.

"Nay, my lady, that is what I would ever say when gazing upon your comeliness—"

"Royce, you horse's arse, be you gone from my lady's side. Your stench will make her swoon."

Genevieve didn't connect the sound of horse's hooves with Kendrick until she saw him sitting astride his mount not three paces from her. Genevieve looked up at him and her mouth fell open again. A ghost horse? Well, she'd seen stranger things.

"Holy moly," she said weakly.

Kendrick winked at his captain. "That's much more complimentary than a mere 'wow.' Don't forget whom she loves, lackwit."

"Kendrick, you buffoon, why would she choose you when you look as if you've recently bathed in the moat and smell just that bad?"

"I sense a slur in among those witless words."

"I daresay you do."

"Then I must demand satisfaction."

"I would be pleased to give it to you."

Kendrick smiled down at Genevieve. "Perhaps you would care to watch me dispatch this cretin in the joust?"

Genevieve couldn't do much besides gape. Had she ever back-talked this man? He looked strong and powerful in jeans and a sweatshirt; he looked menacing and fearsome in mail with his sword at his side and a lance in his hand. How had anyone ever stood against him in battle? Anyone who had seen him bearing down on them at twenty miles an hour would have been a fool not to run for cover.

"Sit on the far side of the garden, love, under the tree. I've had Worthington leave a blanket or two there for your comfort. You'll be perfectly safe. Unlike Royce."

Genevieve hesitated. "He can't hurt you, can he?"

"He won't get close enough to me to accomplish that. And nay, he cannot hurt me, even if by some miracle his lance points anywhere but up at the sky as he lies on his back in a disgraceful cloud of dust."

Royce snorted. "Do you wish to pay me now or later for not humiliating you in front of your lady?"

"Captain," Kendrick warned, "'tis a dangerous path you walk."

"Is that fear I hear in your voice, Seakirk?"

Genevieve walked away before she laughed. There wasn't enough room in the entire expanse of the inner bailey for the two egos involved. She made her way across the dirt field, trying to remind herself that it really was the garden, then bundled up in the two blankets left for her on the bench. She sat back to watch something she had only read about in books.

There was a long wooden rail running down the field, from

the back of the lists to the front. Kendrick rode down to the
end of her right and turned his horse, his lance in his hand.
Royce started at the end to her left. He flipped his helmet
down with his lance, and his horse reared. Kendrick did the
same, then their horses sprang forward. Genevieve felt the
ground rumble beneath her feet and heard the pounding of
hooves as Kendrick and his captain hurtled down opposite
sides of the rail toward each other. They met with a tremendous clash. Royce teetered in his saddle but kept his seat.

Kendrick turned his horse, then went galloping down the
railing again. This time Royce's lance splintered, his shield
went flying out of his hand and he hung on to his seat by his
fingernails. Kendrick wasn't moved. Genevieve had suspected
he was good, but this was tangible proof. It was no wonder
he'd made so much money jousting. She could just imagine
him winning against knight after knight, then herding them all
into a big group and holding them for ransom. How arrogant
he must have sounded as he demanded payment for their release.

The third pass left Royce sprawled in the dirt. Kendrick
didn't even bother to help him up, probably because there was
suddenly a very long line of other challengers. Royce heaved
himself to his feet and trudged across the field to make her a
low bow, then collapse on the bench next to her.

"He's an arrogant whoreson, isn't he?"

"There's a law against self-incrimination, you know," she
said with a smile.

Royce grinned. "Ah, true love speaks. 'Tis surely the only
reason you tolerate his foul temper. I daresay I wouldn't be
equal to the task."

She recognized a lie when she heard one. "Have you known
him long?"

"We squired together, then went to war together. And we've
shared this semblance of life for the past few centuries. Aye,
I've known him long. But how I've borne him for so long is
still a mystery to me."

"You love him very much, don't you?"

Royce coughed. "Love him? Nay, my lady. Tolerate him I do, and nothing more."

"Knights aren't supposed to lie."

"Ah, then I must tell the truth, though I pray you, do not tell him, else he will tease me for it." Royce waited for her nod before he continued. "I had only sisters in my home and when I found Kendrick, it was as if the Good Lord had held him in reserve simply to be my brother. His family was very wealthy and very important in my day, but Kendrick never made me feel as if I came from a sire any less important than his. Even when we squired together, he treated me as an equal, unlike the other lads. When we earned our spurs, I offered myself for his captain, and I've never regretted it. Brothers we were, and the best of friends. My deepest regret over the last seven hundred years is that I could not spend more time with him. Matilda did not even leave us that comfort."

"And you don't mind me elbowing my way into this?" she asked.

"Of course not," Royce said with a grin. "You've improved my lord's temper enormously. My only request is that you keep your eyes open for a maid for me, but make her as beautiful as you are and with as much spirit. I'm powerfully jealous of Kendrick's good fortune."

Genevieve squirmed and looked back at the field. Compliments from Kendrick still made her blush; compliments from a virtual stranger were even harder to take. She watched Kendrick ride to the far end of the jousting rail.

"He's a very good knight, isn't he?"

"There was none to equal him in his day, though his brother Phillip would damn me for saying so, as he thought himself to be the superior warrior." Royce shook his head. "Kendrick possessed an arrogance Phillip could not match even on the best of days."

"I think he's still got it."

"The arrogance?" Royce asked with a smile. "Aye, 'tis true. He's not lost any of his skill either. Watch you how he moves against these who have come to challenge him. And fine warriors they are."

Genevieve watched as Kendrick unseated seven challengers in a row. "Did he make these guys up?"

"I beg pardon?"

"Conjure them up. Like his brother and his cousin."

Royce smiled in amusement. "Nay, my lady, they are just as real as I or my lord. It takes them only moments to gather once they catch wind that Kendrick is training. Before you came to Seakirk they were known to mill about the lists, hoping to entice him into sallying forth and giving them a skirmish or two. Kendrick has forbid them within the gates since you arrived, but I daresay they still wait without each day, hoping for a chance to unseat him."

Genevieve swallowed uncomfortably. "Are they always here?"

"Where else would they go?"

"To haunt some other castle?" she offered.

"When the finest warrior in England resides at Seakirk? Nay, Lady Genevieve, there is no reward for going elsewhere."

Genevieve nodded and watched Kendrick make mincemeat out of another handful of knights dressed in various colors. Kendrick was impressive, though a time or two he swayed in his saddle just as the others did, but not nearly as noticeably.

"Do they ever beat him?"

"Rarely. But when they do, pray you have something to stuff in your ears that night, for the rejoicing will go on 'til dawn." Royce grinned. "I don't have to say what a foul mood that puts my lord in."

"No, you don't," she said dryly. "I can just imagine."

The line at the challenging end was thinning rapidly, and finally it came down to a man who had to be as big as Kendrick, if not bigger. Genevieve chewed on her nails as Kendrick rode against him, finding herself praying that Kendrick would win. The second pass almost unseated her love and Genevieve rose nervously.

Kendrick didn't look at her as he thundered back down the way for the third pass. This time the black knight went tumbling back off his horse in a flurry of cloth and curses. Once he had been assisted up by his fellows, the entire group cursed Kendrick, then made their way grumbling from the lists. Genevieve sat down, relieved. Kendrick rode over to her, leaped from his horse and dropped to one knee before her. He bowed his head.

"My lady."

Genevieve looked down at him, listening to him pant heavily. The sweat positively dripped from him. His clothes were soaked and his hair was plastered to his head.

"Ah," Genevieve began, searching quickly for something appropriate to say, "well-done, brave knight."

"I am your servant."

"Great. Thanks a lot."

Kendrick lifted his head and looked at Royce. "She's not much on lavishing praise, is she?"

"A mere syllable to fall from her lips would be a jewel. And besides, your head is swelled enough."

Kendrick lunged, and Royce laughed and jumped away. Royce made Genevieve a low bow. "I must depart, fair maiden. Should you need me, I am at your service. And remember to start that list of wenches for me, if you please." He bowed to Kendrick, then put his hand over his heart. "My lord, I bid you a very fond *adieu*. Your skill, as always, leaves me breathless."

"Oh, leave, would you?" Kendrick grumbled as he rose to his feet.

Royce's laughter trailed after him as he walked away. Kendrick looked down at Genevieve. "Did he behave himself?"

"He told me how sweet you were when you were young."

"He must be delirious."

"I'm sure you were adorable and Lady Anne could never bring herself to scold you. Even when you took apart the blacksmith's forge."

"She tried very hard not to laugh when my father bellowed at me."

Genevieve rose and smiled up at him. "I wish I had known you then."

"If you had, we would now be going inside and spending the afternoon in bed, for I would have wed you the moment your father let you from his house. In fact, an afternoon in bed sounds like a fine idea to me. I'll clean up and meet you there. After all, I should have some reward for my fine performance this afternoon," he said, nodding as if he expected her to agree with him.

"More praise wouldn't cut it?"

"Nay. It must be an entire afternoon of lying next to you and gazing at your beauty. And then perhaps I'll stay the night. But just to sleep. As if I could do anything else," he muttered.

"Give me a half hour, then I'll praise you to your heart's content. After all, you were wonderful this afternoon. I was very impressed."

He winked at her. "More praise along those lines would be well received later."

"Make it an hour then. I'll need to make a list."

Kendrick entered his bedchamber much later, cleaned up from his late afternoon's exercise, only to find his lady sound asleep. He walked around to her side of the bed, gritted his teeth and strained to pull the covers up over her. She woke just as he was using the remainder of his strength to tuck them up under her chin.

"Thanks," she murmured sleepily.

"My pleasure, beloved."

She opened her eyes and smiled. "I love you."

He leaned over her and made the motion of brushing his lips over hers. "I love you, too, Gen. Go back to sleep."

"You'll stay?"

"The French army couldn't drag me away."

She smiled, then slipped back into slumber. Kendrick kicked off his shoes and vaulted lightly over her to stretch out on the bed. He turned on his side and propped his head up on his palm to better look at his lady.

Her dark hair was spread out over the pillow, looking even darker against the white of the sheet and the fairness of her skin. He let his gaze roam over her face and marveled that she thought herself not beautiful. Aye, the men she'd known had been fools indeed. Not that he was anything less than happy about that. He was pleased, ridiculously so, that she was a virgin, that no man had touched her, that had he been able to wed her, she would have belonged to him and him alone.

One of her hands rested on the comforter, her slender fingers relaxed and uncurled. If he could, he would have put his hands over hers and enjoyed the feel of her slight fingers intertwined with his. The gentleness he would have used as he would have drawn both her hands into his, then placed them about his waist! Aye, Genevieve would have needed gentleness in her wooing, so that he did not intimidate her. What he would have given to have had but an hour to spend with her in mortality!

Would he merely kiss her, caress her mouth with his, tease her tongue into joining his in a mating dance? Or would his self-control shatter and leave him carrying her to his bed, to love her fully, possess her completely?

Or would it be enough to touch her hand? To trail his callused fingers across her palm, then over the softness of her wrist? For once, to know that her skin was truly as smooth as it looked? He closed his eyes briefly and prayed for a miracle. Just once. Just a simple touch.

He stretched out his hand. He left it over hers for several moments, imagining how it would feel to lower his palm and have it cover her hand, not go through it. He could imagine feeling the ridge of her knuckles, the warmth of her skin, the sinews and tendons between her fingers. Now if only he could feel it in truth.

He lowered his hand.

And for a single, boundary-shattering moment, he thought he felt resistance.

Then his hand went through hers and disappeared inside the blanket. He pulled it free as if he'd been burned. He rolled away and cursed silently as an uncomfortable stinging began behind his eyes. *Fool. Dolt. As if you thought things would magically become different!*

"Kendrick?"

He cleared his throat roughly. "What?"

"Are you cold?" she murmured. "You look like you're shivering."

"Why in the world would I be cold when I haven't a body with which to feel a chill?" he barked.

Silence.

Kendrick groaned and turned to face her.

"I'm sorry, love," he whispered hoarsely. "I didn't mean to shout."

She shook her head, then leaned back and blew out the candle on the nightstand. By the faint light of the fire he saw her weary smile as she faced him again.

"We've both had a long day and we're tired."

"Aye," he agreed.

"Things will look better in the morning."

"Aye."

But he sincerely doubted it.

Chapter
Nineteen

Kendrick stood in the shadows of the great hall and watched the party in progress. It had been Genevieve's idea, this reviving of the old customary Christmas celebrations. Kendrick had found himself going along with it, simply because it reminded him of home, and this year was the first year in centuries he had felt homesick.

Villagers had been coming to the keep in the evenings for almost two weeks, partaking of the lord's winter stores as they would have in the old days. Genevieve left the lord's chair empty each night and sat down in the chair next to it, as would have been her place had things been a bit different. Most of the villagers thought her daft. A few, like Mistress Adelaide, thought her actions to be hopelessly romantic. Kendrick had eavesdropped on the good woman when she babbled for a solid evening about the tenderness of the gesture. Little did the villagers know that Kendrick had been sitting in that chair off and on for almost a fortnight, keeping himself invisible.

Genevieve had known the moment he first sat down. He'd spent the rest of the evenings since, whispering into her ear.

She'd blushed at his less-than-gentlemanly suggestions and smiled at his words of love. It had satisfied him.

At first.

Now, things were different. This was Christmas Eve. He should have been in that chair next to her. Instead, he stood in the shadows, like a misbegotten stableboy too ashamed to show himself. He ground his teeth in frustration. Never had he been so dissatisfied with his unlife.

No longer. He could bear it no longer. He'd stewed and fumed and raged for three weeks since the night he had tried to touch his love. He was past reason, past restraint. He would take his rightful place at the table and when the guests were gone, he would take his lady upstairs and give her the gift he had purchased her and ask her the appropriate question. The time for action had come.

Without giving it another thought, he strode from the shadows, stepped up on the dais and walked around the table. Worthington hastily pulled out the chair and Kendrick sat down.

The silence in the hall was deafening.

He felt the eyes of every soul there on him. That made him want to squirm, but he'd come too far to turn back now. He set his jaw and looked at his lady, daring her to say anything against his behavior.

Genevieve merely smiled.

"Good evening, my lord Seakirk."

He nodded imperiously.

Her smile deepened. "Your guests have arrived, my love."

"Aye, I can see that," he nodded again, feeling suddenly unwilling to look anywhere but in her eyes. By the saints, had he gone daft?

"Perhaps you should say a few words. In welcome."

The chair was far enough away from the table that Kendrick could stand without standing through it. He rose to his feet and let his gaze sweep over the crowd.

Half the group fled. Kendrick might have laughed at the scurrying for the door, but it actually hurt his feelings quite a bit. As if he had planned to capture them all and slow-roast them in the hearth!

He opened his mouth to call them back, then shut it. His pride was stung, but it was still there. If they wanted to leave, damn them, then they could. Whoever had the courage to remain would hear his flowery speech and partake of his finest food and drink. The rest of them could go to hell.

The hall door banged shut. Then there was silence. Kendrick looked at the score or two of souls who remained, staring at him with their jaws slack and their eyes wide. They were older folk from the village, along with a few young men and women. Kendrick watched as the remaining villagers got hold of themselves. He was faintly impressed but knew he probably shouldn't have been. The older ones were past being surprised by anything that happened within Seakirk's gates and the young ones were impressionable enough to find it intriguing. Hopefully. At least none of the remaining folk had fainted, though Mistress Adelaide was gazing at him with something akin to worship.

And then, all of the sudden, words deserted him.

This should have been something that came naturally to him. After all, he'd heard his father and grandfather make speeches of this kind numerous times. He'd rehearsed his own speech when the king had awarded him Seakirk, knowing that soon Seakirk would be his and it would be his duty to welcome guests to his hall.

And now, this was truly *his* hall. His lady sat at his side, watching him with love in her eyes. Folk who would have been his peasants, his responsibility in another time, were gathered below the high table, watching him, waiting for some gem of wisdom to fall from his lips.

He cleared his throat.

"I bid you welcome, friends," he began, wanting to wipe his hands on his thighs. Instead, he clasped them behind his back. "With the crowd having thinned so rapidly, there should be an abundance of food and drink for your pleasure." A few of the younger ones grinned at that. The old ones regarded him with the smiles the old reserve for use while indulging young, arrogant men making speeches. Kendrick felt himself begin to relax. There was a bit of respect in their faces too. Aye, the evening wasn't a complete failure after all. He was lord of Seakirk and 'twas obvious that most people thought of him as such. He gave them his most lordly smile. "Make merry, friends, while the evening lasts. Worthington, see to the minstrels and such, that my guests might be entertained."

With that, he sat down, stretched his legs out and assumed the lordly pose his father and grandfather had always assumed at such significant moments. Damnation, but it felt fine!

"Well done," Genevieve whispered. "You were wonderful."

Kendrick smiled at his lady. "Wait until you see what I have for you later, then see what you think."

"Coal for my stocking?"

"Something less personal, surely."

She laughed softly. "You're a terrible tease."

"My lord Seakirk?" a wobbly voice whispered.

Kendrick turned to see Adelaide standing in front of the high table, trembling like a leaf. Oh, the brave woman, coming close in spite of her fear. Kendrick gave her his most charming smile, guaranteed to make any woman over the age of ten swoon. Adelaide swooned right into Worthington's arms. Worthington staggered, then set Adelaide back on her feet and put a goblet of wine into her hands.

"Drink, Miss Adelaide," Worthington instructed.

She drank, her eyes wide over the brim of the cup. When she was finished, she straightened her girth and looked Kendrick over. Kendrick felt like laughing. Ah, but this old woman had spine!

"A pleasure, Mistress Adelaide. My lady has told me much of the wonders in your shop. My only regret is that I cannot come see them myself."

Adelaide's composure was fully regained and she stormed on ahead, as any good foot soldier would have.

"Nonsense, my lord. I'd be pleased to bring you anything that suits your fancy. If Worthington will be so good to help me place the items in my car, I will bring you a few samples of my acquisitions. I daresay you'll need things for the chambers you and your lady are restoring."

"I daresay you're right," Kendrick smiled. "Perhaps after

the new year. And Worthington will be more than willing to aid you however he can. Won't you, Worthington?"

Worthington lifted one silver eyebrow and sent a look that was somewhere between a pleading and a warning. Kendrick had his suspicions that Worthington held a soft spot in his ironhanded soul for Adelaide, and that look confirmed it nicely. Kendrick merely smiled blandly.

Worthington hrumphed. "Come, Mistress Adelaide. I will see you have a fine chair by the fire for the duration of the evening's entertainment. Though I don't see how a minstrel could possibly equal the spectacle we have just witnessed."

Kendrick would have thrown something at his steward had he been capable of it. As he wasn't, he merely sat back and scowled. Only until the next mortal approached, however. Master Wadsworth, the parish priest, Adelaide's brother. Ah, no crosses or holy water. With the likelihood of exorcism very slim, the evening was shaping up quite nicely.

A successfully conducted chat with the priest was obviously all it took for the rest of the company to decide that having a spirit as a host wasn't such a poor thing after all. Kendrick found himself besieged on all sides by villagers wanting to make his acquaintance and see for themselves who had been hiding up at the keep for so many years. He was well aware of Genevieve sitting by his side, and he felt a great amount of pride in knowing she was his lady. Her low husky voice was compelling and her smile sweet and bewitching. Kendrick was rather relieved there was no other man in the room of the right age to court her. He had the feeling he might have had competition.

As midnight approached, the guests began to leave to attend Mass in the village. Kendrick rose long before the hall was empty and looked down at his lady. What he wouldn't have given to have been able to escort her to Mass! He looked at her gravely.

"Do you want to go?"

She shook her head. "Not without you."

He wanted to sweep her up into his arms and carry her up

the stairs. He did the next best thing. He leaned down and whispered in her ear.

"Then let us retire to our chamber, my lady, and I will give you your gift."

"We have to wait until tomorrow," she protested.

"Nay," he said firmly. "Mine will not wait for another dawn."

She looked taken aback, but followed him when he started toward the stairs. They mounted the steps in silence, then Kendrick turned the lights on as they walked down the passageway. Genevieve opened the door to the bedchamber and he allowed it. His strength was better reserved for what he planned to do shortly.

Worthington had managed to slip off and arrange the place before the fire exactly as Kendrick had requested it. Kendrick ushered Genevieve over to the rug thrown down before the hearth, then sat across from her. He waited while she looked around the room, then waited some more for her to notice what sat on the stone of the hearth. It was small, but not so small that she shouldn't be able to see it readily enough.

He didn't have to wait long. She smiled at him, then caught sight of the blue velvet box. Kendrick couldn't have asked for a better reaction. Her mouth fell open. Her hand flew to her throat. She pointed at the box and wrenched her gaze back to his, her mouth working silently for a moment or two.

"Box," he supplied. "Ring box, if you'd rather."

"But . . ."

"Open it," he said, with a smile.

Her hands shook as she picked the box up. Kendrick felt tears begin to form in his eyes. Sweet, beautiful Genevieve, who looked as if he'd just pulled the moon down and presented it to her on a silver platter.

"Oh, Kendrick," she breathed, "it's beautiful."

He ached to hold her, to draw her over onto his lap and put his arms around her. He would have kissed away every tear that fell from her eyes, following them over her cheeks, along her jaw and down her throat. And then he would have buried his face in her hair and relished the feel of her arms around him and the sound of her breath in his ear.

With an effort, he pushed away his foolish dreams. *Take what you can have and be satisfied, Seakirk, for 'tis all you'll get.* He tried not to berate himself for being such a fool to think he and Genevieve could actually live out their lives being this much in love and having nothing but words and glances with which to show it. By the saints, this was an impossible situation!

He came to himself to find that Genevieve was watching him, her expression grave. He shook his head and managed a smile.

"Forgive me," he said quietly, "just idle thoughts." He gestured to the box. "Does it please you?"

"It's the most beautiful ring I've ever seen."

"Perhaps you'd care to know why I bought it?"

She nodded.

"You'll have to sit up in that chair so I can kneel before you properly and tell you the tale. Will you?"

She nodded again, then felt her way back to the chair and pulled herself up into it.

"Take out the ring, beloved," he said softly, rising and standing before her. "And put it in your palm. Nay, the left palm. And do not hide that right hand. 'Tis where a betrothal ring must be worn, don't you know?"

"Oh, Kendrick," she whispered, giving him a watery smile.

He went down on one knee before her, praying he wouldn't start to weep before he'd said the speech he'd been rehearsing for a fortnight.

"Genevieve," he began slowly, gravely, "I'm well aware of how little I have to offer you—nay"—he said, holding up his hand—"give me leave to finish." She nodded, but he knew she wasn't happy with his words. Neither was he, but truth was truth and there was no sense in pretending otherwise. He took a deep breath. "I can offer you a home and my gold—anything you desire, I can provide you. These worldly goods are the only tangible things I possess."

"They don't matter," she broke in.

He smiled dryly. "Then my castle does not please you?"

"Kendrick, you know what I meant."

"Aye, I do," he agreed. "But whether you wish for these things or not, they are yours. And along with these things of the world, I offer you my protection, such as it is. I will do anything within my power to keep you safe. There may come a time when that may mean something to both of us."

"I certainly hope not."

"I agree. Other than that, all I can offer you is my heart," he said softly. "And my love. I will cherish you, Gen, just as much as I would had I arms to hold you and a body to love you with. Not a day will pass that I won't tell you how deeply I love you and how much joy you've brought into my sorry life. Before you, there was naught but darkness. Now there is naught but light. And if I please you, if you feel the same way," he paused and took a deep breath before he finished— and by the saints he was suddenly nervous!—"would you do me the honor of being my wife?"

"Oh, Kendrick," she said with a half-sob. Of happiness or grief, he couldn't tell. She nodded, the tears streaming down her face. "Yes."

"Hold out your ring for me then, love," he said. "And give me your hand."

"Kendrick—"

He ignored her protests and put his fingers on the large diamond ring. It was tempting to jest about the size, that his task would have been easier had the stone been smaller, but he couldn't. This was no time for jesting; it was time to pray he could accomplish the feat he planned.

He poured all his energies into concentrating on the task before him. How many times in life had that concentration been what had unseated an opponent larger than he or kept him on his feet after hours of fighting in the hot Arabian sands when his very soul seemed to be escaping his skin with his sweat? Aye, this was the very same thing. Only this was so much more important. He would put Genevieve's ring on her finger, even if doing so put him in bed for a fortnight.

He lifted it. By the saints, it was enormous! He felt the

sweat break out on his forehead and slip down his temples and cheeks. Genevieve's hand was instantly before him. He flashed her a tight smile for her aid. She likely couldn't see him for her tears; he definitely couldn't see her for the blood that thundered behind his eyes. Sweat drenched his shirt, slipped down his thighs to pool at the back of his knees.

He pushed the ring over her first knuckle. She caught the back of the ring with her thumb and started to pull.

"Don't," he rasped. He met her eyes. "Don't."

Her shoulders began to shake with the force of her tears. Despite that, she held her hand steady. Saints, had he never noticed before how long a woman's finger could be? He gritted his teeth and pushed with all his strength to slip the ring over the last knuckle and into place.

Done.

He collapsed at her feet. She was instantly on the floor, kneeling next to him.

"Oh, Kendrick." She reached out to smooth the hair back from his brow, and her hand went through him. She pulled it back and wrapped her arms around herself. She closed her eyes and cried.

It was agony to sit upright but he did it anyway, ignoring the screaming pain that went through his muscles. Obviously there was enough substance to him that pain was still possible.

"Genevieve," he said hoarsely. "Ah, my Gen, don't weep so when I can't comfort you. I beseech you."

She lifted her head, her hand over her mouth. Her eyes were bloodshot and her cheeks wet with her tears. She took her hand away from her mouth and hesitantly stretched it out.

"I would give anything to touch you," she whispered. He could feel the tightness of her throat from the strained sound of her words. "Just once, Kendrick. Just once." She put her hand against his cheek, against the place where her hand would have rested had he been alive. "Just once."

"Perhaps in time," he offered, knowing he lied but unable to say anything else. It would take a miracle.

Her shoulders slumped. "Kendrick, you're already pale. Come to bed."

He managed a wan smile, despite the tears that flowed down his cheeks. "I should exert myself thusly more often. 'Tis obviously the way to win a place in my lady's bed." He put his hand over hers as it hung in midair next to his cheek. "Tell me the ring pleases you."

"I'll never take it off," she vowed. "Never."

"Do you love me?"

"Desperately."

"Then come to bed and tell me. Come to bed, Genevieve, and we'll turn out all the lights and talk."

She nodded and rose with him. "I'll hurry."

He nodded as he watched her walk across the room to the bathroom. He waited until the door was closed before he turned to the hearth and hung his head.

And wept.

•

Chapter
Twenty

Genevieve stood on the battlements and shivered with the late afternoon chill. The new year had come already and brought with it nothing but grief. She looked down at the beautiful diamond that sparkled in the pale winter sun. Kendrick had touched it. She had felt him take it out of her hand, then slide it onto her finger. Why then couldn't she feel his touch on her skin?

She dropped her hand and fought the urge to weep. She'd done nothing but weep for the past two weeks. Though she'd tried to do it in private, she hadn't been able to hide her lack of appetite or her red nose from her knight. His expression had become grimmer with each passing day. She hadn't seen him smile in a week. It was intolerable! When she'd come home from London she'd known there would be tears. She hadn't anticipated just how many, though. What a terrible miscalculation. It might have been better to not have had him at all than to have him this way.

She put her hand to her mouth in horror. Had she actually thought something so dreadful? She turned and ran from the battlements. A distraction. She had to have some kind of distraction. Kendrick spent most of his waking hours in the lists. Maybe some kind of exercise would soothe her. It couldn't hurt to try.

Kendrick had shown her the back way out of the keep, through the secret tunnel and out from under the outer bailey wall. The path down to the beach was steep but manageable. She picked her way among the rocks, ignoring the mist, ignoring the bitter cold. A run in the sand. That would keep her mind on her feet and off her life.

She ran until she was gasping for air and her muscles were on fire. The mist had turned to rain and it beat down on her mercilessly. She didn't care. The sand was cold and wet under her as she dropped to her hands and knees and panted. When had she become so out of shape?

"So the quarry comes to us."

Genevieve looked up quickly and paled. Two men stood there, dressed in black, their faces hard with wickedness. One of them reached for her and she flung herself backwards, scrambling for her feet.

"Oh, no ye don't, missy," the other said, blocking her way.

Genevieve changed directions and threw herself forward, managing to slip between the men. She jumped to her feet and fled.

"Let 'er run," one of the men said. "I could use the air. 'Aven't ye noticed the fine sea air up 'ere, Davy?"

Kendrick! Genevieve screamed silently. She had the mental picture of him jerking his attention away from the knight who thundered toward him in the lists; Kendrick flew off the back of his horse and landed in the mud on his back, his feet in the air, thanks to the lance catching him full in the chest. She saw him jump to his feet, heard him shout for Nazir and for the other ghosts haunting the outer bailey.

To arms! he shouted. *To me, lads! Seakirk!*

Genevieve cried out in pain as her pursuers tired of the play and grabbed her by the hair. The motion almost snapped her neck. She was flung to the ground and the men stood over her, laughing.

"Nice piece, ain't she, Davy? I says we 'ave 'er now, deliver 'er later. What says ye?"

The other man grinned, revealing a toothless smile. "I'm for ye, Al."

Al slapped the other man. "I told ye not to use me name, ye bugger! 'Ave ye gone mad?"

A mist rose up around them suddenly. The men whirled around in surprise, looking for what had blocked the sun so suddenly and completely.

Gen, on your hands and knees to your left. As far and quickly as you can!

She didn't have to hear that twice. Al and Davy had their knives drawn and she didn't exactly relish the idea of being impaled by one. She scrambled away on her hands and knees, screaming as a blade buried itself in the sand next to her hand. She changed directions and fled until she met water and could go no further. She lay flat on the sand in the surf and prayed.

The sounds of battle raged all around her and the mist was so thick she couldn't see the sun. Ghostly shapes melted in and out of the darkness, men in full battle gear, waving their swords and shouting with wraithlike voices. Al's and Davy's screams were lost in the clamor. Genevieve put her hands over her head and prayed that they would mistake her for driftwood and leave her alone. Why wasn't Worthington calling the police?

The screams faded in time and the mist began to clear. She lifted her head and shrieked at the dark figure standing above her with a shotgun in his hand. Then the sun came through the clouds and she saw the glint of silver hair.

"My lady, come out of the water. You'll catch a chill."

She jerked on Worthington's trousers. "Get down," she hissed. "You'll get killed!"

Worthington took her hand and helped her up. "My lady, the ruffians are seen to. Let His Lordship see you back to the house while I wait here for the authorities."

Kendrick came out of the mist, bloodied from head to toe. She gasped and he swore. Instantly he was back in jeans and sweatshirt.

"Just for show," he said soothingly. "Back to the house, Gen, and into a hot bath. Worthington will see to the prisoners. Worthington, make sure the authorities hold them until Inspector O'Mally can question them. If they seem unwilling to talk, by all means have them brought back here. I daresay I could persuade them to give us the information we need."

Kendrick turned a frown on her as they walked back to the castle. "What in heaven's name were you thinking to come alone here?" he demanded. "Good Lord, Genevieve, 'twas a foolish notion!"

She stopped halfway up the path and glared at him. "I had to walk. You train. Why can't I do the same?"

"Because I can take care of myself!"

"So can I."

"So I see by this morning's events. You will not leave again, Genevieve, without telling me."

"I don't have to answer to you—"

"How am I to protect you when I don't know where you are!"

"Oh, just leave me alone," she moaned miserably, pushing through him and stumbling up the path. "Just leave me alone!" As soon as she was on solid ground, she ran through the tunnel, through the servants' quarters and up the rest of the way to her room. She slammed the door behind her, ran to the bathroom and locked the door behind her. Not that a locked door would have stopped Kendrick.

She dropped her face into her hands and shuddered. As if her life wasn't hard enough with just dealing with her love! Now to have men chasing her, even in her own back yard? She groaned as she pushed away from the door and dragged her soggy body over to the tub.

How much worse could it possibly get?

Kendrick sat in his study, his feet propped up on the stool, his head back against the couch. He'd been sitting in the same place for the past twelve hours, most of the night, waiting for Genevieve to come to him. It had been a vain effort. She had taken a bath, then gone to bed. He couldn't bear to go comfort her. His fear was still too close to the surface for that.

What a disaster. He'd come within inches of losing Genevieve without even being aware of it. And rescuing her had only made matters worse! He was well aware of the ache she felt, the hunger to be held, to be gathered close and kept safe. He understood completely; there were no words to describe how desperately he wished he could oblige her.

A tap sounded on the door. He looked up in surprise. Why, it wasn't even dawn yet. What in the world would she be doing up? He tilted his head back.

"Genevieve?"

The door opened and she looked in. "Still speaking to me?"

He smiled, pained. "Of course, love. By the saints, you're up early!"

She sighed and closed the door behind her. More fetching nightclothes with the slick feet, only this time in green. What he wouldn't have given to have hands with which to pull them off her! She padded over to the couch and sat down. Almost on top of him. Kendrick managed a faint smile. She was obviously so distracted she didn't know what she was doing. Even though she wore his ring on her finger, she was still hopelessly shy. Nay, her usual place was a good hand's breadth away. Marriage likely wouldn't change that any.

"I couldn't sleep," she whispered, lifting her face to his. "I'm sorry about yesterday. I was rude."

"You were upset. I understand."

"I just needed to get out."

"I understand, Gen," he said softly.

"Will we survive this? Are you sure you don't want me to sign the papers—"

"Absolutely not!" He took a deep breath and released it slowly. "I'll take what I have with you. It will be enough."

"But—"

"'Tis a far sight better than the alternative."

She chewed on her lip as she looked up at him. "But you've been so miserable."

"Winter makes me moody."

"It does not."

He dragged his hand through his hair. "I've spent far too much time wishing for what I cannot have, my love. I'll stop. Perhaps later today we'll take up our work on the other chambers again. A distraction is likely what will serve us best for now. And you've a wedding to plan, you know. I've always thought June to be a fine month for nuptials."

She looked down. "When did you plan to marry Matilda?"

"The dead of winter."

That brought a smile to her lips, though she didn't raise her head far enough for him to catch the full effect. "June it is then, my lord."

"Fetch that blanket, my sweet, and come curl up next to me. Shall I wake Worthington and have him build up the fire?"

"No, it's fine," she said, rising and snatching the blanket off the chair near the door. "Let's watch television, Kendrick. I need the distraction."

"It's too early for anything good."

"I don't care," she said, resuming her place next to him. "Just find something."

"I taped the Raiders game. Should we watch it?"

"Later, Kendrick. It's not even breakfast yet. I can't watch football until after I've had something to give me energy."

"All right then, love. You take the remote."

"Control. I like that."

"I knew you would."

She drew the blanket around her, her eyes never leaving his. "You are a wonderful man."

"Tell me more."

"Read my mind. I'm too tired to talk now."

He leaned back against the couch and relented. He'd wring a few compliments out of her later when she was engrossed in something else. The sooner she forgot about her fright yesterday, the better off she'd be. The Inspector would likely show up before noon, and Kendrick didn't want her thinking about that until absolutely necessary.

"Look," she said breathlessly.

Kendrick looked at the screen and rolled his eyes. "It's a

cartoon. Gen, surely there's some football on somewhere in the world. This isn't even a real show."

"It's Cinderella. Possibly the greatest love story of all time."

"The greatest?"

She turned and looked at him. "Besides ours."

Kendrick's chest tightened at the grave smile she wore. "Aye," he said softly, "besides ours."

"Now, be quiet and watch. The prince is very handsome."

"More handsome than I?"

"No one is more handsome than you," she said, her eyes glued to the screen.

He gave in. Had he wished for a distraction? Well, wishes certainly seemed to be coming true at the moment. It was readily apparent that he wasn't going to have Genevieve's full attention until the show was over. Just as well. She was already sighing that romantic sigh of hers, and he had the feeling this cartoon would put her in a fine mood. He fully intended to take advantage of it. Perhaps it would be just the thing to cure him of his own foulness.

The thought of a nap appealed to him until he started to watch the show. The mice with their squeaky voices made him grin and the sight of the fairy godmother made him laugh. There was a caricature of Adelaide, up on the screen for all to see. A pity she wasn't a fairy godmother in truth. Kendrick knew just the wish he would ask for.

Ah, such sweet romance. Tears streamed down Genevieve's face as the show ended and Kendrick blinked furiously to hide his own telltale mistiness. The saints preserve him, he was weeping over a cartoon! He turned to his lady and smiled at her sniffles.

"My Gen, you've such a soft heart."

"It's so beautiful," she said, looking up at him with dreamy eyes. "Don't you think?"

"I do." Damn, was he truly going to weep? He cleared his throat gruffly. "*Now* can I watch the Raiders?"

She leaned her head back against his arm. "Go ahead. Wake me up when it's over."

He nodded and turned the VCR on. The last play-off game.

Ah, the tension the lads must feel. Surely it was something akin to preparing for battle, though the stakes were not nearly as high. Though for some it doubtless felt like life or death. How he would have loved to play the game. Such a pity he and Royce couldn't return to their mortal bodies. They were both young and strong. A career in the NFL wouldn't be unthinkable.

Tied at halftime. Kendrick groaned and leaned his head back against the couch. Of course it couldn't have been a clean, decisive victory. Nay, this would be one of those battles that raged on until the last minute and even then, the victory wouldn't be clear-cut. A rout was what he had needed to see that day. It would have soothed him. He turned off the low sound and let the tape continue. A break in the tension was what he needed.

He closed his eyes and let his mind wander. And wander it did, right back to the cartoon. Ah, the feats the fairy godmother was able to accomplish! Would that such miracles were possible. Perhaps they were, if he just wished hard enough. Just one hour, nay even half an hour. If he could just hold his love in his arms once, long enough to kiss her, to touch her face, to wrap his arms around her and hold her close to his chest. Was that so very much to ask for? Just once? For just a few moments?

Just once. 'Tis all I ask for. Just once.

Of course, it wouldn't happen. He sighed. Miracles didn't happen in these times. He closed his eyes, then shifted his arm. Genevieve's head was putting it to sleep.

He froze.

Genevieve's head was resting against his arm.

Not the couch, but his arm.

He wondered if he would ever again take a normal breath. He was touching her. She was touching him. With care born of sheer panic, he lifted his head and looked down at her. Merciful saints, he could feel her!

He slowly reached out and fingered a lock of her hair. He gasped softly when he felt it slide smoothly between his thumb and middle finger. He held his breath and touched her cheek with his hand. Her skin was smooth as a babe's under his callused palm. The touch woke her and she opened her eyes and smiled up at him.

"Is the game over?" she asked sleepily.

"Nay," he whispered hoarsely. "'Tis but halftime."

"Then why did you wake . . ." The words died on her lips as she realized what was happening. Her astonishment was as great as his. "What's happening?"

"Don't question it. Just let me touch you."

She nodded, wide-eyed as his fingers trailed over her cheek. He traced her mouth with his thumb, over and over again, memorizing the feel of it under his hand. Oh, so very beautiful and so very soft. He slipped his hand along her jaw and into her hair. Soft, silky strands falling over his fingers like spun glass, burning his hands where they touched them.

He had to kiss her. He tipped her face up and covered her mouth softly with his own. He took her gasp into his mouth and gave it back to her as he groaned. Soft, sweet and trembling, aye, he knew that was how her mouth would be. He dropped his other hand behind her back and pulled her closer to him, tilting her head further back and parting her lips with his.

She'd never been kissed properly. He knew it the moment he slid his tongue inside her mouth. Her jerk almost pulled her out of his arms. It would have, had he not been holding her so tightly.

"Sshh," he whispered, leaving her mouth to press his lips against her cheek, her temple, her ear. "*Chérie*, do not fear me. Come back to me, *ma petite*." Ah, how long had it been since he had loved a woman in French, wooed her in his grandfather's tongue, let the silky words drip off his tongue with slow, sensuous abandon?

Yet, it was different this time. This was *his* woman. The words had been made for her ears, his hands had been formed for her sweet body, his mouth made to caress only hers.

"My love," he breathed against her mouth. "Sweet, sweet Genevieve. Tell me this is no dream."

"It's a gift. An impossible gift. How long will it—"

His mouth cut off her words. He couldn't bear to contemplate the possibility of losing her now. If he did, he would kill himself out of grief. He ignored the fears that tormented him and concentrated on the trembling woman in his arms. He parted her lips again and kissed her deeply.

Nay, 'twas too soon. He was far too hasty for her. It was as he'd known all along. Genevieve would take gentle wooing, not a barbaric possession of her mouth and body. Kendrick pulled away and simply gathered her close to his chest, stroking her back soothingly.

"My Gen," he murmured. "How I've longed to hold you in my arms."

"Take me to bed. Now."

He pulled back. "What?" he asked, incredulously.

"While we have the chance, Kendrick." She trembled as badly as she had the first night, when he had almost scared the life from her. "We have to do it now."

"'Tis too soon—"

"There may not be another chance," she said, a frantic look coming to her eye. "Please, Kendrick. I'm not afraid."

That was a lie if he'd ever heard one. He closed his eyes, his common sense warring with his desire.

His desire won. Without warning, he swung her up into his arms and rose, all in one fluid movement. He looked down into her face, his own expression grim.

"This is what you want?"

"Don't you?"

"I want to wed you first," he said hoarsely. "But I fear the time is too short."

"Then love me." She wrapped her arms around his neck and pressed her cheek against his. "Love me while you can."

Ah, sweet Genevieve, so courageous in the face of certain terror. What a brave warrior she was. He could make it good for her, see that it hurt her as little as possible. If he were lucky, he'd be allowed that much time. He strode to the door.

And then he felt Genevieve slip through his arms.

She cried out in pain as she hit the floor, then clutched her wrist to her chest. Kendrick looked down at her, his mouth agape. He reached for her, stretching out his hand to take hers.

And touched nothing.

"Bloody hell," he shouted, clenching his fists to his sides.

Genevieve crawled to her feet and collapsed on the couch, weeping with hoarse sobs that wrenched at his gut like a blade being twisted in his belly.

Kendrick couldn't bear it. He walked through the door and sprinted up to the battlements, waiting until he was there to give vent to his own hoarse cry of anguish. He stood at the wall and wept as the first rays of the sun exploded over the horizon.

Saints above, how much worse could it get?

Genevieve heard the cry echoing in the keep and in her heart. It wasn't fair! Why? she sobbed, lifting her face heavenward. Why did she have him only to have him ripped away? Why had she felt his arms around her for long enough to taste bliss, then find herself thrust down to hell again?

Despair crashed over her like a wave, robbing her of breath. She clawed her way to the surface of her grief only to be cast down to the depths again. She stumbled to her feet, then felt her way to Kendrick's private study. She had to end it. They couldn't go on, not after what had happened. She would sign the papers, give Kendrick his freedom and then she would spend the rest of her life grieving. Perhaps her life would be a very short one. God willing, it *would* be; then she'd hike up her skirts and run right along to heaven where Kendrick would be waiting for her. It would be better than surviving what had suddenly and with certain finality become the most hellish situation she had ever experienced.

She flung open drawers, tossed papers over her shoulders, searching frantically for the deed she knew had to be somewhere in his desk. She rifled through the side drawers, through the middle drawer, through the cubbyholes that contained nothing but notepaper and stamps.

Then she saw it. Under the blotter. She pulled it free, her hands trembling so badly she could hardly hold it. She set it down carefully, then felt blindly for a pen. Just a simple signature. Easily done. She'd signed hundreds of things during the course of her lifetime. She could sign this too.

She put the pen to the signature line. Under the line some-one had typed her name with an old-fashioned typewriter. Genevieve Buchanan. Two simple words. She could do this.

She jerked the pen across the line in a shaky imitation of her name, then threw the pen and the deed across the room. She sank to her knees and wept until she was sick.

It was only the stillness that finally brought her back to reason.

She couldn't hear Kendrick's shout echoing in her mind any longer.

She called to him with her mind as he'd taught her to do.

Silence.

She lay down on the cold stone floor and cried—deep, wrenching sobs of pure, unadulterated grief.

It was over.

He was gone.

Chapter
Twenty-one

The searing pain in his chest was gone. Kendrick's eyes flew
open in surprise. He'd heard the sound of the arrow being released and felt it slam into his chest like a hammer. First there
had been breath-stealing agony, then a sweet darkness that
beckoned to him, promising peace and surcease from pain. But
now he had been restored to life? The very thought made him
panic. He jerked frantically on the chains that bound his wrists
and they fell away as if they had never been there at all. He
freed his ankles just as easily.

Think, de Piaget. Was this another of Matilda's tricks? Did
Richard's men lie in wait above, armed and ready to do battle
with a single, hapless victim? If only Royce and Nazir were
alive! The threesome had escaped more than one impossible
situation. He looked next to him. Their bodies were gone! He
drew his hand over his eyes. By St. George's throat, he was
going daft!

Nay, his captain and his Saracen warrior were dead; he remembered seeing it done. The memory would never fade.

Richard would pay dearly for his sport. He would not find his last captive dispatched so easily this time.

Kendrick espied his mail shirt where it had landed after being stripped from him and flung across the room. He dashed over to his gear, then hurriedly wriggled into his mail and seized the tabard bearing his father's crest. The saints be praised, his sword was there too. He snatched it up, then crept up the stairs with great stealth, knowing full well that the slightest noise could mean certain death.

But—hadn't he died before?

He shook his head sharply, trying to clear away the puzzling thoughts and images that continued to lap at the edges of his senses. There would be time to sort it all out once he was free of Seakirk. He would ride to Artane, gather his brothers and cousins and come back for revenge. Richard had best enjoy his last days on earth. Once Kendrick had him within arm's reach, the man would beg for the mercy of an eternity in hell. Kendrick had never in his life felt such blinding hatred. Aye, the man would pray for death long before it came to him.

The main floor was easily gained and Kendrick cast his eyes about for any sign of Richard's men. There was no one in sight. Then he pulled up short. The last time he saw it, the great hall had been ill-kempt and foul-smelling, worse than the lowest inn he had ever frequented. Now it was clean and fresh-smelling. And what had happened to the rushes?

He smiled bitterly. How kind of Matilda to see to the cleaning so quickly. Of course the floor would have needed a scrubbing after all the men he, Nazir and Royce had killed. Blood and body parts everywhere.

Odder still that the hall was empty. No fires burned in the hearths. No stench of rotting meat from the kitchens assailed his nostrils. Not even a hound dozed on the floor before the fire. It was as if every soul had been plucked from the keep.

Perhaps they were all lying in wait outside. He tightened his grip on his sword. There was only one way to find out. He strode over to the doorway, threw up the bar and jerked it open.

And almost fell over in his shock. By the saints, what had

happened to the lists? He put his hand to his head, trying to stop his vision from blurring. Yesterday he'd ridden into Seakirk's courtyard and sighed at the sorry state of it; now he was looking at a place that had been tended with great care.

He closed the door behind him and leaned back against it. The buildings were still there, looking more worn than before, but in tolerable shape. But instead of dirt surrounding the keep, there was finely laid stone; instead of dirt and sand for the lists, there was sod. And the garden! Saints above, the garden was a fine one!

But it was empty. Kendrick felt very ill at ease. What witchcraft was this? He made his way out to the grass-covered field and looked around him, unable to believe the emptiness of the place.

"Damn you, Richard!" he shouted. "Show yourself! Come and fight me, you coward!"

Nothing. There was no answer.

"You bloody whoreson, come to me!" Kendrick thundered, growing more enraged by the moment. "Come out from behind Matilda's skirts and fight like a man!"

Genevieve's head jerked up at the sound of hoarse shouting. What in the world was going on now? A frown crossed her brow. The thick accent made the man's words almost unintelligible. She rose heavily to her feet and stumbled to the door. It was probably another thug come to try to kidnap her.

She left Kendrick's study and made her way down the hall, picking up her pace as the shouting increased. Good grief, where was Worthington when she needed him? She ran down the stairs and across the great hall. The door was unbarred and she stopped at the sight. What was going on?

She opened the door and peeked out. The shouting continued, louder now that she could hear the voice clearly. It was a voice that sounded remarkably like Kendrick's, only this voice was deeper, fuller, rougher.

As if it came from within a man's chest.

No, it couldn't be. She shook her head as she hastened down the steps. *Don't even think it, Buchanan!* Lord, what a crushing blow that would be! To imagine him alive only to find she was mistaken? No, she wouldn't survive that.

"Damn you, Richard, you bloody whoreson! Show yourself!"

Genevieve gasped, then sped around the side of the keep to the grassy expanse beyond the stone of the courtyard, to the turf near the garden.

Kendrick stood in the middle of that field, shouting hoarsely. She heard him calling for Richard and Matilda. He was dressed in the clothes that should have been upstairs in their fine, glass cases. His jewel-encrusted sword was in his hand; the early morning sun winked off the blade.

Genevieve's breath came in gasps and her heart pounded against her ribs.

Kendrick caught sight of the wench as she rounded the corner of the keep. Then she began to run toward him, calling his name. By the saints, what manner of dress was that? She was covered from neck to feet in green fur, a green he had never before seen in his life. Who was she? A Celtic elf from the Scottish forests?

He took a dozen swift strides and caught her by the arm.

"Who are you, bitch?" he snarled.

"Kendrick," the young woman said frantically, "it's Genevieve. My love, don't you recognize me?"

"How do you know my name?" he demanded, wondering at the strangeness of her accent. And she spoke the peasant's English, and very poorly at that. She was no noblewoman obviously, else she would have spoken French.

"Kendrick, Richard killed you and you were a ghost for seven hundred years."

"Lies," he spat. Saints, the woman was a witch!

"You lived at Seakirk all that time," she rushed on. "I'm the last of the Buchanans and you tried to kill me. We fell in love. This morning we touched for the first time, don't you remember? Then you were a ghost again and it upset me so that I signed the deed to the castle over to you and I thought you'd really died."

The last of the Buchanans? Nay, he knew all the Buchanans, and this wench looked little like them. Jonathan Buchanan, aye, he remembered the lad well. Kendrick saw himself standing over the young man, describing his loved ones in great detail as the lad put Kendrick's description on canvas. He saw himself playing chess with Jonathan and felt the frustration of not being able to touch the pieces.

But how could that be? His fingers worked perfectly well. Then from whence came such a memory?

He shook his head sharply, forcing away the thoughts. By the saints, the witch was weaving her spell already. "You lying wench," he snarled, grabbing her by the arm and yanking her along with him as he strode back to the house. Perhaps if he tossed her in the dungeon, she would be rendered powerless.

"I'm not lying," the young woman said urgently. "I know everything about you. I know you got the long scar on your chest that afternoon when you and Phillip were fighting with swords, after your father told you not to."

Kendrick ignored her and broke into a trot, ignoring the woman when she stumbled. Let her heal herself with her black powers.

"I know how when the king offered you Seakirk, you rode off alone that day to the shore and prayed for guidance about what to do. You saw a vision of Seakirk with a garden where the lists had been, with strangely dressed people traveling in little metal boxes with wheels." A half-sob escaped her lips as she tripped and went down. He hauled her to her feet and continued on his way. "I know that you took that to mean you were to wed Matilda," she gasped. "That those were your descendants many years in the future. You never told that to anyone, Kendrick, but you told it to me."

Kendrick lifted his hand to slap the words from her mouth.

Kendrick, we never strike women, not even in anger. Always remember that as your strength is superior, so must be your control of that strength.

Kendrick's hand hung motionless in the air. By the blessed

name of St. George, this was a witch! What did it matter how
he abused her?

*Not even serving wenches should feel the strength of your
blows, son. A woman, no matter her station in life, is one of
God's gentler creatures. Treat them as such.*

"Damn you, Father, this is different," Kendrick growled
under his breath, but he lowered his hand and instead clamped
it over the witch's mouth. "Silence, witch," he hissed. "The
Devil is your master and I'll not hear any more of your blas-
phemy."

She continued to struggle but his strength was, quite obviously, indeed superior to hers. Though she was tall and slender, there was something about her that made her seem very
fragile. He frowned as he swung her up into his arms and
stalked back to the house. More enchantments. She was doubtless as large as his horse and just that attractive without her
black beguilements to cloak her in loveliness.

The hall was just as empty as he had left it. Again, unbid-
den, a vision came to him. The hall was full of people, dressed
so strangely that he stopped dead in his tracks. Men and
women danced in the most ridiculous-looking clothes he had
ever seen. Collars as wide as his hand, gowns that gave the
women hips the width of trestle tables, coverings for the men
that made their thighs look like fat mutton legs.

Just as quickly, the memory was gone. He was left with a
slight girl in his arms who wept. He hardened his heart, knowing it was her magic that made him want to be kind to her.

Instantly he turned and headed toward the cellar steps. Two
doors? Since when had there been two doors down to the cellar? He surely hadn't noticed that when he came up. Shrug-
ging, he chose the door further away. No one challenged him.

He thumped down the steps, then looked about for somewhere to bind the witch. It would be foolish to leave her hands
free. The saints only knew what sort of mischief she could
conjure up that way. The rings on the walls were his first
choice but her wrists were too slender for them to be of use.
He espied a length of rope on the floor and picked it up. He

dumped the witch to her feet near a pillar and bound her with her arms encircling it behind her.

"Oh, Kendrick," she pleaded, "please wake up!"

"I am awake and none too soon," he snapped. "Where is Richard? I vow I'll see his head on a pike before midday!" He sheathed his sword, then folded his arms across his chest and glared down at her. "The truth, if you're capable of it."

"Richard's dead," she said hoarsely. "So is Matilda. Kendrick, this is 1996. They all died hundreds of years ago."

"Lies," he spat. "What Matilda paid you to use your powers against me was not worth it. I will find Richard and his whore and see them repaid for their sport. You will die, then I will call for my brothers and we will reduce this hall to rubble. Vision or no vision, I will not dwell in a place of evil."

"Kendrick, please," the girl pleaded. "You've lost your memory—" She gasped. "You lost your memory? Kendrick, let me help you get it back! Just listen to me and try to understand my words."

Kendrick put his hands over his ears. By the saints, the wench wanted him to submit to her black art without a fight! She had to die and soon. But with what weapon? There had never been a witch in all his days at Artane, though he had heard of plenty of them being found in Scotland. How did one go about killing a sorceress? By fire?

He shuddered. Even with the innumerable men he had slain crusading, there were some things he simply could not bring himself to do and burning a woman was one of them. Should he cut off her head? He looked at her. Even in the faint torchlight, her beauty was plain to the eye. Enchantment or no, she was a lovely creature to look upon. Nay, he could not decapitate her, nor could he slip his blade into her breast and end her life that way.

He caught sight of the crossbow laying on the floor. Where Richard had dropped it. The bolt was not nocked, as it should have been had it been ready to be fired. He looked to the wall where he had been chained.

"And what of Jonathan? Don't you remember the painting he did of your family? It's in your den upstairs, Kendrick, along with your television and the computer I gave you for Christmas. All you have to do is talk and the computer does what you want. Don't you remember all the games I found to go with it? And don't you remember all the Raiders games we watched on TV . . ."

How odd that the arrow was there. As if it had been discharged from the bow.

But wasn't that exactly what had happened? He had looked Richard full in the face and watched him smile coldly. He had heard the noise of the arrow being released and felt blinding agony as it shattered bone and sinew. He had tasted sharp, metallic blood in his mouth.

"And don't you remember how impossible Nazir was being before we agreed to let him decorate his own room? All the hours we spent putting down markers for the furniture, only to find he'd rearranged them during the night in protest? And all those nights we spent together on the love seat in your den, curled together in front of the fire, talking of hopes and dreams, things we were sure could never come true? And my ring. Don't you remember giving me my ring, Kendrick? You put it on me yourself . . ."

Kendrick put his hand against the wall to steady himself. He had taken the bolt in the chest. Hadn't he? Memories tormented him, like demons in a thick mist who appeared only long enough to make him start after them. He reached for one memory, only to have it elude him and leave him holding onto another. Who was Jonathan Buchanan?

Matilda's grandson. But how would he know that? He felt himself closed inside a prison, without the benefit of touch, taste or smell. He remembered roaming through the keep, seeing the rushes on the floor but not being able to reach down and feel them. The stables were filled with dirty men and horses, but there was no sharp tang of manure and sweat. There was food before him on the board but the smell did not waft upward. His hand encountered nothing when he tried to bring some of it to his mouth.

"Cease!" he thundered, whirling around and gazing at the

girl, who continued to babble nonsense. She was casting a spell on him. "Cease with your prattle and your magics!"

"You love me," she insisted. "Damn you, Kendrick de Piaget, this is our chance and you're blowing it! Remember me, you jerk!"

"The Devil is your master," he hissed, "and I'll hear no more of your lies." He snatched up the arrow and fitted it to the crossbow.

"Kendrick, think of the things you love," she said quickly. "Your Jaguar. My red feety pajamas. Listening to Nazir tell you of the naughty hauntings he's done."

"Call to your master, for you'll join him soon," Kendrick said coldly, as he cranked the metal cable back until it caught.

"Oh, Kendrick," she said softly. "Please remember. Remember that I love you more than life itself. I signed the papers, Kendrick. That's why you came back, I know it! To have a second chance at life, the life Richard stole from you."

Kendrick straightened and took aim.

Kendrick, your duty is to protect women and children.

Not witches. This woman is a witch.

Never sully your honor by hurting a woman to make yourself feel powerful, son. Kill a man when required, but never a woman. They are God's most precious gifts to us.

Father, stop!

Kendrick, how proud I am of you and the man you've become. Remember that your father and I will be waiting for you when your time comes.

Mother, what are you talking about? When what time comes? Kendrick put his hand to his forehead and pressed firmly. What sorcery was this that he should hear his mother's voice speaking such strange words? He looked again at the witch. How full of sadness and regret was her face. What was that other emotion radiating out from her eyes?

Love?

Impossible. It was a spell. She had bewitched him as he stood there, as unsure of himself as a green squire. He again raised the crossbow and looked her in the face.

"Have you any last words?" he asked hoarsely. "Any words of truth?"

Ah, the sadness in her expression!

"Here is truth," she whispered. "I love you, my gallant ghost."

First there was nothing. All emotion and thought receded from his mind like water receding from the shoreline. Then memories crashed over him like a fierce wave. He drew his hand over his eyes, but still they came on. His vision would not clear. The bow clattered from his trembling fingers and he stumbled away, feeling dizzier than he ever had in his life, even after the most fierce and exhausting of battles. And still the memories came.

The birth of Richard and Matilda's child. Watching Nazir stalk the pair and frighten them until they feared to leave their bedchamber. His mother joining him on the battlements, bidding him farewell. His father following soon after. Knowing that his parents were dead and feeling the agony of not being able to follow them.

The mist continued to swirl inside his head. Jonathan Buchanan. The man who had befriended him. Watching Jonathan pass over into a bright light and feeling numb resignation, knowing he was not allowed to follow. Years of darkness, of bitterness, of hatred. Generation after generation of Buchanans passed before his mind's eye. Lady Alice's insistence on learning to play the harp to accompany herself, despite her complete inability to sing. Lady Helen's continual beatings at the hand of her husband and the satisfaction of being able to drive the man daft, then watch him hang himself.

Lady Agatha's flight from the upper window after a particularly horrifying night. Kendrick winced. Had he truly appeared, holding his head under his arm and leaving blood spurting from his severed neck? What had he cared? Again, he felt the rush of all-consuming hatred against a family who had damned him.

He rested against the wall, pressing his face against the cool stone. *Cool stone.* He could feel the damp coolness against his cheek. How long had it been since he had felt anything?

Locked in a vacuum, deprived of the smell of flowers in the springtime, the taste of cold wine on a hot day, the feel of warm steel in his hand and the weight of mail on his back. He had been denied those things year after year, century after century. Until when?

Until Genevieve.

He gasped again as another flood of memories came washing over him. Drenching himself in blood and appearing to her upstairs in his bedchamber, vowing to make her daft. Fighting his grudging admiration when she had the cheek to ignore him. Using all his strength to put her betrothal ring on her finger. Sweet, beloved Genevieve. He whirled and looked at her.

"My God," he whispered.

Genevieve. The one who had given him joy. The one who had loved him and forgiven him for the dreams he had ruthlessly crushed. The one who had given her heart into hands that could never truly hold it. The one who had made him weep ghostly tears for what he could never have with her.

The one who had loved him enough to set him free.

"Genevieve," he said hoarsely.

Genevieve opened her eyes at the sound of her name. She froze and stared at him, as if she thought she were hearing things.

"Genevieve," he breathed.

She closed her eyes and let out a shuddering breath.

"My love, what have I done to you?" Kendrick exclaimed, hastening over to her as quickly as his shaking legs would carry him. He cut the ropes that bound her hands behind her, then caught her as she sagged against him. He gathered her close, rocking her with a desperateness that was echoed in her embrace.

"Oh, Kendrick," she whispered, beginning to weep, "I thought you wouldn't remember me."

"Sweet, sweet Genevieve," he whispered, tightening his arms around her. Merciful God, how close he had come to slaying the very being he loved more than life itself! He felt the hot sting of his own tears and then relished the feel of them coursing down his cheeks.

And then he wept for another reason entirely. He was alive. It was a miracle, an impossible, beyond-all-reason miracle. The curse had been broken and somehow he had been given a second chance at life. How long would it last? The thought pulled him up short. Would he die? How long had he been given?

Please, he prayed silently, *let it be until we are both old and gray. Please don't take this from me so soon.*

A peace stole over him, like a soft mist. It reached down into the innermost depths of his heart and stilled the fears there. Genevieve would be his forever, even past the grave, so what did life matter? But he had the feeling they would both have a great deal of white in their hair before they made their final journey together. He closed his eyes and gave thanks for a second chance. His life and his dreams had been restored and he would never forget the mercy of that gift.

Then his joy bubbled up within him and spilled over, making him laugh. He pushed Genevieve back and took her face in his hands. "*Mon Dieu*, how I love you!" He ran his hands over her face, over her hair, across her shoulders and down her arms. He kissed away her tears, then kissed her mouth. Beloved Genevieve!

She managed to escape his groping hands long enough to fling her arms around his neck. He caught her around the waist again and crushed her to him.

"Your mail!"

"I'm sorry," he grinned, not releasing her.

"I think I'll survive," she gasped.

"I hope so, for I vow I'll never let you from my arms again." He held her as close as he could and closed his eyes, savoring the feeling. How perfectly her slight body fit against his. How blissful was the feeling of her arms around his neck, holding onto him as if she would never relinquish him.

Then his stench hit him square in the nose. "By the saints, Gen, how can you bear my smell?" he gasped, pulling away. "And you're freezing."

"No, don't go yet," she said quickly.

"Oh, I'm not leaving," he reassured her. He hauled her up

into his arms, laughed at being able to accomplish it, then strode toward the dungeon door. He'd always meant to wall up the entrance to the dungeon but now he was glad he'd never gotten around to it. Worthington would have had a hell of a time getting him out. He ran lightly up the steps, relishing the feel of weariness in his muscles and his lady's cold fingers around his neck. "You're chilled, Gen. I daresay you'll need to shower with me to warm up."

"Kendrick!"

"We are betrothed," he grinned, striding down the passageway near the kitchens. "'Tis allowed."

"No way."

She would learn soon enough that he was merely teasing. He knew he would need to take his time with her, but his enthusiasm was too great to give way to reason at the moment. All he wanted to do was strip off his filthy clothes, bathe his sweaty body, then pull his lady back into his arms and keep her there until the priest could be fetched and the ceremony could be performed. Then he would continue to keep her in his arms until she grew used to the feel of him there, then he'd love her until she was breathless. His body stood up and applauded the idea.

Worthington came out into the great hall the same time they did. He was rubbing his eyes. "What is all the confounded racket?" he grumbled.

"Too much wine last night," Kendrick whispered loudly to his lady. "We'd best not demand breakfast quite yet."

Worthington did a double take of Genevieve in Kendrick's arms, then his eyes rolled back in his head and he slipped to the floor with a groan.

"Maybe later," Genevieve agreed.

Kendrick laughed as he stepped over his steward and carried his love across the hall. He would come down later and rouse Worthington, then order him to prepare a meal. For now, he had more important things to do, such as bathe, then kiss his lady senseless a time or two.

Aye, fiction had become reality and how sweet it was.

Chapter
Twenty-two

Genevieve sat on the counter in the bathroom and listened to Kendrick hum a medieval-sounding melody in the shower. It was too much to take in. She *had* felt his arms around her, hadn't she? She had felt his mail dig into her side as he carried her up the stairs. She had put her face against his dusty hair, felt the warmth of his skin beneath her fingertips. He was real, as solid and tangible as she was.

"This was worth waiting for," Kendrick groaned.

How different his voice sounded. Deeper, rougher. She smiled.

"It feels that good?"

"I think it would be better if you were in here with me, but that might be too much pleasure for this first day." He poked his head out from behind the curtain and winked at her. "We'll try it tomorrow."

She watched his fingers as they held the shower curtain. Real, corporeal hands. Hands that had held her, touched her face, traveled over her back and arms as Kendrick felt her to make sure he wasn't dreaming. Hands that could now easily slide her ring onto her hand and brush away her tears.

"Genevieve?"

She looked at his face and smiled weakly. Even with his hair dripping down around his face and dirt on his cheeks, he was beautiful.

"Come here."

She felt a blush begin to stain her cheeks. "Why?"

"Because it's been at least ten minutes since I last touched you. I want to make sure you haven't turned into a figment of my imagination."

She didn't know how he could joke about that, but he did seem determined to make light of it. He'd told her not to worry, that he had been given a second chance, that he would never leave her, but it would be a good long time before she relaxed completely.

Genevieve wiped her hands on her green pajamas as she hopped off the counter. Now to face her other great worry.

Kendrick was real.

That should have had her grinning from ear to ear. Instead, it made her enormously nervous. It was all good and fine to fall in love with a man possessing just slightly more substance than your imagination, to have him whisper things in your ear that made you blush, to imagine how it would feel to have him hold you and kiss you. It was another thing entirely to have that dream made flesh, and have that flesh be full of desires. Good grief, she'd only been kissed once, and that by Kendrick in his study the night before. Yes, they would surely have to wait a few months before they did anything else. Maybe he wouldn't mind putting off their wedding until they had progressed past the hand-holding stage, say in another year or so.

She put her hand into his wet palm and blushed as he raised her fingers to his lips. His lips were soft against her hand, his face rough from his whiskers. She felt butterflies take flight in her stomach as he pulled her even closer and lowered his head to hers.

The door burst open suddenly and Genevieve jumped back. She put her hand to her chest, over her pounding heart, and looked at a wide-eyed, disheveled Worthington. Even his normally obedient white hair was standing up all over his head.

"Am I dreaming?"

Kendrick frowned at him. "Eggs, ham, bacon, porridge, fresh rolls, some of those pancakes Gen likes so much and whatever else is in the icebox. And be quick about it. I'm starving."

Genevieve reached out and caught her butler as he swayed. He looked like he wanted to cry.

"I think I need a brandy," he whispered.

Genevieve understood the feeling completely.

"After you prepare my meal," Kendrick barked. "And I want a chocolate milk shake. Make haste, man. And call down to the village and make sure Adelaide's brother is about. We've a wedding to see accomplished." He shut the shower curtain with a snap.

Worthington put his shoulders back, dragged his hands through his hair and retreated from the bathroom. Genevieve swallowed nervously. A wedding? So soon? She eased herself up onto the counter again. Maybe Kendrick was teasing her.

He shut off the water with a curse.

"These tanks are too bloody small," he grumbled, flinging the curtain back. "How is a body supposed to enjoy a shower that lasts such a short time?"

Genevieve would have answered, but the words got stuck in her throat. Kendrick dragged his hands through his hair, leaving his body fully bared and flexed for her perusal. And what a magnificent body it was. His muscles were sleek and beautiful, not bulky and clumsy. Broad shoulders tapered down over a washboard stomach to slim hips and a flat belly.

She took in the sight of his groin and couldn't stop herself from gaping. Heaven preserve her if he really thought that was going to fit anywhere on her side of the room. The very thought made her want to bolt.

Legs. Yes, look at those legs. Sleek, powerful, tight. Covered with crisp, dark hair. In short, a perfect specimen of a man. Evidently wearing that heavy mail for so many years had certainly paid off. Yes, sir, it certainly had. Now if he would just cover up that finely packaged bit of masculinity so she could breathe again.

"Are you finished yet?"

His voice was laced with lazy amusement. She jerked her gaze back to his and found that his pale eyes were twinkling with unholy merriment. She jumped off the counter and reached for the door. A brawny arm snaked around her waist and she shrieked in spite of herself.

"You aren't going anywhere," he murmured into her ear. "Sit you back on this counter and wait for me."

She pressed her hands against the door and prayed for deliverance. "Hurry and dry off, would you?"

He chuckled as he released her. She heard him drag the towel across his body, then heard his murmur of pleasure. "Very soft cloths."

Genevieve nodded and continued to wait until Kendrick announced that he was finished. She turned around in time to have his towel put into her hands. He looked at her innocently.

"How does one wear that?"

She put it around his waist and tucked it securely, all the while keeping her eyes glued to his. "Like that."

"Thank you," he said solemnly. "Now you will give me a razor? And might I use your toothbrush? I'll send Worthington down for others this afternoon."

The toothbrush was produced and used rather skillfully. Shaving was accomplished in just as efficient a manner, with only a nick or two. She watched him, then blushed as he grinned at her in the mirror. Then his grin turned into a lazy smile that made her knees feel mushy under her. She backed away, intending to slip out the door before he noticed what she was doing. Holy moly, she wasn't ready for this!

"I'm not finished with you," he said in a low voice, catching her around the waist. He lifted her onto the counter then put his hands on either side of her. "Indeed, I've not even begun."

Genevieve wanted to move, but found she couldn't. Her heart beat wildly against her ribs, but whether it was from fear or nervousness, she couldn't tell. Little men made her nervous. Men the size of linebackers made her quake. It wasn't that she'd ever been hurt by one; she'd just never gotten close enough to one to know whether or not he would hurt her.

She had the feeling she was going to find out the truth of the matter immediately.

Genevieve watched as Kendrick took her hand in his, then slowly and carefully touched every part of her skin, starting with her fingers and finishing with her wrists. No scar was overlooked, no burn dismissed. He trailed his fingers over her palm, over knuckles, over the bones in her wrist. Then he brought her hand to his cheek and held it there, closing his eyes and rubbing his face against her palm. He reached for the other hand, then brought her fingers to his lips. He opened his eyes and looked down at her.

"You have beautiful hands."

It was the most astonishing compliment she had ever been given, made all the more remarkable by the fact that for the first time she felt it might be true. He put her hand on her legs, then urged her knees apart until he was standing between her thighs. Her instant protest died when he reached up to touch her hair. And then she forgot everything but the look on his face and the gentle touch of his hand. He fingered a lock of her hair as if he had never before touched anything like it, brought a handful to his nose to inhale the fragrance, then to his lips to taste it.

"Very soft," he murmured as he rubbed several strands against his cheek. "Very beautiful."

Genevieve couldn't move as he put his hands on her shoulders and trailed his thumbs along her collarbones, then up to her throat. His large, warm hands were gentle as he moved them up the sides of her neck and back under her hair. She held her breath as he bent down toward her. She forced herself to keep her eyes open and see him, instead of closing them and perhaps missing part of what was the most astonishing experience of her life.

Kendrick kept one of his hands at the base of her neck while the other came back to cup her cheek. He trailed his fingers over her face, looking intently at her, missing no detail. He traced her eyebrows, her nose, her cheeks, her jaw, her lips, touching her as if he feared he would break her.

"So beautiful," he whispered. He bent closer and smelled her hair again, then dipped his head and inhaled at her neck. "So sweet." He placed his smooth cheek against hers, then turned and pressed the softest of kisses against her ear. "You don't wear perfumed oils, do you?"

She shook her head, mute.

"Don't start," he said, nuzzling her neck with his nose. "You smell too good as is."

Shivers went down her spine at his touch. He kissed the hollow of her cheek, her cheekbones, the corner of her eye. He worked his way down her nose, then over her other cheek and down to her jaw.

"Tilt your head back," he urged softly, putting the flat of his hand behind her head to support it.

She obeyed him, too caught up in his spell to do anything else. "Will you vamp out on me and suck my blood?" she asked, attempting a joke. She knew she would faint soon if something didn't give. His gentleness was completely unnerving her!

He chuckled as he pressed his lips against her throat. "You read too many horror novels, my sweet. And you know I've given up my ghoulish status for good. I'm but a simple man now, held captive by the beauty of his lady."

"I see."

And then words deserted her at the feel of his firm lips against her skin. He left not an inch of her throat unkissed. His hand supported her head while his other arm came around her back and pulled her closer to him. Genevieve felt like a ragdoll in his arms, mindlessly reveling in the strange sensations his kisses brought her.

"How sweet your skin tastes, my Gen, and how salty from your tears. Forgive me for frightening you earlier."

"Forgiven," she breathed.

"Only tears of joy from now on," he murmured as he lifted his head to look down at her. He smiled, then slowly lowered his head and pressed his lips against hers. She closed her eyes and surrendered without a fight.

His exploration was slow and leisurely, but no less thorough. He tasted each part of her lips, nibbling at their fullness, then pressing his lips and the tip of his tongue against the corner of her mouth. When he traced the inner part of her lips with his tongue, she couldn't stop from opening her mouth to him.

He only ventured in far enough to taste the parts of her lips he hadn't reached before. She held her breath as he touched her teeth, then slid his tongue fully into her mouth. That was when the first moan escaped her. The nerves in her stomach sprang to life, making her feel the same jolt as she might have had she been in an elevator dropping down thirty stories. So this was the French kissing her mother had warned her about. Good grief, no wonder! Genevieve felt the soles of her feet begin to tingle.

Kendrick groaned deep in his throat, but his assault became no more forceful. He caressed her tongue with his over and over again, as if he simply could not taste her enough to satisfy himself. Genevieve put her arms around his neck simply to hold on. She opened her mouth further under his, urging him to take more, to give her more of that sweet, seductive heat that flowed so thickly through her veins.

A banging on the door almost sent her through the roof. She jerked back from him so quickly, she smacked her head against the mirror.

"Oh, Genevieve," Kendrick said with a chuckle of miserable laughter, pulling her close and rubbing the back of her head. "Come you here and hold on while I kill whoever has disturbed us." He held her to him with one arm and opened the door. "What do you want, busybody?"

Worthington was once again impeccably groomed. He took in Kendrick's appearance, looking down and clucking his tongue disapprovingly. Genevieve followed Worthington's eyes and more heat flooded to her cheeks when she noted, and who wouldn't have, the prominent bulge beneath Kendrick's towel. The sight gave her the strangest, most unnerving sensation in her stomach. No, that sensation was quite a bit lower than her stomach. She pushed back against the mirror and tried not to squirm when Worthington looked her way. She was certain she looked dazed. Worthington must have agreed because he gave Kendrick a reproving look.

"Your repast is almost prepared, my lord. I think it highly improper that you keep young Genevieve captive while you are so scantily clad."

Kendrick slammed the door in his face.

Worthington's *hrumph* could be heard clearly through the wood. "Ten minutes, my lord, and not a moment longer."

Kendrick looked at Genevieve with a scowl. "I'm going to send him on holiday. Tomorrow."

Genevieve felt a grin creep out. It was the first time she had seen that beloved scowl on those mortal features, and the sight delighted her. Then his scowl turned into a slow, lazy smile and she shook her head quickly. She ducked out of his arms, but Kendrick stopped her before her feet touched the floor.

"Oh, no you don't," he said huskily. "Just where do you think you're going?"

"I need to dress and so do you."

"We have ten more minutes."

"Your eggs will be cold. Let me go, Kendrick."

He took her face in his hands and lifted her eyes to his. A gentle smile curved over his lips.

"Thank you. You have given me great pleasure this morning."

She blushed and tried to pull away but he shook his head. He bent and brushed his lips across hers.

"I am in earnest."

"I haven't even showered yet, or washed my face—"

His expression sobered. "You don't desire me, then?"

"Kendrick," she squirmed.

"You're just nervous?"

She nodded.

"Gen, I haven't changed."

"You're a bit more substantial than you used to be, Kendrick."

"Call me *my love*, as you used to," he said softly. "Unless it no longer pleases you."

She hesitantly put her arms around his neck.

"I love you and I'm not afraid of you. My love," she added.

"Maybe you'd like to have me take a turn on that counter you're sitting on after breakfast?" he suggested politely. "Just to give me a closer look, of course."

"If you want."

"Don't sound so enthused," he said dryly.

"I didn't mean it like that."

"I did but attempt a poor jest. Come with me, my love."

She followed him out into the bedroom. They had kept clothes in his size in a trunk for appearance's sake, and Genevieve dug through it until she came up with things she hoped would fit. Kendrick had lost his towel somewhere between the bathroom and the bedroom and stood waiting patiently by the bed in all his glory. Genevieve blushed as she shoved the clothes into his hands.

"Good luck."

She retrieved her own garments and bolted for the bathroom. After a quick cold shower, she hastily put on underclothes, then washed her face and brushed her teeth. She had just pulled her jeans up over her hips when Kendrick opened the door, still naked, with a pair of jockey shorts in his hands. Whatever question he'd had died on his lips at the sight of her. He looked at her bare feet, then let his gaze roam over her legs, linger for some time at the fly of her jeans, which she hadn't gotten quite buttoned up, and then stop at her lacy bra. Genevieve crossed her arms over her breasts but he was instantly standing before her, pulling her arms away. He reached out hesitantly and fingered the elastic of the strap, then trailed his fingers down until they lightly brushed over the lace covering the top of her breast.

He pulled his hand away suddenly and turned. "Hurry," he said hoarsely.

Genevieve yanked a T-shirt and sweater down over her head, buttoned up her jeans and dragged a brush through her hair. Shoes would have to wait. The sooner Kendrick was covered up, the better she'd like it. She left the bathroom to find him sitting on the bed. He caught sight of her, then held out the briefs. And he scowled.

"Are these what I think they are?"

She nodded, biting her lip to keep from smiling.

"Well, they're too small. I'll be gelded by noon if I wear them."

She laughed, then jumped away as he reached out to swat her. "You stay there. I'll see what else I can find."

A few more minutes spent rummaging in his trunk produced a pair of boxer shorts. Kendrick nodded approvingly and put them on. Jeans and a sweatshirt completed his outfit. He wanted to go barefoot but she convinced him tennis shoes would be a better choice.

He caught her hand as they left the room. "You needn't make me sit on the counter in the bathroom this afternoon." He dropped her hand and shoved his hands into his pockets as if he'd been doing it all his life. "If it does not please you."

She looked up at him solemnly. "You think entirely too much, Kendrick de Piaget."

"I'll stop thinking if you'll stop fearing me."

"I'm trying."

"I love you, Gen. I'd never hurt you. How can you think that?"

She had the feeling that little-boy pout was going to get her every time. She gave in and put her arms around his waist, albeit hesitantly. When he didn't move, she took her courage in hand and snuggled a bit closer to him. He was all muscle, but comfortable enough. She laid her head against his chest, then relaxed as he put his arms around her and began to gently stroke her back.

She was just starting to get the hang of the hugging business when Kendrick's stomach growled loudly. She pulled her head back and found that he was blushing.

"I forgot you were hungry," she said, feeling his blush somehow begin to plaster itself to her cheeks.

"That's a very good sign."

She blushed some more and nodded, feeling utterly foolish.

Kendrick only smiled gently and kissed her quickly on the forehead.

"Food first, then perhaps we'll come back to this very spot and I'll pout some more for you. You liked it, didn't you?"

Genevieve wasn't about to tell him what she liked, as she had the feeling he'd know it anyway. She took his hand and let him lead her down the hall. Her gallant ghost was hungry and she wasn't going to stand in the path of his breakfast.

Chapter
Twenty-three

Kendrick's mind reeled. Smells assaulted him from every angle: the shampoo he had used, the soap Genevieve used to wash her face with, the fabric of his sweatshirt, the charring wood in the hearths below, the delicacies Worthington was cooking. He had to force himself not to bolt down the stairs and fall upon the food like a savage.

And the feel of things! He trailed his fingers along the smooth stone as they walked down the curving staircase. He smiled in appreciation of the softness of Genevieve's hand curled in his, their fingers laced together. The sweatshirt was smooth against his chest, the jeans a bit rough as they pulled at the hair on his legs. The rubber of his shoes squeaked as he walked down the steps.

A gust of cool air hit him full in the face as they rounded the last of the steps. He gasped and pulled up short.

"Kendrick?"

He looked down at Genevieve. "Drafty old pile of stones, isn't it?"

"I suppose you hadn't noticed before."

He grinned as he scooped her up into his arms. "Nay, saucy wench, I hadn't noticed before."

She put her arms around his neck. He noticed her hesitancy, but pretended to pay it no heed. She would accustom herself to him in time.

"Don't drop me."

He smiled. "A knight never drops his lady. It's bad form." He winked at her, then descended the remaining steps to his great hall. Already Genevieve came more readily into his arms. Aye, she would grow accustomed to him soon enough.

There was so much to touch and smell, he hardly knew where to begin. He let Genevieve slip down to her feet, then took her hand and dragged her along behind him. First there were the tapestries. Faintly rough under his fingers, a good woolly sort of feeling. So delightfully musty smelling. Then the stone of the hearth. Aye, it was well cut and well laid. He put his hand to the cold stone of the mantel, then smiled as the warmth from the fire hit him. How much he had missed even such simple pleasures. What was more soothing than a hot fire and warm wine after a morning in the lists in the dead of winter when a man's body heat never quite warmed up his mail? And how refreshing it was to spend hours under the hot sun, fighting or training, then find a cool barrel of rainwater handy for dunking the head?

He paused, catching another whiff of Worthington's work. Without saying a word, he pulled Genevieve toward the kitchen. What heavenly smells.

"Not so fast," Genevieve laughed, running to keep up with his long strides.

Kendrick only threw her a smile and kept on. By the saints, he was starved! He plunked his lady down into a chair, then advanced on the ovens. Reaching out to steal a flat cake only earned him a sharp rap with a spoon from his steward.

"Sit down and wait, as befits gentlefolk."

Kendrick opened his mouth to retort, then felt Genevieve tug on his arm. He turned his frown on her, but she wasn't impressed. He grumbled at her as she led him over to the table and pushed him down in a chair.

"Behave."

He sat back with another frown, vowing under his breath to eat the table if sustenance wasn't supplied posthaste. He watched as Genevieve picked up a plate and walked over to the stove. He suppressed the urge to rise, haul her against him and ravage her mouth. His blood was still fired with the sweet kisses he'd stolen up in the bathroom. With any luck at all, he'd have more of them as quickly as possible. Surely Genevieve would see her way clear to indulge him in that, wouldn't she?

"Worthington," Genevieve said as she began to fill the plate, "he's liable to skewer us and set us to roast over the fire if we're not careful. I think we'll have to forgo politeness in favor of safety this morning."

Kendrick flexed his fingers as she set down a plate heaped full of various exceedingly edible-looking provisions in front of him. She caught his hand as he reached out to snatch a tasty-looking bit of meat.

"Silverware, Kendrick."

He looked dubiously at the fork she offered him. "Never saw the need for those. We didn't have them in my day."

"Well, your day is now 1996 and we use forks. And that's spicy sausage you're eyeing. It'll burn your mouth."

"I am perfectly capable of deciding what I will and will not eat," he said, ignoring the fork, reaching for a link with his fingers and popping it in his mouth. It was blisteringly hot and so spicy that his eyes began to water. He stubbornly continued to chew, blinking rapidly. By the saints, his mouth was on fire! Genevieve laughed and handed him a glass of milk. He downed it in a single gulp.

"Wonderful," he gasped.

She pulled out the chair on his right and dropped down into it. "You'd better fry up more of that sausage, Worthington. His Lordship loves it."

Kendrick flashed her a scowl before he turned back to his plate and examined what was left. He tore off a hunk of bread and munched on it as he tried to decide what would be the least humiliating of the meats to try next. Not having paid attention to mortal fodder for the past few centuries had left him feeling rather ignorant. At least the bread was something he knew how to eat. And how fine it was, completely free of the rocks and dirt that had always seasoned the bread he had eaten during his time.

"Try the ham," Genevieve suggested. "Smoked, but fairly mild."

He took her suggestion and knew heaven the moment the meat touched his tongue. He closed his eyes and groaned as he chewed.

"That good?"

He looked up to find Genevieve smiling at him gently.

"Bliss," he sighed.

Suddenly, her eyes filled with tears. He washed down the contents of his mouth with another swig of milk, deciding right then that he definitely preferred ale, then pulled Genevieve into his arms. She began to weep; great, heaving sobs of pure misery.

"Genevieve, by the saints, what ails you? Are my manners so poor?"

That jest only served to make her weep the more. He looked at Worthington who held up his hands in a helpless gesture. Kendrick tucked his lady's head into the crook of his neck and began to rock her slowly.

"My love, what troubles you so?" he whispered.

"I'm so afraid," she said, clutching him as if she feared hell itself planned to instantly spirit him away.

"Of what? There's nothing to fear."

"What if something happens to you?"

"My sweet Gen, nothing is going to happen to me. Didn't I ask you to trust me? I've been given another chance. *We've* been given another chance. I'll be right here by you for the rest of your life. We have years to do all the things we talked about doing: traveling, restoring old castles, having children."

"Excuse me, Your Lordship, but how many children?" Worthington interrupted dryly.

"How many would it take to make you daft?" Kendrick said, fighting his smile.

"If they were to be anything like their sire, the thought of even one makes me shudder."

Kendrick chuckled and gave Genevieve a squeeze. "Do you hear, my love? Wouldn't it please you to make our illustrious busybody daft? How will we do that if I'm not here to father a few children by you?" She didn't answer, but at least her tears were beginning to cease. "Gen, I will not leave you. I vow it. You'll doubtless be enormously weary of me by the time we're old."

She pulled back and shook her head. "I could never grow tired of you."

He put his finger under her chin and tipped her face up for his kiss. Such sweet lips, wet with salty tears. He wondered if he would ever taste her mouth enough to satisfy himself.

"My lady, you'll never know just how long it will take to tire of His Lordship if you do not feed him."

Genevieve pulled back and smiled up at Kendrick. "I think that's a fancy way of reminding me that your breakfast is getting cold."

Kendrick gave Worthington a dark look. "What he's trying to tell me is how desperately he needs an extended holiday."

Worthington set down more dishes piled high with pancakes, eggs, rolls and fruit. "You would starve without me."

Genevieve smiled. "Worthington, I'll cook for him for a bit."

"And I'll help her," Kendrick said firmly. "After the wedding tomorrow, you're officially on holiday. Take a cruise. Go to the Colonies, or the south of France. I'll pay for whatever you want."

"Anything?" Worthington said, his ears perking up.

"Aye," Kendrick grumbled. "You deserve it. Go make your plans. I'll clean up the kitchen."

Worthington didn't need to hear that twice. He was nothing but a flurry of coattails as he scuttled from the kitchen. Kendrick reached for the eggs and began inhaling them.

"Tomorrow?"

He stopped chewing. "Too soon?"

Genevieve shook her head, but he knew that the thought

made her nervous. He settled her more comfortably in his lap
and began chewing again.

"We don't have to consummate the marriage right away,"
he offered.

She gulped and said nothing.

After he'd stuffed three slices of ham into his mouth at
once, he gave the matter more thought. He could wait to love
her. For a few more hours. Surely by then she would have
grown accustomed to him.

Or so he hoped.

Kendrick spent the rest of the afternoon planning. Organiz-
ing sieges had always been one of his strengths and he put that
skill to good use in planning his wedding. He tucked
Genevieve into bed for a nap, then set to work arranging all
the proper documents and procuring Adelaide's brother for the
ceremony.

And then he spent the remainder of the afternoon trying to
get over the shock of having watched Royce and Nazir walk
into the hall, as tangible as he was. They spent the afternoon in
the kitchen, discussing both the significance of Genevieve's
having signed the deed and the definite improvements that had
been made in mortal fodder since the Middle Ages. By the
time night fell, Kendrick had broken up two fights between his
captain and his Saracen, eaten enough to make himself sick
and put the finishing touches on the ceremony to be performed
the next day. He'd assured himself again that Genevieve's
wedding present had been prepared as he'd requested, then
sent his lady off to bed.

By the time he retired, he was wide-awake and frustrated.
He could hear Genevieve tossing restively in the next chamber. He wanted to go to her, but knew better than to do it.
There was something troubling her, something she obviously
didn't want to share with him. Not that he'd had time to question her. Nay, he'd been far too busy plotting and planning.
And he was currently suffering because of it. If only she
would trust him! Didn't she know he loved her more than life,
that there wasn't anything he wouldn't do to make her happy?

He sighed. Tomorrow they would be wed, then he would eject all the guests from his hall and have a very long talk with his lady and find out just what sorts of things were going through her overactive mind. A pity his return to life had signaled an end to his mind-reading capabilities. They certainly would have made things a great deal simpler.

He closed his eyes. Tomorrow. He would solve all their problems tomorrow.

Chapter
Twenty-four

Genevieve tiptoed into Kendrick's chamber, wanting to make sure he slept soundly. The light from the candle by his bed cast warm shadows over him. How innocent he looked in sleep, almost harmless. She reached out to smooth the hair back from his face.

Her hand went through him and touched the pillow.

"Kendrick!" she screamed. He didn't move. She tried to shake him but her hands clutched nothing. "Kendrick!" she screamed, over and over again, overcome by the terror she had been fighting all day. "Kendrick!" she sobbed, clutching at shoulders that were not there.

"Genevieve, wake up!"

She opened her eyes. Kendrick had his hands on her shoulder, shaking her. She sat up with a cry and threw her arms around him.

"Oh, Kendrick, I dreamed you were a ghost again. I tried to wake you, to touch you, but I couldn't feel you!"

Kendrick pulled her from her bed, swung her up in his arms

and strode from the guest room. "We'll go lie down and I'll hold you. That will soothe you."

He was naked. Lie down with a naked man? The thought was like a bucket of ice water thrown in her face. Her reason, and her apprehension, returned with a rush.

"Oh, but I'm all right," she said quickly. "Kendrick, take me back. I can't sleep with you tonight."

"I'll not take you, Genevieve."

"But—"

"Enough," he said firmly. "I've spent the past two hours tossing and turning and listening to you do the same. This is foolishness."

She couldn't argue with him. It had taken her two hours to fall into a very uneasy sleep and that sleep had resulted in a horrifying nightmare. Perhaps if she held onto his hand while they slept, her fears would be eased.

Kendrick shut the bedroom door behind them and walked to the bed. He pulled back the covers and laid her down. Even by the faint light of the dying fire in the hearth, she caught a full view of his nakedness. She jerked the covers over her head.

"Put some clothes on," she whispered frantically.

She heard him sigh heavily, rummage around in the room, curse heartily as he stubbed his toe, then sigh again as he slid under the covers next to her.

"Are these strange, thick hose without feet enough or must I dress completely?" he grumbled.

She threw the covers off and escaped the bed on the other side, tears of humiliation already stinging her eyes. Kendrick caught her before she reached the door. He turned her around and gathered her close.

"Forgive me, Genevieve. 'Twas a foolish thing to say."

"Let me go. I'll go back to my own room and you can sleep however you want."

Kendrick was silent but he did not release her. Finally the soothing motion of his hand skimming over her hair teased her into relaxing. She leaned against his broad chest, his warm skin and the steady beating of his heart soothing her further. He put his arm around her shoulders and led her over to the hearth. After tossing another pair of logs onto the fire, he sat down in the large chair and drew her down onto his lap. He put his hand under her chin and lifted her face up.

"Having a body again has allowed me to slip into old habits," he said softly. "In my time, I never wore a stitch of clothing to sleep in. After wearing mail day and night while I was away and not changing clothes for weeks on end, being free of the confinement was a heady pleasure."

"You can sleep however you—"

He put his hand over her mouth.

"It was thoughtless of me to parade about naked before you. I should not have done it this morning after I showered, nor should I have done it tonight. This morning I was teasing you and tonight I was in too much haste to gain your room to think of clothing. The fault is mine."

"I don't mean to be a prude," she whispered.

"It is proper that you are shy. I am a thoughtless knave to have embarrassed you thusly." He leaned forward and pressed his lips against her cheek. "Forgive me."

"Why are you so sweet?"

"I do it to redeem myself for all the times I have been so impossible."

"You've never been impossible."

"Give me a chance," he said, in a stage whisper. He pressed his lips against her hair. "Let's go wash away those tears, then go to bed. You don't want your eyes to be red tomorrow. Royce will challenge me on the spot if he thinks I've driven you to weep already."

She nodded and rose. Kendrick took her hand and led her to the bathroom. He flipped on the light, then winced right along with her at the brightness.

"Candles were easier on the eye," he muttered as he wetted a washcloth.

"I believe it," she agreed as he tilted her face up and gently washed her cheeks and eyes. He patted her face dry with a soft cloth, then flicked off the light. Genevieve followed him back into the bedroom, then slipped under the covers and shivered as Kendrick banked the fire. He came back to her and sat down on the edge of the bed.

"Afraid of ghosts?" he teased.

"I still don't think I've forgiven you for the arrow coming out of your chest. That was disgusting."

He grinned. "I thought it marginally clever. I didn't even get a good scream out of you."

"You didn't deserve one, you jerk. I hope it was the most unsatisfying week of your life."

"It was." He leaned over and pressed a kiss against her forehead. "Go to sleep, my love. I'll keep watch."

"Where?"

"By the fire," he said, rising.

"But you can't sleep there."

"You would rather have me in your bed?"

Genevieve searched for something to say besides the truth.

"Your silence answers for you, my lady."

"Oh, Kendrick, it isn't you." Then she felt herself blush. "Well, it is you. Sort of."

"There is no law that says the marriage must be consummated tomorrow night."

"It has to happen sometime."

"You flatter me. Nay, I know," he said gruffly, as she started to rise, "you did not intend it thusly."

Genevieve wanted to say something to reassure him, but came up with nothing. The shocks she'd endured that day had taken their toll on her. The knowledge that she would actually be married the next day was the final straw. It wasn't the marriage that made her nervous; it was the after part. Kendrick had been a good sport about it that day, but probably only because he'd been too busy putting out fires to pay her much attention. Tomorrow everyone would leave and she would be alone with him. She knew he would never hurt her, but he would certainly want to be close to her. Physically. Intimately.

The thought made her want to bolt.

She watched him sit down in front of the fire and stretch out his long legs.

"Kendrick?"

"Aye."

"Will it hurt?"

He paused. "A bit."

He obviously knew what she was talking about. "A bit?" she prodded.

"Somewhere between *ouch* and *slit my throat, if you please.*"

Oh, goodness.

Kendrick stood at the altar of his chapel and held his lady's hand in his. This was the moment he'd thought would never come. Genevieve was his. He looked down at her surreptitiously and felt his heart swell within him. How beautiful she looked in the antique wedding dress Adelaide had provided. Her hair was piled atop her head with a few tendrils hanging down in ringlets over her neck and temples. Kendrick's fingers itched to take it down and bury his hands in it. Sweet, sweet Genevieve.

He was given leave to kiss her and he did, though not nearly as thoroughly as he would have liked. For one thing, she was stiff as a sword in his arms. Perhaps it was wedding jitters. Goodness knows he might have felt them himself, had he not been so eager to bind her to him. Genevieve was different, though. He knew he made her nervous, but had no idea how to ease her fears. If their marriage was to be something other than in name only, he would have to bed her. Though the very thought sent blood rushing to strategic parts of his anatomy, it likely sent fear rushing through her veins.

Patience, Seakirk. It would take patience to show her he could bring her pleasure. And he was a patient man. He'd waited seven hundred years for her. What was a few more days?

He held one of his wife's icy hands between his own and strove to warm it. It was useless. She was as skittish as a mare in a stable full of randy stallions. As if he intended to bed her on the spot!

Patience. He had enough, didn't he?

By late afternoon, he was busy shooing everyone from the keep. Worthington was certain he and Genevieve would starve and had made Adelaide promise to check on them every other day. Worthington was planning a cruise to the Greek islands but had promised to call from each port. Kendrick told him not to bother.

Royce was looking forward to a fortnight or two spent boarding at Adelaide's and being introduced to all the eligible maidens in the area. He had been the first one out the door when the time to leave had come. Nazir, on the other hand, did *not* want to go. He wasn't at all enthusiastic about the prospect of staying with Mistress Adelaide, as he was sure the woman would poison him if given the chance. Kendrick smothered his smile at the looks his brave Saracen and Mistress Adelaide were exchanging. He sincerely hoped she had insurance for her shop. It was impossible to predict what mischief Nazir could combine.

Kendrick stood on the top step of the hall and watched as the procession drove off. He rolled his eyes as Nazir threw Genevieve one last pleading look from the back window.

"However many children we have, we may as well add one more to the number," he grumbled.

"Nazir is hopelessly fond of you."

"Nay, he's fond of you. I daresay he thinks to have you wrapped about his little finger. If he wants something, he heads straight for the soft touch in the family."

"Soft touch? How un-medieval of you, my lord."

"You want medieval?" he asked politely. "Why didn't you say so?"

Without warning, he dumped her over his shoulder and strode back into the house, pausing only long enough to lock and bolt the doors to the great hall.

"Kendrick, I'll throw up on you."

He hastily rearranged her in his arms. "You've a weak stomach, my love."

"I'm starving. Have we eaten today?"

He smiled as he started toward the stairs. "I'm rubbing off on you. Let's change and then perhaps we'll come back down and have a second dinner. I could eat one without too much trouble." *Good, Seakirk. Distract her with food.* The less she thought about what was to come, the better off she'd be.

Once they reached their bedroom, Genevieve made a bee-line for the bathroom. Kendrick stripped off his medieval garb, clothing that had been cleaned and mended just for the wedding, and donned his favorite pair of sweat bottoms. Exceedingly comfortable garments. He didn't care for the way they left his feet exposed, but socks took care of that easily enough.

He waited for Genevieve to reappear. Then he waited some more. No water was running in the bathroom. What was she doing? He paced for another quarter hour until he could bear it no longer. He strode over to the door and knocked.

"Gen?"

"Coming," she said weakly.

The water turned on immediately and he heard soft splashing noises.

"Gen, can I come in?"

"Sure," she said. Her voice cracked on the word.

Kendrick opened the door swiftly, then caught sight of her white face. Oh, why had he never tried to seduce an unwilling virgin before now? It would have made the task ahead so much easier.

He left the door open as he approached. No sense in making her feel as if she had no escape. He stopped a foot in front of her and held out his hand.

"Come to me, wife," he said soothingly. "You look chilled."

She put her hand into his with all the enthusiasm of a woman digging into the garbage disposal for a lost earring. Kendrick knew that exact look because he'd seen her dig for one in the kitchen the week before. He tried not to let that wound his pride.

He drew her carefully into his arms and clenched his jaw when her icy fingers came into contact with his bare back. By the saints, the woman's fingers rivaled ice cubes!

"Genevieve," he whispered, pained, "I won't hurt you."

She nodded, her head jerking.

"Sweetheart, please relax." He pulled back and tipped her face up, giving her his most winsome smile. It was a smile that showed off his dimple to its greatest advantage. He knew that, because he'd spent a goodly amount of time practicing while looking in a polished silver platter during his youth.

It had absolutely no effect on his wife.

He sighed, then swept her up into his arms. When words failed, action was the only recourse. He carried her to the bed, laid her down, then stretched out beside her. She sat up, her feet already moving down toward the floor.

"Genevieve—"

"I forgot something."

"You forgot nothing. Come you here." He tugged her back down. "Don't move," he ordered as he leaned down and pulled up the blanket. He covered them both, then drew her into his arms. "Genevieve, by the saints, I've no plans to ravish you. Let me warm you, then we'll turn our minds to other things."

Her trembles only increased. "What other things?"

Kendrick sighed in exasperation. "Food, for pity's sake!"

She started to cry.

He started to swear.

"Genevieve, by all the saints above, get hold of yourself!"

"I can't do this," she wept. "Kendrick, I just can't do this yet."

"We don't have to—"

"I'm so s-sorry," she hiccuped. "I thought I c-could. R-really."

Kendrick drew her closer, but that only made her trembles increase. By St. George's bones, that wounded him! He was the one person she should have felt the safest with, yet his embrace terrified her.

He released her slowly and didn't stop her when she turned away. Her tears wrenched at his heart, even more so because he knew he was the cause of them.

He listened to her weep far into the evening, then remained motionless behind her as she finally drifted off into an exhausted sleep.

Patience? He smiled grimly. He hadn't possessed a smidgen of it. He'd been too eager to wed her to give her time to adjust truly to the changes in their lives. Aye, and he'd been eager to bed her. In fact, he was still eager. His body clamored for his attention, reminding him uncomfortably of just how pleasant making love could be. And to love Genevieve? Ah, that thought put him in agony. To feel her naked body pressed against his, her slender fingers tangled in his hair. To hear her soft moans of pleasure and her words of love whispered in his ear. Imagining it, when she lay only inches from him, was sheer torture!

But it was torture entirely of his own making. He should have given her time to adjust. He'd known just how little experience she'd had with men. Aye, she'd accepted him willingly enough before, but he'd been only slightly more substantial than the knight of her dreams. And now? Now, he was flesh and blood, bone and sinew, possessing desires that she didn't understand and couldn't help but fear. And instead of thinking with his head, he'd thought with another part of his anatomy and hurried her along through a wedding she'd obviously not enjoyed and into a wedding night she'd been terrified of. And now she lay exhausted from weeping.

Pitiful, Seakirk.

He waited until dawn, then rose and carefully gathered his clothes. With any luck, Genevieve would sleep far into the morning and not miss him until he was already gone.

If it was time she needed, then it was time she would have.

Chapter
Twenty-five

"Kendrick?"

Genevieve put her head inside his study door. Empty. She entered the room and closed the door behind her. No reason to panic yet—just because she'd woken to find herself alone with no sign whatsoever of her husband. Maybe he was out riding. He hadn't had time to do so since his return to life, and she knew he was itching to be back up in the saddle.

She walked into his private den and sat down at his desk. She leaned back and looked up at the portrait of his family. How happy they looked. And how content Lady Anne looked, in spite of the fact that Lord Robin looked every bit as lusty as his son. Genevieve felt herself blush uncomfortably. How had Anne managed to, well, do it?

Genevieve groaned and put her head down on Kendrick's desk. What a disaster. Last night wasn't how it was supposed to have happened. She had planned to be warm and loving, stoically braving any pain to give Kendrick pleasure. Somehow, things had gone horribly wrong.

It had started the moment reality had set in. She'd let herself be caught up in the fact that Kendrick was now a corporeal man and would expect things she didn't think she could give. Even if she'd wanted to talk to him about it, which she hadn't, she wouldn't have had the chance. She knew Kendrick had lots on his mind—goodness knows he had his hands full just controlling Royce and Nazir. That couldn't have been helped. She wasn't particularly proud of her reaction once he'd woken her from her nightmare, but what did he expect? For her to jump in bed with him right away?

The more she'd thought about making love with him, the more nervous she'd become. Her wedding had been a joke. Her lips had been so tight with strain, she'd barely managed a coherent "I do." And then last night! She had the feeling that her falling to pieces wasn't exactly how Kendrick had envisioned his wedding night proceeding. It hadn't been her ideal dream either. If only they'd had more time, just a few days to start over and get to know each other as two normal people did, with stolen touches and kisses building to intimacy, instead of merely a few words spoken over their heads and then instant union . . .

Unfortunately, there hadn't been the luxury of time. She was just going to have to get hold of herself and stop acting like a child. She was a married woman, for heaven's sake. She loved Kendrick. Making love with him would be wonderful.

And there was another, more startling revelation she had come to, a realization that had begun when she'd thought Kendrick had been turned back into a ghost.

Her dream hadn't been taken away. It had been fulfilled. Kendrick, the knight of her dreams, had been made flesh. And for the first time since the change, she couldn't have been happier about it.

She wanted him to know about it. Immediately. She rose from the desk, waved to his family and left the study. Maybe he was downstairs in the kitchen fixing himself a snack. If there was one thing the man could do, it was eat.

The kitchen was empty. So was the great hall. Genevieve felt her palms grow damp. It wasn't possible that something had happened to him. Oh, not now, not after she'd come to her senses, not after she'd realized truly how deeply she loved him.

She checked the other bedrooms. Nothing. She even checked the door downstairs she still couldn't open. It was a door off the great hall leading to a room she had seen only once, a smaller room, almost like a family room. It had been locked since before Christmas and Genevieve had heard all sorts of pounding going on inside, usually at night. Trying to get Kendrick to divulge all the details had been even harder than trying to get Worthington to do the same. She stood at the door and pounded, calling Kendrick's name.

No answer.

All right, this wasn't funny anymore. She ran to the front door, opened it, and sprinted down the steps. It was bitterly cold outside but it didn't faze her. She ran to the stables. Nothing but horses. Not even the groom was there to answer her questions. She sat down on a bale of hay and thought about crying. She would have, too, if she hadn't been so upset. It was impossible! She had had Kendrick long enough to marry him, push him away for a night, and lose him?

She couldn't believe it. There had to be another explanation. Maybe he'd gone to the village for something. He had probably left her a note and she had been too distraught to find it.

The phone was ringing when she entered the hall. She ran to the kitchen and reached for the portable on the counter. The unit was there but the phone was gone. She followed the sound of the ringing through the kitchen and into the pantry. The shelves revealed nothing but food.

Aha! She shoved her hand into a pile of folded towels and came up with the handset.

"Hello?" she said breathlessly.

"Uh, Lady Seakirk, this is Johnny. At the outer gates?"

Genevieve's chest tightened. Great. More thugs at the doors.

"Yes? What is it?"

"My lady, I doubt you'll believe this . . ."

Wonderful. Maybe they were coming in by the truckload this time. It was tempting to hoist a white flag.

"But there's a man here at the gates on a horse."

A horse?

"A horse?" she echoed herself.

"Aye, milady. And dressed all in armor the man is."

Genevieve put her hand over her chest; her heart thumped against it furiously. "Well, why don't you ask him who he is?"

Johnny covered the phone with his hand and took her suggestion, except he bellowed his question. There was silence, then his voice back on the line.

"My lady, he says he's come awooin' and 'tis none of my bloody business who he is."

Genevieve felt a giddy relief flood through her veins.

"My lady, I hate to spoil the surprise, but I'm sure 'tis His Lordship. There's not another in the area with quite the same frown. And he threatened to send me packing if I didn't open up to him right quick."

"Then by all means," she said, starting to feel light-headed, "let him in."

She put the phone down slowly, not needing to hear any explanation for what Kendrick was doing. Damn him, he'd listened to her dreams that one day in his den, the first time she'd touched his hand. A blush of mortification warred fiercely with a blush of pleasure. So he was coming to see her as he would have in his time.

A dress. She needed a dress. She fled from the kitchen, across the great hall, up the stairs and down the corridor to her bedroom. Adelaide had given her a medieval costume as a wedding gift. Genevieve knew she'd have a heck of a time getting the dress on, but she'd do it. With any luck, Kendrick would ride slowly and she'd be ready for him.

It was a simple, straight sheath with a generous amount of material. She cinched the leather belt around her waist and let it fall down over her hips as she'd seen it worn in pictures. No time for something to cover her hair with. Kendrick would just pull it off anyway.

Shoes. Damn, where were her shoes? She searched frantically for the little slippers Adelaide had given her. Not to be found. She shoved her hand in the armoire and pulled out the first thing her hands encountered.

Her pink bunny slippers.

Well, they'd never show. She shoved her feet into them and slipped and slid as she ran for the great hall. *Please let him ride slowly.* She wanted to be at the top of the steps when he rode into the courtyard.

She came to a skidding halt a hand's breadth from the front door. After panting for a moment or two, she pulled open the door and looked out. The portcullis for the inner bailey was just being raised and a lone horseman rode underneath it. Genevieve closed the door behind her and composed herself on the top step.

It was Kendrick. He wore his mail coif pushed back off his head, revealing his long, dark hair. She easily recognized the gray cloth of his tabard and the lion embroidered in black. She never would have mistaken that lion for another, especially with the color of its eye. The sunlight glanced off his sword, setting fire to the emerald in the hilt. Genevieve swallowed, wishing her mouth weren't so dry. How in the world could any woman have resisted him? She felt terrible about having done it the night before. She had probably missed out on the night of her life.

Kendrick came to a halt near the bottom step, sat back and stared at her. For a split second, she wondered if he'd lost his memory again. Then the slightest of smiles crossed his lips. He lifted his hand and crooked his finger at her.

She walked down the stairs on shaking legs, stopping next to his horse. He looked down at her.

"I understand Her Ladyship has an abundance of dragons to be slain. I've come to do the deed."

She smiled. "There are several, brave knight, and I think it will take quite a few days to do it. I don't suppose you'd want to stick around, would you?"

"Aye, I would."

He wasn't moving. Well, perhaps he needed prodding.

"Should we seal the bargain with a handshake?"

"Something less personal, to be sure."

Sweet Kendrick. "A kiss then?"

He scowled down at her. "Aye, that will do. Come up here, wench. 'Twould take too much energy to dismount and ravish you."

He held down his hand. She took it, then lifted her skirts and put her foot on his. Kendrick hauled her up and into his arms. Genevieve put her arms around his neck, then pressed her face in his hair.

"I'm sorry," she whispered. "About last night."

He pulled back to look at her. "For as well as we know each other, it hasn't prepared us to be lovers, has it?"

She shook her head, slowly.

"Then we'll see to that, too." He pressed his lips gently against her forehead. "Let me tend my stallion, then I'll join you inside."

"I'll come with you," she volunteered.

A wry smile touched his lips. "Then you missed me this morning?"

"Very much."

He turned the horse around with his knees, then clucked his tongue. Genevieve wrapped her arms around his neck and held on.

"We aren't galloping, my love."

"No, but we're a long way off the ground."

"And here I thought you just didn't want me escaping."

"Kendrick, has anyone ever told you that you do a lot of fishing?"

"Fishing?"

"For compliments."

"I do not."

"Yes, you do. All the time. Am I so stingy with them?" She looked up into his pale green eyes and groaned. "No, don't start with the pouting again. I compliment you more than is good for you. You're not suffering any."

"A knight can never have too many compliments from his lady," he said solemnly.

He swung down from his horse once they reached the stables, held up his arms for her, then stopped. He lifted the hem of her dress and caught an eyeful of her slippers. He grinned up at her.

"My wife, the fashion plate."

His wife. Maybe it was just beginning to sink in, or maybe it was that he had dressed up in his uncomfortable mail to make her feel like a damsel in distress, or maybe it was his dimple peeking out at her so mischievously. Whatever the reason, his term sounded heavenly and she couldn't stop smiling.

"I was in a hurry."

He tugged on one of her toes. "To see anyone I know?"

"You're fishing again."

"I can't help it." He swung her down into his arms. "Sit you on this bale of hay and admire my fine form while I see to my mount. And keep your feet up. You don't want your bunnies getting damp."

Genevieve sat back against the opposite stall door and felt herself be carried back in time hundreds of years. The sounds that filled the air were of mail and leather creaking, the soft stamping and snorting of the horses around her and Kendrick's deep whisper as he talked to his horse in French. Her husband's first language was Norman French; how astonishing! It made her wish the boundaries of time would thin just long enough for them to escape back into his world. How would it have been to have Kendrick as her knight in truth? To know that her safety, even her very life, depended on his skill?

And how would it have been to ride with him to Artane and meet his family? Would his parents have cared for her at all, or would they have wished Kendrick had chosen another? She was almost tempted to ask him to take her there anyway, so she could see where he had grown up. Unfortunately, the castle was probably not even close to what it had looked like in the Middle Ages. It might be too painful for him to see it changed.

"Genevieve?"

She looked up and caught her breath. It wasn't that she wasn't accustomed to his handsomeness, or his finely built body. She was. She was also very familiar with that knee-buckling, sexy smile of his. No, her abrupt loss of breath had nothing to do with those things. Or perhaps everything to do with those things.

This man was hers.

And he wanted to woo her.

He walked over to her purposefully, hauled her up into his arms and gave her a mock frown.

"I hunger, wench."

She put her arms around his neck. "Well? What are you going to hunt us for dinner?"

"I'll slay a few steaks from the freezer."

"You're so brave."

"Ah, a compliment," he said, sounding supremely pleased. "I would have more of them. Perhaps while I am in the act of subduing the refrigerator with my sword. My prowess in battle was always greatly revered."

She smiled and pressed her lips against his cheek. "I'll cook supper. I doubt you'll have the strength after all your efforts in gathering the goods."

He only grunted again, arrogantly, and strode back to the house.

Kendrick sat at the long kitchen table with his legs stretched out and watched his wife as she puttered about in her medieval gown with those ridiculous slippers. Kendrick felt a surge of affection for her well up inside him and he couldn't help but act on it. He jumped to his feet, whirled her around and planted a smacking kiss on her startled mouth.

"You are adorable," he grinned.

She laughed at him. "Why?"

"Because you just are." He kissed her again quickly, spun her back around and threw himself back down in his chair. Genevieve put her hand to her head, obviously to stop it from spinning, then looked over her shoulder at him.

"Are you feeling all right?"

He smiled and nodded. What he wanted to do was get up again and kiss her senseless. Instead, he remained firmly planted in his chair. He wasn't going to make the same mistake again. He would woo Genevieve de Piaget until she was positively dizzy from his efforts, but he wouldn't touch her until she touched him first. It might take him a month to woo her to his bed, but he could wait. Having her come to him willingly was worth any amount of patience.

Heaven help him.

He sat back and smiled, deciding that things were going rather well so far. It had been an hour since he'd swept his love up onto his horse and in that hour Genevieve had laughed more than she had in the past week. He'd made a fool of himself by stalking the refrigerator with his sword, then doing the same to the microwave until he'd announced that they were both properly intimidated. Genevieve had laughed so hard, she'd cried. He would have stalked the rest of the appliances if he'd thought she might have found it amusing.

He lifted his arms to stretch, then realized he couldn't. By the saints, when was the last time he'd forgotten he was wearing mail? Not even on the Crusade had it become such a part of him. He rose and walked over to his wife.

"Would you excuse me a moment?" he asked politely. "I am in desperate need of a stretch after my hard exercise in this kitchen today and my mail hampers me greatly."

She only smiled blandly. Kendrick had the presence of mind to be pleased with her lack of reaction. At least she didn't expect him to come back down naked and ravish her on the table. He stroked his chin as he left the kitchen. Now, that was a fine idea. Perhaps his lady wouldn't be opposed to it in a few months. Of course, Worthington would have to be sent on holiday again for them to have enough privacy, but Kendrick had the feeling the old busybody would find traveling much too much to his liking to protest being sent away again. Aye, a bit of loving while there was chocolate ice cream well within reach wasn't a poor idea at all.

Getting his mail shirt off was a trick, but not completely beyond him. It was a relief to have the weight off his back. He shoved his legs into a pair of soft jeans and dug into his trunk for some kind of tunic. He pulled out a sweatshirt with the Raiders logo on it and smiled at the sight. When had Genevieve done this? Perhaps she wasn't as opposed to him as she seemed.

Nay, that was unfair. She loved him. She had always been shy and likely still would be. For all he knew, he intimidated her with his size alone. A pity she hadn't known his mother. He could call to mind scores of memories of his mother tilting her head back to shout at his father, who stood a good head and a half taller than she and doubled her in weight. But his father wouldn't have hurt her for any money. Why, 'twould have been unthinkable! He would have sooner cut down his sons than lay a hand on his lady. A pity Genevieve had never witnessed the like. She would have realized that he shared his father's sentiments.

He hastened from the room and ran down the stairs and across the great hall to the kitchen. He could smell the seasoned meat and his mouth had already started to water. If he weren't careful, he would be the size of his horse soon.

Genevieve was just setting down a chocolate milk shake at his place when he walked into the kitchen. He immediately rounded the table and wrapped his hands around the glass. Genevieve put her palm over the top and held the goblet to the table.

"No."

"Aye."

"Kendrick, not before supper."

"I can decide for myself."

"No, you can't."

"Aye, I can."

She frowned.

Take no prisoners, Seakirk. He leaned over and captured her mouth with his. He didn't try to force her mouth open, he simply covered her mouth with his and kissed her. She didn't pull away. In fact, she lost her balance and leaned into him. He didn't catch her. He pulled back and looked to see if his assault had achieved the desired result.

His lady was clutching the side of the table with both hands, her eyes closed, her mouth parted slightly. Oh, and his milk shake was now free. He downed the contents in one slow, throat- and brain-numbing draught, then set the glass down with a bang. He burped discreetly, to his ears anyway, and sat down with a satisfied grunt.

Genevieve opened her eyes and looked down at him.

"You, my lord, are a barbarian."

He tried to look offended. "I burped discreetly." By the saints, she looked like she was ready to faint!

"I wasn't talking about that."

He lifted one eyebrow and affected a casual pose. "Oh?"

She put her fingers to her lips and turned around to fetch a plate. Kendrick smothered his smile and jumped to grab a platter of vegetables that was nigh onto slipping from his lady's fingers. He set it on the table and then put Genevieve in her chair. She didn't look capable of getting there herself. Well, at least she wasn't bolting. Perhaps he could keep her dazed long enough to teach her to trust him.

Dinner was a silent affair. Kendrick was far too busy eating to talk and Genevieve looked to be too bemused. She toyed with her food as she leaned her chin on her hand and watched him devour his supper. He finished with all haste, then looked around for more. She smiled at him and pushed her plate over.

He consumed his second meal more slowly, mainly because Genevieve was watching him and he became uncomfortably aware of his table manners. Silverware had never been much of a concern for him in the past. A man didn't live out-of-doors for months on end and worry about offending his comrades' sensibilities. Kendrick ate with his hands, using his knife only when his teeth wouldn't suffice. Just how did a man wield a fork without looking like a dolt? He looked up at Genevieve with a pained smile.

"Forgive me."

"Why? You're doing fine."

"I'm embarrassing myself."

She shook her head and came to stand behind him. She put her hand over his left hand. "Hold the fork like this. Once the meat is cut, either keep it in this hand or switch, whatever is more comfortable. Got it?"

"Ah, nay," he said quickly, as she moved away. Deception

wasn't a sin when it was used to keep your wife near you, was it? "Show me again, Gen. Just another time or two."

Needless to say, he finished the rest of his meal with Genevieve's help. He was disappointed when he had to admit he hadn't the room for anything else. Genevieve started to pick up the plates, but he stopped her.

"Love, that gown can't be as comfortable as jeans. Go change. I'll clean up here."

"Kendrick, I can do it."

"Nay, you cooked. I'll clean up."

"You don't know how to run the dishwasher."

"How difficult can it be? The plates go in dirty and come out clean. Even a medieval barbarian can comprehend the simplicity of that."

She leaned over to kiss his cheek. "I was just teasing about the barbarian thing."

"I think not."

"Kendrick—"

He smiled. "You like me this way, I know. I'm not offended."

"Good. And thanks for doing the dishes. You're a very chivalrous knight."

Once she was gone, he released a most satisfying burp and then set to his work. Placing the plates in the dishwasher was insultingly simple and he marveled that he didn't need to even clean them off first. How civilized man had become to invent a machine that could chew up bones, chunks of vegetables and crusts of bread, yet still deliver clean dishes an hour later. He had trouble initially with understanding which way to place the plates and mentally chided himself for not having paid closer attention to the commercials on television that might have shown him how to accomplish the feat. Well, everything lined up fairly well and the door closed readily enough. What else could anyone ask for? The machine made terrible noises when he turned it on but perhaps that was how it was supposed to sound.

Kendrick walked to the door of the kitchen and looked out into the great hall. Genevieve still hadn't descended. He paused. He was full, but another milk shake would certainly suit him. Perhaps he would make one for his lady while he was at it. She was powerfully fond of the concoctions and he understood fully the reasons why.

The blender. Another modern miracle. He plugged the beast into the outlet, then searched for the glass beaker. He espied it sitting upside down on a cloth near the sink, along with its blades and such. Fitting it together was accomplished easily enough and he rested the glass on the white base. After fetching his ingredients, he searched for a spoon and set to work. It was slow going, likely because he ate more ice cream than he put into the blender. No matter, for there was plenty in reserve. Genevieve's command had obviously made an impression on Worthington, for the freezer was stocked to the brim with all manner of chocolate ice creams. Though he preferred the chocolate with the chunks in it, all he could find was the smooth variety. Olde Fashioned, it was called. He snorted. Ice cream with bugs and rocks in it would have been Olde Fashioned.

He heaped several spoonfuls of the ice cream into the blender, then added what he thought to be an appropriate amount of milk. Hopefully it wasn't enough to make the shake runny. If there was anything he couldn't abide, it was a runny shake.

He looked at the blender, sizing up the enemy and wondering why it looked so incomplete. The white base with its buttons, the glass with its metal curved piece, and the contents. He looked over at the towel. Nothing there but a bit of black plastic and some silverware. He shrugged and turned back to his minor appliance. Now, the buttons were a puzzle but surely they meant what they said. Low? Nay, that sounded far too slow. High was what he needed. The ice cream was hard and would take a great amount of strength to soften it into a thick liquid. Feeling rather pleased with himself and his prowess in the kitchen, he held onto the white base of the blender and pressed down on the correct button.

There was a tremendous gurgle.

And then an explosion of ice cream and milk.

Onto every surface of the kitchen, including him.

"Merde!" Kendrick bellowed. "Bloody whoreson, what possesses you!"

The machine stopped. Kendrick wiped the ice cream from his eyes and blinked. Genevieve was holding out the black plastic object.

"You forgot the lid."

Her eyes twinkled madly and her lips twitched, as if she strruggled mightily not to throw back her head and howl with laughter. Kendrick felt a severe blush stain his cheeks, though his lady wouldn't have noticed, thanks to the chocolate mess that covered him from the waist up. Well, his choice was either to laugh or weep. A giggle escaped his wife and that was all it took. She held her sides and doubled over as peal after peal of laughter left her gasping for air. All Kendrick had to do was envision the sight that had greeted her to make him laugh just as heartily. By the saints, he was a buffoon!

Genevieve shook her head as she reached into one of the cabinets and pulled out a clean towel. "Kendrick, you're drenched. Let me get some of this off you. On second thought, go take a shower. I'll clean up the kitchen. And what is that terrible noise?"

Before Kendrick had time to argue with her about cleaning the kitchen, she had shut off the dishwasher and looked inside.

Well, no wonder the infernal thing had been making such a racket. All the crockery was broken! He padded over and squatted down next to the open door.

"There is something amiss with this beast," he said, clucking his tongue. "Look what's happened!"

Genevieve laid her hand on his head gently. "Kendrick, you have to scrape off the plates before you put them inside. And you can't put in bones, my love. The dishwasher doesn't like them."

He realized immediately the enormity of his mistake. He lifted his eyes and looked up at her, pained.

"Perhaps I'm not at my best in the kitchens."

She bent and kissed the end of his nose. "Maybe not, but you look adorable wearing a chocolate milk shake."

"And this machine here?"

"We'll get someone to come fix it tomorrow. You'll know what to do with it the next time."

He closed the door and rose with a sigh. "Let me build you a fire in the hall, love, then I'll come clean this mess. 'Twas my doing, after all."

"Don't be silly. I'll help. Worthington keeps more towels in the pantry. Grab a few and we'll have the kitchen back in shape in no time."

Kendrick had to admit that his lady was a swift cleaner. He made a rather ineffectual attempt at helping her, making more mess than he cleaned up. He was more than willing to sit when she pushed him down into a chair, though he silently promised to cook her a few meals in repayment for her aid. She'd need her strength if she were to survive his wooing.

He closed his eyes as he listened to her walk over to the sink and turn on the faucet. He heard the sound of a cloth being wrung out and assumed she had done it prior to laying it out to dry.

Until he felt her nudge his knees apart. His eyes flew open. She smiled and drew her hand over his brow, closing his eyes. Kendrick groaned when he felt the soft, warm cloth against his skin.

"Oh, Genevieve."

"Kendrick, it's going to take more than a simple face washing to get you clean. I think you should go take a shower."

"Whatever you want, Gen."

But he didn't move and she didn't stop her ministrations. Kendrick hardly dared breathe, afraid he would frighten her away. By the saints, how he loved the feeling of her hand on his skin, even though the thin cloth was in the way. He was half tempted to make another mess just so she'd have to fuss over him.

But when she pulled away, he didn't protest. He was a patient man. He would wait until she came to him. She'd washed his face. That was a fine beginning, wasn't it? He opened his eyes and smiled up at her.

"Thank you."

"You're welcome."

"I think I must bathe."

"You are looking a bit crusty around the gills."

He rose. "You'll wait for me?"

"Here?"

"I'll build you a fire in the hall. Then I have a surprise for you." He was tempted to take her hand, but he refrained. Best not to push things. He led her out into the hall, built up the fire in the hearth, then made her a bow. "I will return posthaste, my lady. To show you your wedding gift."

Her mouth hung open. "But, Kendrick, I don't have anything for you!"

He bent and pressed a gentle kiss against her forehead. "You are my wedding gift, Genevieve. I could ask for nothing more."

With that, he straightened and walked away. And he suppressed the powerful urge to peek around the corner of the stairs and see what her reaction had been.

He hoped she was smiling.

He held out his hand and pulled her to her f

something I want to discuss with you."

"What?"

"I'm not sure I want to spend any time

Genevieve didn't have to hear his r

had happened there: touching him

ing him ripped away; signing a

want to be there again either

"I understand," she nod

"But the great hall is

"We could fix u

solar on the third

"I've a solu

and put it i

Gene

coul

Genevi
was! Sh____ _____ gaping at the blender as it exploded upward like a volcano would forever remain etched vividly in her mind. If she hadn't known it would have wounded his pride, she would have shouted with laughter right then and there. And that bewildered look he'd worn when she'd handed him the blender lid. She laughed again. Sweet, charming Kendrick. How could anyone resist him?

She chuckled to herself until she heard him thumping down the stairs. He sauntered over to her, then stopped and inclined his head.

"I believe the crust is gone now, my lady."

"You poor thing," she said, feeling another grin escape. "I should have shown you how to use the blender before I left."

He scowled. "I knew it was missing something important but damn me if I wasn't too stupid to latch on to what."

"It's that modern technology, Kendrick. You can't run a blender; I can't run a VCR. It's a trade-off."

eet. "That's

in my study again."

easons. Too many things

or the first time, then hav-

way the castle. No, she didn't

ded.

far too drafty for us."

one of the other rooms. Or maybe the

floor? It overlooks the ocean."

tion already." He pulled a key out of his pocket

to her palm. "Your wedding gift."

eve knew instantly that the key was for the room she

n't open. She met his eyes. He smiled encouragingly.

Go on. See if it pleases you."

She walked casually over to the door, when in reality she wanted to run there. The lock turned easily and she opened the door and pushed it back.

It was her library. It was dark and inviting and just exactly how she'd pictured it. She whirled around and looked at Kendrick.

"You saw this in my mind."

"Guilty as charged."

"Oh, Kendrick." She threw her arms around his neck and hugged him. "I love it!"

"How can you tell? You've hardly looked it over."

She smiled again at his teasing tone, then pushed out of his arms to look at her wedding gift. Beautiful dark wood furniture and floor-to-ceiling bookshelves. Deep, forest-green carpet. An enormous fireplace. Comfortable chairs done in black watch plaid. Brass lamps.

And more books than she could count. It would take her a lifetime to read them all.

"Don't even think of sequestering yourself in here to read all these titles," Kendrick growled softly. "I do not take well to being ignored."

She laughed as she walked over to one of the shelves and trailed her fingers over the bindings. "All my favorite authors. How did you know?"

"I ransacked your memory one night while you slept. Genevieve, did you hear what I just said?"

"Of course, husband."

"Then repeat it back to me. And put down that book!"

She grinned at him. "An entire library at my disposal and you thought I wouldn't read anything?"

He growled and advanced. She put a chair between them.

"Come on, Kendrick. Just a few books a day."

"One a week."

"Five a week."

"By the saints, Genevieve, 'tis far too many!"

"I'll read while you're in the lists."

He folded his arms over his chest. "I'd rather have you watching me in the lists."

"Every day?"

"The thought is so tedious it makes you yawn already?"

"Can I bring a book?"

"Nay, you cannot bring a book. And put that one you hold in your hands away. I did not bring you here to share you with some dead fool's drivel."

"Gee, Kendrick, it looks pretty interesting—" She shrieked and jumped away laughing as he vaulted easily over the back of the chair. He caught her and pinned her up against the bookshelf.

"How does it look now?"

"Really dull," she breathed.

He took the book out of her hand and replaced it on the shelf. "Well-spoken."

"Boy, you're demanding. Has anyone ever told you that?"

"Many times. And always in the most complimentary of tones."

She tried to think of something else clever to say, but words had suddenly and quite completely deserted her. She could only stare up at her husband, acutely aware that he was standing only an inch or two away from her, that his hands were resting on either side of her against the shelves, that he dwarfed her in size. Though he'd always looked substantial to her while he was a ghost, having him as a living, breathing body was rather overwhelming. She saw the rise and fall of his chest, heard the faint sound of his breathing, felt the heat from his body radiate out and warm her. She knew how his arms would feel around her, how wonderfully cherished she felt when pressed close against that hard chest.

She also knew that he was waiting for her to do something about it. After all, was he really so different than he had been before? Despite the obvious differences, he was still Kendrick. He was still the knight who had offered her his castle and his heart after she'd poured out her soul to him. He was still the man who'd used all his strength to put a simple ring on her finger. He was the one who'd teased her, driven her crazy with his demands for her attention, protected her from the bad guys. And he was the one who loved her. He'd put his dream on hold to give her hers, and to keep her near him. Did having a body change him so much?

It didn't. Even though she wasn't quite sure how to proceed and she knew she'd probably make a fool of herself a dozen times over, she would give it a try. After all, how hard could seducing her husband be? It wasn't as though he wasn't willing.

She kept her eyes locked with his and slowly lifted her hands to put them on his shoulders. He didn't move, didn't blink. At least he wasn't running the other way. She leaned up on her toes to kiss him. She couldn't reach. He didn't offer to help. She dropped back to her heels and frowned up at him.

"You could bend down."

"As my lady wishes." He lowered his head obligingly.

Now, that was better. She put her hands on his shoulders again and lifted herself up on tiptoe to meet his lips. Just the touch of them sent tingles down her spine. She kissed him again, then another time, wondering why he wasn't responding. She opened her eyes and looked at him.

"You could put your arms around me, you know."

"All you have to do is tell me what you want."

Oh, so that was his game. Maybe it wasn't such a bad game,

specially since it wouldn't last too long. Kendrick bragged about his patience, but Genevieve knew he didn't have all that much of it. She smiled smugly, enjoying the power she had over him.

"If that's the case," she said imperiously, "then I want you to put your arms around me and hold me close."

"Of course, Your Ladyship," he said humbly, putting his arms around her.

Genevieve frowned. Now, that was an impersonal embrace if she'd ever felt one. "With feeling, Kendrick."

"I'm feeling you quite well, my lady."

She rolled her eyes. "And here I thought you wanted to be my love slave."

He dropped to his knees. "Command me," he said earnestly.

She laughed as she smoothed the hair out of his eyes. "I thought you were supposed to be wooing me."

"I changed my mind. I'd much rather have you woo me."

"I don't have the faintest idea how."

"You were doing a fine job a few moments ago."

"You liked it?"

He looked off into space, as if he pondered her question deeply. "It was less painful than a flogging, but not quite as wonderful as a bowl of chocolate-chocolate-chip ice cream with whipping cream atop it."

"Less painful than a flogging?" she echoed.

"Much less."

She shut her mouth with a snap. Then she took him by the hand, pulled him up and led him over to the long couch placed strategically close to the hearth.

"Sit."

He sat obediently.

"Don't move."

"Not even to build you a fire?"

"I think I might be too tempted to roast you over it."

"It would add greatly to the ambience, my lady."

"Oh, all right. Just keep the tools out of my reach."

"Where are you going?"

"To fix you some pleasure," she muttered under her breath as she stomped out of the library. She slammed a few doors

and drawers as she fixed him a large bowl of ice cream and
scooped enough whipping cream on top to choke a horse. Or a
medieval barbarian. Less painful than a flogging! She was
tempted to go back and kiss him senseless. On second thought,
that wasn't a bad idea at all. She snatched up the bowl and
spoon and walked purposefully back to her library.

Kendrick didn't flinch when she slammed the door, but he
would have been a fool not to know something was up.
Genevieve slapped the bowl down on the table next to his arm,
took him by the front of his shirt and jerked him to her.

"Less painful than a flogging?" she snapped. "I'll show you
less painful than a flogging, buster."

She buried one of her hands in his hair and tilted his head
back, then pulled him even closer to her by the front of his
shirt. She bent her head and swooped down on his lips with
passion worthy of the silver screen. It didn't bother her that he
was too surprised to respond. By the time she got done with
him, chocolate-chocolate-chip ice cream would be as appealing as soggy asparagus.

Not being exactly sure how to proceed in wooing her husband, she improvised. People were always slanting their
mouths over other people's mouths, then delving inside with
their tongues. It couldn't hurt to try. So she tilted her head and
slanted her mouth over Kendrick's. He didn't wrap his arms
around her, but his breath caught. Mr. Unaffected was not as
unaffected as he seemed. Encouraged, Genevieve slipped her
fingers further into his hair and slanted her mouth over his
more forcefully. It was an easy thing to part his lips and she
plunged ahead, hoping she wouldn't make a fool of herself.

The moment she touched his tongue, she groaned. Kendrick
refrained from comment but his breath caught again and she
could feel his heart thumping wildly in his chest. *All right, pretend you aren't affected and see what it gets you.* She pushed
him back against the back of the couch and followed him, leaning on one knee. She buried both of her hands in his long, silky
hair and continued to assault his mouth, pretending that she
knew exactly what she was doing. And though Kendrick might
have been sitting there like a bump on a log, his tongue cer-

ainly made up for the rest of his body's passiveness. Genevieve groaned every time his tongue tangled with hers, drawing her further into his mouth, loving her sweetly and passionately. But no matter how fully his tongue mated with hers, he simply would not follow her back into her mouth. Well, that was fine with her. This was her lesson she was teaching. Maybe in a few hours, she would demand that he kiss her the way he'd kissed her in the bathroom the day before their wedding. For now, she wanted Kendrick to realize she meant business.

She tore her mouth away from his, stood up and reached for the bowl of ice cream. She placed it ungently into his limp palms, then looked at him. He looked dazed. And flushed. Genevieve smiled smugly as she walked over to the wall and looked for something to read. It would have to be something that didn't take any intelligence whatsoever because she couldn't see straight, much less think that way. After choosing an appropriately pulpy detective novel, she sat down on the end of the couch furthest away from Kendrick. She stretched out her feet and wiggled her toes in front of the fire.

"Eat your ice cream," she said, unconcerned, as she opened her book and stuck her nose in it.

"I don't think I want it anymore."

"I didn't ask for your opinion."

Out of the corner of her eye, she saw him move closer. She doggedly tried to make sense of the first page of the book. It was impossible. Three bodies already? In two paragraphs? How in the world was she supposed to keep all those names straight?

A spoon appeared in front of her. "A taste, my lady?"

She ate it to humor him. "Tastes a little dull to me."

"Aye," he agreed, "to me too."

More bodies. In the library this time. It might not turn out to be half bad after all. Of course, it was very difficult to concentrate with Kendrick spooning ice cream into her mouth every thirty seconds. After about five minutes of rereading the same paragraph and being uncomfortably aware of the man feeding her, Genevieve realized she wasn't going to be doing any reading that evening. But there was no sense in letting

Kendrick realize that. She stole a look at him as he set the bowl aside and saw that he was starting to scowl.

He stretched out on the couch and put his head in her lap, elbowing his way under her book. She ignored him. He captured one of her hands and put it on top of his head and made dragging motions with it, suggesting oh-so-subtly that she comb his hair with her fingers. Genevieve humored him, but refrained from looking at him. She still hadn't quite forgiven him for the flogging remark.

"Genevieve?"

She pursed her lips and kept reading.

"You've been on page two for almost a half hour now. How is it you ever finish anything when you read so slowly?"

"I'm savoring it."

He took the book and flung it across the room. "Savor something else."

"More ice cream?"

His expression darkened. "Nay."

"Another book?"

"Damnation, Genevieve, you're vexing me apurpose!"

"It's better than a flogging, isn't it?" she asked sweetly.

He scowled. "I was teasing you."

"I know."

He took her other hand and brought it to his lips. "Woo me," he cajoled. "I'll woo you tomorrow in payment."

"I think I'd rather have ice cream."

"Genevieve . . ."

She put her hand over his mouth. "Just kidding. I'll woo you. What do you want?"

"For you to comb my hair."

He wanted plenty more than that; she could see it in his eyes. "That's it?"

"Perhaps another chaste kiss or two."

"Nothing else?"

"Nothing else."

She bent her head and kissed his lips softly. Oh, she could certainly acquire an addiction to his mouth easily enough. She kissed him again, then leaned back and began to drag her fingers through his hair.

"I should get a brush."

"Your fingers suit me perfectly."

Genevieve had to admit Kendrick was suiting her perfectly too. Now if he would just do her the favor of sweeping her into his arms and kissing her, she'd be perfectly happy.

Instead, he fell asleep.

Why she was surprised, she didn't know. She chalked it up to too much pleasure from having his hair combed. Well, at least it gave her ample opportunity to get used to the feeling of his head on her legs and his fingers imprisoning one of her hands. She slouched down more comfortably and idly toyed with a lock of her husband's hair. It was hard to believe that she'd felt such bone-numbing fear the night before. As if Kendrick would actually hurt her.

She sighed. Perhaps her ease came from knowing he wouldn't make love to her that night. She wasn't exactly sure how she knew that, but she did. Perhaps it was the restraint he'd shown while she was kissing him. It had affected him. She hadn't been able to resist a surreptitious look at his lap. Men were so patently unable to hide their reactions. Even so, Kendrick had still let her feel like she was in control. She blessed him silently for it. He was right when he'd said that all their time together hadn't prepared them to be lovers. She knew him well emotionally and mentally, but physically? Not at all. The only remedy for that was time. How like Kendrick to want to give her that time.

She smoothed his hair back from his brow. "I love you," she whispered.

"I love you, too," he whispered back.

She gasped. "You're awake?"

He opened one eye and looked up at her. "Aye. And wondering if you'd fallen asleep. My hair suffers from your inattention."

She smothered a yawn with her hand. "Sorry. My hand got tired."

He reached up and captured that hand, then kissed her palm.

"Thoughtless of me not to realize it. But you've given me great pleasure this evening. Shall I cook you a late supper in payment?"

"Thanks, but I think I'll take a rain check. I'm really tired."

He smiled gently. "It has been an exhausting few days, my love." He sat up, then rose slowly to his feet, stretching. "Let me see you to your room. Sleep is no doubt what you need."

Her room? Naw, he didn't mean that. He meant their room. Genevieve allowed him to pull her to her feet. She was obviously so tired, she was hearing things. Kendrick's hand was warm around hers as he led her from the library, through the great hall and up the stairs to the second floor. Walking down the hall with him reminded her how terrified she'd been the first couple of nights in the castle. Now she felt like nothing could harm her. It had everything to do with the powerful knight walking next to her. If anyone could protect her from thugs, it was Kendrick.

He stopped her at the bedroom door, then turned her to him with his hands on her shoulders. He pressed a kiss on her forehead.

"Good night, my love."

She frowned. "Aren't you coming to bed?"

"I must go back down and bank the fire. Then I think I may have to make myself a small snack."

"But you're coming later, right?"

He shook his head.

She shook her head too, not understanding. "But why not? You aren't going to stay up all night watching movies or something, are you?"

He slipped his hands up her neck and tilted her face further up with his thumbs. "I'll not come to your bed, Genevieve, unless I come to it truly. And I don't think you're ready for that quite yet."

"Oh."

"Good night, my love."

"But," she blurted out, "there isn't anywhere else to sleep."

He kissed her chastely, then he pulled away.

"Oh, no you don't," she protested, throwing her arms around his neck and holding on. "That wasn't satisfying at all."

He frowned, then wrapped his arms around her and pulled her tightly against him. "Not satisfying? You leave me in agony on the couch downstairs, cast a bowl of ice cream onto my lap and tell me to eat it, and now you talk to me of dissatisfaction? My lady, you don't know the meaning of the word!"

Oh, yes she did. She leaned up on her toes and planted her mouth on his. Then she slanted it. Then she opened it and didn't give him much choice but to do the same. He groaned, a satisfying, heartfelt groan that made her want to grin. She kissed him thoroughly, learning to relish the feel of his hard unyielding body pressed tightly against hers. Yes, there was nothing quite like being locked in Kendrick's embrace and knowing he didn't want to let her escape.

She kissed him until her toes curled up in her shoes and her knees began to tingle. When Kendrick began to sway unsteadily, she knew the time for halting had come. She pushed out of his arms and smiled up at him, loving the dazed look on his face.

"That, my lord, is satisfaction."

Then she breezed into her room and shut the door in his face. She leaned back against it and put her hand over her heart, wincing at the erratic pounding in her chest. Satisfaction? She felt like she'd just run a marathon!

"Genevieve?"

His growl came through the door clearly.

"Yes, husband."

"I'll repay you for your sport."

I sincerely hope you will, she thought with a smile. "Good night, Kendrick."

He grunted.

"Sweet dreams," she added.

"This is war," he said distinctly.

"Don't let the bedbugs bite."

He cursed, fortunately in old French, but she had the feeling she figured prominently in his slander. His curses faded as he walked away from her room, leaving Genevieve smiling broadly.

War? Oh, she certainly hoped so.

Chapter
Twenty-seven

"You fool!"

Bryan winced at the force of the shout. He held the phone away from his ear as Mr. Maledica swore vigorously for several minutes in a language Bryan couldn't understand, and didn't want to learn. It sounded like French, but it was a dialect he had never heard. He didn't want to speculate about which slum his employer had been in to learn it.

"God's teeth, McShane, you are the most incompetent little swine I've ever known! How difficult could it possibly be to hire a mercenary or two and send them in to snatch a witless girl? A ten-year-old child could execute this plan with more skill!"

"Y-yes, sir," Bryan said, his teeth beginning to chatter. *Chin up, lion. At least Maledica doesn't have his fingers around your throat.*

"Must I do your thinking for you?"

"I t-tried, sir—"

"And failed miserably!"

Bryan's teeth chattered some more. "Of course, sir."

"Now, hear me well, little mouse. I don't want to have word reach me of another of your failures. You will find a way to capture Miss Buchanan, even if you must do so with your own two hands, is that clear? 'Tis obvious that after your last bungling attempt, she will be slow to leave the keep. I daresay you haven't any choice but to follow her inside."

Bryan winced.

"No more failures, McShane."

"No, sir."

The line was disconnected abruptly and so loudly that Bryan's ear rang. He fumbled with the receiver several times before he managed to replace it in its cradle.

So Maledica wanted him to go inside Seakirk. Bryan broke out into a cold sweat. God help him, he didn't want to! De Piaget had told him not to come back, and Bryan knew he hadn't been making idle conversation. He'd never get past the gate guards, and, if he did, he'd never make it back out of the castle alive.

No, he couldn't do this personally. He would go as far as the village, but no further. He would have to find someone capable this time, perhaps someone less easy to bribe but less prone to the vapors, unlike his last two thugs. A pity he couldn't find a man of the cloth to exorcise Kendrick; that would certainly make things easier.

His lion sat up and roared encouragingly.

Bryan smiled for the first time in ten years.

Chapter
Twenty-eight

Genevieve woke to the sound of faint noise. Well, maybe Kendrick had called someone in to fix the dishwasher. She rolled from her bed, showered and dressed, then ran downstairs.

"*Merde!*"

So, Kendrick was cooking again. She poked her head inside the kitchen.

"Damnation, burned again!"

Genevieve ducked as a frisbee-size pancake, charred to a beautiful black, went sailing over her head and slammed against the wall behind her. Kendrick had another one on his spatula, primed and ready for launch. He saw her and lowered his arm.

"Good morrow to you," he snapped.

Genevieve fought her smile and walked over to him, ignoring the kitchen full of smoke. She calmly turned on the vent over the stove, took the spatula from Kendrick's hand and flipped the burned pancake into the sink. Then she stuck her finger in the batter and tasted it.

"Kendrick, it's wonderful!"

"Aye, a pity neither of us will ever know just how fine. Damn me, but these bloody wretches burn before I can get my spoon under them!"

"You have the heat up too far. Medium is hot enough. If you keep it on high, one side burns and the other side stays raw."

"I know that!"

"Are you sure you want pancakes?"

Kendrick stomped over to the freezer, jerked out a carton of ice cream and threw her a glare before he cursed his way out of the kitchen.

And so progressed the day. Kendrick wanted to go riding; a storm of epic proportions arrived and thwarted his plans. He wanted to drive to the village; the car wouldn't start. He wanted chocolate-chip cookies; the brown sugar was as solid as marble and just that impossible to soften. Genevieve could only laugh helplessly at his frustration. In payment, he dumped her over his shoulder, hauled her into the library and tickled her in front of the fire until she was sobbing with laughter.

Genevieve thought his frustration an amusing thing until he left her at her door again that night. He kissed her until her knees buckled, then turned her around and pushed her gently inside the room. She had too much pride to beg him to kiss her just a few more times. Though the outcome of the war was yet to be decided, she knew he'd scored a victory that night.

Genevieve shivered as she sat on a bale of hay and watched Kendrick brush his horse. Actually, his horse was simply the horse he had chosen a week ago, on the day he had come back to life. During his ghostly years he had overseen the filling of his stables and now possessed a dozen of the finest horses on the island. Or so he claimed. Genevieve didn't have any reason to doubt him. The animal currently being groomed was a magnificent beast, huge, strong, and as black as midnight.

Kendrick hummed as he worked, his hands smoothing over the silky flanks, combing the mane into a waterfall of darkness. Genevieve closed her eyes and pretended that his hands were skimming over her skin. He was driving her crazy! It had been almost a week since their wedding and it had been the longest week of her life. He never touched her until they were upstairs in front of their bedroom door and then he more than made up for spending the day pushing her away. They'd been there in the hallway for over an hour the night before, kissing and caressing and teasing each other into a frenzy. Genevieve had tried to pull him inside the bedchamber with her, but he wouldn't come. If she heard him tell her one more time that he was sure she wasn't ready yet, she'd haul off and slug him.

The stall door closed with a soft bang and Kendrick wiped his hands on his jeans.

"Ready to go back?"

She nodded, her teeth beginning to chatter. She slipped her hand into his and sidled up to him as they walked back to the hall. Having his arms around her certainly would have taken the edge off the chill.

"You know," she began casually, "the ground sure is wet."

He smiled down at her, the twilight casting most of his face in shadows. "It is."

"Gosh, there are even puddles here and there. I could get my feet wet."

"'Tis a good thing you wore your galoshes. And your slicker. Bloody frigid out tonight."

"I would be a lot warmer if you'd carry me."

"Can't. I've got a sore back."

"You lie like a rug."

He laughed and squeezed her hand. "I'm covered with dust and horsehair. I didn't think you'd wish to be covered by the same thing."

She almost said that what she wanted was to be covered by his big, warm body, but it sounded a bit too earthy even for her recently acquired lustful state of mind. She had her doubts it would impress Kendrick. He'd probably tell her that was a sure sign she wasn't ready for anything.

A shower, her red feety pajamas and a delicious meal of imported super-chunk peanut butter sandwiches weren't enough to improve her mood. She scowled at her husband through dinner, then scowled at him as he walked with her up the stairs.

But when he took her in his arms at the door, she didn't have the energy to scowl anymore. She melted against him, loving the feel of his tongue caressing hers, his hands in her hair, his hard frame pressing her back up against the door. She wrapped her arms around his neck and stood up on her toes to better reach his mouth. His shoulders were tense beneath her wrists and the muscles in his neck were taut. She wove her fingers into his hair and pulled his mouth down harder against hers. It occurred to her, in the back of her mind, that she had changed very much from just a week ago, but she didn't give it too much thought. Entertaining intelligent thought while Kendrick was working his magic on her mouth was completely beyond her.

His hands slipped from her hair and she pulled her head back to protest. Before she could open her mouth, he had pinned her against the wall firmly and had captured her mouth again. She had no idea what he intended until she felt his hands on her ribs. Even through the thick flannel she could feel his touch burning her.

Then one of his hands moved to the zipper of her pajamas. She would have helped him find it if she'd been able to unclench her hands from his hair. Luckily, he didn't need any help. Soon the hiss of a zipper opening greeted her ears as cold air greeted her bare skin. Cold air was immediately followed by warm hands. Her breaths became moans and her knees became mush. If he hadn't been pinning her against the door with his hips and legs, she would have collapsed. She was torn between the feelings his mouth was arousing and the feelings his hands began to arouse. All she knew was that she never wanted any of the feelings to end.

Which was, of course, precisely what happened. First he slipped his hands around to her back, then he moved his head to rest it on her shoulder. He merely stood there, breathing hard, holding her so close he robbed her of air.

"Kendrick," she squeaked.

"Aye?" he asked gruffly.

"Why did you stop?"

He pulled back and put his hand on her zipper, then he stopped and looked at her. With a low moan, he brought the edges of the garment together and zipped it closed. Then he put his hand behind her head and pressed his lips to her forehead.

"I love you," he said.

"Please don't stop."

"I have to."

"Kendrick!"

He kissed her swiftly, then turned and walked down the hall.

"Kendrick! Damn you, come back here!"

He turned slowly. "I can't. Genevieve, you aren't ready—"

"If you tell me one more time I'm not ready, I swear I'll pick up that broadsword of yours and geld you, you jerk!"

He winced. "And we certainly wouldn't want that."

"Kendrick!"

He made her a low bow and turned, disappearing down the winding staircase. Genevieve stomped into her room and slammed the door shut. How could he do this to her? If this were really a war, she'd done nothing but lie down and let him walk all over her. It was going to stop. She'd give him a taste of his own medicine. Right after she had a cold shower and a terrible night's sleep.

She walked to the bathroom, already planning her attack.

Kendrick parked the car, gave it a pat on the hood for starting and behaving so nicely on the trip to the village, then ran lightly up the steps to his hall. He held a single red rose in his right hand. It was hardly enough to appease his wife, but it might be a start in the right direction.

He made his way into the kitchen, the smells of supper drawing him as though he were a starving waif. He walked in, did a double take, then stopped so suddenly he almost lost his balance. Was that Genevieve? With those ridiculous beasts in her hair? He approached hesitantly, wondering just what had possessed his wife to wrap her hair in such a fashion. She turned around and looked at him blandly. He gasped. Her face was blue!

"What," he asked in a strangled voice, "have you done to yourself, wife?"

"I'm wearing a beauty mask."

A beauty mask? Kendrick wasn't about to ask for the details. He laid the rose down on the table. "What are those animals in your hair?"

"Curlers."

"They look painful."

"They are."

"Why are you doing this?"

"The honeymoon's over, buster. This is real life. I do this all the time."

He sat down at the table with a thump. She did this all the time? He couldn't bring himself to believe it.

And then it hit him. She was trying to score a point against him. Ah, well, perhaps he deserved it. It had been his intention to make her desire for him greater than her fear of the bedding. Obviously he'd been a bit too thorough. Her threat to geld him still rang clearly in his mind.

Perhaps he could talk her into washing all the blue mud off her face, then he'd be her willing slave for the rest of the evening. That prospect brightened his outlook considerably.

He waited until after supper before he broached the subject.

"Love, that beautiful mask must be uncomfortable."

"It is."

How to phrase his request delicately? No idea. So, having no other choice, he forged ahead boldly.

"Wash it off and I'll do your bidding for the rest of the night," he offered.

She lifted one eyebrow. The mask cracked in a few places and several chips landed in her lap.

"Anything?"

"Anything."

She pushed away from the table. "I'll come clean up the mess later."

"I'll see to it." He smiled at her hesitation. "I'll rinse off the plates first and I won't put any bones down the garbage disposal. I've learned my lesson." The smirks and snickers of the repairmen still stung his pride when he thought about them too long.

"If you're sure."

"Oh, I'm very sure. Make haste, wife, before you scatter blue slivers all over the house."

She nodded and rose, her ridiculous headwear looking like a misshapen crown. Kendrick chuckled once she had gone. Ridiculous or not, his wife was adorable. He chuckled some more as he cleaned up the kitchen with skill Worthington would have admired; then he retired to the library. After building up the fire, he sat down on the couch, enjoying a few moments of peace in which to contemplate what sorts of delightful things his wife might require of him. He prayed she would make it something that required his undivided attention for a lengthy amount of time. Perhaps she would care to have her hair brushed. And then her shoulders rubbed. Who knew what that could lead to. Kendrick closed his eyes and smiled broadly. Ah, this evening could finish well indeed.

The door behind him closed with a soft click. He didn't move. Just a few more seconds of precious strategy-planning time, then an assault on the quarry. With any luck, Genevieve would be too distracted to realize what he was doing until he had her in his arms and was well on his way to giving her pleasure. Genevieve cleared her throat softly. Kendrick opened his eyes and looked at her.

And rational thought deserted him.

Merciful saints above, she was a vision. Where she had purchased the flimsy gown (and he hesitated to give the scant sheath such an elaborate title) was a mystery, but it had been a fine purchase indeed. It couldn't have been any more transparent or it would have greatly resembled that plastic wrap in the kitchen that was forever folding over onto itself and making him daft. His usual remedy was to fling the entire roll away. Oh, how he wanted to do the same thing with his wife's gown.

She moved to stand in front of the fire. "It's a bit chilly," she said, in a low, husky voice.

Kendrick couldn't agree. A sudden, stifling heat flooded his veins. Obviously Genevieve didn't know that the firelight behind her revealed all of her curves. He looked up at her face, framed by that glorious mane of hair, then began to suspect she knew exactly what the light was doing to her garb. He felt his mouth go dry. Since when had his wife turned into a siren? Was it the beautiful mask? Nay, she had been as beautiful last night as she was tonight. The gown? Nay, not that either. She was just as fetching in her red nightclothes. Whatever it was, he wanted to find out firsthand just how deep the change went. He held out his hand.

"Come here."

"No."

He frowned. That wasn't the answer he had been expecting. "Why not?"

"The fire is warm."

"I'll keep you just as warm, my lady. I vow it."

"My lord, you seem to have forgotten our bargain."

"What bargain?" By the saints, the flimsy robe couldn't be enough to keep her warm. If she would just come a bit closer . . .

"You are at my mercy tonight, Kendrick. I'd like you to remember that."

He swallowed with difficulty. Surely she didn't mean to torture him. Then again, why not? Hadn't he done the same to her all week?

"Genevieve, I beg you to take pity on me."

"I'll think about it. Later."

She turned and walked toward a bookcase. Kendrick jumped to his feet and blocked her path.

"Genevieve."

She moved past him. He tried to cut her off at the couch only to have her change directions again. He trailed her over to the desk that sat against the wall to the far left of the hearth. She reached for pen and stationery. He made a flying leap for the surface and managed to plant himself there, on top of her sheaf of writing paper.

"You could have broken the desk," she chided.

"Aye, and had it cheerfully fixed, surely."

She regarded him long, her arms folded over her chest, her head tilted to one side.

"You aren't being very obedient, Kendrick."

"My greatest fault. Punish me by kissing me senseless."

The corner of her mouth twitched. "I should punish you by ignoring you."

"Nay, love, I adore being ignored. You know that surely. Rather you should pay attention to me. Close attention. The very thought of your scrutiny makes me shudder." He looked at her hopefully, nodding slowly. She didn't start nodding with him. Damn, where had his plan to make her desire him run afoul of such trouble?

She reached out and fingered the collar of his oxford shirt. "You did promise me obedience, Kendrick."

"Aye." Would that she'd order him to strip on the spot!

"And you agreed to do whatever I asked. Anything."

"Aye, I did."

"Then I ask you not to touch me."

His face, and his hopes, fell. Past his feet, past the floor beneath him, straight to hell. It was all he could do not to weep.

"If you will it so," he managed, finally.

"I do," she said, unconcerned. She stepped back a pace from him and smiled serenely. "There's a favorite saying in antique shops back in America."

"What?" he asked, unable to muster up any enthusiasm for conversation. Didn't the woman know she had just broken his heart? His one desire—aye, his fondest wish—had been to love her truly, to bring her pleasure, to possess her fully and by so doing, allow her to possess him in like manner. And now she couldn't bear the feel of his hands.

" 'Look but don't touch.' "

He lifted his eyes and his jaw hung slack. He watched as the gossamer robe slipped down Genevieve's arms and pooled at her feet. Nightclothes? What dolt had ever termed what little she was wearing *nightclothes?* Kendrick continued to gape at her as she moved to stand between his knees.

"Sit up straight, Kendrick."

He sat bolt upright, trying not to flinch at her fingers' movements against his throat. He gaped some more as he looked down and watched her unbutton his shirt. She pulled it free of his jeans, unbuttoned the cuffs and slipped it down off his arms. It joined her robe on the floor.

Then he felt the touch of her slender hands on his bare shoulders. He looked up and met her eyes. There was hesitancy there, in direct contrast with the expression of bravado she wore. In an instant, he understood what she was doing.

His wife was seducing him.

And in another blinding flash, he realized what she intended to do once he was down on his knees begging her to carry him to bed.

She was going to turn and walk away.

Heaven help him, she wanted revenge. Well, she could have it, for about ten paces. Then, assuming she hadn't tied him up and left him to rot, he would scoop her up, carry her to his bed and love her until they both couldn't move. Revenge? Ah, what a sweet sound.

Her fingers brushed down over his chest, over the scars scattered here and there, along the scar Phillip had given him. Her hands trembled. Kendrick closed his eyes and tried to look pained. Genevieve was touching him. How he'd longed for this. He sucked in his breath as her hands smoothed across his belly, then back up over his ribs. *Ah, Genevieve, don't stop!*

She didn't. She ran her hands over the muscles in his arms, coming down to touch his hands that rested on his thighs. He opened his eyes and watched her look down. He knew the moment her gaze drifted over his groin because color immediately sprang to her cheeks. He closed his eyes and tried to look miserable.

"Are you enjoying this?" she asked, suspiciously.

" 'Tis torture. Plain and simple torture."

He peeked out of one eye and saw her frown.

"You wouldn't lie, would you?"

"Moi? Never."

"Good." She beckoned with her finger. "Come closer. I'm going to torment you with kisses now and I don't want it hurting my back."

It was his pleasure to do whatever she wanted. He hooked the chair behind her with his foot and brought it closer to his love, then rested his feet on it. She was, quite conveniently, trapped between his legs, the desk and the chair, but he pretended not to notice.

"Close your eyes, Kendrick."

He obeyed, dutifully. And he groaned silently when her lips brushed across his. Already his hands were itching to wander purposefully over her body. He clasped his hands behind his back in an effort to behave. And then he stopped thinking about anything but Genevieve's mouth against his, Genevieve's fingers sliding into his hair, the faint scent of her soap and skin. She hesitantly parted his lips and began to kiss him deeply. He groaned before he could stop himself, then opened one eye a bit to see how she had reacted to that slip. Her eyes were closed and she wore a look of intense concentration. He felt a smile start in his knees and work its way up. She was distracted. Maybe she wouldn't notice if he just happened to put his arms around her in a friendly embrace. He unclasped his hands.

She left his mouth and kissed her way up his neck.

His fingers twitched.

She nibbled his earlobe.

His fingers, and his toes, curled fiercely.

"Are you suffering yet?" she breathed into his ear.

"I don't think you understand who you're tormenting," he rasped. "Know you not that I was one of the fiercest warriors of my day?" *Aye, that's why I'm fair ready to weep so you'll help me to the floor and bed me immediately.*

"You promised you wouldn't touch me. You're a very honorable knight, my lord."

"Honor be damned," he squeaked as she gently touched her tongue to his ear. "By the saints, Genevieve, cease!"

She pulled back and smiled at him. "All right." She pushed past his leg and walked away.

"Oh, no you don't," he said, shaking his head to clear it. "You vowed to torture me and you've hardly finished."

"You told me to stop. Kendrick, you promised not to touch me!"

"What I want to do is wring your neck!"

"All the more reason to keep your hands to yourself."

Kendrick pinned her against a bookcase, holding her captive with a hand on either side of her body. He scowled down at her.

"I do not like this."

"Tough."

"You're making me daft!"

"You've been pushing me away for a week and I'm getting back at you. Now, I want you to suffer! I'm not quite through torturing you, so keep your hands off me until I'm finished."

Kendrick scowled some more, then an idea born of sheer desperation came to him. He pushed back from the bookcase.

"Don't move."

"Where are you going?"

"I'm taking my hands somewhere where they won't be tempted to throttle you. But I'll be back."

He stomped across the library, leaving her standing near the fire. So she didn't want him to touch her, did she? That meant only his bare hands—and he knew just how to solve that.

Chapter
Twenty-nine

Genevieve watched Kendrick go, then snatched up her robe, wondering if she'd pushed him just a bit too far. Well, he deserved it. A girl could only be expected to take so much before she had to give something back. And she'd taken plenty.

But the seduction hadn't quite worked as she'd wanted it to. She'd wanted to have him sweating profusely, begging her to have mercy and let him hold her. Making him want to strangle her had not been the desired result.

The door behind her slammed and she whirled around to see her husband standing there glowering.

He was wearing oven mitts.

He looked so ridiculous that she laughed. Kendrick advanced with the light of battle burning brightly in his eyes. Genevieve laughed again, turning to dart away from him. That lasted only three steps before she tangled her foot in the robe and went sprawling. Kendrick caught her around the waist and pulled her back to her feet, then turned her around in his arms so fast her head spun. She put her hand to her temple and looked up at him, waiting for him to come back into focus.

"Thanks," she said weakly.

"You put your robe back on."

"Well, yes . . ."

Mitted hands pushed it down off her shoulders.

"Kendrick, you're getting stroganoff on me."

"Tough."

She laughed again, until her back connected with the wall and she realized she had nowhere to run. Kendrick put a crusty, mitted paw under her chin and lifted her face up.

"You never said anything about kissing," he growled.

She could only gulp in response.

He bent his head and boldly captured her lips with his, as a good warrior would. Genevieve closed her eyes and opened her mouth to his searching tongue, then made a grab for his shoulders once passion tackled the backs of her knees. He caught her to him and wrapped his arms gently around her. His kisses turned as gentle as his embrace.

"This is madness," he whispered against her mouth.

"I wanted to get you back," she said, opening her eyes. "You teased me unmercifully this past week."

"I was trying to make you want me more than you feared me."

"I never was afraid of you, Kendrick."

"You have no reason to be. I'll take you gently, Genevieve, as gently as I know how."

Genevieve looked up. Kendrick merely stood where he was. Waiting. Genevieve swallowed. Well, it looked like the war was coming to an end.

"Now?" she asked.

He nodded.

"Here?"

He shook his head. "Nay, not here, my love. Upstairs."

And still he waited. Genevieve didn't have to give it any more thought. She took a deep breath and nodded.

"Upstairs, then."

Kendrick tossed the oven mitts onto a chair. He put one arm

under her shoulders and the other under her knees and lifted her off the ground. Genevieve wrapped her arms around his neck and closed her eyes as he carried her through the great hall and up the stairs.

As they passed down the hallway, Genevieve remembered the times Kendrick had frightened her there. Never in her wildest imaginings had she entertained the thought that someday he would be hers, that he would be carrying her to their bedroom to make love to her.

He paused in front of the door and met her eyes. "You're certain?"

"Kendrick, whatever happened to the ruthless warrior who took what he pleased, when he felt like it?"

He shook his head. "Not tonight, Genevieve. Tomorrow, if it amuses you, but not tonight."

She'd seen the teasing side of him, the tormented side of him, the infuriated side of him, but she'd never seen the quietly determined man holding her in his arms. She wasn't sure how to treat him.

"Kendrick, smile for me."

He pushed open the door and carried her inside. He walked over to the fireplace and let her slide to her feet. She watched him build the fire, then rise and turn to her.

"Genevieve," he said gravely, putting his hands on her arms, "I want to love you well. I feel like I've waited seven hundred years for this moment and now that 'tis come, I find myself feeling as clumsy and callow as a squire."

"You didn't drop me on the way here. That's a good sign."

"I suppose it is."

"I think you'll do a great job."

That made him laugh softly. He took her hand. "Come lie with me, my love. I want to hold you in my arms, in my bed, in my bedchamber."

She walked with him, then shivered as he picked her up in his arms and laid her on the quilt. Genevieve watched as he kicked off his shoes, pulled off his socks, then stood over her in nothing but his jeans. Genevieve looked at him, remembering the first time she had faced him, the night he had come to her with the knife. She smiled at the memory. How beautiful he had been, all muscle and strength. And now that gorgeous man was flesh and blood and he was going to make her his. Kendrick stretched out next to her and drew her close.

She lay with her head on his shoulder, her hand resting over his heart, for several minutes. She relished the feel of his hand skimming over her hair and the warmth of his body driving away the remaining chill in her body. And when he rolled her over onto her back, she went willingly.

"I love you," he whispered.

"I love you, too."

"Let me make you mine, Gen. Let me love you truly."

In answer, she put her arms around his neck and pulled him down to her. He kissed her, slow, lingering kisses that left her breathless. His hands traveled over her body, cautiously at first, then more boldly as he realized she was stiffening only with passion. Genevieve blushed as their remaining clothing somehow found its way to the floor, then other things clamored for her attention.

It was the oddest sensation, having his naked body pressed against hers, but she soon grew accustomed to it. She couldn't breathe when he moved on top of her, but she didn't mind that much either, being far too caught up in knowing that the moment of truth had finally arrived.

And then she froze.

"Kendrick, the door is open."

"What?"

She looked at his face. He was flushed. And he looked a bit dazed.

"The door."

"Aye?"

"It's open." She looked pointedly at the door, hoping he would take the hint. "You know." She lowered her voice. "I don't think we want an audience."

He dropped his head to her shoulder and groaned. "We are in the midst of mind-numbing passion and you are thinking of ghosts?"

"You never know who is out there. Please?"

"Very well, my lady." He rolled away and walked to the door. "I've no more stomach for that than you."

The door shut with a click.

The ghosts in the hall grumbled.

"We should've stood them up," the first said, with a regretful shake of his head.

"Aye, 'twas done so in my day," another said. "Take 'em to the bedchamber to start with. Then strip 'em and stand 'em up facing each other, nice and polite like. Then have 'em take a good look at each other 'afore the bedding, leavin' the poor wretches a last chance to bolt."

"I would've run the other way, had anyone bloody bothered to do the like for me," a third muttered, sounding exceedingly sorry that hadn't happened. "By the saints, that woman of mine had knobby knees!"

They discussed that for a good while before subsiding into further grumbling.

"Spoiled my evenin', 'e did, by shuttin' us out."

"Aye, and I coulda used a bit of sport—"

Lady Henrietta Buchanan folded her arms across her substantial bosom and frowned at the men crowded in the hall.

"You've seen enough, the lot of you. Be off with you and leave the lord and his lady in peace."

"But how will we know—"

"Aye, I've a mind to see the sheets—"

Her ladyship's frown was formidable. "You'll see no more tonight and you'll see nothing tomorrow."

"Come on, lads," one disgruntled soldier muttered. "She's left us with no choice but to haunt the tavern. Let's be off."

Lady Henrietta tapped her ghostly slipper until the corridor was cleared, then hrumphed in satisfaction. She'd always thought Kendrick to be a rather handsome lad, even if he had frightened her into the vapors on more than one occasion in her life. He had certainly become much more polite since his marriage. Henrietta was also enormously pleased with Genevieve. How lovely that the last of the Buchanans had turned out to be a nice young woman, in spite of her upbringing in the Colonies. Helping the pair have peace on this their first night of, well . . . Henrietta fanned her burning cheeks. Yes, it was the least she could do.

After one last piercing glance down the hallway to make certain the revelers were dispersed, Lady Henrietta returned to her tapestry frame in the upper solar, leaving the lovers to their night's work.

Kendrick scratched his heel with the big toe of his other foot as he stood before the stove and concentrated on breakfast. He was cooking breakfast to distract himself. What he wanted to be doing was loving his lady. He had the feeling she might not appreciate it quite yet. He grinned to himself as he swirled the eggs around in the pan with the spatula. They had spent most of the night awake, talking and snuggling. And touching. Kendrick had been well aware of how greatly the first time had pained her. And that thought pained him.

He had done his best to make up for it that morning, taking her slowly and gently. He smiled to himself as he peeled the eggs away from the side of the skillet. He would never forget the look on her face when she'd first found her pleasure. Though he'd wanted to laugh at her astonishment, her expression of wonder had touched his heart and humbled him. So he'd gathered her close and promised her the world and all good things in it. How he loved her!

He jumped when he felt arms go around him, then winced at the icy fingers on his chest.

"Morning, you," Genevieve whispered.

"I didn't hear you come in."

"You were laughing at your eggs. Did they say something funny?"

Kendrick turned around and tipped her face up with one finger. "Teasing me already this fine morn? I daresay you must be pleased with yourself over something. What could it be?"

Her blush was enchanting. Kendrick wrapped one of his arms around her and pulled her close to his boxer-clad form. When Genevieve encountered his aroused condition, her mouth fell open and she gaped up at him. Kendrick smiled sheepishly.

"Can't help it. Look what you've reduced me to."

She blushed again, deeper, and pressed her face against his chest. "I didn't mean to."

"I think you did," he whispered, bending to press his lips against her ear. "I think 'tis a nefarious plot to starve me to death. Or is it merely a scheme to steal my breakfast by distracting me with other things? And what could those other things possibly be? Let me think—"

She turned her head and kissed him. He knew she was doing it to silence him and save herself further embarrassment, but it achieved another end entirely. He stood perfectly still and let her have her way with his mouth. His only movement was to reach behind him and turn off the burner on the stove. Wouldn't want the hall to burn to cinders because he was too busy distracting his lady to watch the fire.

The moment he touched her tongue, he was lost. He groaned as he pulled her more closely against him. She wrapped her arms around his neck and buried her hands in his hair. Kendrick fought the buckling of his knees. Before she was truly awake was obviously the time to seduce his lady. He shivered as she dragged her fingernails over his shoulders and down his chest.

"Our breakfast will be chilled," he said hoarsely.

"We'll make more."

"You aren't awake enough to make that decision."

"I'm wide awake, Kendrick. And I think I'm ready to try this again."

He groaned. "Oh, Genevieve."

"Do I need to carry you?"

He took her hand and pulled her to the door, stopping every few paces to kiss her again. He led her over to the library, through the main chamber, then opened the door to the viewing room. He pushed the remote off the couch and pushed his lady down gently, following her immediately.

He touched her slowly, carefully, until her breath began to come in soft gasps. He kissed her mouth, her neck, her breasts, pretending not to notice her blush. Even in the faint light coming from the library he could see her color. And he found it bewitching.

He moved over her, determined to go even more slowly, to fill her fully. He stretched out full-length atop her, then bent his head and kissed her until he felt her initial tension become a tension of a different sort entirely. And then he slowly, carefully and gently took her, telling her again and again how much he loved her. Perhaps later they would laugh as they loved. Now, it was too new, too fragile. When she could accept all of him without stiffening as she did now, aye, then he would make her laugh while he loved her. Now all he wanted to do was make sure she didn't weep.

"It's better," she whispered.

He smiled against her neck. "Aye."

"Are you happy with me this morning?"

He lifted his head and looked down at her. An odd question. "Aye. Why wouldn't I be?"

"You aren't groaning."

"I'm too busy trying not to hurt you for any groaning."

"You're doing a fine job of not," she said, blushing.

"Am I? Then let me see if I can bring you pleasure."

He covered her mouth with his and continued on with his intention. Her gasps stole his breath. He kept on, gently teasing her all the way to pleasure. When she found it, she dug her fingernails into his back and moved beneath him with an unconscious seductiveness that was his undoing. He lost his control before she had regained hers. He reined himself in, so as not to hurt her, than collapsed against her, wanting to weep.

"Genevieve?" he rasped when he felt her tears against his neck.

She shook her head and held him tightly to her. "Don't leave me."

"Never." He stayed right where he was and wrapped his arms around her, trying not to crush her. He held her until her tears had ceased and she was merely dragging her hand across his back rhythmically. "Genevieve?"

"Yes, Kendrick."

"Did I hurt you?"

"No, Kendrick."

"Why did you weep?"

"Because I love you."

He smiled. "Am I crushing you?"

"No. I like you here. You'll stay awhile, won't you?"

"I'll stay forever if you wish it."

"I do."

Kendrick did his best to keep some of his weight on his elbows so Genevieve could still breathe. And he smiled. He'd loved his lady well, bringing her pleasure. Not a bad accomplishment before breakfast. He grinned against Genevieve's neck. Who knew what he could accomplish before lunch?

Chapter Thirty

Kendrick shut off the shower, relishing the feel of actually having used hot water for a change. He dried off, then put on what Genevieve called biker shorts. They were tight and bound his thigh muscles well. Perfect for training. A pity they wouldn't come off easily. The more easily taken off, the better, as his fondest wish was to be in bed with his lady for as long as possible, as naked as possible.

Unfortunately Genevieve was still sleeping. Kendrick left the bathroom and looked down at his love. She was exhausted, and no wonder. Over the past week they'd done little but make love, eat and sleep, though sleeping was only done when they couldn't keep their eyes open. Not that he was complaining, no indeed. But Genevieve needed sleep and he intended that she have it.

He donned his high-top sneakers and fetched his sword from where it leaned against his trunk. A morning spent training with Royce was what he needed. Then perhaps he would plead soreness and Genevieve could be persuaded to come into the bathroom with him again. She had refused ever since he'd teased her about the noise of her passion. Just the memory of that sweet afternoon sent heat rushing through his veins.

The phone rang as he entered the kitchen. Perhaps Royce was reading his mind after all. He picked up the receiver.

"Aye?"

"Lord Seakirk? Ah, it's Inspector O'Mally, Your Lordship. I came up to question the lads who gave your lady a bit of trouble the fortnight past and thought I might come by and give you some news."

Kendrick paused, faced with two alternatives. One was spending the morning listening to the Inspector ramble on about things he didn't wish to think about. The other was training with Royce, then fixing his love a meal, carrying her into her library and making love to her again on that extra-large sofa in the soundproof viewing room.

There just wasn't a choice.

"You can tell me over the phone."

"I spoke to Worthington, my lord, and he informed me of your nuptials and of the recent cure of your affliction."

"Affliction?" Kendrick echoed.

"The one that forced you to refrain from touching anyone?" The Inspector chuckled, albeit weakly. "To be honest, Your Lordship, I'd entertained the idea that you were a ghost." He was silent for several moments. "But such things surely aren't possible. This is the twentieth century, after all."

Affliction? Leave it to Worthington to make it sound as if he'd had the bloody plague!

"Ah, well," Kendrick said gruffly, scrambling for something to say, "'tis the miracle of modern medicine."

"Your tale of being born in the thirteenth century was told very well. I must confess I believed it fully. And what I saw in your hall that day—"

"Mirrors," Kendrick lied. "Eccentricities of the nobility and all."

"Indeed," the Inspector chuckled. "Now, on to other matters, if you will. When should I pop in for our visit?"

Bloody hell, the man was persistent. Kendrick sighed deeply.

"Over the phone, man. I'm too busy for an audience today."

Inspector O'Mally's sigh was faint, but audible. "Very well then, my lord. It would appear that the two lads were from a nearby village and had been hired by a man from London. They wouldn't divulge his name and I'm of the opinion that they didn't have it to give. He paid them via a package posted in London. It will be next to impossible to determine who sent the package. They received a telephone call but we traced it to a booth in London, not a flat. The caller was a man with a nasal voice, but no other distinguishing patterns of speech and such."

"London," Kendrick mused. "I know few there. Have you run checks on them? Anyone with an abundance of funds and a reason to want Genevieve dead?"

"The only person you and Lady Seakirk have in common is Bryan McShane, my lord. I called his secretary and was told he was out of the office the week the funds and instructions were posted."

Kendrick stroked his chin thoughtfully. Bryan McShane? Impossible. The man was a pitiful rabbit. And he was paid far too well to attempt anything so foolish. How could he profit by hurting Genevieve?

"Nay, my good man, he has no reason to want to hurt my lady. It has to be someone else."

"I will of course keep looking, but I'll keep my eye on this young McShane, my lord, if you don't mind. You never know just what lurks inside the criminal mind."

"You do that," Kendrick agreed. "Ring me when you have tidings."

He hung up. Bryan McShane? Preposterous. The man was afraid of his own shadow. He wouldn't have the courage to look at a thug, much less hire one. Kendrick shook his head and put the matter out of his mind. He was perfectly capable of protecting Genevieve and he fully intended to do so. The next lad who tried to harm her would find out firsthand just how fierce he was.

He had just put his finger to the phone to dial when he heard the light thump of bunny-covered feet and knew that his lady had arrived. He hung up the phone and waited for her.

She wore an oversized sleep shirt that hung to her knees and proudly declared that she'd fallen and couldn't reach her snooze alarm; and, of course, she was wearing her pink slippers with the ridiculous ears that flopped over her toes. Kendrick opened his arms and she walked right into them. He gathered her close and rocked her as she yawned against his chest.

"Poor lamb," he chuckled. "Too early?"

"The sun isn't even up."

"It's almost ten, Genevieve."

"It still looks dark to me."

"That's because your eyes are closed."

"Do you have to be so damned cheerful so early?"

He laughed at her disgruntled tone and lifted her face up to kiss her. She melted against him and he groaned as she wrapped her arms around him. There was nothing quite like a sleepy Genevieve to get a man's blood boiling first thing in the morning. He'd experienced it just the morning before. He'd merely leaned over and breathed a good morrow into her ear. The next thing he'd known, she'd wrapped her arms around him and proceeded to give him sleepy kisses until he'd had no choice but to let her seduce him. And seduce him she had, not even opening her eyes. He'd expected her to then roll over and fall back asleep. Instead, she'd finally opened her eyes, given him a sleepy grin and asked him what he planned on fixing her for breakfast after that fine dessert.

Kendrick grinned against her mouth, then pulled back and turned her around, swatting her gently.

"I'm going to train for an hour or two. Go back to bed."

"You'll wake me up soon?"

"In two hours. Go back upstairs before you fall asleep on your feet."

"Be careful," she said, feeling her way to the door. "Wouldn't want you to cut off anything important."

Kendrick barked out a laugh as Genevieve disappeared. He toyed with the idea of following her, then forced himself to think of how fat and lazy he'd become. He needed to train. Two hours, then the rest of the afternoon spent lazing with his love on whatever comfortable horizontal surface they could find.

He dialed Adelaide's number, then asked for Royce.

"Kendrick, you fool, what are you doing?"

"Giving my lady a bit of peace. Have someone drive you home. I want to train."

"I have a motorcycle. Bought it yesterday. I think you're mad to choose me over your lady, but I'll be there posthaste."

"I'm not choosing you, dolt," Kendrick grumbled, but Royce had already hung up. He hung up the phone and stretched, then bent and tried to work the kinks out of his muscles. It had been over a week since he'd ridden, much less picked up a sword. Royce would find him poor sport indeed.

He took his blade and went to sit out on the front steps of his hall. It was cold out, but he forced himself to ignore it. How soft he'd become in unlife. He'd never before paid much heed to the cold; warring had never been a comfortable proposition and he had learned early on not to complain of it. He smiled. How easy it was to complain now, especially since a hot fire and his love waited within.

He lifted an eyebrow as the portcullis was raised and a motorcycle roared through the gate. Kendrick grinned as Royce came to a halt before him. His captain was clad all in black with his sword attached to the back of his vehicle like a flagpole. Royce dismounted, took off his helmet and smirked.

"You look like a lazy whelp, Kendrick. Get you to your feet and let's have a bit of play this morn."

Kendrick rose and stretched. "Insults will not work with me. I'm far too contented for that."

Royce stripped off his jacket and peeled away NBA-style warm-ups. Clad in nothing but shorts and a T-shirt, he picked up his sword and motioned with it.

"Tell me of it while we work. Tales of your fetching bride

might be enough to distract me, and distracting me is surely the only way you'll make even a respectable showing."

Kendrick picked up his sheathed weapon and grinned as he clapped Royce on the back. "Flattery always was your strong suit, my friend. And I'll not share the secrets of my marriage bed with you. But I will hear of your conquests in the village. How do you find twentieth-century wenches?"

"Very much to my liking, but I daresay I'll never understand the concept of dating. They require all manner of gifts, meals and wooing and then I'm favored with naught but a kiss, if that."

Kendrick laughed. "You should have passed more of your time watching television, Royce. That's how 'tis done nowadays. And I'll thank you not to ruin any virgins. I don't fancy a line of furious fathers at my door each morn."

"I'll do my best to humor you."

They walked around the side of the hall opposite the garden. Kendrick was tempted to have the grass pulled up and the lists reinstated. Nay, it was best to put sand down in the outer bailey. He and Royce would need room to train, and the inner bailey seemed too confining. He sighed as he pulled his sword from the scabbard and tossed the sheath aside. How strange life was going to be without a garrison of men to train with each day, without the worries of defending his keep against enemies, without wondering how he could balance what the soil could produce with what his people needed to survive. How easy life had become since his time.

He realized he was staring blindly only when Royce put his hand on his shoulder and shook him.

"Kendrick? Dreaming of your lady?"

Kendrick shook his head. "Times have changed, my friend."

Royce smiled. "I understand your meaning, my lord. I'll miss the roughness of our life."

"Liar. You complained each time we went into battle."

"I don't know how you'd know. You were complaining much louder than I and doubtless couldn't hear anything but your own whine."

Kendrick sighed. "I won't miss the killing, but I'll miss the excitement."

"And the cold, and the poor food, and the diseases, and the danger, and the leeches. I can understand why."

"That isn't the point."

"We'll simply need to find something to take the place of it," Royce said, stepping back and drawing his sword. "Perhaps we'll recruit a few lads from the village who wish to be trained and pass a few hours each day that way. As for the rest, we'll take up other things to fill our days. I daresay skiing wouldn't be a bad sport. I've always been fond of speed."

Kendrick fended off Royce's attack with ease born of years of practice. In the back of his mind, he noted that he wasn't nearly as out of shape as he'd thought himself and that pleased him. Aye, perhaps a sport was the thing. In truth, he'd gained so much more than he'd given up.

He laughed at the thought. There was no comparing it. He had a strong body. He had a well-built keep and a bank full of money. And he had Genevieve. Anything else was merely a luxury.

"I'm not so poor a swordsman," Royce growled.

Kendrick blinked, then realized his captain had thought he laughed at him. "It wasn't you, Royce."

Royce grunted and renewed his assault. "Wipe the smirk off your face, Seakirk, lest you force me to do the deed myself."

Kendrick laughed again. He relished the feel of his muscles working as he wielded his heavy broadsword. He grinned at the shocks that went up his arm each time his blade connected with Royce's. Nay, he'd lost nothing and gained so much.

He parried with Royce until his arms began to ache and the sun was past the point of noon. He cried peace and Royce collapsed back on the grass.

"The saints be praised," he gasped. "I think I prefer being a spirit to having this pain of sore muscles."

"Of course you don't," Kendrick said, holding down his hand and hauling his captain to his feet. "A fine showing, little lad. I'll even let you stay for lunch as a reward."

"Only if Genevieve is cooking. I'd rather starve than eat your fare."

Kendrick grinned as he resheathed his sword. "I've become a fine cook. Even Genevieve says my milk shakes are beyond compare."

Royce pointed out to him all the reasons Genevieve would have for flattering his ego and Kendrick laughed at all of them until they approached the corner of the hall. He put his finger to his lips. Royce stopped alongside him and they carefully looked around to the steps.

"By St. George's bones, it's a priest," Royce whispered. "Likely come to exorcise you."

Kendrick elbowed his captain in the ribs. "'Tis likely your stench he comes to rid us of. Be you silent!"

He leaned closer and listened intently.

"You're kidding, right?" Genevieve was saying.

"My lady, I was sent by a concerned acquaintance who bid me see what I could do about easing the disturbance in your hall."

"Disturbance?"

The priest cleared his throat. "The restless spirit, my lady. Might I come in?"

Kendrick frowned. "It doesn't sound like a bloody priest to me," he muttered.

"More like a thief," Royce agreed.

Kendrick pulled back and looked at his captain. Royce raised a single eyebrow in question, a smile tugging at his mouth. Kendrick stroked his chin thoughtfully.

"There is a side door to the kitchen."

"Aye, there is."

"I daresay there's enough ketchup in the ice box to cover at least one of us. That would look ghoulish enough."

"Nay, then your lady would have to clean it up. I say battle gear would be sufficient."

Kendrick nodded and they backed away carefully from the side of the house.

Slipping through the great hall was a trick. Fortunately, Genevieve had let the man in, but kept him near the fron door. Kendrick and Royce ran up the steps to the third floor and down to Kendrick's study.

Ten minutes later they were clomping down the stairs in full gear. Kendrick let his mace thump down the stairs behind him, Royce was making ghostly wails and moans as they went. Kendrick thought it a bit much, but he wasn't going to rob Royce of his sport.

They reached the great hall and Kendrick had a hard time not grinning at his lady. She was leaning back against the hall door, her arms folded across her chest, her expression one of warning.

"Bolt the door, Genevieve," he boomed.

She hesitated.

"Bolt the door!" he thundered, raising his sword and waving it menacingly.

She obeyed, rolling her eyes.

And then the priest pulled a knife. Kendrick didn't think, he merely reacted. He had his own knife out of his belt and flying from his hand in the blink of an eye. The blade caught the man in the shoulder just as he threw his own blade.

"Bloody hell!" Royce bellowed.

Kendrick pinned the priest against the door with his sword at the man's throat.

"Royce?"

"In my shoulder. Nothing serious."

Kendrick looked at Genevieve who had gone white as a sheet. "Love, call the authorities. Inspector O'Mally is down in the village. He'll be interested in this man of the cloth, I'll warrant."

Once she had disappeared into the kitchen, Kendrick looked back at his captive. He removed his sword from the man's throat, then pulled his knife free.

"I'm bleedin' to death!" the man exclaimed.

"You'll live. Now, who are you? And don't bother me with lies about your being a priest."

"I'm not talkin' to anyone but my lawyer."

Kendrick caught the man by the throat and lifted him up off the ground. "If you don't tell me what I want to know, you

won't be alive to talk to a lawyer. Only my comrade and I ar
in this room with you. You wounded him. You don't think
could run you through and claim self-defense?"

"Who are you?" the man gasped.

"Kendrick de Piaget, earl of Seakirk. Your executioner i
you don't loosen your tongue."

"You're supposed to be a ghost!"

"Do I feel like a ghost to you? Nay, I do not. But you'll cer
tainly be naught but spirit if you don't answer my questions
What are you doing here?"

"Trying to exorcise you!"

"*Merde,*" Kendrick growled. "The real reason." He droppe
the man back against the door and brought up his blade to th
man's throat. "Talk while you still have a voice to use." Whe
the man still seemed unwilling to speak, Kendrick carefull
slit the false clergy collar and flung it away with a flick of hi
wrist.

"I was to kidnap the woman," the man blurted out. "An
carry her down to the village. Mr. McShane said I'd have n
trouble getting her. Bloody hell, he's a liar!"

"Bryan McShane?" Kendrick said. "What in the world doe
he want with Genevieve?"

The man shook his head gingerly. "I'd not be knowing tha
Your Lordship. I'm just a workin' man, my lord, tryin' to fee
my family."

Kendrick frowned. "Perhaps you'll earn your bread in a dif
ferent manner from now on, old man. Now, where were you t
meet our illustrious Master McShane?"

"At the inn. The first room on the left at the top of the stair.
He said he'd be waitin' for me."

"Let's not keep him waiting any longer than necessary
shall we? Royce, where is Genevieve?"

"I'm right here," she said, coming across the room.

"Bind Royce's arm, would you? We'll carry him down t
hospital and then take care of Master McShane."

Kendrick kept his eyes on his prisoner as he listened t
Royce mutter and curse under his breath. Genevieve wasn
making a sound. Then he felt himself pushed aside, an

Royce's fist connected with the false father's face. Kendrick contemplated telling his captain to stop, then discarded the idea. He would have been doing the same thing if he hadn't just found himself with an armful of wife.

"I can't believe this," she whispered hoarsely. "Bryan McShane? What could he possibly want with me?"

"We'll know soon enough, love," Kendrick said, trying to keep the anger out of his voice. Bryan McShane was a dead man. He was likely behind all of Genevieve's frights and he would most certainly pay for his sport.

"Royce, he's senseless," Kendrick said, reaching out to grab hold of his captain's arm. "Leave him be. With any luck, we'll see the Inspector on our way into the village and he can relieve us of this burden."

Royce hefted the man over his shoulder and carried him down the steps.

"Don't bleed on my car," Kendrick warned as Royce climbed into the back seat with the senseless priest.

"Kendrick, your concern is touching."

Kendrick flashed him a smile in the rearview mirror. Royce winked in return and Kendrick knew his friend would survive. Now he had to concentrate his energies on finding Bryan McShane and keeping him alive long enough to put him through hell.

The thought was singularly appealing.

Chapter
Thirty-one

Bryan pulled his hat lower over his eyes and slumped down in his seat. Taking the train had been a flash of inspiration. Taking it to Scotland instead of down to London had been nothing short of brilliant. First to Edinburgh, then on an airplane to America. The thought of living in the States terrified him—those pesky Americans with their uncivilized ways—but he would bear it. At least he would be alive to bear it. A lucky thing he had recently placed all his money in a Swiss bank account. Having to go back to dig in his mattress would have been unfortunate indeed.

The clackety-clack of the train should have soothed him, but instead it startled him continuously. His feet would have sounded like that while they banged against the wall as he hung a foot off the ground with Maledica's fingers around his throat. He pulled at the collar of his shirt uncomfortably. God help him.

He exited the train several hours later on shaky legs. The thought of taking a bus to the airport didn't appeal. What he wanted to do was take a cab and collapse in the back of it. He stumbled to the curb and opened the door. Good: it was empty. He wasn't so far gone that he'd lost his caution.

"The airport," he said, falling back against the seat. "And step on it."

The far door opened and he shook his head, his eyes still closed. "I don't want to share."

"Where you're going, little mouse, there's only one to a box."

Bryan opened his mouth to scream. Maledica stifled the scream with his hand.

"A deserted alley will do nicely," Maledica said to the cabby, tossing him a handful of hundred-pound notes. "Discretion is the key. If you'll wait, I'll pay you to drive me to the airport. Or has my servant already done that? How convenient."

Bryan closed his eyes, knowing it was too late to pray, too late to do anything but enjoy his last few moments on earth and grieve a bit for the lion who had never truly come out in him. Perhaps he'd have a chance beyond the Pearly Gates, as he was sure he'd be entering them shortly.

A pity, really. Among other things, he certainly would have liked to see Maledica pitted against Lord Seakirk, especially now that he'd seen the ghost climb out of the car back at the village and realized that de Piaget was no longer merely a spirit.

The car stopped in darkness.

Bryan sighed as he felt his fear rush through him like a roar.

And then he felt hands go around his throat.

And he knew no more.

Chapter
Thirty-two

Genevieve looked up as Kendrick came from Royce's hospital room. He was smiling faintly and she relaxed.

"He's all right?"

"Aye. 'Twas but a paltry wound. I survived much worse and made not nearly the noise as I was being stitched up. My captain is a woman."

"I heard that," a voice called from within the room.

Kendrick smiled as he pulled Genevieve to her feet. "He fears I will shame him before that little wench down yonder, see her? My marriage has truly affected him, for he told me he's fallen in love and will wed her before spring."

"It's the Florence Nightingale syndrome," Genevieve smiled. "Happens to a lot of patients."

"Indeed?" Kendrick stretched, then made a face of pain. "My muscles seem to be a bit sore from the afternoon's exertion. I don't suppose you would care to be nursemaid to me tonight, would you?"

"Depends on what you'll give me for doing it."

Kendrick only smiled as they continued on down the corridor, but Genevieve didn't mistake it for anything but a promise. She put her arm around his waist and hugged him as they left the building. How close she had come to losing him without even being aware of it. The last thing she had expected from the "priest" was to see him pull a knife out of his pocket.

She closed her eyes and let the purr of the motor soothe her as Kendrick drove them home. He was tense. She could feel that without touching him. She supposed he had his reasons, as did she. Knowing that Bryan McShane wanted her was unnerving to say the least, especially since he was nowhere to be found. She hoped he had decided his plan wasn't worth pursuing and had left the country.

She opened her eyes as the car crossed over the drawbridge, then sat up and peered out the window. She could have sworn she saw shapes in the darkness.

"Kendrick," she began, then she shrieked as he slowed the car to a stop. There was a man standing no more than ten paces away, dressed in full armor. His sword was in front of him, point down in the dirt, and he rested his hands on the hilt.

Kendrick reached for the door handle.

"Don't," she pleaded. "Oh, Kendrick, lock the door and let's turn around."

Kendrick smiled faintly. "Don't fret, beloved. I know the man. The ghost, rather."

"But—"

He leaned over and kissed her. "All is well. Lock the door behind me."

He got out of the car. She locked the door, then leaned forward and rested her hand on the horn. If the other man made any suspicious moves Kendrick couldn't see, she'd warn him.

Her husband walked purposefully toward the ghost, then stopped. They were turned at an angle so Genevieve could see their profiles. The ghost was intimidating, but Kendrick more so. He looked as arrogant and formidable as if he were lord of the keep and the man facing him a mere servant.

Perhaps that was the truth. Genevieve felt the tension drain from her as the ghost did nothing but answer the questions Kendrick put to him. Finally he made Kendrick a low bow and disappeared into the darkness. Kendrick walked back to the car and Genevieve unlocked the doors for him.

"Who was that?"

"Stephen of Burwyck-on-the-Sea. He was one of my father's vassals' sons in life. I daresay you'll never see him up close." Kendrick winked at her. "He's very shy."

"He looks fairly fierce."

"As fierce as I?"

She smiled and patted his leg. "Of course not. That's why he was bowing to you, not the other way around. It's obvious he knows who is lord here. What was he doing?"

"Keeping watch for me. I didn't like the thought of bringing you back to an empty hall so I bid him see to any visitors."

"Were there any?"

"Stephen regretted to say that there weren't."

Genevieve smiled and leaned her head back against the seat. "You really do have some questionable friends, my lord."

He returned her smile and pulled up to the hall. He opened the door, then came around to fetch her. Genevieve went into his arms when he pulled her from the car.

"Kendrick, you could have died—"

He kissed her. "Hush, love. Nothing will happen to me. Well, I might freeze to death if we stand out here much longer. Let us go inside and I'll build you a fire in our bedchamber. Or, if you like, we'll put blankets on the floor, and play camping in the library. We do have the ingredients for s'mores, don't we?"

"I wouldn't dare be without them."

"Then I'll fetch what's necessary from the kitchen and wait for you in the library. Run on and change into something more comfortable."

Genevieve nodded. She made it halfway up the stairs before she realized she was frightened witless. She fled down the hallway to her bedroom, flicked on the lights and slammed the door behind her. Her room was empty and she heaved a sigh of relief. She changed quickly into a nightshirt and ran from the room. She slipped and slid all the way down the hall, down the stairs and across the great hall. Kendrick caught her at the door to the library.

"Whoa," he chuckled, "why are you running?"

"It was dark up there."

He gave her a squeeze. "The front door is bolted and everything else is secure." He pulled her into the library and locked the door. "Now you are my prisoner for the night. What wicked things should I do with you?"

Genevieve couldn't smile. "Kendrick, I'm worried."

He took her hand and led her over to the fluffy comforter he'd spread out before the fire. He sat and pulled her down with him. His expression was grave.

"I can protect you."

"It's not me I'm worried about," she exclaimed. "What if something happened to you?"

He shook his head, as if he couldn't believe what he was hearing. "Genevieve, McShane doesn't want me."

"You don't know that."

Kendrick smiled dryly. "And that is why he tried to kidnap you three times instead of me? Gen, don't think about it any more. I've doubled the security on the hall, both mortal and not-so-mortal. There isn't a soul who'll walk on Seakirk's land that I don't know of it immediately. You'll be perfectly safe while I go out and do some investigating—"

"The hell you will," she interrupted.

"Now, Gen—"

"Don't even think about it," she said, taking hold of the front of his sweater. "You let the police handle this." He opened his mouth to protest, but she shook her head. "If you so much as look like you're trying to get involved in this, I'll divorce you."

He blinked. "What?"

"You heard me. These aren't the Middle Ages, Kendrick, and you aren't a mercenary. The detectives are trained to deal with this sort of thing and you aren't."

"I am a fine warrior," he said stiffly.

"I'm not talking about that. I'm talking about a man possibly coming at you with a gun. It's a different world. Leave the investigating to those who do it all the time. You stay here and keep an eye on your family because your family loves you very much and doesn't want to lose you."

She was prepared to argue much harder, but Kendrick didn't seem to need any more convincing. He obviously wasn't happy with what she'd said, but she could see in his eyes that he recognized the truth of it. Genevieve put her arms around his neck and hugged him.

"I love you. I don't want to lose you."

"If it were a fight in the lists, I could best any knave," he muttered.

"I know that, my lord."

"Indeed, I would relish such a challenge."

"And you'd do a great job of it, too," she agreed. "And I'd be there, cheering you on."

"I am a superior warrior," he reminded her.

Genevieve smiled. "Of course you are, my lord. You're superior in quite a few areas. Roast a few marshmallows for me and allow me to praise your prowess at the cooking fire. Then I just might praise your prowess in other activities."

Kendrick drew her onto his lap and cradled her. "I'm not going to let you out of my arms until this mystery is solved." He pressed his lips against her hair. "I'll keep you safe, you'll see. I'm handy enough with a gun, if need be."

"A gun? Where did you learn that?"

"I'm not completely behind the times."

"Well, don't you dare start carrying one." She frowned at him, then felt her frown fade at the worry she saw in his eyes. "Stop," she whispered. "Everything will be okay. The Inspector will figure it out. Then our lives will get down to normal and we'll grow old and probably boring together."

He smiled and kissed her softly. "We'll never grow boring for I have the distinct feeling our lives will never be normal."

"We don't have a very good track record, do we?"

He laughed. "Nay, my sweet, we do not. But I wouldn't trade our meeting and courtship for anything. It's only made me appreciate you all the more. Now," he said, putting her gently off his lap, "hand me a skewer and prepare yourself to praise my skill with camping cooking, for I daresay there isn't another who can do a s'more up the way I can."

Genevieve handed him two metal fondue forks and the bag of marshmallows. Then she leaned back on her hands and watched him as he stripped off his sweater and shirt, shoes and socks and set to work. She suppressed the urge to pinch herself to make sure she wasn't dreaming. How often did wishes come true? Not often enough but they certainly had for her.

She hugged her knees to her chest as she watched him and marveled over his finely honed body. She smiled when he looked over his shoulder at her and winked. Then she grinned when he began fishing for compliments again. Her joy was almost enough to make her glad he'd gone through seven centuries of hell. She couldn't imagine loving anyone else. How had she ever survived without him?

She leaned up and put her arms around his neck. "I love you," she whispered in his ear.

"Tell me again."

She leaned over his shoulder and kissed his cheek. "I love you. And I'm glad you waited for me. You've made me enormously happy."

"And you me."

She rubbed her cheek against his, smiling at the sandpapery feeling, then kissed her way back to his ear.

"Genevieve—"

"Hush. Pay attention to your marshmallow."

She took his earlobe between her teeth and nibbled. He shivered. Finding that reaction to her liking, she gently traced his ear with her tongue. His breath caught. Genevieve trailed her fingers over his chest, grinning to herself at the way his muscles jumped. Seducing Kendrick was just so darned rewarding. The man was patently unable to hide his reactions. He would have made a terrible poker player.

"Kendrick," she breathed into his ear.

"Aye?" His voice had taken on a decidedly hoarse quality.

"Your snack is on fire."

"Damn."

He blew out the flames, then set the skewers down on the hearth. Then he folded his hands primly in his lap and remained where he was.

"I regret the interruption," he said solemnly.

"I'll bet you do, buster," she grinned. She pulled him back, then pushed him down on the comforter. His eyes were twinkling as she sat on his stomach and leaned down to kiss him. "You look rather smug."

"Smug? Nay, merely content. I like it when you seduce me."

"There's no seduction implied here, my lord. I'm flat out having my way with you."

"Then, by all means, have away."

That was another thing about seducing Kendrick. He was always so willing to pitch in and help. He was more than happy to help her off with her pajamas and very cooperative about taking off his own remaining clothes. And Genevieve never thought to wonder how he received her caresses, for he was certainly disposed to telling her how wonderful she made him feel. If anything, he made her blush with his praise.

Genevieve was fairly pleased with herself too, as she held onto her love while he was caught up in the throes of passion. She had bedded her husband properly and damn, it was a fine accomplishment.

She started to pull away, but Kendrick wrapped his arms around her.

"Not yet."

"You want me to stay?"

"That's why I'm holding you in an inescapable embrace. You aren't uncomfortable anywhere, are you?"

"Not in the least."

"Then stay yet awhile," he murmured, leaning up to kiss her softly. "Put your head on my shoulder and let me relish the feel of you in my arms. Have I ever told you just how deeply I love you? Or that I would cheerfully wait another seven hundred years to have you if I had to?"

"Oh, don't say that," she said quickly. "I wouldn't want to test it."

She ducked her head and pressed her lips against his neck. It didn't matter if he was teasing her; that he'd found her bungling touch pleasing was enough. Of course, he'd flinched good and hard when she'd smacked his you-know-what with her knee, but he'd seemed to have forgotten the pain quickly enough. With practice, she might even be able to not hurt him before she made love to him.

Twenty minutes later, she had recaptured her 49ers nightshirt and was scratching her husband's broad back as he worked on their snack. She wasn't quite sure how she'd gotten roped into servitude, but she was sure it had been an underhanded maneuver on Kendrick's part. Not that she minded all that much. His skin was smooth and his groans were music to her ears. His back was free of all but the most minor of scars, except for the Infidel's bite over his kidney and a long, thin mark over his shoulder blade.

"Where did you get this one?" she asked as she traced it with her finger.

"I don't think you want to know all the sordid details."

"Something wicked to confess, Sir Kendrick?"

"Would it help to know she's dead?"

Genevieve laughed. "Go on. I can take it."

"In truth," he said, turning to face her, "there's little to take. I was at court, a few years after the Crusade, a year or two before my murder, when I met a woman. Not a beautiful woman, not even a woman who stirred my blood. Indeed, I came to her room at her invitation but could not bed her for I could muster up nothing more than a sisterly affection for her. She was the king's ward, a homely thing whose parents had been slain while traveling from Wales. We came to an agreement, she and I, that we would keep each other company and laugh together at the intrigues of court life. And for a fortnight, we did just that."

"You were very sweet."

"Does this mean you won't sentence me to a life of celebacy?"

She smiled and shook her head. "So, you befriended this homely orphan and then what happened?"

"Well, one evening the king held a feast, over and above the feasts that were held each night for his pleasure. And it was during this feast that my newly acquired friend, Lianna, was insulted. I, being the fool I was, challenged the knave and found myself contemplating a morning in the lists."

"To defend her honor?"

"Aye."

Genevieve smiled lovingly. "You were so gallant."

"I was an idiot."

"It was a very chivalrous thing to do. So then you had to meet this guy in the lists. Did you know him?"

"Aye," Kendrick sighed, "he was my cousin, William of Sedgwick."

"And you knew him previously?"

"Aye, we had met a time or two. Even had I not known him, I knew his reputation, and it was a poor one. His treatment of Lianna should have warned me further of his true character, but I thought that on the king's field he would at least behave honorably."

Her eyes widened. "He gave you that scar."

"Aye, he did. We battled with lances first and I bested him fairly, though it was an effort as he was a fine warrior. By the time I dismounted in front of the king's pavilion and knelt to my leige lord, the blood was thundering in my ears so badly I could barely hear the cheers of the crowd. I didn't notice that their cheers had turned to cries of warning until Lianna tumbled over the railing in her haste to save me. I ducked and William's blade only glanced off my shoulder, instead of plunging through my heart as had been his intent. I turned and fought him until he was bleeding from every bit of exposed skin and had no more energy to come at me. The king banished him for his treachery. William vowed revenge, but I never saw him again. 'Tis a safe bet he went to his grave despising me, though he should have rather despised himself for his lack of honor. A man fairly bested does not strike the victor once his back is turned."

"Wow," she whispered. "You were very lucky. I hope you rewarded Lianna properly."

"Actually, the king tried to reward me by giving her to me to wife. My younger brother Jason, who always did have a discerning soul, offered himself in my stead. Of course, it hardly hurt his feelings any that Lianna's dowry consisted of more fiefs than Jason could count."

"Greedy little guy."

Kendrick smiled. "Actually, he couldn't have cared less. He sired himself a dozen children and gave away fiefs as fast as the wee ones could come of age and claim them. Then he and Lianna sequestered themselves in their favorite keep and lived out the rest of their lives in bliss."

"Then I suppose it was a good thing for me that marriage was just a *bit too confining* for your taste, as you put it."

He leaned forward and kissed her softly. "Actually, I was saving myself for you. You were waiting for me, weren't you?"

She went willingly into his embrace. "You know I was. I couldn't have asked for a braver, more chivalrous knight."

"Nor I for a more beautiful, bewitching lady." He put his s'more down on the hearth and drew her onto his lap. "I'll keep you safe, my Gen. I vow it with my life."

Genevieve closed her eyes and wrapped her arms tightly around his neck. The possibility of Kendrick losing his life terrified her. How had Anne borne having Kendrick's father leave to go to war?

Genevieve sighed deeply as Kendrick's hand skimming over her back began to relax her. It wouldn't come to that. The Inspector would find Bryan and put him in jail, then she and Kendrick would get down to living a normal, everyday, wonderfully uneventful existence.

Chapter
Thirty-three

Genevieve frowned. The button to the drop-drawer of her green feety pajamas was nowhere to be found. She'd looked in her drawers, under the bed, in the trunk where Kendrick had hidden a good portion of her clothes, and in the bathroom, which was the last place she'd worn her green ones before Kendrick had pulled them off her with all due haste. But even in the bathroom she'd felt a draft up her back; surely the button had been long gone before that.

She thought back over the places she'd been in the past two weeks, wondering just which room would contain her missing lime-green button. Other than one evening last week, she hadn't worn her pajamas since the day . . . the day Kendrick had come back to life. She shivered at the memory of him carrying her down to the basement and tying her to the post. Thank heavens he'd regained his memory before he'd done something *she* would have regretted.

She left her bedroom and made her way down through the great hall and to the cellar. She was half tempted to make Kendrick come with her, but he was outside playing with

Royce and she didn't want to disturb him. His captain had called earlier and invited him to a few hours in the lists. Kendrick had made a production of not wanting to go, but Genevieve knew better. She'd sent him off with a smile, glad to have the chance to retrieve all her clothes while he was out.

A blast of icy wind startled her as she opened the cellar door and she almost closed it again and headed for higher ground. But no, that was stupid. There was nothing down there but a few spiders. That and probably a few stray ghosts. Those she could handle. Kendrick's entourage seemed to grow by the day. The men didn't come inside the hall as far as she knew, but she had certainly caught herself walking through a few of them outside. Just yesterday she'd bumped into Sir Stephen, who had blushed clear to the roots of his ghostly hair, babbled an incoherent apology, then turned and fled.

She turned on the light and descended the steps, ignoring the chills that went down her spine. It wasn't as though she were descending into a roomful of coffins. She smiled confidently as she put her foot on the cement floor. Piece of cake. She walked over to the stone pillar and looked around it. She even went so far as to get down on her hands and knees and search.

"Success." She picked up the button and started to rise, then something light colored caught her eye. She knelt again and reached around the post. It was a piece of paper, so old it almost crumbled to dust in her hands. She carefully picked it up and climbed back up the stairs.

She laid the piece of parchment out on the kitchen table and looked at it. The wax seal was broken and badly chipped but she still saw the ornate shape of what could have been a dragon. A dragon? She shook her head in wonder and carefully unfolded the note.

She squinted and struggled to make out the letters. Now, if it had been in English, she might have been able to understand it. But she made out the word *je* and knew it was French. Why that surprised her, she didn't know. Searching carefully through the characters revealed the names William de Sedgwick and Richard de York.

William of Sedgwick?

Genevieve pulled away from the paper as if it had suddenly come alive. A letter from Richard to William? No, William's signature was at the bottom. She felt the hair stand up on the back of her neck. It defied logic, but she had the distinct feeling this might explain what had happened all those centuries ago.

She ran from the kitchen. Kendrick could interrupt his training for this.

"Kendrick!"

Kendrick stopped in mid-stroke and looked up to see Genevieve running across the grass. He leaned on his sword and stared at her, unable to fight his smile. Would he ever become accustomed to the fact that this adorable creature was his? He wiped his face on his shirt, then resheathed his sword. He wanted two free hands to capture his woman with. The moment she was within reach, he grabbed her. She squirmed out of his arms.

"Not now. I found something downstairs you have to come look at right away."

"A new place to make love?" he inquired politely with a wink thrown Royce's way.

Genevieve made a sound of impatience before she took his hand and started to drag him back to the house. "This is serious."

"So is making love."

"Kendrick!"

Royce laughed as he clapped a hand on Kendrick's shoulder. "Marriage has left you with nothing but one thought in your head, my lord. I vow you were never so concerned with the fairer sex when last we were alive."

"'Tis my sweet Genevieve who distracts me so."

"I can see why."

Kendrick scowled at his captain and considered halting and giving Royce a few bruises in warning, but Genevieve was single-minded in her desire to see him back inside the house. He threw Royce a dark look as he jogged to keep up with his love.

She pulled him all the way to the kitchen table, then pointed at the piece of parchment laying there.

"Read this."

Kendrick started to pick up the epistle, then saw the condition of the paper. Much too frail for handling. He bent over and quickly read the missive.

First the blood drained from his face, then he felt it all pool in his ears. The thundering deafened him.

Royce gasped from over his shoulder. "The bloody whoreson!"

Kendrick swayed and instantly felt Genevieve's hands helping him down into a chair.

"Kendrick, what does it say?"

Kendrick shook his head. Words were beyond him. He read the letter again.

I, William of Sedgwick, send greetings to you, Richard of York, and by this writing seal with blood our bargain. Once I receive word that Kendrick of Artane is en route to Seakirk, I will arrive with the promised sum of ten thousand marks of silver. Once he has been slain and I have seen for myself that your lady Matilda has worked her dark magic on him, the silver shall be yours. Once the deed is accomplished, I will escort your lady to her coven and pay her another five thousand marks of silver for setting in motion the spell which will give me power over death. These things I promise and bargain for, setting my hand to this epistle in blood, in the Year of Our Lord, 1260.

"Oh, merciful saints," he whispered hoarsely. He looked up at Royce. "I can't believe it."

"What does it say?" Genevieve asked, frantically. "Damn it, will one of you translate it for me?"

Kendrick shook his head. "Ask Royce. I'm not equal to the task."

Royce translated it dutifully. Kendrick barely had the presence of mind to catch his lady when her knees buckled.

"William? The one who came at you in the lists?"

"The very same," Kendrick said, drawing her down onto his lap. "I never thought he would go this far."

"How far did he go?"

"He sold his soul to a coven of witches in return for power over death, just as he said in the letter."

"But what does that mean? He didn't die? Or is he a ghost? Or is it that he merely wanted you to be bound to Seakirk?"

Kendrick shrugged helplessly. "I have no idea. It could mean anything."

"Merciful saints above," Royce said hoarsely. "Then Sedgwick could still be roaming about the island. The saints preserve us if he is! Who knows what kind of mischief he's wrought."

"Indeed," Kendrick nodded. The thought was truly mindboggling. Perhaps some of the ghostly lads would know more. *Sir Stephen, come to me,* he called, pleased his mental powers still worked with his ghostly garrison. He drummed his fingers on the table and waited for his newly acquired vassal to come to him. It had felt odd the day before to have Stephen kneel and pledge him fealty. Kendrick had his suspicions that part of the reason the man had done it was that he was infatuated with Genevieve, but so be it. The more men Kendrick had looking after his lady, the better he'd like it.

He kept Genevieve on his lap as Stephen appeared and made him a bow. The lad studiously avoided looking at Genevieve, and Kendrick suppressed his smile. He'd never met anyone quite as shy as the man before him.

"Sir Stephen, I've a task for you. You remember William of Sedgwick, do you not?"

"Aye, my lord. A dishonorable whoreson if ever there were one." He looked quickly at Genevieve and blushed hotly. "I beg your pardon, my lady."

"I agree completely," Genevieve said, tightening her arm around Kendrick's shoulders.

Kendrick looked at his man. "I've reason to believe that he somehow escaped death by selling his soul. Do you remember his visage?"

"Aye. A blue eye and a brown, my lord. Most disturbing."

"That is our man. What I require is that you question the lads, discreetly of course, to learn if they have seen anyone resembling him. If any feel the need to roam, send them roaming. You I will require to remain here. I'll not have my lady unprotected."

"It would be an honor, my lord Seakirk, to serve you however I may. You'll have my report as soon I've learned aught."

"I'll expect nothing less. You may go."

Stephen bowed again, then tripped over his ghostly feet a time or two and escaped out the side door. Kendrick smoothed his hand over Genevieve's hair.

"Your beauty makes my men clumsy, my love. 'Tis a wonder I can put one foot in front of the other."

She didn't return his smile. "This is worse than I ever imagined, Kendrick. What if William is still alive?"

"Then we'll find him and I'll challenge him to meet me in the lists."

"But after what he did the last time—"

"I'm forewarned this time. He'll not best me."

Genevieve looked at him with troubled eyes. "Maybe it's all a joke."

Kendrick shook his head. "Nay, the letter clearly states that he paid Richard of York ten thousand marks of silver, not a small sum I might add, to do me in. And I daresay he achieved his end of escaping death by forfeiting another five thousand marks of silver to the coven of witches at the abbey."

"Witches?" she echoed. "At an abbey?"

"A rumor in my time, but obviously not far from the truth." He dragged his hand through his hair and released his breath slowly. "I wish I had but one more go at him in the lists!"

"He's long dead, Kendrick," she said gently. "There are no such things as witches. It's probably just a sick joke. Let that be enough for you."

"His head on a pike would be enough for me," Kendrick grumbled. He looked at Genevieve and his expression softened. "Doubtless you're right, my love. I'll let it go. After I thrash Royce in the lists." He kissed her, then rose. "Come with me, Royce. Have the car keys handy, Gen. We'll likely have to carry Royce to hospital once I'm through with him."

Royce snorted as he followed Kendrick from the kitchen. "What a dreamer you are, my lord. I daresay your sweet bride will exert herself greatly to put your soft pudge into the car, as I fully intend to humiliate you this morn. Perhaps you should spare her the effort and concede the match now?"

"Kendrick," Genevieve called, "don't forget you promised to take me to Adelaide's this afternoon. Nazir has already called me twice this morning, wondering when I was coming into town."

"Give me an hour to train, then I'll shower and take you. I'll buy you lunch too, if you think up a few pretty insults for Royce."

Genevieve only grinned and waved him away. Kendrick kept up his chatter with Royce until they were outside, then he continued to talk as they made their way across to the inner bailey wall. Royce's grin immediately faded to concern once Kendrick turned to him.

"Kendrick, you don't suppose it's true, do you?" he said in a hushed voice. "That he bought your death?"

"Aye, I believe that readily enough," Kendrick replied, looking about casually. No sense in babbling his innermost thoughts to an audience. "And I daresay I believe the other just as readily."

"But why would he do it?"

"Don't you want immortality?" Kendrick said, swinging his gaze back to his captain's. "Despite the obvious difficulties, haven't you enjoyed the past seven hundred years? Didn't you watch in awe the first time you saw a moving picture or a rocket blast off into space? Didn't you weep the first time you heard Mozart's symphonies? Didn't you long to drive a car, fly in a plane, sail on a ship? Why would anyone have willingly chosen death, when those were the alternatives?"

"Ah, but none of those things was worth the price of my soul," Royce said. "And are those pleasures of mortality worth the cost of being separated from family that has passed on before? If something happened to Genevieve, would you sell your soul to tarry here without her, or would you accept death when it came, knowing that your joy would be full when you saw your love again?"

Kendrick smiled. "You know my answer to that. But 'tis of William we speak. He had no family, no lover, no friends. He was shamed, shunned, exiled. Think you he wouldn't have scld his soul for revenge?"

"God help us if he did."

"Aye," Kendrick agreed. "But surely he is nothing more than a mortal man. I can best him. We will find him and I will challenge him to face me over lances."

"And when you best him, what then? Will you send him away?"

"He won't be alive to walk away."

"Kendrick, I daresay I needn't tell you how your lady will react to the news that you intend to fight to the death. Don't force me to take your place at her side once you're gone."

"As if she'd have you."

"Many wenches would take me, and willingly too."

"The blind and daft ones."

Royce drew his sword and lashed out. Kendrick only had time to jump back and draw his own blade before his captain was coming at him furiously. Kendrick didn't even have time to grin at Royce's ferociousness. All he could do was concentrate fully on keeping his captain at bay. Perhaps it was best. It took his mind off his problems, the main one being how he would find William of Sedgwick. Killing him was a different matter entirely. Murder was a slap-on-the-wrist offense in medieval times, when it could be proved that it was actually murder and not self-defense or good business. Modern man was a sight more particular about his affairs.

Well, that would come later. Now the task was to find William, then understand what he wanted. And hope he could be bested.

*   *   *

An hour later, Kendrick descended the stairs to his great hall and heard the babble of male voices coming from the kitchen. He sprinted the distance, his heart thumping wildly against his chest. If anything had happened to Genevieve . . .

"Well, I don't think I could relate it to anything you'd understand."

That was Genevieve's voice.

"It looks powerfully sticky. What does it taste like?"

Kendrick pulled up short at the doorway to the kitchen. He was so surprised by what he saw, he couldn't find his wits to scatter the souls with a bellow.

No less than half his ghostly garrison was in his kitchen. Some sat on the counters, others sat at the table, still others hugged the walls. And all of them were watching Genevieve finish off half a peanut butter and jelly sandwich. Even more astonishing was the fact that she looked perfectly at ease, as if she were holding court and these were her loyal and harmless court jesters. Kendrick leaned against the doorframe and looked over the band.

There was Stephen, of course, standing behind his lady with his sword in his hand, looking mightily fierce, as if he intended to behead the first lout to even belch without permission.

Ah, then Colin of Berkhamshire, a seasoned warrior of forty-five summers who had cut such a swath through Germany that Kendrick was certain the republic was still reeling from the aftershocks. And there he sat on Genevieve's left, behaving as prettily as if he'd been born and reared in a sewing circle.

Oh, and not to forget Robert of Conyers. Kendrick smirked. Genevieve would think twice about chatting with him so easily if she'd had half an inkling of the man's fierceness on the battlefield. Kendrick had watched him lay waste to half a garrison by himself, be wounded half a dozen times, yet rise from his bed the next day to fight again. And there he sat, hanging on Genevieve's every word as if he'd never before heard a man talk.

"Well, it is kind of sticky, but that's just the nature of it,"

Genevieve said, washing down her sandwich with a swig of milk. "And it tastes like peanuts. Does anyone know what peanuts are?"

There was much low murmuring, as if the lackwits actually discussed amongst themselves whether or not they had tasted such a thing. Robert of Conyers spoke up.

"Nay, milady, we've no such knowledge. Can you not liken it to something else?"

"I'm afraid not. It's a one-of-a-kind taste. But you guys recognize milk, don't you?"

"Mead?" Colin asked doubtfully. "I much prefer ale."

"So does Kendrick, and for breakfast too, if you can believe it."

"And what does my lord Kendrick think of these peanut-jelly concoctions?" Robert asked. "Does he find them to his liking?"

Kendrick frowned. "As she said before, 'tis nothing you would understand. If you lads have finished with my lady, I've a mind to have her to myself. Now."

The kitchen emptied so quickly, Kendrick had to hold onto the doorframe to keep his balance. It was a good thing his lads were ghosts, else he might have been trampled in the stampede. Once the dust had settled, he looked over to see Stephen still at his post. Stephen sheathed his sword and crossed the room, where he made Kendrick a low bow.

"Your lady is safely delivered to you, my lord. And I have no word on our quarry. I will inform you when I have tidings."

Kendrick nodded imperiously and Stephen departed. Kendrick sauntered over to the table and looked down at his love.

"Wooing the garrison, my lady?"

"They invited themselves," she smiled. "A great bunch of guys, huh?"

Kendrick laughed. And this from the woman who could hardly bear to hold hands with him a few weeks ago? How much she had changed.

"If you only knew just how fierce they were," he said with a smile. "But you seem to have tamed them nicely. Now, must I call them back, or can you make do with me for the rest of the afternoon?"

She rose and hugged him. "How green your eyes have become, my lord."

"They have always been green."

"I know," she smiled. She kissed him softly. "Let's go check on Nazir, then come home. I made the boys promise not to come in unless they were invited. I need privacy to seduce you, Kendrick. And I'm thinking I'll be needing a whole lot of privacy tonight."

She patted him on the behind as she passed him. Kendrick laughed to himself at the come-hither look she cast him over her shoulder on her way out of the kitchen. Aye, things had changed indeed.

The village looked the same as when he last saw it. He couldn't stop himself from looking at each man who passed, though, wondering if he would recognize his old enemy. He saw no one suspicious. Nazir was overjoyed to see Genevieve and threw himself at her feet, begging her to release him from punishment. Kendrick had a hard time not laughing at the horror stories Nazir spouted, merely to garner sympathy.

Nazir's pleading was in vain. Kendrick extricated Genevieve from his servant's clutches soon enough and promised Nazir all manner of gifts and privileges if he would merely behave himself for another week. Worthington would return from his cruise by then and be ready to babysit. Kendrick knew he wasn't equal to the task and he didn't want Genevieve using her time that way, especially when there were far more important things for her to be doing.

He had planned to let her seduce him after they returned to the hall, but when they returned, he found himself with a different desire entirely. He bolted the hall door, then carried his lady up the stairs before she could protest. Once they were safely ensconced in their bedchamber, he undressed her, then fell with her to the bed. It was the most passionate experience

f his long life and he almost fainted with his release.
Genevieve wept.

Then they burrowed under the covers and Kendrick held his
ove as she drifted off to sleep.

He spent the night awake. He examined his situation from a
undred different angles and racked his brain for a suitable
trategy. At least Genevieve was relatively safe. The good In-
pector would take care of finding Bryan McShane and that
ould be solved.

Or would it?

Kendrick sat bolt upright, his mind working furiously. Bryan's
uperior's name was W. S. Maledica. *Maledica?* How could
e have been so stupid? Maledica, from malediction? A curse?
He clapped his hand to his head. By the saints, he was a fool!
He'd never thought to question the man's initials, but he had
he feeling that when he called the office in the morning, he'd
nd they stood for William Sedgwick. But why? Why had
ryan McShane been so eager to have Genevieve? Correction,
hy had William sent Bryan to kidnap Genevieve? What did
he have he could want?

Or was it another angle entirely? Did William know how
uch Genevieve meant to him? Was William merely using
er as another means of tormenting him? But how could
William possibly know just how deeply he loved Genevieve?
r that they had been wed? Or that he now possessed a body
f flesh and bones?

Kendrick lay back down slowly, taking a deep breath and
eleasing it. So many questions and so few answers. He would
ave to redouble his efforts to find William. And if worse
ame to worse, he would lure him to Seakirk and kill him
ithin the walls. That would be fitting, wouldn't it?

Assuming, that is, that he could be killed.

Kendrick gathered his lady close and closed his eyes.

Heaven help him.

Chapter
Thirty-four

Genevieve walked into the house, wondering if her feet we
touching the ground. She'd gone to the doctor, thinking sl
had the flu and wanting to know why it had lasted so lon
She'd never considered the possibility of a child, though wl
she hadn't was a good question. She and Kendrick had be
married two months. And now a baby. She grinned as sl
hugged herself and danced all the way to the kitche
Kendrick would be thrilled.

Wouldn't he?

Yes, he would. Just last night she'd been poring over a bo
of heraldry with him. Kendrick had shown her his family
coat of arms, and how he would change it now that he w
lord of his own keep. His sons and daughters would bear
each a bit differently according to their birth order. She had
missed the note of wistfulness in his voice when he'd contem
plated such a thing.

He'd also shown her the coat of arms for Sedwick.
dragon rampant. Genevieve had gotten shivers at just the sig
of it. William couldn't be still alive. If he were, she sincere

oped he'd chosen some nice warm place like Africa to call
ome. Anywhere far away from England.

Genevieve walked into the kitchen and saw the note on the
efrigerator. Kendrick's bold scrawl greeted her eyes.

> *My Gen, Royce and I've gone riding, as you in-*
> *structed us to do before you left. I hope you passed your*
> *time at Adelaide's pleasantly and came home with a few*
> *fine acquisitions for your trouble. I'll be home before*
> *noon.*

> *Kendrick*

It was only eleven, giving her enough time to bake a batch
f cookies and maybe catch a chapter or two of the novel
Kendrick continued to try to hide from her. She lifted the lid
n the cookie jar. She pulled her book out, smiling as she did
o.

"Subtle, Seakirk," she said, dryly. "So you want your cook-
es, do you?"

"Not that he'll have a mouth with which to eat them," a
eep voice rumbled from the doorway.

Genevieve whirled around, her hand at her throat. Then she
asped. There, standing at the door to her kitchen, was a man
a full battle gear. Heavy chain mail covered his arms and
gs; a helmet rested on his head; his long sword hung by his
de, well within reach of his gloved hands. He stared at her
om out of one blue eye and one brown. Embroidered on his
ircoat was a mythical creature depicted in a fighting stance,
olored in black and red.

A dragon.

It was William of Sedgwick's crest. Genevieve gasped again
d looked around frantically for a weapon. She lunged for the
ock of knives and came up with a meat cleaver. Thick fin-
rs went around her wrist, squeezing until she had no choice
it to drop the knife. She tried kicking. William caught her
cross the cheek and sent her sprawling. He hauled her up and
nned her against the wall. Genevieve couldn't find any

breath for screaming. The man was easily as tall as Kendric
and just as broad. And he looked like he'd like to kill her.

"Who are you?" she whispered.

"I'm surprised de Piaget hasn't told you about me. I van
quished him at a tourney many years ago and he, being th
woman he is, cried foul."

"That's not how I hear the story—" She gasped as his fir
gers tightened around her throat. "Saw . . . scar o
his . . . back."

"Sleeping with a ghost, my dear? How quaint."

"He's not—" She shut her mouth with a snap.

William's eyes narrowed. "He's not what?"

"Nothing."

He buried his hand in her hair. "I have a deed for you
sign, sweet wench, then I believe I'll have you a time or tw
Won't that please His Lordship well?" William laughe
loudly. "God's teeth, what a fine jest! Not only will I have h
castle, but I'll have his woman too, all while he sits unable
do anything about it." He pulled her toward the door. "Whe
is your illustrious lover? Off haunting the stables like the mi
begotten cur he is?"

Genevieve didn't answer. She had to find a way to wa
Kendrick. William held her by the hair once they were ou
side, then reached in his car and retrieved his briefcase. F
opened it and pulled out a deed to the castle.

"Sign it."

"Why should I?"

"Because once I own Seakirk, de Piaget will never have it
William smiled pleasantly. "Won't that be a fine jest? He
bound to Seakirk only for so long as he doesn't own the cas
legally. And now I will be the one to hold the deed." F
laughed again. "Ah, to see him in a hell of my making has a
ways been my fondest desire."

"He wasn't the coward—"

William slammed her against the car so hard, she lost h
breath. "Foolish bitch! You've no idea how I suffered. N
lands were stripped from me. My title was taken away and r
family shunned me. I was forbidden to compete in any tov

ney, not only in England but in Normandy and France. God's bones, woman, I was reduced to begging! It took me years to earn the silver to pay for de Piaget's demise and I paid for the silver in blood. Now sign the damned paper and let us be done with it!"

"She's already signed one deed. She has no need to sign another."

Genevieve looked up to see Kendrick sitting on his horse not twenty paces away. And surrounding him, as far as the eye could see, were other mounted men, all dressed in full battle regalia. Genevieve couldn't tell which ones were ghosts and which ones weren't.

"Let her go, Sedgwick."

William was so stunned that Genevieve managed to slip from his grasp before he was the wiser. She ran around to the other side of the car, watching William to make sure he didn't chase her. He didn't. He shut his briefcase and laughed.

"Ah, de Piaget, you always did have a fine sense of humor. As if you actually thought your pitiful presence would intimidate me. Now, listen closely while I tell you of my plans. First I'll have your wench a few times. You can stay and watch if you like. Indeed, I insist upon it. The men are welcome to remain also. I always did like performing before a crowd."

Kendrick only smiled blandly. "And your performances were always so entertaining, as I remember. I daresay the king didn't care for them, though."

William's eyes narrowed. "Once I've finished raping your woman, I'll have her sign the deed. You didn't know what young Master McShane's real mission was, did you? A pity he met his end a few days past. I never did care for cowards."

"Didn't you? Couldn't you stomach seeing in others what others saw in you?"

William spat at Kendrick's feet.

"Once the castle is mine, you'll never be free of it. The last of the Buchanans will die, eventually, when I've tired of her. Then the estate will belong to me. I might even live here with you, Kendrick. We'll pass the rest of eternity, me in delight, you in hell. Ah, such sweet revenge."

Genevieve had never wished for anything more than she wished for a tranquilizer gun at that moment. She would have shot William in the backside and had the authorities haul him off to jail. An eternity behind bars was what the man deserved.

William turned and looked at her. "And now for my sport. You're a comely thing, Mistress Genevieve. A bit spirited for my taste, but you'll be broken soon enough." He started around the front of the car and Genevieve bolted toward Kendrick. He leaped down from his saddle and pulled her behind him. He drew his sword and held it out. William laughed and walked right into it. Kendrick lifted the point so it only impaled his enemy in the shoulder, not in the heart.

William jerked back in surprise. Then he laughed. "How long can you hold your weapon, pitiful spirit? Another few moments until your strength runs out?" He laughed again. "A pity, de Piaget. You know, don't you, that the only way I can die is by your hand. 'Twas Matilda's idea and I thought it to be a fine jest. As if you could actually hold a blade long enough to do the deed!" He laughed again, heartily.

Kendrick slapped William across the face with the flat of his blade.

"I told you: Genevieve signed the deed giving the castle to me. In return, I was given back my life, the life you stole from me." Kendrick smiled, but his eyes were hard. "Now, old friend, I think it time we face each other in the lists again. Only this time, the king will not be here to save your worthless neck."

William shook his head in disbelief. He pushed the sword away and reached out to push Kendrick. When he encountered a solid form, his eyes widened and he jerked back.

"St. Michael's bones," he said, his voice hoarse. Then he gathered his composure and laughed. It was a forced laugh but a laugh nonetheless. "Very well, then. How shall we do this? Guns?"

"Lances. Royce, fetch William a horse. Nazir, come you close and make certain he possesses no other weapons but his foul stench."

Kendrick pulled Genevieve behind him as she tried to look around him.

"Now is not the time, Genevieve. Wait until Nazir can escort you back to the house."

"I'm not going in the house," she said tightly. "Don't waste your energy trying to make me."

Kendrick conceded the battle quickly. He waited until Nazir had finished frisking William before he beckoned to his servant. "Take her to the outer bailey and watch over her. I don't need to tell you what will be your fate if she's harmed."

"Of course, Master."

Kendrick kept his eyes glued to William as Genevieve retreated with Nazir. He waited again while a saddled horse was brought for William's pleasure. Kendrick noted the beads of sweat on William's brow and noted that they increased when several garrison knights surrounded him at twenty paces. A bloody good thing William couldn't tell a spirit from a mortal.

Once William was mounted, Kendrick motioned him on ahead, surrounding him by mailed knights with grim expressions. He followed, noting that Royce had fetched several lances and was carrying them. He'd likely need all of them, though he sincerely hoped it came down to a battle with swords. He had a scar or two to repay William for.

He saw Genevieve the moment he came from under the tunnel. She was backed up against the wall with Nazir in front of her and a dozen lads surrounding her. Kendrick felt a trickle of tension ease from him. At least Genevieve would be safe. His greatest fear was gone.

Now, there was only room for rage. William would pay for seven hundred years of living in hell. Kendrick took a lance from Royce and positioned himself at one end of the field. He waited until William had turned his horse, then Royce called the start. Kendrick jerked up his shield and lowered his lance, concentrating on nothing but the area of chest left exposed behind William's shield.

They came together in a tremendous crash. William teetered, but regained his balance. Kendrick turned his horse, thundered back down the way and took another lance. His destrier leaped

forward and its hooves pounded against the turf. Kendrick
aimed for the middle of William's shield this time and smiled
grimly when William went tumbling off the back of his horse.
Kendrick dismounted and sent his horse backing away with a
sharp command. He crossed the field to his opponent, feeling
the old battle fever come upon him as it hadn't done for seven
centuries. His rage boiled within him but his head was clear.
The world took on a surreal quality, movements became
slowed, the only sound he heard was the blood thundering in
his ears. His reflexes were quick and sure, so much quicker
that to his mind William looked like a bumbling page.

He toyed with William, cutting him, taunting him, infuriat-
ing him. Aye, once this whoreson was dead, there would be no
more need for Genevieve to fear, no reason for her to run
shrieking down the stairs because she thought she saw something in the shadows. Aye, William's death would bring an
end to many things.

William finally released a bellow of rage and came at
Kendrick in a fury. Though it was tempting to drag it out
longer, Kendrick was acutely aware of Genevieve watching
him. It was bad enough that she would watch him take another
man's life. He couldn't go so far as to enjoy it.

He knocked away William's shield and slipped his blade
between William's ribs.

"Die," Kendrick said.

"You'll die, too," William gasped. "That was the rest of the
curse."

Kendrick froze.

William crumpled to the ground and Kendrick jerked his
sword free, then he let it slip from his fingers. He watched in
horrified fascination as William disintegrated before his very
eyes, becoming the seven-hundred-year-old corpse he should
have been. A bit of breeze blew down from the north, picking
up the ashes and scattering them about. Soon there was nothing but bones covered by mail.

Kendrick looked quickly at his own hands. They were normal. He looked up as Genevieve ran across the field toward
him. He held out his hands and backed away, unwilling to

know the truth. Aye, he looked normal enough, but what was the truth of the matter? Would Genevieve leap into his arms and fall to the ground? Did William know something he didn't?

Genevieve ignored him and threw herself at him.

And, for an instant, Kendrick imagined that he couldn't feel her.

And then he felt hot tears on his skin and realized they were his lady's. Her slender arms were around his neck; her lithe body was pressed up against his. The saints be praised William had been a liar to the end!

"You're bleeding, Kendrick."

Kendrick knew he was bloodied, but the blood was William's, not his. He wrapped his arms around Genevieve and held her close, not caring that he soiled her greatly.

"I'm unhurt," he said, sending a prayer of thanks heavenward. "'Tis over, my love. William is gone and he'll not trouble us again. 'Tis his blood, not mine, that covers me."

She didn't believe him, if the strength of her embrace told anything. He held her to him and looked over her head as Royce approached. He smiled at his friend.

"Now we can both rest easy."

Royce returned his smile. "A fine showing, my friend. Have you a preference for what I do with the remains?"

"None. Just don't bury him on my land."

"I wouldn't think to. Take your lady inside, Kendrick. I think she's seen enough for the day."

Kendrick nodded. He stripped off his bloody tabard, then pulled Genevieve back to the house with him.

It was over, and Genevieve was still his.

Kendrick smiled.

Three hours later, Kendrick's smile had turned into a disgruntled frown. The entire camp had returned to the keep and he found he missed greatly having privacy with his lady. Genevieve had already held court with all the garrison knights and assured them she was whole.

Now she was holding court with their own household members, standing at the kitchen counter next to a bowl of chocolate-chip cookie dough, waiting for a batch of cookies to come from the oven. Worthington was sitting at the table, along with Royce and Nazir, and the trio was demanding all manner of details about her activities over the past month. Genevieve was blushing furiously and fielding the questions quite poorly, to Kendrick's way of thinking. The annoying clucking noises Worthington was making only added to his irritation. He was half tempted to send the three of them on holiday for a year or two. Perhaps by then he might not be so distraught over the division of Genevieve's attentions.

Though Kendrick had the feeling even sharing her with any possible children would not sit too well with him at first. Aye, he'd become besotted indeed, and everyone knew it. Damn Royce if he wasn't smirking like the lackwitted dolt he was. Kendrick focused his attentions on his lady and ignored his comrades.

She looked pale. He knew he shouldn't have been surprised, what with all she'd been through over the past few weeks. He frowned as she consumed another spoonful of dough. It couldn't be good for her. In fact, she was turning positively green.

He'd barely opened his mouth to comment on that when Genevieve tossed the spoon into the mixing bowl and fled from the kitchen. Kendrick leaped to his feet to follow her, only to find three other men in his way.

"She's *my* wife," he bellowed, shoving them aside. He sprinted back to the bathroom off the kitchen and knocked on the door. "Genevieve?"

"Go away," she said miserably. "I'm sick."

He could hear that readily enough, and the sound made him queasy. He took a deep breath and opened the door. Genevieve was just turning on the faucet to rinse out her mouth. Kendrick stood at the doorway, feeling altogether helpless. He waited until Genevieve finished, then turned her gently around and pulled her into his arms.

"I'll take you up to bed."

"No, I'm fine, really," she said, pushing back and looking up at him with a smile. "I've got to make your cookies now."

She pushed out of his arms, took his hand and led him back to the kitchen. Kendrick followed, wondering what contrary spirit was possessing his wife at present. He allowed her to push him down in the chair and then looked at his mates.

"She says she's fine."

"Of course she is," Worthington said, as if he knew exactly what he was talking about. "The nausea isn't continual. Isn't that so, Lady Genevieve?"

Genevieve threw an oven mitt at their steward. Kendrick blinked, then looked at Royce who was chuckling.

"Foul tempered, too. Ah, Kendrick, what fine months lie in wait for you ahead."

"Shut up, Royce," Genevieve said, casting a warning look his way.

"As you wish, my lady."

"Would anyone care to tell me what's going on?" Kendrick growled. "Nazir?"

Nazir rose. He made Genevieve a low bow. "I will be upstairs, reaccustoming myself to my chamber. With your permission, Mistress?"

"I think I'll do the same," Royce said, rising and stretching. "You are going to put me up here, aren't you, Kendrick? Genevieve promised you wouldn't make me sleep out in the stables. But I won't take the chamber next to yours. You'll probably want to do that room in soft colors and—"

"Royce," Genevieve said, turning and shaking her wooden spoon at him, "don't make me get Kendrick's sword and use it on you."

Royce held up his hands and backed out of the kitchen. Kendrick looked at Worthington.

"Well? Aren't you going to leave too?"

"And miss this announcement? I should think not."

Genevieve cleared her throat. "Kendrick said you could have his study upstairs, Worthington. Maybe you should go check out the television."

"Announcement?" Kendrick echoed, rising. "Worthington, what are you—" Worthington walked away before Kendrick could finish. He turned to Genevieve. "What was he talking about?"

Genevieve put down her spoon and came to him. She pushed him down gently into his chair, then put her hands on his shoulders. By the saints, was she telling him she was going to leave him? Those were tears already welling up in her eyes. Kendrick steeled himself for the worst.

"We're going to have a baby."

Kendrick felt his mouth drop open. For the first time in both his life and unlife, he was speechless. There were so many emotions running through him that he hardly knew how to identify them, much less give them the attention they deserved. Surprise, elation, panic and a humbling emotion he couldn't identify at all.

"A babe?" he said, and his voice broke.

"Tell me you're pleased."

Kendrick looked up at his love and felt his eyes mist over. He rose and gathered her close.

"I'm afraid I'd break you if I hugged you as fiercely as I wish," he said, hoarsely. "Oh, Genevieve, I can't believe it!" He tilted his head back and laughed for joy. Then he lifted his love's face up and kissed her soundly. He realized Genevieve was still on her feet so he pushed her down into a chair and then started to pace.

"Of course, you'll rest from now on. No more mornings learning to ride, no more trips to town. I don't know that I trust the car to get you there and back safely. Reading may not be too taxing, but I'll have to give it more thought. Carrying a child is hard on a woman, Genevieve, and I'll not lose you because of a babe. Too many men must remarry because they lose their wives in childbirth. I've waited seven centuries for you, I'll not give you up so soon.

"Royce and Nazir will have to move. Perhaps down to the village. We'll hire a nanny and a wet nurse so you needn't exert yourself. And I'll keep the garrison outside, perhaps even beyond the inner bailey. I'll not have their rough talk and play disturbing you. And the nursery! Aye, we'll have to do that up soon enough. Perhaps I'll hire a chef. I don't think

Worthington can feed you as you need to be fed. A chef from Italy perhaps. They seem to have fine, strong children there. And no more of that peanut butter concoction. I can't believe it's good for a body—"

"Kendrick?"

"Nor any more of that cookie dough. Ice cream is definitely forbidden you. Nay, my love, plenty of rest and as little exercise as possible. I don't want my babe causing you any more grief than necessary—"

"Kendrick!"

He stopped his pacing and looked down at her. "Aye?"

"Come down here where I can see you."

He knelt down before her. "Aye?" Anything she desired, that he would fetch for her, willingly.

"Royce and Nazir stay. They belong here as much as we do."

"But—"

"And you're not going to hire a cook. That would hurt Worthington's feelings. I don't need a chef from Italy. The garrison knights may come and go as they please, just as long as they stop following me into the bathroom to watch me throw up. That embarrasses me."

"They do what!" he thundered.

Genevieve put her hand over his mouth. "I won't ride anymore, but I'm going to exercise and you're going to do it with me, even if it means walking around the garden a hundred times a day. I promised Adelaide I'd come to her shop an afternoon a week and watch it for her and I fully intend to do that." She paused for breath. "What else did you say?"

Kendrick took her hand and kissed it before he rested his elbows lightly on her legs and put his hands on her waist.

"A great deal of nonsense, I'm certain."

She leaned forward and kissed him softly. "You are happy, aren't you?"

"Very. Are you?"

"You know I am."

"Why didn't you tell me sooner?"

"I thought it was the flu. I just went to the doctor this morn-

ing. He told me to just do what I've been doing so far and I'll
be fine." She smiled serenely. "Now our lives will finally get
back to normal. Isn't that great?"

"Aye, my love, it is."

"Your cookies are burning, Kendrick."

"Let them burn. I have plans for you in your library at the
moment."

"You could at least turn off the oven on your way by."

Kendrick did, then picked his lady up in his arms. "Would
milady protest if I loved her sweetly in her library?"

"I would relish the experience," she said, her eyes sparkling.

"I would too. And then later you'll have a nice warm bath
and a nap. Nay, I think perhaps a bit of supper before you
sleep. You'll need your strength."

"Kendrick, you have the potential to become a terrible nag."

He grinned as he carried her across the great hall and into
her library. He agreed with her wholeheartedly but couldn't
bring himself to apologize for it. He was alive to nag his lady
and that was a most precious gift. She would bear him a child
and he would keep them both safe.

"Kendrick?"

He set her down and locked the library door behind him.
"Aye?"

"I love you, you know."

He smiled and bent his head to kiss her. "Aye, I know. And
I love you."

"Do you think our lives will finally get down to normal
now?"

He drew her close and rested his chin atop her head. "Aye,
my love, I do."

His lady snuggled closer and wrapped her arms around him.
Kendrick closed his eyes and smiled. From now on, nothing
but happiness, nothing but days and nights of loving, nothing
but Genevieve filling his life with joy.

Ah, how sweet were the gifts he'd been given.

Epilogue

Considering all the people gathered in the great hall, there should have been an enormous amount of noise. Instead, there was silence, except for the occasional creak of a chair or a deep sigh. The souls, housed in bodies or not as the case might be, were awaiting tidings, and praying those tidings would be good ones. It had been a night of waiting, of listening first to the muffled moans of pain that carried down to the hall, then straining to hear any sound at all.

Suddenly there was the sound of swiftly descending feet, and a disheveled, imperfectly groomed Worthington appeared at the bottom of the steps, his weathered face alight with pride and relief.

"A man-child," he announced, as boastfully as if he'd sired and birthed the lad himself.

"Worthington!"

The bellow from upstairs sent Worthington scurrying out of sight again.

The crowd wasn't sure if relief or more praying was called for. Mistress Adelaide began to weep.

Only a score of moments passed before the footsteps were heard again. Worthington appeared, looking even more disheveled than before.

"Another boy! Her Ladyship has borne His Lordship a pair of lads!"

"Worthington!"

The crowd, to a soul, leaped to its feet and began to pace. Two children? And another bellow? Then the folk held their breath as Worthington appeared a third time.

"Another babe. A lad. God help me if there's another!"

Worthington pitched forward and hit the floor with a weary thump. Mistress Adelaide, used to dealing with crises of all sorts and varieties after enduring Nazir for almost a month, took charge and saw to the emptying of the hall and the preparation of a nourishing meal for Her Ladyship. It was only after it had been sent up that she roused her beau and told him that he would only have three young charges to look after.

Worthington sighed in relief.

Genevieve woke, weary but happy. She looked to her left and saw Kendrick sitting in a comfortable chair, asleep. He was holding onto his three week-old sons, one in his left arm, one in the crook of his right and the other on his thighs. Genevieve turned onto her side, surprised at how easily she did it. Natural childbirth hadn't been in her plans but her labor had started before she could get to the hospital. The doctor had been sent for and had arrived almost immediately, half the village trailing in his wake.

Triplets hadn't been in her plans either, as she had been assured she only carried twins. Kendrick had been so surprised, he'd come close to tearing his hair out. He hadn't been much help, as he had spent more of his time bellowing at the doctor than helping her with her breathing. But she'd understood it had been his fear for her that had made him so irrational, and loved him all the more for it.

She sat up and swung her legs over the side of the bed. Uncomfortable, but not painful. She reached over and touched Kendrick's knee.

"Sweetheart?"

He opened his eyes immediately and sat up, causing two of his sleeping sons to make little complaining snorts. Genevieve took number three and cradled him close, but her eyes were on her husband.

"You need to come lie down."

Kendrick adjusted his babes. "I'm bonding, Gen."

"You're snoring, love. None of us can sleep for all the noise."

"The lads seem to be holding up well."

Genevieve smiled. They were. They were beautiful babies, with abundant dark hair and delightfully soft little faces that Kendrick boasted resembled him remarkably well at such a tender age. She leaned forward gingerly and kissed her husband.

"They look more like you with every passing hour. And they certainly sound like you when they're bellowing for their supper."

"Aye," Kendrick said, with a proud grin. "Fine, strong sons."

"We'll christen them tomorrow?"

"Nay, Genevieve. Next week, when you're better rested. Just because I have three wee ones to keep in line now doesn't mean you'll escape my scrutiny. You'll stay in bed until I think you sound enough to rise. I'm perfectly content to stay here and see that you obey me."

He certainly seemed to be. He hadn't left her side since the birth. Then again, he'd been by her side consistently since she'd told him she was pregnant. She hadn't complained and didn't intend to start now.

"Next week, then," she agreed.

"Lie back down, Gen. The lads and I will join you for a nap. And perhaps lunch later."

Genevieve lay back down and rested her youngest son next to her. Kendrick brought the other babies over and placed them next to their brother. He stretched out his long form on the bed and reached over to take her hand.

"Thank you."

She smiled. "You're pleased with them?"

"Aye. Royce is already making swords—"

"Kendrick!"

He grinned. "Wooden ones, love. And I promise I'll not let them have them 'til they're ready, though I was but three when I first held one."

She put his palm against her cheek. "You seem to have survived well enough, I guess."

"I'll watch over the lads well." He leaned over the lads in question and kissed her softly. "Are you happy, my Gen? Happy you wed me?"

"You know I am."

"And you're happy with our sons?"

"Very."

He kissed her again, then lay his head back down. "At this rate, we might produce a dozen children in no time at all."

"Don't even think it. They'd all be boys and nag me just as badly as their father does."

"You love my nagging, you love my arrogance and you love my scowls."

"Maybe."

"I know it."

She looked at him closely. "Don't tell me you found a way to read my mind again."

He grinned. "I might have. I miss that, you know. I loved watching you dream about me."

"Would you trade that for what you have now?"

"You know the answer to that. I'm blind with love for my lady and deeply humbled at the gift she's just recently given me. There is nothing in this life or the next that could replace that."

Genevieve looked at her husband and felt love well up in her heart for the adorable, grumbly, impossible knight who had turned her life upside down, then righted it, planting himself square in the middle of her heart. Nothing could make her move him. He was her joy and she wouldn't have traded him for anything.

She watched as he closed his eyes, his fingers still intertwined with hers. His arm rested lightly over their sons, Robin, Phillip and Jason; named after the men in Kendrick's family. Already Kendrick had chosen godfathers for the boys: Royce, Nazir and Worthington. Worthington was already clucking over young Jason like a mother hen. Genevieve had the feeling the youngest of the triplets would be by far the most spoiled. Royce and Nazir were far more concerned about their godsons' training than whether or not the babes were dressed warmly or held often enough. Kendrick oversaw the group of six with the authority of a king.

Not even their unearthly garrison had been idle. Genevieve had woken one afternoon to find her room filled with illusory flowers, courtesy of Sir Stephen. Guards, usually headed up by the fierce Colin of Berkhamshire, stood at her door when Kendrick was anywhere but by her side. Robert of Conyers had even begged an audience with her the day before when her sons had been wailing for all they were worth and she'd been near tears trying to soothe them. He'd produced a lute and sung sweetly until the boys were quieted. Having a ghostly garrison at her disposal was becoming altogether too convenient.

She came to herself when she realized Kendrick was staring at her. She smiled reflexively.

"What?"

"You're too far away," he said. "My lads are but a week old and already I'm jealous of them."

Somehow, that didn't bother her that much, perhaps because she knew it wasn't exactly the truth. Kendrick adored his sons. But it was also rather nice to have him missing her. She pulled her hand from his.

"Put the pillows where you're lying. That will keep them from rolling off the bed. I can move over a bit."

"Not too much. I've a mind to snuggle close to you."

Genevieve smiled as he rose and made a barrier with a pillow. He moved his sons away from her, then walked around the bed and lifted her over. Genevieve closed her eyes and smiled as he settled down behind her and wrapped his arm around her waist. His chest was warm against her back and his arm heavy and secure.

"Genevieve?"

"Yes, husband."

"Do you remember how I told you a few months back that I thought our lives would finally settle down?"

"I do."

He paused. "I daresay it isn't going to happen. Will that grieve you?"

When something not normal included triplet boys, a garrison of ghosts, a despotic butler, a petulant Saracen, a raucous guard captain and a husband who was the most chivalrous knight ever created, a man who loved her and cherished her more than she ever dreamed anyone could—would that grieve her?

"Not in the least, my lord. Not in the least."

*Turn the page for a preview
of Lynn Kurland's
novel . . .*

THE VERY THOUGHT OF YOU

*Available in paperback
from Berkley Books*

The Highlands, Scotland
February 1998

The horse scrunched up his nose, tossed his head in obvious discomfort, and then sneezed.

Alexander Smith opened his mouth to curse, then realized the precariousness of his situation. He grasped the top edge of the stall door and very deliberately clamped his lips shut. He blinked furiously to clear his eyes of a substance he didn't want to examine too closely.

He should have stayed in bed.

He'd known that, of course, from the moment he'd woken. His first clue had been the sound of rain on the roof—day fifty-six of the Scottish deluge. His next warning had been shivering through a cold shower, courtesy of his younger brother. The final straw had been counting on a breakfast of sausage, eggs, and fried potatoes only to find nothing but dangerously aged cottage cheese and on-the-verge-of-turning-green bread in the fridge. By the grease stains on his brother's chin, Alex had known immediately where to lay the blame.

And now this.

He looked down at his snotty shirt and wondered just how long it would take for it to crust over so he wouldn't drip all over the house.

His horse, looking much more comfortable and rather contrite, bumped him companionably with his nose.

"Beast, Beast," Alex said, carefully dragging his sleeve across his mouth, "do you really think I can go out looking like this? What if we run into some beautiful Scottish girl? What kind of impression are we going to make?"

Beast ducked his head in obvious shame.

Alex grunted. "That's right. Well, have a nice day. I'm sure you will, now you can breathe again. I'm going back to bed."

It seemed the safest alternative.

He wiped his face with a patch of clean shirttail, then left the stables and walked across the courtyard. The castle rose up before him, an impenetrable wall of gray stone relieved only by a few windows on the second floor. His brother-in-law Jamie had spent a fortune seeing the keep restored and the results were chilling. Alex could almost see medieval Scottish clansmen bursting out the front door in their plaids, brandishing their swords and screaming like banshees.

Alex entered the hall and pulled the door shut behind him with a bang. Once his eyes adjusted to the interior light, he saw his younger brother sitting in front of the hearth, warming his toes by the fire. Alex marched across the great hall, prepared to give the runt a second installment in the berating he'd given him earlier. He didn't want another Saturday starting out like this—*sans* hot water and saturated fat.

Zachary glanced up from his book, took one look at Alex, and started to laugh.

"Gggrrrr," Alex said, wondering if strangling his brother would be half as satisfying as just contemplating it was.

"Good grief," Zachary gasped out between guffaws. "What'd you have—an encounter with the Blob?"

Alex gritted his teeth. "How'd you like to have an encounter with my fists?"

"Eeuw," Zachary said with a shudder. "Maybe after you clean up."

"As if I could," Alex growled.

"What's your problem? I had plenty of hot water."

"I know!"

Zachary only blinked innocently. Then he rubbed his disgustingly well-fed belly. "There's nothing left in the fridge, you know," he said.

"And whose fault do you think that is?" Alex demanded.

Zach sighed again, the mournful sigh of a man left home alone with nothing to graze upon. "Man, I hate it when Jamie and Elizabeth go out of town. The least they could have done was leave Patrick or Joshua behind. Josh makes great desserts." He looked at Alex narrowly. "Why'd I get stuck with just you? You won't even keep the fridge stocked."

Alex relived briefly in his mind some of the more choice experiences he'd had pummeling his baby brother. His irritation momentarily soothed by those warm and fuzzy memories, he managed to speak very calmly. "And what's wrong with you that you can't go to the store?"

Zach settled himself more comfortably into his chair and moved his toes closer to the fire. "I'm too busy. You go instead. And get something good. None of that health food garbage."

Alex mentally counted to ten. When that didn't work, he set his sights on a larger number.

"Oh, and Alex? I'd go shower first if I were you." He looked at Alex and started to grin again. "Really. I think it would be the right thing to do."

Alex wanted more than anything to wring his brother's neck in payment for ruining his Saturday morning and to stop the brat's giggles. Unfortunately, his shirt was beginning to crust over and he was starting to itch.

"I'll go to the store later," he growled, contenting himself with giving Zachary a murderous look and a smart cuff to the ear on his way to the stairs. With any luck there would be hot water by now.

He rummaged around in the armoire for clean clothes, then headed for his bathroom. He was just reaching into the shower for the taps when the phone started to ring. He ignored it and turned on the water. He hesitantly put his fingers under the spray and smiled in faint surprise at the increasingly warm temperature. Maybe things were starting to look up.

He started to strip when he realized he had no towel. He had a vague memory of having flung it into the hamper in disgust after his earlier foray into chilly waters. After turning off the shower to conserve what precious hot water there was, he opened the bathroom door only to hear the phone still ringing. Alex growled in frustration.

"Zach, get the phone!" he yelled.

The phone continued to ring. Alex cursed as he gingerly rebuttoned his shirt, then made his way into his brother-in-law's study.

"What?" he barked into the receiver.

"Nice to talk to you too, buddy," a male voice said with a laugh. "All that lovely Scottish scenery getting to you?"

Alex rolled his eyes heavenward. His day had just taken a decided turn for the worse. "Tony, what do you want?"

"What, no chitchat?"

"Not with you, thanks anyway."

"How's Elizabeth?" Tony continued. "The baby? Your barbarian brother-in-law?"

"My sister's fine, her baby is fine, and Jamie is fine. Now what the hell do you want?"

"Well, since you asked," Tony said with a strained laugh, "I'll get right to it. We need your services."

Leave it to Tony not to mince words. Alex took a deep breath.

"Tony, I quit eight months ago. I haven't changed my mind."

"But you haven't heard the deal on this one, my friend."

"I don't want to hear."

Tony made a sound of impatience. "It's the sweetest takeover I've ever seen. Smooth, easy. They'll never see it coming. I've already got controlling interest. I just need you to come in and close the deal. It will make you richer than your wildest dreams.''

''I'm already richer than my wildest dreams, Tony.''

''You can always use more—''

''No. Don't call me again.''

''Alex—''

''Don't.'' Alex hung up the phone.

He leaned back and let out his breath slowly. Was it possible he had ever enjoyed any of this?

Unfortunately, he could remember all too well just how enjoyable it had been. And he remembered just as clearly how it had all started. Anthony DiSalvio had hired him fresh out of law school, when Alex had still been green and full of chivalry. He'd become a lawyer to save the world from injustice. And then Tony, a senior partner, had come to him with a special assignment. Alex had been flattered beyond belief. A little corporate raiding, a take-over done by the book; it had been a rush. He'd saved all the little guys by getting rid of the big bad guys.

He'd been a smashing success.

It had gone to his head.

He'd woken up seven years later. It had taken his sister's mysterious disappearance to make him take a good hard look at what he was doing with his own life; he hadn't liked what he'd seen. He had become a pirate—a very rich pirate, but a pirate nonetheless. The little guys had become lost in the shuffle. Alex had raided just for the sheer sport of it, and for the money. He'd started out to save the world from injustice; instead he'd wound up being the cause of more injustice than he cared to think about.

So he'd walked away. Far away from New York and London and all the places where he'd hoisted the skull and crossbones. Leave it to Tony not to take his blunt and offensive resignation seriously.

''I need a change of scenery,'' he said to the contents of Jamie's study. ''To somewhere sunny, like the Baha-mas.''

Maybe Jamie had a few travel books on the shelf above his desk. Alex put off his shower a few minutes more in deference to Jamie's private library. Surely there was some destination detailed there that would interest him. He had the time for a vacation. He certainly had the need for one.

He ran a finger along the spine of each book above Jamie's desk, mentally checking off the ones he'd read.

Then he stopped.

Trails Through Time. Now, this was a new one. Alex pulled the book down and opened it. He read the inside jacket. "In *Trails Through Time* author Stephen McAfee takes the reader on a marvelous journey down roads in Britain, from Roman times to the present day."

Interesting. Alex flipped through the pages, then stopped when something slipped out and landed on the desk with a soft *plop*. Alex put the book aside and reached for the folded piece of paper. It was very worn, as if it had been folded and unfolded dozens of times. He gingerly straightened it out, then looked at it in astonishment. It was a treasure map. Considering the day he was having, he was fairly impressed with his ability to recognize that.

Not that he should have been surprised. He'd been an Eagle Scout, after all, and one famous for his mapmaking skills. Add to that the board and plunder skills he'd acquired after law school and he had the piracy category all sewn up. This was, however, one of the oddest maps Alex had ever seen in his long and illustrious career.

There were the normal things, of course: requisite directional arrows, landmarks aplenty. In fact, the landmarks looked suspiciously like the surrounding countryside. Yes, Jamie's mountains were there to the north. The castle sat prominently in the middle of the map, with the meadow below it due south. There was the forest to the west and another part of forest to the south. And that squiggle over there had to be the stream that fed into the pond not far from the garden. Alex stared at it for several minutes wondering what looked so strange.

Then it hit him.

There wasn't just one X marking the spot. There were several.

To another man, such a flagrant disregard for treasure-mapmaking standards might have only indicated slight befuddlement on the part of the mapmaker. But Alex wasn't just another man. And the mapmaker was his brother-in-law, James MacLeod. And Jamie wasn't befuddled, he was an honest-to-goodness, former mediev—

Alex put on the mental brakes before he traveled any further down that well-worn path. Traveling down *any* path Jamie was associated with was hazardous to one's health. Maybe Jamie had just been scribbling in his spare time.

Unfortunately, those didn't look like scribbles. Alex looked at the map again and frowned at what was very deliberately scrawled next to the X's in Jamie's bold handwriting.

Medieval England.

17th Century Barbados.

The Future.

It couldn't mean what he thought it meant. The map was just Jamie's doodles. People didn't just walk over certain spots in the ground and up and disappear.

Though Barbados didn't sound too bad at the moment. At least it would be sunny there. And look, there it was, due north of Medieval England. Alex left the map sitting prominently on top of the book where Jamie couldn't help but notice that Alex had seen it. He would realize he'd been caught, and Alex would enjoy the opportunity to give Jamie a thorough ribbing. Heaven knew he deserved it.

Could it be true? Alex turned the possibility over in his mind. Barbados at least would be a pleasant change of scenery. What could it hurt to just go have a look and indulge in the fantasy for an hour or so? He had a great imagination. He could hang out under a tree and pretend he was loitering on some sunny beach. Maybe he'd even pretend he'd traveled there, just to see if he could rattle Jamie. Yes, the morning was starting to shape up nicely.

Alex left the study, grabbed his coat, and headed downstairs. He was still covered with horse snot, but there was no sense in getting cleaned up now. He wouldn't need his shirt much longer because he'd be sunning himself on a nice beach, watching bikini-clad women strut their stuff in front of him—or at least pretending to do so. Given the fact that he hadn't seen blue Scottish sky in weeks, Barbados was starting to sound mighty nice.

If there just wasn't that disconcerting seventeenth-century business attached.

Alex plowed into his brother at the bottom of the steps.

"Hey," Zachary said, annoyed, "watch it. You're going to get me dirty and I have a date."

Alex steadied himself with a hand on the wall. Zachary had a date? Alex hadn't had a date in eight months, and he was the owner of a huge portfolio and worked out every day to keep his body from turning to fat. Zachary was a semi-starving former student who ate junk food in front of the television and grew things on paper plates under his bed. How was this possible?

"With whom?" Alex asked, stunned.

Zachary smirked. "Fiona MacAllister."

Alex reeled like a drunken man.

"Fiona?" he gasped.

"Yeah," Zachary said with a shrug. "You snooze, you lose, bro. And *I* wasn't snoozing. I gotta go get cleaned up." He gave Alex's crusty shirt a pointed look before he mounted the stairs and disappeared out of sight.

Alex shook his head. Fiona MacAllister was the grocer's daughter. Alex had been planning to ask her out for weeks. He'd just been waiting until he thought she might be used to him. After all, he was a rich and powerful former corporate raider, and he hadn't wanted her to want him just for his money.

Alex pushed away from the wall. There was something very wrong in the world when his brother could get a girl to go out with him and he couldn't.

He made one last detour to the kitchen on the off chance

that some undiscovered cache of junk food was hiding there. He rummaged through the pantry and found his secret box of Ding-Dongs still safely hiding behind a container of oatmeal and a bag of rice. It was a good thing Zachary never came close to anything resembling a raw ingredient. Alex indulged himself immediately and tucked a second snack into his coat pocket. One never knew what one might find for dinner on the beach. No sense in not being prepared.

He shut the hall door behind him and put on his coat. As he walked across the courtyard to the stables, the rain increased with every step he took. It wasn't a good sign, but he ignored it. Within minutes he had Beast saddled and was heading out the front gate.

He turned back to the north to look at the mountains behind the estate, with their last dustings of snow. Spring was right around the corner. He could smell it. He followed his nose as it pointed him to the west where a little stream ran into the pond which sat serenely next to the garden. Jamie had certainly done a good job reproducing that stream on the map. And there lay Barbados just past Medieval England on the other side of the pond.

Alex felt an uncomfortable tingle in the air and frowned. He could believe anything of the forest on the other side of the keep, but this bit of ground in front of him? There were no gateways to the past lurking under those boughs. Maybe his sister Elizabeth was just using the map for one of the romance novels she wrote.

Alex urged his horse forward, wondering as he did so just what he thought he was doing out in the rain on a horse who had a cold, following directions on a map made by his lunatic brother-in-law. He was losing it. It was the only answer. His breakfast of fermented cottage cheese had obviously had adverse effects on his common sense. Even the thought of mentally spending a morning in Barbados was starting to sound unappealing. He would probably be better off calling a travel agent.

But he had already come this far; there was no sense in

turning back now. He continued on his way under the boughs of the rowan trees. The silence was palpable. A chill went down his spine. Alex pulled his collar closer to his neck and gave himself a hard mental shake.

All the same, he wondered just how Jamie had discovered all that business about those little gates.

Probably better not to know.

The trees thinned and suddenly gave way to an intimate little glade. The forest floor was carpeted with moss and clover and a large circle of plants. Elizabeth called it a faery ring. Alex looked narrowly at it. Was this the gate? Was it possible? He shook his head. It just couldn't be anything more than a very simple ring in the grass.

Right?